Unvarnished

Balance Blade Chronicles
Book 1

James O'Rell

To my wife, Mounika

Without your support

This would not be possible

I love you

Check out Blade's Edge Media website and on social media

x: @BladesEdgeMedia

Facebook: Blade's Edge Media

Instagram: BladesEdgeMedia

BlueSky: @BladesEdgeMedia.bsky.social

Read the prequel to Unvarnished: Gemini Dilemma

On https://bladesedgemedia.com

Prologue

Night fell upon the Kingdom of Morander; threatening clouds blocked out the light the moon tried in vain to shine. The castle town buzzed with movement, its steep mountainous walls reflecting the lights of the many torches carried by numerous messengers. The castle city was chiseled into the mountain, a testament to the country's might. Its many stone ramparts, carved from the mountain, with bricks from area quarries to supplement what couldn't be etched from the existing stone. The storm clouds that hung over the city flashed thunderless lightning, warning of the storm that was to come.

The great nation's citizens chattered with apprehension in its many pubs and homes, awaiting their great king's rumored announcement. They whispered in hushed tones, afraid the magic-using monsters that populated the mountains to the north might harken their worried words.

A woman left the castle, wrapping herself in a brown cloak as she mounted a horse. She pushed the steed into a gallop, blowing past the guards at the gate, leaving the castle behind her. The lady pushed her stead to its maximum speed, forcing it to keep ahead of the riders that would be in pursuit. The woman continuously glanced behind her but saw no one in the distance. Even though she saw nothing, it did not stop her from pushing her horse to its limits.

The woman traveled north into what used to be the Kingdom of the Ginta. She followed the mountain range the castle was nestled in until the new elevation caused her ears to pop. This mountain range looked like any other, carved from millions of years of erosion. The closer the woman rode to the mountain, the less dense the forest was and the rockier the terrain became, making it difficult for the horse to keep up its current speed. The woman showed no mercy on the animal and pushed it harder.

She leaped from her mount when she reached a small cottage at the base of one of the mountains. It was a simple hut built with only materials on hand. She burst through the door.

Before the woman exhaled another breath, cold steel graced her neck.

"Who are you, and what are you doing in our home?" the sword wielder hissed softly.

"Karan, it is me, Jalnis!" the intruder exclaimed in a hush.

"Jalnis?" Karan replied, pulling her sword from the woman's neck. "What are you doing here?"

Jalnis stepped into the doorway and shut the door behind her, sealing the room in darkness. Karan's trained eyes could still see Jalnis in perfect detail with the small amount of available light. Under her cloak was the elaborate dress of a lady of the court, tailored in shades of light blue and trimmed with gold. Her hair was lavishly decorated and styled with gold butterfly pins, most of which are now clung to her hair by a strand or two, with her hair twisting around others, creating a sandy-blond and golden mess.

Karan gazed into Jalnis' emerald eyes, and it was plain to see that the years were catching up with her. Her face started showing the wrinkles the highborn fought so hard to hide. Jalnis' chest heaved from the ride, and it almost seemed she would fall over on the spot.

"It's Karagan; he's on his way here. He plans to kill you, your children, and your husband. King Gregor has proclaimed that all magic has been banned and that the Kar'kel and Tala'har who use it will be destroyed. "

"So, our leader will execute the king's will?" Karan growled. "He is Tala'har! This makes little sense."

"It does not have to. Get your young ones and husband and go. It will be best if I am not here when my husband arrives."

"I will pray for you, Jalnis; thank you," Karan replied.

"I'm off to warn the other Kar'kel and Tala'har," she declared as she left the small hut.

"Hey, honey," a sleepy male voice muttered from the darkness. "What is going on?"

"It is time, Karan," another voice spoke, resonating from Karan's mind.

"Trebor, we need to leave."

In a few moments, in a flurry of action, the small family, a man, a woman, and two girls, were on the road, carrying almost nothing from their small hut. Karan held the hand of her oldest daughter, who held the hand of the youngest. The husband of the family, dressed in a long, simple robe, lagged. He stumbled his way through the paths, tripping on almost every root and stick.

"Where are we escaping to?" the Trebor asked.

"I do not know, but I can show us the way if that makes any sense," Karan said.

"Lead the way, love. If anyone can lead us to safety, it is you."

The wood surrounding them was quiet, a sure sign that something was wrong in Karan's mind. She felt as if there was someone, or something, waiting for her and her family. She looked back at her two children. One was almost a woman, while the other was just finding the world. She hated the idea of pulling them from the only home they ever knew, but it was better than dying at the hands of a man they called 'uncle.'

After hours of running, avoiding town after town, they entered a dark, deep, thick forest. The lack of light from the moon made the dense woodland feel like an impenetrable wall of foliage. A quiet breeze floated through the air and guided unseen branches back and forth; only their creaking signified their presence.

"Mom, we must turn back," the older daughter warned. "This is Elven Territory. They will kill us on sight… and that's if we're lucky."

"The elves won't bother us on this night, Gwyneth," Karan replied and turned to keep moving.

"Love, before we go any further, we've got to rest," the father said. "The girls aren't going to say it, but I can see it in their eyes. They are exhausted. We need to stop."

Karan turned to her children. Her eldest stood tall, barely showing any signs of fatigue. The girl wore a massive pack containing most of the essentials the family brought along, and her sword hung at her side. The youngest child's chest heaved, and her pale skin shone with the sweat that soaked her brow and dark hair.

"Karri, can you go on?" Karan asked the child.

3

Karri opened her mouth but never received the chance to speak.

"Mom, you know as well as I do she could be dying, and she'd never admit to it," the oldest cut off the young one.

"You have time to stop and rest," the same feminine voice as before echoed into Karan's mind.

"I suppose you are right. We stop and rest," Karan resigned

"Mom, I'm fine," the little one protested.

"No, your sister and father are right; we stop here. The heat is already hard enough on you, let alone the fast pace we've been keeping."

"Mother! How am I ever going to be a good Tala'har if you baby me," she whined.

"You'll be stronger in the future, Karri, I promise," her father comforted.

The family ventured off the path and found a small cave to take refuge. Karan stepped out of the cave as her family settled in, walked toward the path, climbed a tree, and waited. Just as she reached a perch, water began to pour from the night sky.

The father put his hand toward his wife, grabbed at the air, and slowly moved his hand back toward his chest. Karan floated out of the tree and back into the cave. As she found herself back in the cave, she was hanging upside-down, long brown hair dangling from her head like a waterfall. The girls couldn't help but giggle.

"What are you doing, Trebor?" she growled.

"Keeping you safe," he grinned.

"That's my job," she hissed.

"Yes, but you can't do your job if you get soaked and catch your death of cold. Besides, the rain affords us needed rest. If my brother is coming after us, he wouldn't be foolish enough to ride in this heavy rain. He'd kill himself and his horses."

"Fine, I'll stay in the cave," she spat as she crossed her arms.

4

Trebor stared at her momentarily as Karri and Gwyneth continued to laugh.

"You can put me down now," Karan sneered.

"Oh, I'm sorry, love. I enjoy peering at you upside-down. I'd say more, but the children are here."

Karan rolled her eyes as Gwyneth put a finger down her throat and mockingly gagged. Karan was gently turned right-side up and placed on her feet with the simple movement of her husband's hand.

The family waited out the rain in the small cave. Karan would occasionally peer out to see if she could see anything at all, but little was visible through the downpour. She turned back to check on her family. Trebor was seated on the left side of the cave, with his back up against the wall and head pointed to the ceiling. Gwyneth and Karri were on the other side of the cave, Karri tucked under her big sister's arm, fast asleep.

Morning came and went, with the rain still echoing throughout the small cave. Trebor pulled some jerky from his pack and shared it with the girls. When he offered it to Karan, she waved it away with a stroke of her hand.

"You seem rather unshaken for someone who just found out their brother wants to kill him," Karan commented.

"It doesn't surprise me," Trebor sighed. "Ever since he lost his charge, he has been different. I knew something such as this would happen one day."

"I thought the prince was Uncle Karagan's charge, and he's not dead," Gwyneth interjected.

"The prince is his second charge," Karan spat.

"I thought Tala'har only get one charge. Why does Uncle Karagan get two," Karri asked.

"That's right, we do get just one charge. And only one," Karan explained. "Yet, when they discovered the young prince had magic, your uncle insisted on protecting the prince as if he was a Kar'kel, like your father. He claimed it would make Moranderians and their king more tolerant of those with magic."

5

"Doesn't seem to turn out that way," Trebor sighed. "It seems that all he has managed to do is expose our existence and place a target on our heads."

"Should we really run?" Gwyneth questioned. "Aren't we turning our backs on our own?"

"Jalnis made it out like he was specifically targeting us. Also—" Karan drew in a deep breath before releasing her following few words in an exasperated sigh. "I knew it would come to this one day."

"You knew something about this?" Trebor's eyes looked as if they were to pop from his head.

"This is a day I have been waiting for ever since I received the Dharg'syth," she said while gesturing to the large, folded scythe that hung on her back. "It is only given to the Tala'har who has the most important and difficult duty. I would one day take my family to another world. Please do not ask where I received this information; trust me, it is true. You girls are the future. If we stay to fight and lose even one of you, all might be lost."

"So, is that why I don't have a charge?" Gwyneth demanded.

"I'm afraid so," Karan said.

"Where did you—" Gwyneth began.

"Your mother asked for our trust, and I will give it to her. I expect the same from you, Gwyneth. This leads me to believe that you girls will protect someone special."

"Yes... a Dalan'tari, as they say in the old tongue or we say now, Balanced One," Karan revealed with an expulsion of air.

Trebor stared at her, mouth agape. Gwyneth huffed and crossed her arms.

"Do they even exist? I thought they were an old wives' tale spun by Kar'kel and Tala'har mothers to scare their children into not abusing their magic," Gwyneth rolled her eyes.

"I believe you, Momma," Karri added excitedly.

"It's not that I don't, Mother. It just sounds a little—grand. Aren't Balanced Ones supposed to be protectors of creation, who even police the

6

gods?" Gwyneth struggled. "How could we even be worthy protectors of even the earthly incarnate of something so powerful?"

"I cannot answer that, Gwyneth, but I have the utmost faith in my daughters," Karan said. "And what you say about them is true, and the stories your father told you about them, even the ones I told you were total hogwash, are also true."

"Karan, you've never led me wrong. There have been times when I couldn't fathom how you were aware of the things you knew, and I understand you don't want to talk about that. That is fine. If that is our destiny, we should meet it head-on," Trebor stood and took his wife's hands.

"Thank you; I do need all of your trust."

"You have mine, Momma," Gwyneth nodded.

"Don't forget mine!" Karri exclaimed.

The rain stopped just after Karri's declaration. The sun peaked out of the clouds and caused a blinding light show on the forest foliage. Light bounced from leaf to leaf, making the light almost intolerable. The beauty of the scene masked the severe nature of the circumstances.

"Let's go. If they are chasing us, they are most likely on horseback, and it won't take them long to catch up," Karan said.

As the family stepped out of the cave, a vast shadow obscured the light in the forest. Karan pushed her family back into the cave as her eyes were drawn upward, catching a brief glimpse of a large, ashen-colored creature that flew above.

"What was that?" Gwyneth whispered. "Mom, was that a feral dragon?"

"I've never seen one that big... or of that color," Karan whispered in return.

"I'm not scared of no dragon!" Karri declared.

"I've heard stories of ancient, mythical dragons," Trebor explained. "They were larger and far more powerful than the current feral or Hinacar

Dragons breeds. These dragons could assume human form, or whatever form they chose, for that matter. Many of them were avatars of specific elements."

"You are just going to scare the children," Karan sighed. "I wouldn't jump to those sorts of conclusions, Trebor. Let us continue to move and watch the skies."

"I'm still not afraid of no dragon," Karri mumbled.

The family passed through the dense forests of the Elven Territories without seeing a single elf. The dragon that passed above had not been seen again. The family followed Karan as she navigated small paths through dense foliage that no horse could travel through without serious injury. As they traversed the Elven Territories, night began to fall. The forest around them again became unnaturally quiet. The family traveled for hours, seeing no one on the paths they took, but they could smell the residuals of human encampments in the forest, signaling their passage of the Elven Lands.

Karan stopped dead in her tracks and put her hand up for the others to do the same. Karan's sharp ears picked up almost deaf footsteps gracing the tree branches behind them. She knew something or someone was striding near-silently from branch to branch.

"Run," she yelled, clutching Gwyneth's hand and sprinting. Gwyneth tightened her grip on Karri and dragged her along at a breakneck speed the child's tiny legs could barely keep up with. Trebor also ran, trying not to let his long robe trip him.

As they fled, beams of light sizzled by as Karan felt one graze her cheek, leaving a bright scarlet streak behind. She sensed another blast coming. She used her free arm to push Gwyneth out of the way, and it harmlessly hit the scythe on Karan's back.

Karan took a moment to glance back and saw a dark blur approaching from the rear. It was moving far faster than she could force her family to move. She looked ahead and saw their destination: another cave in the woods. She realized that whoever or whatever was chasing them would catch them long before they reached the cave.

Karan slid and spun around, coming to a halt, which allowed her family to pass. She brought her scythe off her back and met the pursuer head-on. As her foe approached her, she realized it was a man in dark armor. The armor perplexed her. She had never seen such a suit.

Karan felt her scythe connect with the stranger's hidden hand blades, which shot out of the tops of his armored gloves. She reeled back from the force of the collision, sliding to a stop with her right knee to the ground. She prepared to meet the attacker's next charge with her weapon held in front of her.

"Karan, go!" her husband hollered as she slid to a halt.

"But, I can't..." she muttered. "I'm your Tala'har."

"Go! The future and destiny of our children are far more important than my life. Only you can teach them what they need to know to meet their destiny. I love you all, don't forget that."

More light beams rained down on them. Trebor shot a hand toward his children, creating a shield that deflected numerous close blasts.

"Go, my dear," the voice in Karan's head rang again. "This is how things must be. I am sorry. His death will not be in vain. Go through the portal in the cave; there is safety and a friend on the other side."

Karan turned away from the stranger as tears fell from her eyes. She snatched Gwyneth's hand, which was still latched on to Karri. She dragged them into the unnaturally dark cave.

What remained of the family stumbled through unnatural darkness until the twilight light almost blinded them. They staggered out of a similar cave opening in a strange setting.

The area around them was a series of grassy knolls. To their left was a strange conglomeration of metal bars built into a dome-like structure over a sandy lot. In another sandy area, swings hung by strong, metal chains on a structure of long metal tubes.

A figure appeared from the shadow of a nearby tree. She was a short, semi-stout woman dressed in a lavender skirt and light purple blouse. Her hair was dark brown and tied neatly behind her head. She smiled gently at the family.

Karri dropped to her knees and began to bawl; Gwyneth sunk to her knees and drew the child close as tears fell from her eyes as well.

"The Tara'vir family, I presume?" the portly woman said.

"Yes," Karan's eyes darted around, still adjusting to the light, searching for threats.

Karan could feel the air crackle around this new stranger in the odd clothing.

"You need not fear; I've been sent to aid you," the woman said. "I'm sure you have plenty of questions that will be answered in time. We should get you out of this public place and into less conspicuous clothing. For now, welcome to Earth."

Chapter 1

I felt like I was slowly falling from that muggy night sky that watched over the park and landed gently back into my bed.

"Carrie! Wake up! You're going to be late for school!"

My mother's caw yanked my consciousness back into this reality. I sat up in my bed, disoriented. I would have said what I had seen was a recollection of my past, but it was more than that. I was watching it from afar, only able to observe the unfolding events. Some of them were events I was previously not privy to. It dawned on me how strange it was to see my younger self from the outside. It felt like I was watching a movie. I relived the scene of my father's death a dozen times in my dreams before, but never like this. I shook off the gloom and slid my feet out of bed to start the day.

Chapter 2

I watched the world speed by as if I were a bullet capable of shattering the existence of some poor soul. I observed the landscape through the glass of my mother's car side window. I put my hand over my eyes, trying to block the Miami sun. The areas we drove through did not look much different from any neighborhood I had seen since I arrived in this strange world. The only real difference was the occasional palm tree planted alongside the road. Many of the houses we drove by were nearly identical, a reminder of rapid development in this suburb outside of a metropolis of frolicking and excess. It was enough to make me gag.

"Dear, did you put on that new sunblock I bought you?" my mother's lyrical yet nagging voice vibrated from the driver's seat.

"Yeah, Mom, I put it on," I replied.

"Good. I don't want you coming home looking like you just escaped from the kitchen of some seafood restaurant," she said.

"Don't worry about it, Mom; I'll be fine," I yawned.

"That skin of yours is very fair, and Miami is much different from Seattle," she reminded.

"Yeah, Mom, I know."

"You have that form you're supposed to bring with you, right?"

"Yeah, it's right here," I dug the paper out of my bag. I took a close look at it.

"You spelled your name with two 'a's again. You're not 'Karan' anymore, you're Karen," I sighed.

"Be a dear and correct it for me."

I removed a pen from my bookbag and added the extra line that turned an 'a' into an 'e'.

"Hey... do you feel that? I'm unsure what I'm sensing, but it's huge. It's tough to pinpoint its exact location," I admitted.

"Yes, I've sensed it since we came into the area. Your charge is here, somewhere," Mom answered.

"Do you know how old my charge is supposed to be?" I inquired.

"Yes, the person in question is supposed to be about your age, according to what I've been told," Mom said as she turned the wheel, pulling into the sizeable U-shaped driveway in front of the school. Above the entryway covering, the name Marshall High School was displayed in white lettering.

"Could it be possible that the person is here? At school?" I asked.

"I suppose that wouldn't be completely out of the realm of possibility. Keep your eyes open," she said with her usual wide smile.

"I will, Mom. Thanks for the ride," I said also with a big smile.

"No problem. Have a good first day at school," she said, waving her hand forward, signaling me to get moving.

I stepped out of the car into my brand-new world. I grabbed my little black tote and closed the car door. My new environment was full of students of all races and colors. It was a variable human rainbow on the lawn of the school. The sky was blue and cloudless, with the occasional seabird screeching as it flew overhead. The building seemed to be getting old; it might have been built sometime in the early 1980's. It looked like every other institution I had been to here on Earth. I dreaded the sight of it.

The presence I felt in the car was even stronger here. Whoever my charge was, they were close by. The thought of meeting them gave me goosebumps. I pulled my phone from my pocket. It was a recently made smartphone designed as a flip phone. I never liked the idea of a bare, unprotected screen. I stared at the phone intently, feeling I should be calling someone, informing them of this new revelation. Yet, my mother already knew, and I had no idea how to contact my sister. I knew I wanted to call someone but couldn't place who.

I shrugged off the strange feeling of forgetfulness and walked up to the main doors. None of the many students who loitered on the staircase said a word to me. As I approached the door, a smallish, slightly rotund woman stood in the doorway. She wore a deep lavender pantsuit with a small rosary around her neck for garnish. She held her hands folded in front of her. Her cheeks nearly collided with her eyes as she flashed me a compact but friendly grin.

13

"Good morning, Carrie. I hope you have a wonderful day at school," she said, her grin beaming brighter than before.

"Morning' Ju…dy… I mean Principal Angler," I said.

"Here is the form you needed to be signed," I said, handing her the document I had corrected.

"So, she managed to spell both of your names right this time," Judy remarked.

"Nope, I had to fix hers," I laughed.

"Well, 'Karan' will always be 'Karan,' at least in her head. Anywho, I hope you enjoy your stay at our school," Judy said, bent closer to me. "I hope your mother can keep her feet in one place long enough for you to graduate."

I bent closer to her, "I don't foresee that being a problem."

"What do you mean?"

I looked around and realized that students were filtering into the school around us, "I'll tell you later when we are alone."

"Understood," she said with a smile before returning to me to look further down the hallway.

"Your homeroom should be the last door, on the left. You better hurry; Mrs. Jenkins has a distaste for tardy students, even if they are new here. I swear sometimes, I should just put that old coot in retirement…"

Judy stopped mid-sentence, turned to face me, and said, "Well, I've said too much. Tootles!" She said nothing else as she turned and walked down the hall.

"Tootles…" I growled to myself. "I swear it's like she knows I hate that fucking word. Oh well."

I started my way down the crowded halls of the aging school, taking in each sight. I was hoping to find something, anything of interest.

"This place was as boring as a bunch of old coots playing shuffleboard," I thought as I listened to the near-deafening and mind-numbing chatter of the barely sapient excuses for human beings that surrounded me.

14

The usual varieties of school-age archetypes were all here, even though they were from every race and color. Jocks were hanging out in a crowd on one end of the hall. On the other side, judging by the number of bottle-blondes, were a bunch of cheerleaders who were busy gawking at said jocks. I passed the cheerleaders and jocks, getting a few nasty looks from the cheerleaders, most likely because of my dark clothing and black lipstick. I then found a large four-way intersection that appeared to be everyone's favorite hangout while not in class.

I glanced around before going any further. I analyzed the place and made mental notes of any security liabilities. It was an open area, meaning if anyone picked a fight, I would have a decent amount of room to maneuver, as long as it wasn't as crowded as it is today. I wouldn't say I liked even the idea of running from a fight, but it might be best with this many people congregating here, especially if I was facing many opponents. My sister and mother would probably think it would be best to run, no matter what, with this large crowd. That is the difference between us. I'm too aggressive to be a good Tala'har.

Scanning the crowd with my spiritual eye, I found little of note. All had relatively faint auras, and slight hints of color were like an overlay over what was physically there. As I strolled, nothing wasn't anything unusual here, leaving me uneasy. I caught the brief presence of a yellow aura with a darker one that appeared attached to it, but even those auras vanished as the student moved farther down the hall. As I moved down the hall, the massive presence I had felt since arriving in Miami was becoming even more noticeable.

A bright aura caught my attention as I continued to my left. To my left was a duo of natural blondes, whom I assumed were sisters because they looked similar. These two were nothing but curves, being extremely well-developed for high school students. Both had slightly fair skin with crystal-clear complexions. The one with a single ponytail wore nothing but a tube top and a short, black leather miniskirt. The other had shorter hair and was nearly a foot shorter; they wore a similar outfit except for a black leather jacket over the tube top. She had one hand behind her back, making a male masturbatory gesture, signaling to any who could see that she was pretty bored of the other blonde's incessant chatter. Her deep blue eyes gleamed as she sent a wink and a flirty smile my way as she caught me gawking at her. I smiled back.

Those two girls were different than the other students. The tall one lacked an aura entirely, which wasn't possible for a living being. I then remembered Judy's wasn't visible, and I had never really figured out a way to ask her why. The short one had an aura that was even more vibrant than what I had seen with my own family, who all had brighter auras than anyone I had seen in this world. Her aura's color was a vibrant pink, a color usually associated with someone who loved life and whose very purpose was to bring joy to others while having fun themselves. That was what my mother had told me of those with pink auras, at least. She seemed cool enough, not to mention being amazingly attractive, and was obviously special in some way. I made a mental note to speak with her later.

The sound of students chanting "Fight, Fight, Fight" and a bunch of students rushing by broke me out of my admiration for the short girl. Not far from the sisters was a group of students in a circle. I stood on my toes to see what was going on. A red-haired, freckle-covered mammoth of a girl was fighting a tall blonde girl who didn't look entirely different from the other two girls I had just seen. My eyes opened wide as I realized who I was staring at. As a punch connected with her jaw, she made no expression, only stared at the chubby girl with boredom and disinterest.

The girl who was punched had an aura that was the color of an inferno, and it drowned out the energy of anyone close by. There was no question she was the one...

I pushed through the crowd as fast as I could and caught the next punch in my hand. The red-haired girl glared at me, eyes wide open and teeth clenched.

"Who the fuck do you think you are?" she said.

"Someone who's not fond of little bullies picking on people who won't fight back," I said. I snuck a glance at her out of the corner of my eye. I was shocked at how beautiful she was. Crystalline blue eyes looked to the ground as a small amount of blood oozed onto smooth, fair skin. Her skin was not like mine, so extremely white to the point where half an hour in the sun would fry it to a nice crisp; but instead, she was a lively tone of fair skin, very much like the sisters down the hall. She stood almost a foot higher than me, and I am not short, either. She was nothing but muscle and curves hidden under baggy clothing and a slightly slouched posture. Her blonde hair was far longer than the other two blonde girls, going to the small of her back. It wasn't messy, but it looked like it was just allowed to grow, never really styled. This somehow added to her somewhat 'wild' beauty. This goddess of a girl was allowing the child of a bully to push her around.

"This is going to end... right now," I thought as I still held the girl's fist. I pushed the girl back with only a tiny amount of force. It was enough to send the little ginger stumbling back a few feet. Had a couple of other girls not stepped out of the way, this massive tub of lard would have smashed them.

"You are so going to pay for that," the fat little lard ass snorted.

"Bring it, bitch," I replied with a grin.

"I'm not worth defending," the tall girl mumbled from behind me.

"I'll be the judge of that," I said. It then occurred to me that I was being rather harsh to this bully, mostly in my head. It was a low blow even for me to make fun of someone's weight, yet I couldn't help myself. I felt ashamed and knew someone would be disappointed in me, but I couldn't fathom who. Again, I felt like I was forgetting something. Even if it was only in my head, this was not a part of me that I wanted this tall girl to see. It was a part of me I wanted to be buried in the past.

The little red-headed wrecking ball attempted to ram me. I stepped to the side, and the tall girl did the same. The bully was victim to her own momentum and slammed right into one of the jocks and almost fell on top of him as she tumbled to the ground.

She stood up and shook off the pain, ignoring the sneering guy she had smashed into. Her face was beet red and soaked in sweat, matching her moisture-dripping hair. She shook her head, unleashing the sweat from that disgusting rat's nest. She cocked her fist and came at me with a punch.

Just as the little brat's punch went into the air, it fell limp to the girl's side as Principal Angler pushed her way to the front of the crowd.

"There is absolutely nothing to see here; all of you better get to class, or every one of you will be in for detention!"

As the crowd dispersed, the principal turned her attention to the ginger and me, "Susie and Carrie, my office, right now!"

She turned to the tall girl. "Autumn, dear, I wish to see you too. You're not in any trouble."

The three of us followed the principal to her office. Between exchanging glares with the bully, I snuck another look at Autumn. The slouching

17

posture she carried herself with was probably her attempt at not attracting attention. I couldn't fathom why someone who could clearly stand up for herself let this bully beat on her. I put that question on my mental checklist of questions to ask Judy.

The school halls were an institutional white that drove me up the wall. The place looked more like a hospital than a school, much like many other schools I had attended since I came to Earth. Everything in the school was immaculate, yet the clocks in the school were broken. They were flashing some error message or stuck on an incorrect time. There were tiles on the floor that were missing, and some of the lockers were dented from years of abuse. This seemed like the kind of ship Judy would run, extremely clean but falling apart.

The halls were empty, except for a few stragglers still trying to sneak into class unnoticed. We approached the door with the word 'Principal' in bold, capital letters. Under the title, in smaller print, was the name 'Judy Lynn Angler.'"

"Autumn, you stay here while I have a word with these two young ladies," Judy said.

Autumn nodded in understanding as the three of us went into the office.

Judy's office was small but tidy. Bookshelves were in every bit of free space. On these shelves were books or small porcelain Hummel figurines of children and animals in scenes such as ice skating and snowball fights. I only knew what brand of figurine they were because Judy loved to drone on about them while we were staying with her. I could never understand why she kept them in her office. I couldn't figure out if I was in a gift shop or a principal's office.

Two chairs were placed in front of the desk.

"Sit!" the principal commanded.

Susie and I sat down. I glanced over to her and saw the chair's metal legs bending because of the weight her gigantic ass exerted on the chair. I had to stifle a laugh, and it was followed by shame once again. I turned my attention to Judy. Susie rolled her eyes while waiting for Judy to navigate the cramped space surrounding her desk. She finally took her seat and glared at us with eyes wide open.

18

"First and foremost, Susie, you should know better. You and I have extensively discussed picking on other students, especially Miss Alexander. I don't know how to get it to you," the principal said.

Susie glanced over at me, "She started it."

"No, you started picking on Autumn. I know the scenario all too well. Miss Abbey thought it wasn't right you were doing such a thing and decided to stop you," Angler said as she continued to look wide-eyed at Susie, as she almost blindly worked with the computer sitting in front of her on the desk.

"But... but, how do you know that?!" Susie stuttered.

Principal Angler turned the computer's monitor toward us, playing a video of Susie punching Autumn in the jaw. The rest played out as the principal turned her monitor back toward her. It served the little cunt right to be caught in the act.

"No more excuses. Next time I catch you picking on Autumn, I'll let it continue. I only stop you for your safety," Judy said.

"What the hell do you mean by that?" Susie growled.

"Simple," the principal directed her gaze into Susie's eyes. "In eighth grade, a girl tried to punch Autumn Alexander like you did today. Instead of taking the punch like she does with you, she caught the girl's fist and broke her hand. Maybe I'll just let Autumn's tolerance of you wane so she does the same with you. It seems you'll only learn if Autumn beats you bloody!" Judy was now heaving heavily and standing from her chair, palms flat on her desk.

"But... but... but..." Susie stumbled.

"But nothing!" Judy exhaled at an even louder volume. She took a deep breath. "I'm going to let you go with a week of detention. Next time, if you pull something like this on any student, I'm suspending you, and I'll send your mother a full recording of all your exploits. Do I make myself clear?"

"Yes, ma'am," Susie said as she gazed wide-eyed at the principal.

"Now, get out of my sight! You can take the rest of the day off to reflect on the changes you will have to make in your life!" Judy snarled.

Susie silently stood up and quickly stomped out of the office. I was looking at the principal with only one eye. I had never seen her so angry. I nervously played with the silver ring with a gryphon's head on my left hand.

The office was quiet for a moment. I began to worry about Judy's love of rules. Even when I was a child, she set down a strict set of rules while we stayed with her. She caught me snatching a cookie before dinner time. My mother was happy to let Judy deal out a bit of discipline. I was the one washing dishes for a week afterward. I had begun to worry that her natural adherence to rules would overtake my close ties to Judy. I couldn't afford to get kicked out of this school. I needed to be close to Autumn as much as possible.

Judy took deep breaths, trying to calm herself. As I played with my ring, I decided to break the silence.

"Is all of what you said true? About Autumn breaking a girl's hand?" I asked as I stopped fiddling with my ring and looked at Judy with both eyes.

Judy let out a deep breath, "Yes, it is. She felt the girl was a threat to her. She took the girl's hand when the punch was thrown and broke it in the palm of her own. Autumn is an experienced martial artist and is more than capable of defending herself."

"Then why does she just let Susie do that to her?" I asked.

"That is how her parents taught her to deal with such situations after she broke that girl's hand. Autumn's parents knew it would be difficult to justify Autumn using force, so they just told her to accept what the other students do to her, at least that is what I assume."

"She could at least evade the attacks," I replied. "Anyone with that sort of skill obviously could."

"That's what she did in the beginning. That infuriated the bullies more, and they continued to come after her. She must have decided to take whatever punishment comes at her because they eventually get bored of hitting her if she doesn't respond. Susie is one of those special cases. The more Autumn doesn't respond, the more it infuriates her."

"Why do people pick on her?" I asked. "Have you looked at her? At any other school, she would be 'Miss Popularity.'

20

"Ah, that has to do with her cousin, Sophia. Sophia has always had something against her. She is the most popular girl in school and uses her status to spread rumors and to pick on Autumn verbally. Even she isn't stupid enough to directly try to harm Autumn. She knows better than Susie. I would watch my back if I were you. Susie holds grudges, and she will probably try to harm you next," Judy warned.

"I'm not too worried about it," I said as I crossed my legs and put my hands together. The room was quiet again. I began to worry Judy was coming up with a punishment for me.

"As for today's encounter, I have no choice but to give you a detention. School policy calls for punishment, but you'll be serving it with me, so you'll be free to do what you wish in the confines of my office," she declared.

"I understand," I said, letting out a sigh of relief. Judy will be Judy, principal or not. I was just happy she didn't go full force on me.

"I appreciate what you did for Autumn today," the principal's smile widened. "I just ask that next time, you try not to punch or hurt Susie in any way. This way, I can at least have a logical reason to avoid punishing you."

"Do what you have to," I smiled. "I cannot stop defending her anytime soon."

"Really? What makes you so committed so quickly?" Judy said with eyes wide open again, mouth halfway ajar.

"Because it's my duty," I answered.

"I know she's one of us, Carrie, but that doesn't mean it's your duty to defend her," the principal's ajar expression turned to a smile once again.

"Oh, that's not why it's my duty. I'm pretty sure she's the one my mom, sister, and I have been searching for," I said. I mentally froze for a moment… one of us? That was the biggest shock of all.

"You mean she's a…" the principal started me out of deep contemplation.

"Don't say it!" I cut her off in a whisper. "We can't guarantee we're not being listened to. And I'm unsure if Autumn can hear us since she's outside the door. It's not my job to tell her what she is. Her parents must do that. We can't be certain she knows yet. I will see if Autumn will be willing to come by my house so that I can introduce her to my mother. I need her to make sure for me, but I'm almost certain she is the one we've been looking for."

"Oh, dear. I completely forgot she was there. I should have sent her to the nurse; Susie makes me so angry. And I understand. I will try harder not to punish you for doing your duty," Judy's eyes narrowed, and her voice softened. "If this is true, I pity the poor girl. Being one of her power is a heavy destiny, and I wouldn't take it on for the world."

"I know how you feel, but it is my destiny and duty to meet whatever she has to face head-on alongside her," I said. I wanted to burst inside but knew now was not the time.

Chapter 3

Judy requested that I open the office door. I stretched over to the knob, turned it, and pushed it ajar.

"Autumn, dear, please come in here," Judy called.

Autumn stepped into the room. Her eyes were firmly planted to the floor as she said, "Yes, Principal Angler?"

"Please, Autumn, sit down."

Autumn sat down where Susie had been seated. Being so close to her gave me goosebumps.

"There is a favor I must ask of you if you are up to it. Susie didn't hurt you too much, did she?"

"No, ma'am, I'm fine," Autumn said, eyes still looking down as she sat beside me. Her face was still stained with the blood from her lip, which had stopped bleeding.

"Oh dear, how careless of me! I should've sent you to the nurse while I spoke to Susie. Would you like to go get cleaned up first?"

"I'm fine," she rebuked. "It looks worse than it is. It doesn't hurt. Nothing she ever does really hurts me."

I've punched my share of people and taken my share of hits. She was hit fairly hard. Something felt off about her claiming it didn't hurt. I figured she was putting on a brave face.

"Well, that's good," Judy said. "Autumn Alexander, this is Carrie Abbey. She's new to our school, and I would appreciate it if you showed her around the school."

"With all due respect, ma'am," Autumn finally looked up, "aren't I the wrong person to show her around due to my... reputation? It's bad enough she stuck up for me, but to be seen in public with me..."

She looked like a beaten puppy, and this twisted school was her abusive master. The puppy and the master would learn a lesson if I had any say. I didn't leave my home world, being chased by dragons and men in strange armor, to watch my charge go through hell in her daily life.

"I don't care what people think of me, so it's cool. If they have something to say, I'll…" I growled.

"Oh, Miss Abbey, I don't think it's necessary to go into what you 'will' do, now?" Judy cut me off.

"I suppose not," I said. "But really, I don't care what these people think of me. I'll do what I please; no one will tell me otherwise."

Autumn sighed and shrugged, "Well, if it's what you want."

"Yes, yes it is," I said, looking her in the eyes for the first time. I pulled myself back from the gaze almost as soon as it started. My heart began to pound.

"Autumn, get cleaned up, and then you and Carrie can go to homeroom. If I'm not mistaken, you are both in the same homeroom. Oh, and make sure to return here and pick up your pass; I don't want that old coot sending you back to me," Judy said.

Autumn nodded, and we both left the principal's office. Autumn began leading us to the bathroom, eyes still planted downward. She slumped even further, hunching her shoulders forward as she walked.

A moment of silence passed. I had no notion of what to say to her. It was the most extended moment of my life. I wanted to explode with exhilaration. I had been waiting all my life to meet her, and when the time came, I was flabbergasted. There was so much I wanted to tell her but couldn't. I had no idea how much she knew. It was not my job to tell her what she was. It was my job to protect her.

"Why did you do that? You know, fight Susie? You don't even know me; why would you stick up for me?" Autumn questioned with eyes still planted on the floor.

"I already said why. I don't like watching people pick on people who won't fight back," I answered.

"I just feel bad about it," Autumn said.

"Oh, the detention, don't worry about that. Judy and I go way back; it'll be fun," I laughed.

24

"No, not that. Well, that too, but thanks to me, you have zero chance of making any friends at this school," Autumn sighed.

"So, you won't be my friend?" I turned to her and put my hands on my hips. I couldn't help but snicker.

"No… that's not what I mean… of course… I would… I was talking about…" Autumn said.

I stepped before her and put my hand on her shoulder, "Sweetheart, chill. I was kidding; I know what you meant. I don't give a rat's ass. If people want to be my friend, they'll be my friend. If they don't, who gives a shit, it's their loss."

"I guess you could see it that way," Autumn said as she removed her eyes from direct contact.

"Let's hurry and get you cleaned up. I hear our homeroom teacher gets crabby when people are late," I said.

"You don't know the half of it. One time, she spent the whole class lecturing my cousin, Cristy, about being on time. While Mrs. Jenkins' back was turned, she kept making these obscene hand gestures."

"You mean the short one?" I said.

"Yeah, how did you know?" Autumn said.

"I saw her and your other cousin talking. At least I assumed they were your family because you guys look so much alike," I said. "She made those gestures as your other cousin rambled on about something stupid."

"I don't look like them…" Autumn closed her eyes.

"Have you looked in the mirror lately?" I replied.

"Yeah, but they are…" she stuttered again.

"Let's not worry about that right now," I said. "You need to get that blood off your face. I should do some freshening up, too."

"Oh…" Autumn looked up finally and realized we were standing in front of the women's restroom.

We stepped into the restroom and found it deserted. I turned to the mirror, pulled out my black lipstick, and touched up the small places where the pink shone through. I turned to Autumn, who was washing her face.

"Want to try some?" I asked, holding the lipstick vertically in my hand.

"No, thank you," Autumn said as she dried her face.

"Yeah, I guess you're right; we would need to dye your hair for it to work. Then we would probably look like goth sisters," I grinned.

Autumn smiled slightly as she threw the towel away.

"We better get going," she said.

"Yeah, but before the end of this year, I'm going to get this lipstick on your lips one way or another," I said. I then fathomed the other possible interpretations of what I said and blushed for probably the first time in my life.

Autumn shrugged her shoulders, "We'll see. I've never really been much for makeup."

A mental sigh of relief ran through my mind. I was glad she did not pick up on the other possible connotations of that 'innocent' comment. I knew at that point I needed to get my mind out of the gutter.

Autumn and I walked down the hallway back the way we came. I was still completely unaware of where I was going. A blizzard of thoughts ran through my mind. I wiped my brow and found sweat on my hand. The halls were cool enough, but was the bathroom? I wasn't sure. I walked as I thought I was following Autumn, but then I felt a tug on my sleeve. I had almost walked into a closed door.

"Oops," I said as I corrected my path and went around to the open door in the set of double doors. I began to worry that the heat of this place was affecting my ability to function. It reminded me of when we were escaping to Earth. On the way, we had to stop for the night because I couldn't continue, partly due to the heat. I felt ashamed for a moment but then remembered the rain would have stopped us if my failure hadn't.

"Are you okay?" Autumn said.

"Yeah, I'm fine. I'm just adjusting. I'm sure I'll be able to navigate this school blindfolded soon."

26

"That's not really what I meant, but I'm okay," she put on a fake smile. I could see the worry in her eyes. I couldn't imagine why she should be worried about someone she just met, but I shrugged it off as a good thing.

Soon enough, we saw Judy waiting outside her office with a few papers. She moved forward to greet us.

"Autumn, this is for you, and Carrie, these are for you. You two better hurry; I can hear that old bitty complaining already," Judy said.

We were both given a late excuse, but I was also handed a note for the teacher and a detention. Nothing was said as we strolled down the hallway. I had no inclination where I was going, so I was stuck following Autumn, which I was not comfortable with. It was a Tala'har's job to lead the way, not to trail their charge. That way, we could confront a threat if one appeared in our path.

I took a deep breath and closed my eyes, trying to see what I could see with my third eye. The problematic part was I saw nothing but Autumn's fiery, almost blinding aura. I wondered if its sheer magnitude prevented me from seeing anything else when I was this close to her. That would not make matters easy when it came to identifying threats.

We finally found our way to the door of the class. Autumn opened the door and stepped into the room, ducking to avoid blocking the students' view of the board and the teacher. I found an empty seat next to Autumn, which wasn't difficult because Autumn sat in the front row, where all the seats around her were vacant. I did not enjoy being in the front of the class, but this was no longer about me; it was about her. If danger appeared and I was unable to reach her in time, I would never forgive myself.

I looked up and spied the teacher, apparently named Mrs. Jenkins, glaring at me. I handed her the late excuse paper and the note, which she silently took a moment to read. When Judy said she was an old bitty, she wasn't kidding. This old crow looked like she was just a step or two away from the grave. She wore a simple light blue dress that came down to her ankles and covered her frail, thin arms. Her ankles alone looked so weak that they appeared as if they could snap at any time, sending the old scarecrow crashing down. Her face was amassed with wrinkles, and her massive glasses did nothing but magnify them. Her hazel eyes glowered at me, and she likely judged me based on my appearance, like many other people her age seemed to do. She could see the detention in my hand, and I was certain she had it in her head that I was a troublemaker that would need to be put in check.

"It seems we have a new student," the crow finally squawked. "Class, this is Carrie Abbey. Please treat her with the same respect you treat the other students."

I took this moment to glance back and found Autumn's cousin Cristy. As expected, she was sitting in the back of the class with crossed legs propped up the desk as she loudly chewed and smacked gum.

Mrs. Jenkins turned to Cristy the way an overworked parent stares daggers at their child, "Miss Cristy Alexander, how many times must I reprimand you about putting your legs up on your desk? I have already given up trying to keep you from chewing gum in my classroom, but I will not tolerate your feet on the desk. Would you behave this way in your own home?"

"Pretty much," Cristy answered, not moving an inch.

Mrs. Jenkins shook her head and mumbled, "Ask a stupid question and get a stupid answer."

I had to stifle a laugh. It was apparent that the rest of the class hadn't caught what the teacher said, or they would have laughed, too.

The old teacher turned her attention to me, "Carrie, please see me after class to get a textbook."

"Not a problem," I replied.

After what seemed like three hours, the class was finally over. Autumn was about to walk out of class by herself, so I snatched her arm.

"Remember? The principal said to show me around," I said while attempting to make the smirk on my face extremely evident.

"Oh, yeah. Sorry, force of habit," Autumn said. "Not used to having to wait for anyone."

"It's cool; I'll be right there," I said as I approached the teacher. Autumn went over to the door and stood slightly outside it.

"Hi, Mrs. Jenkins. Can I get my textbook now?" I said, playing the good student.

"Miss Abbey, let us get a few things straight. I won't tolerate tardiness. I don't care if that soft principal excuses you. I cannot give you a detention, but you will get extra homework if you are late for my class again. I would be having this talk with Miss Alexander over there, too, but I suspect you were why she was late. She's never late, you see."

"I understand, Mrs. Jenkins," I affirmed, screaming internally to verbally rip this bitch apart.

"You better," she croaked. "I also noticed your detention. That's exceedingly rare on a young lady's first day at a new school. Care to explain?"

I sighed. I wasn't expecting to get reamed out about something that wasn't even this bitch's business, but I decided to humor her. Usually, I would have torn her a new one for treating me this way, but the last thing I needed was to get kicked out of this school. I needed to be as close to Autumn as possible. No place was safe for someone such as her.

"I caught Susie picking on Autumn, so I stepped in," I said.

"Oh," the old woman folded her hands and put them under her chin. "Why would you do such a thing?"

"I felt like it, no particular reason. I didn't think it was right," I replied.

"Did you know Miss Alexander beforehand?" she looked at me with half-open eyes, hands still under her chin.

"No, ma'am, I've never seen her before today," I said.

"I understand. You see, Miss Abbey, Miss Alexander has no friends at this school. My eyesight may be failing, but a blind man could see that. Your standing up for her is a testament to your character. On first impression, I misjudged you. I thought your detention was for picking on her, being that is what everyone else seems to do."

"I've noticed," I said.

"And when you stepped in, did Susan get hurt?" she asked with eyebrows raised.

"Yes, ma'am," I said.

"Ah," the old woman shook her head. She leaned in on her desk, getting closer to me.

"Just between you and me, the little brat deserved anything you gave her. If I were her mother, I would've beaten the bullying out of her years ago, but alas, spare the rod, spoil the child, especially that child."

I was speechless. In the prior moment, she reprimanded me. Now, she was confiding in me, something that she probably wouldn't say to anyone. It seemed everything about this school wasn't what it appeared to be.

"I better get going; I don't want to be late for my next class," I said.

"Yes, of course. Have a good day," the old woman said.

I met Autumn in the hall with my little black tote draping more heavily off my back. I tried to avoid looking at her in those crystalline blue eyes but not to look away to offend her. I was uncertain why she unnerved me, but I was sure I did the same to her. Friendship was a new thing to her.

"So, what's next for you?" Autumn asked.

I pulled my schedule out of my pocket and examined it.

"Looks like I am going to Graphic Arts with Harper," I said.

"Really?" Autumn said with eyes wide open, "That's really funny because I have that class too." Autumn peeked at my schedule. "Wow, how crazy. We were given the exact same schedule, right down to the lunch break and the study hall."

"That's weird," I said. I wasn't naive enough to think this was a coincidence.

The sun rose in the air as if to spite me. Yet, for once, I was glad I was out in the world, in the daytime, because if I weren't, I wouldn't have been there to meet Autumn. It was my destiny and not my place to argue with that, sun or no sun.

At exactly noon, the bell rang, signifying it was time for lunch. Autumn waited for me as I spoke with the third new teacher of the day and took my textbook. I exited the room, and Autumn led us onward. Where there was a slight bounce in her step before the last class, now, it was replaced with tiny footsteps and a gaze that was yet again anchored to the ground.

"Hey, is something wrong?" I inquired.

"No, not all," she lied. "Why do you ask?"

"You just appear to be down," I said.

Autumn took a deep breath, "I'm not exactly happy about going to lunch. I never am."

I was about to ask why, but I already knew the answer.

"Hey, things will be different today; I'm here," I reassured.

"Yeah, but I think this is where we should part," Autumn said, not looking anywhere near me.

"Let me guess: it's because you don't want my reputation being damaged by most of the school seeing me sitting with you," I said.

"You got it," she admitted.

"Autumn, I told you before," I said, expelling a sigh along with it; "I don't care what people think of me. If you haven't figured it out yet, I'm a bit of a black sheep myself. I've bounced from school to school, either getting kicked out or my mother getting bored of the surroundings and moves. I don't give a damn what these people think of me. You are cool, and I want to sit with you, end of story."

"You mean that?" she gasped while finally looking at me. For some inexplicable reason, it took every bit of resolve within me not to look away.

"What? That you're cool? Of course, I don't say things I don't mean," I forced myself to return her gaze with a smile.

"Alright, if this is really what you want," she conceded, her gaze returning to the floor.

I stepped up, put my hand on her chin, and lifted her gaze.

"You have no reason to keep looking to the ground like that. Don't worry about them," I reassured.

She moved my hands and sighed, "Alright, I'll try it your way."

31

Chapter 4

Without another word, she led me forward down what seemed like a never-ending hall until, on our left, we saw five sets of double doors. The doors were all propped open with wooden wedges, exposing groups of round tables littered across a hardwood floor. Students filled most of the tables; thus, the lunch line was short. I went ahead of Autumn and stepped into the lunchroom. Around me, I could see girls gossiping amongst each other as I walked by their tables. Autumn's cousins were seated in the center of the lunchroom at a table filled to the brim with students. One busily chatted with those around her, while the shorter one looked like she would fall asleep and slam her head directly into her lunch.

I moved into the lunch line and grabbed a tray. Autumn slunk in behind me, attempting to look as small as her six-foot, five-inch frame would allow. The food was average school fair. Today's lovely piece of crap was pizza, accompanied by corn on the cob that looked like it had been boiled for way too long and green beans that came straight from the can.

"Pizza, please," I said to the lunch lady whose unibrow scrunched when she saw me.

Without a word, she slapped a square piece of pizza on a cardboard plate and waved me on. I snatched a milk from the cooler and proceeded to the end of the lunch line. Autumn shook her head when offered a pizza slice and moved on. She also picked up a box of milk. I paid for my pizza and waited for Autumn.

"So, where shall we sit?" I asked as she moved up alongside me.

Autumn said nothing but stepped toward the table near the faculty and immediately seated herself. I wasn't fond of sitting this close to authority, but I understood why Autumn chose it. It was probably the only way she would ever get a semi-peaceful lunch.

I put my lunch on the table, put my tote on the chair next to me, and opened my milk carton. I popped a straw in and looked around. Autumn pulled a bagged lunch from her book bag and began to eat. She was again trying to make herself as tiny as possible, with her eyes facing the table. I saw the girls whispering again, pondering what a new person would want to do with the least popular person in school. I could see them clicking around on their smartphones, probably spreading some vile gossip about Autumn and the new girl.

I turned to glance at the table where Autumn's cousins were seated. I could see Sophia, the taller one, standing up while the shorter cousin, Cristy, was trying to get her to sit back down. I had a feeling I knew what was about to happen.

Sophia sauntered our way despite her sister's words.

"Here she comes," Autumn put her head down.

Sophia stepped up behind me. I didn't even turn to look at her.

"Excuse me, new girl. Carrie, is it? Can I have a word with you?" she snipped. I turned to see the little slut with her arms crossed and a sneer on her face.

"Sure," I said. "I'll be right back, Autumn."

Autumn nodded, and I stood up and followed Sophia out of Autumn's and the teachers' earshot. Sophia changed her posture, put her hands behind her back, and adorned an obviously false smile. She leaned in closer to me.

"Look, I don't know if anyone told you," she said. "My cousin isn't the type of girl you want to get mixed…"

"I don't want to hear your mouth," I said. "Don't waste your breath. Your lies won't work on me."

"Lies?" Sophia turned her head slightly with her mouth and eyes wide open.

"Yeah, lies," I said and then sipped my milk. "So, you can go back to your clique of groupies and tell them how filthy I am or some other shit you'll probably come up with. Go ahead and spread it on the socials too, just to be thorough. I don't care what you or anyone else here thinks of me, so you can just kiss my pale ass, you little whore."

"Why…I…" the tramp growled.

"Oh, and by the way," I said as I leaned closer to her sneering face. "If I catch you saying nasty things either to Autumn or behind her back, I will pound you into the dirt, face first. She may not want to hurt you because you're family, but I have no problem smashing up that pretty little face of yours."

Sophia said nothing but stood rigid, heaving. Her fists were shaking, and her teeth were clenched. I saw her eyes glance over to the table of teachers, who seemed to have taken an interest in our conversation. I took this opportunity to turn around and start back to the table.

"Tootles!" I chirped. As I walked back to the table, I mentally reprimanded myself for using that godforsaken word, but it was worth it to piss off that little skank. I glanced back and saw Sophia stomp back to her table, still heaving, shaking, and grinding her nails into her palms at her sides. Autumn gawked at me with their mouth half open.

"What did you say to her?" Autumn asked, removing her head slightly from the table. "I've never seen her that angry."

"Oh, nothing she didn't already have coming," I said right before I took a bite of my pizza.

Autumn sank her head to the table and mumbled, "I'm sure she's over there thinking of some other way to make my life miserable."

"She can only make you as miserable as you let her," I said, mouth still full of pizza.

"Yeah… but..." Autumn stuttered.

"But nothing! I understand it's hard being alone in a place that hates you. I will be here, so you don't have to worry about anyone else but us. Just ignore the rest of them and their bullshit."

Autumn stared at me, eyes wide open and mouth partially agape. She looked like a deer in headlights. "You mean that? You're not just here because the principal wanted me to show you around? I assumed we would go our separate ways after today."

"Nope, don't want to. I want to hang around you. I'm not sure how many times I will have to grind it into your head. You seem nice enough and are the most genuine person in this hellhole. Everyone else seems to be pretending to be something to try to impress someone and such. You hold yourself back because you don't want to attract attention, but you have always been alone here, so I can't blame you for that."

34

"Thanks…" she exhaled. "I just don't want people to do to you what they do to me."

"I wouldn't worry about that," I smirked. "People tend to learn to their place around me."

"Carrie," Autumn's eyes began to water. "You're the first person that's been nice to me in a long time." Tears began to drop from her eyes, and she held her head down to the table.

I stood up, walked around the table, and sat beside her.

"I just wanted to say, 'thank you,'" she continued to cry.

"Hey, hey, it's okay. You don't have to cry," I said. I put my arms around her and squeezed. She shook for a moment and then continued to cry. I looked up and saw Sophia glaring at me with arms and legs crossed, flipping her high-heeled shoe up and down on her foot.

I left my embrace of her and stood up. I retrieved some napkins from the center of the table. I sat down next to Autumn again and handed them to her.

"Thank you," she said again as she dried her eyes.

As the day dragged on, class after class, it felt like I was living in an endless cycling laundry machine. When the final bell rang, Autumn remained planted instead of getting up from her seat, as she usually did after a class.

After speaking to the teacher and receiving my sixth textbook for the day, I met up with Autumn, who had not left her seat.

"Is there a reason you're not getting up?" I said.

"Well… I prefer to wait until the halls empty out," Autumn nearly whispered.

"This is your school as much as theirs," I sighed.

"I know that," she let her gaze fall to the floor again.

"Come on, then," I tugged at her arm. "I need someone to walk me home. If I don't have someone to navigate these streets with me, I'll be cooked like some shellfish by the time I get home."

Autumn's lips curled upward at the one end, "Okay, let's go."

We departed the classroom, book bags in tow. Students were either doing one of two things. Some rushed out of the building, and others stuck about the halls in small and medium-sized groups, making meaningless conversation. Autumn and I weaved our way through the congestion of teens. Nearly every student we passed either sneered or looked away from her. I bared my teeth to a few but tried to ignore the rest. It was best not to allow Autumn to see that their looks affected me.

We finally shoved our way through the crowds and were confronted with Sophia, backed by her little posse of kissasses. Her sister stood a couple of steps back, hand on her forehead, again shaking her head.

"Look, bitch," Sophia snarled. "You and I have to talk."

I crossed my arms and looked Sophia directly in her eyes, "Go for it, but I don't have all day, Barbie."

Sophia hissed in a low tone, "New girl, this is my school, you hear me? The boys love me, the girls fear me. With one word, I can ensure a chick doesn't get a date or lose every friend she ever made. With one word, I can ensure guys get pounded by the football team until they are in the hospital. I won't allow you to disrespect me in my school. You hear me, new girl?"

I stepped within inches of Sophia, "And you listen to me, cunt. I don't give a shit what you do. Make sure I don't get a date while I'm at this hellhole, I don't give a crap. You can have everyone hate me like you have managed to do to your own family; I don't give a damn. You can send the whole fucking football team after me, go for it. I'll send them home crying to their mothers."

I leaned in even closer, "You see, I don't think you know who you're messing with. I don't give a fuck. Remember that. I do what I please, and I don't let little whores like you boss me around."

I turned to Autumn, "Come on, let's go. You and I have better things to do than to listen to the ramblings of some plastic doll that's been played with way too much."

I sidestepped her little group, and Autumn quickly followed. As we passed by Cristy, she looked up at me and let out a grin, which I returned. At that point, I was certain she was cool.

"Why didn't any of you say anything?" I could hear Sophia howling as we left.

36

"That chick is scary," I heard one of Sophia's male groupies say. I couldn't help but laugh.

"And what about you, my darling little sister?!" I heard Sophia say.

"Oh, go fuck yourself," Cristy sneered just before we walked out of earshot.

We weaved out of the school to find the sun beaming down upon us. I put my hands over my eyes to shield them from the orange-glowing bastard in the sky. I hated the daylight and the sun, but I wouldn't have traded anything in the world at that point.

"So, where do you live?" Autumn said.

"Elm... it's not far. Do you know where that is?" I said.

"Yeah, and it's not too far from my house," Autumn said.

"Carrie?" she stopped in her tracks.

"Yeah," I replied.

"Why are you so hell-bent on standing up for me? You just met me today," she questioned.

"I thought we already covered this," I said. "You're cool, and they are a bunch of phonies. Enough said."

"Not that I'm calling you a liar, but I don't really believe you. No, wait, that's not accurate. Of course, I believe you. Well, I don't think you're telling me everything."

I was frozen in my tracks, and my mind went blank. I wasn't expecting this at all. I had to think fast. It then hit me. I surveyed the environment to see if anyone was in the vicinity.

"It's because I know you're immortal," I said once I had confirmed that we were alone.

"You... do?" she said. Her mouth was agape, and she held her hands to her chest. With the way her eyes were open, it looked as if she had seen a ghost.

"I also know Judy is immortal, and I know this because I am, too," I said. "She's been a family friend for a long time."

Autumn finally expelled the breath she had been holding.

"We immortal girls need to look out for each other, and I've never had a friend that I wasn't afraid I would outlive. That's hard to find, and being alone is scary." Tears were now streaming down from my eyes. "I don't want to be alone, Autumn." These tears were far from false, and my reason wasn't either.

Autumn was now the one to wrap her arms around me, "You don't have to be alone, ever. I'll be there; you have my word. When an Alexander gives you her word, her word is her bond."

A small smile came across my face amongst the tears that streamed over it.

Chapter 5

As I attempted to pass under every tree, savoring every drop of shade I could muster, we finally found our way to my house. My neighborhood was like any other in the grand ole United States of America. The houses looked all the same, a staple of rapid suburban development. They were all adorned with either tan or white siding, had two floors, and had the typical two windows on the front, complete with hanging baskets of flowers outside.

Some of my neighbors were out tending to their lawns, which appeared not to need tending. Children frolicked in sprinklers or tiny pools in other yards, and their parents monitored their every move. But some played unsupervised in the streets, kicking balls or skipping rope. The whole scene, so meticulously 'perfect,' made me queasy. Perfection, I knew, was a rare sight. It was often a mask, hiding a harsher reality than what's found in the grittiest inner-city neighborhoods.

My mom had to choose the craziest-colored house on the block. It was a neon shade of pink, utterly disgusting in my book. The home was a chaotic mess from even the outside since Mom had yet to hang curtains on the windows, so at night, you could see right in. All you would see were piles of boxes in the living room. My house was a massive zit on the face of Americana itself.

Yet, despite its garish pink hue, I was relieved to be back in my home. With all its flaws, my home was a sanctuary of 'reality' amidst the illusions that this strange world had thrust upon me.

My expression went vacant, and my mind filled with memories of the home I was torn away from at a tender age. I reminisced about the authentic, genuine people I left behind, unsure if they still existed in that world. The ache of missing it all was unbearable. Above all, the absence of one of the few people who journeyed with me to this world, my sister, was a constant, painful reminder.

"Carrie? You okay?" Autumn broke me out of my train of thought.

"Oh, sorry about that. I was daydreaming there for a second. Want to come in for a few?" I invited.

"Well, I guess," Autumn said. "If you just give me a minute, I must call my mom. She has mapped out how long it takes me to get home, and I will be late. She won't get mad, but she'll worry about me, and I don't want her to do that."

"I can get that. Mom lets me do whatever I want, and she doesn't worry. I can see why yours would worry with that piece of hell we call school."

Being Autumn was on a million hit lists that she was probably unaware of, I was not surprised her mother would be so concerned.

Autumn retrieved a flip-style cell phone from her pocket. I immediately observed that it was either cheap or ancient. While most people carry touch-screen smartphones, Autumn's phone looked like a blast from the early 2000s. She pulled up her mother's number and then looked at me.

"I keep trying to talk them out of making me keep this phone; we really can't afford it," she sighed.

In a few moments, I heard a melodic voice answer the phone.

"Hi, Mom," she said. "Hey, I'm going to be a little late coming home."

The voice on the phone toned down its perky chirp.

"No, Mom, there is no trouble," she said. "I am just walking a friend home. She wants me to come in for a while."

Not a sound came from the phone.

"Mom, you there?" Autumn said.

If joy could be expressed in a single tone of voice, it emanated from that phone.

"Okay, Mom, I won't stay out too late," she said. I'll talk to you later. Bye."

I heard Autumn's mother say 'goodbye' and then she shut the clamshell phone.

"Okay, now prepare yourself," I warned. "My mom is a bit kooky."

"I think I can handle it," Autumn smiled. "I guessed that from the neon-pink paint on the house. No one has lived in this house for years. It looks like no one wanted to live in a neon-pink house, although it could easily be repainted."

"Yeah, but Mom digs the color. I hate it, of course. She is all about bright pastels and neon colors. I swear if she could live her life as a neon highlighter pen, she would."

"I suppose there could be worse traits to have in a mother," Autumn laughed.

"Yeah, I'm pretty lucky in that respect. She is a pretty cool mom. Now let us get inside before I bake to a golden brown."

Autumn giggled and followed me into the house. Once inside, I searched the living room, around the stacks and stacks of boxes to find my mother. Apparently, she wasn't among them.

"Mom, I'm home, and I have someone I would like you to meet!" I said.

My mother appeared from the kitchen. She was slightly shorter than me, with dark brown hair and eyes similar to mine, which were hazel but not quite as bright. She smiled broadly with ruby lips. She wore dark blue sweatpants and a white apron covering a bright green tank top. I glanced at her feet and saw her wearing hot pink high-heeled shoes. I rolled my eyes. It figured she had to be wearing the most ridiculous thing she owned.

"Oh, hi, dear. You're home. Who's your friend?" she asked, in her usual 'mother hen' tone.

"Autumn, this is my mother, Karen Abbey. Mom, this is Autumn Alexander," I said.

"Oh, are you two in class together?" Mom asked with an even wider smile.

"You could say that," I said. "It's bizarre, Mom; we are in every class together. Isn't that funny?"

"Yes, Carrie, yes, yes, it is," she agreed, not flinching. Turning her attention to Autumn, she said, "It's nice to meet you."

"You as well," Autumn said.

"So, I see you're wearing your favorite heels. Planning for a night out on the town?" I said.

"Absolutely. You know me so well. Maybe you and your new friend should go out; it might do you both some good," my mom said.

"I don't know, it's up to Autumn. Do you want to go do something, Autumn?" I said.

"Uh...well... yeah, I guess. I would have to stop at home first, though," she said.

"Good, then it's settled," Mom clapped her hands excitedly. "Autumn, I hate to do this to you, but if you'll be a dear, go outside and wait for Carrie. I must have some words with her in private. Don't worry, she's not in trouble."

"Sure, Mrs. Abbey," Autumn said.

"Oh, don't call me 'Mrs. Abbey', please. Karen will do. It makes me feel so old. I asked Carrie to stop calling me 'Mom,' but even if you have only known her for a day, you probably have learned how stubborn she can be."

Autumn laughed, "Yeah, I guess so. I'll be outside." Autumn stepped out of the house. I turned to my mother.

"So, you knew all along and didn't tell me! Judy was in on it, too, huh? I would have liked to have known, to be prepared!" I snarled. I wasn't sure if I was angry with my mother, but I felt like getting an attitude with her anyway.

"I didn't want you to worry. Plus, when we moved here, you would have searched her out and shadowed her for days before you met her at school. This way, you had a more natural introduction. I was only doing what was best for you," she clucked.

I sighed, "I still would have liked to have been prepared. How long have you known?"

"Before we moved here," Mom said. "Let's just say I have my sources."

"Wait... this is where we came to Earth, isn't it? All this work, and we are fucking back where we started. What the hell, Mom!"

"She wasn't here when we first arrived, I'm sure of it," Mom defended. "It's a massive coincidence; that's all I know to say."

I took a deep breath and exhaled, "So, what do I do now? I'm not sure if she knows what she is."

"You're just going to have to stick as close as possible until we know for sure. It's up to her parents to reveal her destiny. We are only here to protect her."

"Yeah, but she needs to be protected right now," I said.

"From what?" Mom gasped.

"That school, it's taking a beating on her. Her cousin has made everyone hate her."

"That's horrible," my mother replied. "Still, I'm sure it is nothing you cannot handle."

"And... I've been having problems with my spiritual sight when I'm close to her."

"I noticed that when she came in. That could be problematic, but I believe you'll overcome it."

"To make matters worse, I had a close call on the way home. She wanted to know why I was willing to stick up for her. She didn't believe what I had told her before was all there was to it, so I said it was because she was immortal and I needed a friend who wouldn't die on me. Judy did tell you she is one of us, right?"

"Yes, Judy did tell me that," Mom said. "I didn't think those beings would ever be allowed to be immortal because they must be incarnated in certain places to do certain things. That is just the way the universe works. One being immortal seems contrary to what they are designed to do."

"Did Judy happen to mention where Autumn's family got their immortality from? Was it that weird ambrosia stuff she made us eat when we arrived?"

"She didn't say," Mom answered.

"No matter, at least I don't have to worry about being alone anymore," I said. "I know that's a problem if you don't have a man in your life."

"Yes, very much so," my mother sighed. Her stature slumped momentarily, and then she popped back up straight. "Yes, you're going to need money if you're going to go do something tonight, aren't you?"

"Yeah, I suppose."

She pranced over to the sofa, picked up a small neon purple purse, and pulled a wad of money out of it, "Here, take this."

"Isn't this a little much?" My eyes popped open. "I'm not going to Cancun, you know."

"Yes, but you never know," she shook her head. "I've always been a bit too conservative with our money. Now, I won't be as much, so you do what you like with that. Remember that if you come back with any of it, I will send you back out to spend it."

"Oh, yes, Mother, smashing idea. Make me go back out into that oven they call Miami more than I must," I rolled my eyes. "Well, I better get out there. I know she's lived here for a while, but the heat is murder on anyone."

"Bye, Sweetie! Have fun! You know I will!" my mother called as I shut the door.

Autumn was out in the driveway, examining our car. She was hunched over, examining every angle it, eyes wide open.

"Like the car?" I said to her.

"Yeah... it's awesome. The new Lamborghini Diablo; I thought they didn't even put these into production; this is the concept car. I didn't think I would ever see one in person. I'm not sure how I missed it when we came in. Guess the house drew my attention."

"Don't ask me how Mom got ahold of it; I don't have the foggiest. And for some reason, she's been a bit frivolous with the money lately. She said I can drive it whenever, so some night when she's not going out, you and me can hit the town in style. I'm glad I talked her into leaving it in black; you don't want to know the color to which she wanted to subject this poor car."

Autumn laughed and said, "What do you want to do tonight? I'm not much fun, so I don't know what there is to do around here."

44

"Come on, this is Miami! There has got to be stuff to do around here. People from up north come here to party, so we should have no problem finding something to do."

"Okay, like I said before, I need to stop back at my house," Autumn reminded. "Mom will want to see me, and she'll want to meet you."

It was only a five-minute walk, and we stood before Alexander's pearl white house. It appeared as if it was right out of a Norman Rockwell painting. It was a picture-perfect piece of Americana, with actual tasteful garden ornaments such as realistic-looking snails, ceramic frogs on lily pads, and other similar items. The house's coat of paint gleamed and appeared to have been repainted recently. To complete the image, a white picket fence surrounded the property that came up to about my waist. The lawn was recently mowed and seemed extremely healthy, obviously not over-kept like many of our neighbors. Nothing was out of place.

I glanced over to the street and saw a white sports car. It was a model and make that I didn't recognize. In fact, it looked entirely custom, for it lacked any manufacturer insignias.

Autumn also saw it, sighed, and said, "Let's go, but I'm warning you. My uncle is here... and he is... interesting. Try not to kill him, please."

"I didn't kill your cousin, did I?" I replied.

"Yeah, but like father, like daughter," she warned. I wouldn't say I liked the sound of that.

Autumn opened the door for me, and I went ahead of her. The living room we found ourselves in wasn't much larger than the one at my house, but it was a very different room. Like the outside of the house, this room was extremely tidy. On the couch were throw pillows and a cover, all of which appeared to be hand-knitted. Even the drapes on the window were all handmade and were colored a light shade of blue, which let the Miami sun pass gently through. The room was also painted a light shade of blue, similar to the drapes. On the left side of the room was a bookshelf filled to the brim with books. I could see that most books had something to do with combat, such as 'The Art of War,' which seemed slightly out of place in such a peaceful environment. Usually, an environment like this would make me feel ill to my stomach, yet there was something extremely inviting about this place.

From the kitchen, I could see a woman of medium height approaching. As she came into complete view, my mouth opened wide. She was almost the spitting image of Autumn, just much smaller, about a few inches shorter than me. She wore an immaculate, flowing white dress that came down to her knees. Her slipper shoes were the exact same shade as her dress. Her long, blonde hair was tied back in an elaborate ponytail that came down to the small of her back, with a white ribbon tied on the end. Not a hair was out of place on this woman. Gorgeous was the only word I could think of to describe her.

"Mom, this is Carrie. Carrie, this is my mother, Cassandra Alexander," Autumn introduced.

"Cassy, is that worthless daughter of yours home?" a male voice called from the kitchen.

A loud crack was heard from the same direction, "How many times do I have to tell you, Joseph!" The voice was like Cassandra's but far harsher.

A short man appeared from the kitchen, rubbing his right shoulder. He was nearly half a foot shorter than Cassandra. He wore a simple T-shirt and jeans and had short, parted-down-the-middle, light gray hair. His eyes found their way to me, and he let out a cocky smirk. His gleaming blue eyes darted to Autumn, and he let out a barely audible hiss.

The woman that followed him was Cassandra's height and caused me to do a double take. Autumn and her mother may have looked very much alike, but this other woman and Cassandra were identical twins. This woman looked like Cassandra but the two were like night and day. Cassandra was meticulously neat, whereas this woman was less so. Her red sun dress was slightly wrinkled, and her hair was shorter, only going down to her shoulders, and was a bit wild but not disheveled. She sported a pair of red-framed sunglasses on the front top of her head. Whereas Cassandra only wore a simple wedding band, this woman had rings of all different stones and materials on each finger and a bracelet studded with diamonds on her right wrist. She was well-toned but not slightly muscular like Cassandra. She walked with a saunter of the hips, whereas Cassandra moved with the air of nobility. She was Marilyn Monroe, whereas Cassandra was Jackie Kennedy.

"Wow, it looks like Autumn brought home a fox," the short man remarked. "Hey darling, what are you doing hanging around with a loser like my niece?" he said as he examined me. No wonder Autumn asked me not to kill him; I was already two steps from lunging across the room.

The woman in red crossed her arms and rolled her eyes. In the half-moment that I had taken my eyes off Cassandra, she stood before the short man, her hands around his neck, thumbs on his Adam's Apple. She lifted him half a foot in the air and brought him to eye level.

"Listen to me, Joseph," she said, no longer speaking in her previous melodious, birdlike tone. Her voice became darker as she glared at him, "How many times do I have to tell you not to berate my daughter in my presence? I know you are incapable of stopping because your peon of a brain cannot handle such a change, but the least you could do is have the grace to say these things behind our backs. If that is too much for you, which I suspect it is, at the very least, not in front of Autumn's friend. Do I make myself clear?"

"Yeah… sure," Joseph choked.

"Good," she chirped, returning to her melodious voice. She dropped him to the ground abruptly. When his feet hit the ground, he stumbled back, using the wall to steady himself.

"Come on, Meg, let's go home. Cassandra is obviously on the rag," Joseph said as he weaved around me and Autumn to the door with Meg trailing behind. Joseph opened the door for Meg, and she stepped out. He turned to me, closed his fist, extended his pinky and thumb, and held them to his ear and mouth, signaling me to call him. Meg saw this, exhaled a frustrated breath, and bashed Joseph in the head. He held his head with one hand and shut the door with the other. What a fucking piece of work.

"I do apologize for that," Cassandra said. "Autumn's uncle needs to be kept in check while my husband is away. He never learns unless I do those sorts of things."

"It's okay, Mrs. Alexander," I said. "I thought it was funny. Men need to be kept in check once in a while."

"I still can't figure out how my sister tolerates him. I apologize also for his words to you. That was uncalled for," Cassandra put her hand on her forehead.

"Like I said, it's okay. I've heard worse," I replied.

"Mom, I have some great news," Autumn beamed a smile for the first time all day. "We aren't the only immortals in the area besides Principal Angler. Carrie and her mother are like us, too!"

"That's wonderful," Cassandra gleamed. "I know how hard it is to even get an education without people asking too many questions. I'm glad that you two found each other. Maybe we can invite Carrie and her mother over for dinner sometime."

"Yeah, that would be great. She'd love that, although she might clash with your house. My mother is a fashion nightmare," I laughed.

"I'm sure she's just fine," Cassandra grinned.

"Oh, and about dinner," Autumn said. "Carrie and I are going to go out. She wants me to show her around town."

"Do you have money?" Cassandra said.

"Yes, when do I ever go anywhere to spend it?" Autumn laughed.

The sound of the back door opening and shutting echoed through the house. Water was expelling from the kitchen sink.

"William, darling, is that you?" Cassandra called out.

"Yes, love," a male voice replied.

"Good. I'm glad you came home. We have someone to introduce you to," Cassandra said.

A tall man, at least by most people's standards, stepped into the living room. He was dressed in a dirty gray shirt and overalls. He held a gritty yellow hard hat in one hand. He was very muscular and had large hands. Long, messy hair hung down from his head, nearly as black as mine. He still stood a few inches shorter than Autumn. I couldn't help it. My eyes were fixed on his face. He was clearly of some Asian descent but also had very European features.

"Who is this lovely young lady?" the tall man said.

"This is Carrie," Cassandra introduced. "She and her mother just moved into the area, and they are like us. It's rare to find another immortal family so close to us."

"Yes, it is a pleasure, Carrie," William held out his hand to me. Looking like a complete jackass, I timidly took his hand and shook it like a kindergartener shakes their teacher's hand for the first time. I couldn't help it. I was still astonished by William's appearance. If Autumn and her mother were goddesses, he was a god.

"Well, the girls need to get going," Cassandra said. "Autumn has a lot of town to show Carrie, and they should start immediately. Don't be in a hurry to come home; stay out as late as you like."

"It was wonderful meeting you, Carrie. I hope to see you again," William bowed in the traditional Japanese manner.

I did my best to return his bow with one of my own, "Trust me, this won't be the last of me." I stood up to my full height. "Come on, Autumn, let's hit the town!"

Chapter 6

We stepped out of the Alexander house and into the spring sun. The sky was still blue even though the sun had sunk a bit. I glanced at Autumn, who seemed uncertain about what to do next. An awkward silence followed.

"Not that I'm a 'shopping' kind of girl, but do you know if there is a mall around here?" I said.

"Yes, there is one not too far from here. We can catch one of the buses, and we should be there within the hour," Autumn explained. She was no longer gazing toward the ground. I just realized that ever since we had left school, she hadn't walked with her eyes averted to the ground. She seemed to be more outgoing and less reserved. I was not fond of what that place did to her.

Autumn guided me down the street to a bus stop. She sat on the bench, and I sat beside her.

"So, what's your life like, Carrie? You have been asking me about myself all day but haven't given me a chance to learn about you. Where did you live before here?"

"Seattle," I said. "Guess Mom was looking for more sun and a chance to snag herself some spring break college guys. I swear that woman is insatiable. I know she runs around with a lot of guys, but she never brings them home. I've never seen her with another man, but I know she's often with a lot of them."

"There you go again," Autumn said. "I asked about you and got an answer, but then you started talking about your mom. What about you? Did you have friends in Seattle? A boyfriend you had to leave or something?"

"No, none of that, really," I said. Something about the statement felt off, but I dismissed the feeling and pressed on. "I'm always the girl people like, but they fear. No one ever wants to get too close to me most of the time. I've been with some guys, I'm not exactly Virgin Mary, if you know what I mean, but I've never had a boyfriend. Could never take the chance in falling for someone, you know. If Mom decides to move, that pretty much kills relationships." I kept feeling like something was wrong with what I was telling Autumn, but I couldn't place my finger on it.

"I see," Autumn said. "That must have been a hard life."

"Not really, it was all I ever knew," I said.

"Was?" Autumn said. "You mean it's over with, you know, the whole nomadic thing?"

"Yep, Mom said she's done moving. I was shocked, but she said she has found what she's been looking for here in Miami, whatever that is."

"I guess some people just have to find the right place," Autumn said. "I haven't always lived here myself. My mother and father moved here when I was in middle school... I guess that's inaccurate; I was homeschooled before coming here. We used to live in Western Pennsylvania, out in the country. Mom and Dad wanted to be close to the rest of the family, which had taken up residence here."

"That seems to have screwed you, if you don't mind me saying. I mean, look what it's got you."

"I don't hold it against them, though," she sighed. "They ask me all the time if I want to go back. We still have the old house back there. I always tell them no, that life is easier for them here. There isn't a lot of work there."

"Do you ever think about yourself?" I questioned.

She gazed at me, mouth slightly ajar. "Well, I guess I do... once in a while."

I shook my head at her and raised my eyebrows, "You know, you are a terrible liar."

Autumn exhaled, "Yes, I know. Mom says that to me, too. Yet, whenever it comes down to it, I always think of everyone else."

"I guess that's not such a bad trait when it comes to people you care about. You need to learn when to not worry about others and when not to. Your 'give a shit' switch is always stuck 'on,' girl, and we need to fix that."

"I get what you're saying," Autumn looked down. "I suppose that would be more difficult than any training Dad could put me through."

"You train? What sort of training? You don't mind me asking, do you?"

"Of course, I don't mind if you ask. My Dad teaches me the 'Ways of the Blade' and other such skills. He's nearly three hundred years old. He grew up and fought in the Warring States Period in Japan."

"Ah, sounds like hell," I said.

"It probably was. He fought to end the constant squabbling of the local governments, but once the constant string of small wars was finally over, he left like so many others."

"So, he was a samurai?" I asked.

"No, he was trained as a warrior by my grandfather. My grandfather is actually a shinobi by trade, but Dad always excelled in standard combat, you know, sword to sword. He was always a bit too big to sneak around, but he can do it if he really wants to."

"That's really cool," I said. "What about your mom? I mean, after what I saw her do to your uncle, she's a badass in her own right."

"Mom is pretty strong," Autumn agreed. "She never really studied combat formally, like Dad and me. My mother is a skilled medic, and of course, medics on the battlefield are just as fair game as everyone else, so she became skilled with a bladed crossbow and shield. My father befriended a nobleman who controlled the Greek island my mother and her family lived on. When the isle came under attack, my father agreed to help lead the nobleman's forces, and that's how he met my mother." Autumn stopped for a moment, "What about your mom? Here I am talking about myself again, and you've said nothing about yourself."

"Well, not much to tell. Mom doesn't talk much. She has a way of weaving out of questions. My father has passed away; that's about all I can really say."

"Oh, I'm sorry to hear that," Autumn said. "It's pretty obvious she can be a bit evasive."

"You're telling me. She always has her secrets," I said. At that moment, I realized that my relationship with Autumn was becoming no different than Mom's relationship with me. I knew I would have my secrets from her, at least for a while. I also knew I'd be able to tell her everything one day. Well, mostly everything.

The bus finally arrived at the stop and opened its doors. An older woman struggled to descend the stairs, and without being asked, Autumn took her hand to help her down. The woman thanked her as we boarded the bus. It was mostly empty, with only a few passengers remaining. For a city bus, it was surprisingly

52

clean, especially considering the many grungy city buses I had encountered before.

Autumn took a seat in the back of the bus, and I sat down next to her. She stared out the window, eyes open and a slight smile on her face. She was an entirely different person when she was not in school.

Autumn silently watched the world go by, and I observed her doing it. I was more than happy to do nothing but watch her. I should have been observing the surroundings and getting my bearings. Yet, at that point, I just wanted to witness her. She was unlike anyone I had ever met. There was far more to her than what was on the surface. It was apparent just by the look in her eyes, this 'eyes always moving, never slowing their scanning' look, that she was always thinking, always calculating something. Her mind always seemed to be going a million miles a minute. I wondered if she knew what she was and what her destiny held in store.

The ride concluded sooner than I expected, signaled by the bus coming to a stop. Both the back and front doors opened, and a few people stood up to exit through the rear doors.

I finally glanced out the window and found we were directly in front of one of the largest malls I had ever seen. The place seemed to span nearly infinitely in each direction. Part of me didn't want to know how far deep the place went back.

As we exited the bus, Autumn asked, "So, is there anything in particular you are looking for here?"

"Not really," I said. "Maybe some new stuff for my room; I threw away quite a bit when we moved. Mom was in a hurry for some reason." I understood why, although I wasn't about to tell Autumn. Not yet. I glanced over at her as I opened the door to the mall for her, "Are you planning on buying anything?"

"No, I'm just browsing," Autumn said, nodding a 'thank you' and stepping through.

"Browsing? I thought you had money."

"Well, I do, but not money I want to spend," she said.

"Saving for something?" I replied.

"No, not really; I'm just kind of frugal, I guess. I don't need anything, so I don't buy anything."

"Okay, I guess that makes sense," I said. Judging by her faded jeans and T-shirt, which was now, on closer inspection, an old Jimi Hendrix shirt, she clearly needed new clothes badly.

"If you don't spend your money, what do you do with it? I don't mean to be nosy or anything; I'm just curious."

Autumn smiled and giggled, "Actually, I sneak it into Mom's purse when she's not looking. Like I said, I don't need it, and between you and me, my parents aren't exactly in the best financial condition."

"Is this supposed to be a secret?"

"Sort of, well... to my uncles, it is. They would try to shove money down my parents' throats if they knew how bad off we are," she said.

"You mean that uncle I just met? He would try to help your family?" I said, my eyes wide open and my mouth almost circular.

"He's like that with his money. He may be a jerk to me, but when it comes to my father and mother, he does care about them. He and my father go back centuries and were friends even before they married twin sisters."

"I guess everyone has to have some redeeming quality," I conceded. "Yet, I assume they do not want to take his help?"

"Yeah, that's right. The same goes with my Uncle Dan, my dad's fraternal twin. They are too proud to take help from the family; it's just something that has always been that way."

"Pride makes us do stupid things. Not that I'm calling your parents stupid."

"I wasn't going to take it that way," Autumn said with a smile. "So, if I don't give back the money they give me, who knows where we might be? I prefer to eat than to have stuff."

"No arguments here," I agreed.

The mall was just as massive on the inside as it was on the outside. It buzzed with people from a wide array of ethnic backgrounds: Caucasian,

Hispanic, African American, Middle Eastern, and Asian, among others. It felt like every nationality was represented. The stores were spread across multiple levels, each one illuminated by vibrant neon signs. An escalator connected the ground floor to the second level, and in the distance, I spotted another escalator leading to yet another floor of storefronts. Flat-panel monitors adorned the walls, displaying advertisements for various products in the otherwise empty space. The entire place resembled a glowing neon carnival. Normally, such places made me feel uneasy, but on that particular day, I had an ulterior motive.

"This might take a while," I said, expelling a huff of air.

"Why? Is there any other reason beyond the fact that this mall is gigantic?" Autumn said.

"Yeah, I've got a lot of stuff to buy, and Mom gave me a ton of money. She said I had better not come home with any of this money left, or she would send me back out tomorrow to spend more. I can't stomach another visit to a place like this so soon."

"Oh," Autumn said and then started to laugh. "It's funny, you know. Most parents don't want their kids coming home broke, but yours says don't come home until you spent it all."

"I told you she was a kook. Would you be willing to help me?"

"Sure, you name it," Autumn said. Her eyes were wide open as she anticipated the chance to help me.

"I have an idea. How about I buy you something?" I said.

"No, you don't need to," Autumn declined. "I wouldn't feel right without earning it somehow."

"Did I say you weren't going earn it?" I looked at her with eyebrows down, my lips curled up on each end. "You see, I've always been the little sister. My sister spent most of my childhood dressing me up, and I'd like to know what it feels like. Here's the deal. You let me dress you up like a doll, and I'll buy you something, and that something is of my choosing.

"Okay..." Autumn said, tilting her head to the left and back a bit. "Carrie, did anyone ever tell you that you are one strange individual?"

My lips curled even tighter, "I hear it all the time."

Chapter 7

Our first stop was a small boutique that sold goth apparel. Some people were shocked that the whole 'goth' thing had lasted as long as it did, but I wasn't. There will always be angry people who want to wear black. I'm one of those people, although I had never felt more alive in my life than I did at that point.

I wasn't comfortable without my sword. It was challenging to carry a sword around Miami and expect people not to ask questions. And Autumn's way of blocking out my spiritual sight was unnerving. Yet, I couldn't have been more excited. I was now on duty for the first time in my life. Although, if something were to happen, I wasn't sure about my ability to protect Autumn. Not that Autumn was defenseless; I knew better. My mother always taught me to never take my charge's abilities for granted. Even if she had godlike powers, I should still be the first to confront a threat.

I browsed the goth store to find something that would fit me. Fortunately, my size wasn't exactly typical, so most of the good clothes were available. I was relatively tall and had a waist, so the super scrawny girls couldn't fit into my stuff, and the average girl couldn't either. While looking for clothes for myself, I kept an eye on Autumn, who was also browsing the shop. I picked out a pair of baggy pants, complete with metal rings and chains, and a black T-shirt with the chest of a human skeleton on it. I also picked up a black plaid skirt and a black tube top that read 'Go Away!'. I stepped into the dressing room at the back of the store and quickly changed my clothes.

"How do these look?" I stepped out of the dressing room in the pants and T-shirt.

"That looks really good," Autumn said with a quiet voice.

"I like it because the shit fits just right, hugs to me without suffocating. I'm going to try on the other outfit; stay right there!" I said. I stepped out of the dressing room in the skirt and tube top in no more than a moment. "So, what do you think?" I said.

Autumn's eyes lowered to the ground, "Wow, Carrie, you look terrific in that. You're really pretty; you can pull it off."

"So, are you trying to say you're not?" I said with my hand on my hip, shaking my head.

"Well, yeah. I mean, I'm nowhere near as pretty as you. That's why I was shocked you would even talk to me. Most people want nothing to do with me," she said, eyes slinking even further to the ground.

"Autumn, that's not because you're ugly or anything to do with you. It has to do with that bitch of a cousin of yours.

"So, what are you trying to say?"

"I'm saying you are pretty, too," I reassured.

"That's why you want to dress me up?" she questioned. "So that you can prove to me that I'm pretty?"

"Can't keep anything from you, can I?"

"I guess. I don't think it's going to work. I mean, it's not up to me to decide if I'm attractive or not; it's up to other people."

"That's what you think. I'm going to show you one of these days what's wrong with that type of thinking," I replied.

I turned from Autumn and pulled the curtain shut. I put on my clothes and exited the dressing room. I took the clothing I wanted and left it with the cashier.

"Can you help me find something for my friend? She's... well, tall," I said to the cashier.

The female clerk with the ring on her lip and the dark eyeliner looked at Autumn and said, "You're telling me. What do you have in mind?"

I stepped toward the cashier and whispered my idea. Autumn crossed her arms, rolled her eyes, and smiled slightly. Then, I pulled away from the cashier.

"I think I have something in the back. When we got it in, I didn't think we'd ever find someone who could fit into it. I'll be back," the cashier said as she walked to the store's back and entered a door marked 'Employees Only.'

"What did you do?" Autumn said to me with a jokingly scolding tone.

"You'll just have to see. It probably isn't your style, but I want to see it on you anyway."

Autumn smiled and shook her head.

"Hey, give me a break; I was the little sister. It was always my sister dressing me in stuff. Oddly, her fashion sense stuck with me," I defended.

"Where is your sister now?" Autumn asked.

"Who knows?" I shrugged my shoulders. "Last time I heard, she picked up some boyfriend that was in the army. Figures she would go for some army guy."

"My brother is in the army," Autumn said. "He is skilled with the blade, just like the rest of the family, but he's willing to use a gun if it means protecting the place he loves. While he is out making a difference, the rest of us are just back here, surviving."

"Don't look at it like that; you'll get your turn; I just know it. And I doubt you'll have to join the army, either," I said. I thought it was safe to say she had no idea what she was.

"I found it!" the cashier exclaimed as she pranced into the room. "It's been back there a few years, but I think it's still pretty awesome, so you should try it on."

Autumn examined the dress, glanced at the cashier, looked at me, and then turned back to the dress. She then said, "Do I have to?"

"You said you want to help me out. This would help me out. Come on, loosen up a little. It's not like it will stick to your skin or anything like that," I teased.

"Alright, here I go," Autumn stepped into the dressing room.

After a few bumping thuds and noises of ruffling clothes, all movement in the dressing room ceased.

"There, I tried it on," Autumn pouted.

"Come on out," I said.

"Do I have to?" Autumn whined.

"Yes, now get out here, silly," I replied.

Autumn emerged in the black silk dress. The dress was primarily black lace. It had shoulders but left Autumn's sternum exposed and showed off a decent amount of cleavage. Autumn held her eyes to the ground again, trying not to look anyone in the eyes. Her figure was astonishing. Like her cousins, she was far more developed than your average sixteen-year-old. I was just surprised her baggy clothing could hide it as well as it did. She had the sort of body that both porn stars and models would be jealous of.

"Wow... Autumn... you look... awesome," I stumbled, attempting not to let too much of my attraction for her slip out. Fortunately, she was too embarrassed to notice.

"You're just saying that," Autumn denied, cheeks red.

"No, dude, she's not," the cashier said. "I'll be first to admit that dress doesn't look like it's your style, but you do look good in it."

A smile came to my face. I pulled two hair ties out of my pockets, took Autumn's hair, and put them in dual ponytails.

"Who does she look like?" I asked the cashier.

"Oh, my god, I know," the cashier replied, putting her hands over her mouth. "Misa Amani from Death Note! A really tall Misa."

"Bingo, except Autumn's far smarter than Misa; she was a bit of a dingbat," I laughed.

"I do?" Autumn turned to the mirror and studied her reflection.

"You're familiar with Death Note, Autumn?" I asked.

"Yes, Mom would play the DVDs for me when I was younger. It was about a young man who found the Death Note, which would kill anyone whose name was written within it. After watching, we would talk about what happened in each episode. We did that with a lot of anime and other shows. She would always teach me lessons from them."

That entirely made sense. Death Note was about doing evil things for the greater good. The user of the Death Note, Light Yagami, tried to create a utopia by killing off all the criminals in the world, but in the process, he became obsessed with his goal. The reason why Cassandra Alexander chose to expose

59

her daughter to this violent story was simple. It taught that using power to do horrible things to control the world never works, a path and decision Autumn may face one day. She would be the one with the terrible power, and she would have to choose what to do with that power. Showing her an animated version of what could happen with such power must have been the most effective way to approach the subject without telling Autumn too much and scaring her.

"Autumn, what did Misa do for a living in Death Note?" I asked.

"If I remember right, she was an idol... pretty much just a model that spends most her time doing advertising," Autumn replied, still looking in the mirror.

"That's right. What does that mean if you look like Misa in that dress?" I said.

"You're not going to get me to say it or believe it," Autumn declared.

"They don't pick ugly idols, you know," I sighed.

"Can I take it off now?"

"Sure, sorry to put you through so much for my curiosity," I said.

"It's okay, it is kind of fun, in a way," Autumn said as she pulled the curtain.

Autumn and I left the gothic shop and went to other stores, picking out items for my room. I found one of those novelty stores, where most of the merchandise made Autumn blush. I picked out a few posters. The ones I had brought with me had been destroyed thanks to the hasty move. One was a dark forest scene with a scantily clad dark fairy, which reminded me of one of the stories that my father used to tell. My mother told him not to fill our heads with those same stories. I picked up a small statue of a gray dragon, which caused me to reminisce about the massive dragon that flew over our heads on our escape. I also purchased many fun bumper stickers that I would haphazardly plaster on my wall between my posters.

I decided not to humiliate Autumn any further. She stood quietly as I chose things for myself, offering her opinions if I asked for them.

"Okay, I think I've had enough of this place," I said. "Did you see anything you liked?"

"I don't know," Autumn said. "I'm not used to shopping. I go to thrift stores when my clothes become too tattered to be repaired. There isn't much selection at those places."

"Yeah, I get you. I won't make you pick out something; I understand this isn't something you're used to. I'll save it for your birthday or something," I said. "When is that, by the way?"

"September twenty-second," she said.

I laughed, "The first day of Fall, I get it. Also, that makes you a Virgo, which is totally you."

"I've been told that before," she grinned.

"Constantly concerned with doing the right thing, yep, that's a Virgo," I continued to laugh. "Mine is October thirty-first. I was born on Halloween, and my sister is so jealous. Also, that makes me a Scorpio, and that's me; desire is what I live for."

"It seems like you were born goth," Autumn said.

"Yep, would seem so," I said. "Let's get out of here before any of these douchebags start trying to ask us out."

As we exited the mall, I turned to Autumn and asked, "So, where is a good place to get chow around here?"

"There is a good pizza place close to here, but..."

"But what?" I questioned.

"But... my cousin tends to hang out there. I prefer to avoid her," Autumn's gaze again looked to the pavement, the same as she had when we were back in school.

"Autumn, you can't let that bitch tell you where you can and can't go. This is a free country."

"Yes, but just because you can go someplace doesn't mean you should. I could also jump into a shark tank, but you don't see me doing that."

"True, but humans don't belong in the tank with a shark. On the other hand, you have every right to go to eat wherever you like, even if it's your cousins' hang out."

"I guess so," Autumn looked to the floor once again. "If you really want to, let's go.

Chapter 8

Autumn and I took a brief walk down the street and soon spotted a small pizza joint on the right side of the road. It was a quiet establishment amidst the bustling Miami nightlife. The stone building stood alone, flanked by alleys on both sides. Its tan exterior and brown shingles gave it a somewhat unassuming appearance—more of a hidden gem than a showy restaurant. It had the charm of a local dive that only residents truly appreciated for its high-quality food.

As we approached the pizza parlor, I saw Autumn reverting to that girl I had seen at school. I didn't want that, but at the same time, I knew it was vital for her to know that her cousin didn't control her life. Often, protecting someone requires you to put them in the one place they really don't want to be.

I opened the door for Autumn, and she stepped inside. The entire place resembled a scene from the 1950s, complete with black checkered floors and various pieces of Americana like a print of the famous painting "Crack the Whip" and some works by Norman Rockwell. The tables, booths, and stools boasted shiny metal frames covered in cherry red pleather. In one corner of the restaurant stood an old-fashioned jukebox that looked vintage, but was playing the latest terrible pop music, which I usually tried to drown out with hard metal in my head.

I could see Autumn's eyes searching the shop for her cousin. I saw the smug bitch the moment I walked in the door, laughing and carrying on with her douche friends. Autumn turned to the door, and I gripped her arm.

"Don't let her control your life. You have every right to be here as much as she does."

"I know, but is it worth the trouble?" she replied.

"Autumn, you're rolling with me now. That means we go where we want, do what we please, and no one is going to tell us otherwise, especially that two-bit whore."

"I guess so. I mean..." Autumn stuttered

I put my index finger gently on her mouth to quiet her, "It's going to be okay. You have every right to be here. You don't have to say anything unless you want to. I'll deal with her."

I took Autumn by the wrist with two fingers and led her to a table. Just touching her caused me to blush, which, fortunately for me, her sheer discomfort caused her not to notice. I sat down at a table, and she followed suit as I placed my bags from the mall on the floor. The waitress, a girl from our math class, approached with a scowl.

"Look, I'd appreciate it if you guys left. I don't need Sophia stealing my boyfriend because I'm forced to wait on you and her..." she scowled harder in Autumn's direction.

Autumn's eyes sunk to the table.

"Listen here, you little tramp," I snarled. "I don't care if Sophia threatens to kill your family and your firstborn fucking child, you're going to wait on us, or I'm going to have a fucking word with your boss, comprende?"

The waitress sighed, "Fine, what do you want?"

"I'll take a cola to start with. How about you, Autumn?"

"Just water, please," Autumn's eyes sunk even lower to the floor.

The waitress stormed off. I made a mental note not to leave a tip. I turned to Autumn. It wasn't right that she had to endure this. My focus immediately shifted to the table with Sophia and her friends. The bitch was already out of her chair and looked ready to 'whore' her way over to us. I could see her sister shaking her head.

Sophia sauntered to our table, ignoring her sister's dissuasion. This time she was dressed even more like a whore than she was at school. It was a similar outfit, tube top and miniskirt, but the skirt was even shorter, and the top covered even less. Her heels were ungodly high, making an already leggy blonde appear even taller.

After what felt like an eternity, she finally arrived at our table. She glared at Autumn, who was trying even harder to be unseen.

"Autumn, what the fuck? I thought you and I had a talk the last time you showed up here. I don't need my disease-ridden cousin here cramping my style. Get out if you know what's good for you."

Sophia turned to me and opened her mouth to speak. Instead of her voice, the loud, piercing sound of a small dog's bark escaped her throat. The ambient chatter of the restaurant was silenced, with all eyes glued to her. She cleared her throat and tried to continue, but the same sound of a dog came out of her mouth instead of words.

Sophia kept trying to speak, but the only thing that escaped her throat was her best impression of the ear-piercing shrill of a small canine. She covered her mouth and bolted out of the pizzeria. Her entire table was stunned. They remained silent and stared at each other, confused.

Cristy stood up and turned to the table, "I think it's best the rest of you get the fuck outta here," she said. Without hesitation, the group popped up from their table and began to evacuate like a mob of meerkats alerted to the presence of a predator.

"What about the check?" one of the boys muttered.

Cristy turned to him and curled her lip in a snarl, "I got it." Without a word, the entire group evaporated from the restaurant.

Cristy walked over to our table. She was far shorter than her sister and Autumn and didn't try to use heels to make herself taller. She wore the same black leather jacket, tube top, and skirt she had worn earlier that day at school. There was something infinitely sexier about this girl in comparison to her sister, even though they looked so similar. Just like Autumn's aunt and mother, they were worlds apart. Cristy seemed to have a sense of style that her sister lacked.

"Can I sit down?" Cristy asked.

"I don't know," I said. "Ask Autumn."

Cristy looked to Autumn, but before she could say a word, Autumn muttered, "Sure."

Cristy turned a chair backward and straddled it, letting her short legs dangle under it, "I need to talk with you guys. Not the talk my bitchy sister was trying to have, a real talk."

"What's up," I inquired.

Cristy turned to Autumn, "Autumn, I don't know how to ask this." Cristy took a deep breath. "I don't deserve it, but I will ask anyway. Can you forgive me? For all the shit I've stood by and watched and let happen? Can you forgive me for being a bitch?"

Autumn's eyes rose from the table and finally met Cristy's, "This is some kind of joke, right?"

"No, it's not. Since you moved here, I've let my sister walk all over you. I've tried to talk her out of it, but she never listens. That's no excuse. I've sat by and watched it happen nonetheless."

"What made you do this?" Autumn asked. "Before today, you never seemed to say a word whenever Sophia was..." Autumn left the rest of the sentence to the wind.

"It was when I saw Carrie beat the crap out of that fat bitch. A complete stranger came and stood up for you. Yet, here I am, your cousin by blood, and I did nothing but watch. That shit isn't cool. Our mothers are sisters. We should be close friends, not whatever the fuck we've been up to this point."

I couldn't help but smile. I prided myself on being able to pick out bullshit, and this wasn't it. Cristy was, in her own way, bearing her soul. She still couldn't manage to look Autumn directly in the eyes. I could see the shame wash over her face. I just hoped Autumn was smart enough to see what I saw.

"Can you forgive me, cous'?" Cristy said.

"Sure," Autumn said simply.

"That's it?" Cristy said. "No conditions, no 'I have to carry your books around for the next month because of the bitch I've been'?"

"My forgiveness doesn't come with conditions," Autumn declared.

"Okay," Cristy took a deep breath, "Next question. Can I be your friend?"

"My friend?" the color drained out of Autumn's face.

"Yeah, you know, amigos, tomodachi, you know, friends?" she said.

"I... guess..." Autumn's expression of shock lingered on her face.

"Sweet," Cristy smiled. "How about you, Carrie? You're one of the biggest badasses I've ever encountered; how about it? Friends?"

"Sure, why not," I nodded my head. "You seem pretty cool. I respect any woman that can make a table full of people scramble by her word alone."

"Great," Cristy's smile now beamed. Before she could say anything, the waitress returned with the drinks."

"Oh, hi, Cristy," she said timidly.

"Tiff, what's with the face?" Cristy said.

"Oh...nothing," Tiffany said as she put the drinks down.

"If you're worried about my sister, don't be. I'll keep her in fucking check. I expect that when my cousin comes here, you treat her and Carrie like royalty."

"Sure, Cristy," Tiffany nervously nodded.

"And if my sis' tries anything with your man, I will personally kick her ass. I'm sick of her shit." Cristy reached into her jacket pocket, pulled out a credit card, and handed it to Tiffany.

"Put my table's check, and this one's on my card along with a big ass tip for yourself. I don't give a shit if it's two hundred dollars."

"You're joking, right?" Tiffany's eyes popped open.

Cristy fully turned to the waitress, "Does this face look like it's messing around?"

"No, okay, whatever you say," she said as she pulled out her tablet and pen. "What would you guys like?"

"Autumn, you order; I don't know what's good here," I said.

"I guess a sixteen-inch deluxe," Autumn said. If she looked confused before, now she was downright flabbergasted.

"I'll get that right in," Tiffany said. She walked back toward the kitchen.

"So, what have you guys been up to?" Cristy turned back to us.

"Just shopping," I sighed.

"Oh yeah, that mall is ridiculous," Cristy laughed.

"Cristy," Autumn muttered.

"Yeah?" she replied.

"You're serious about all this, right?" Autumn said.

Cristy leaned back, put her feet on the table, and grinned, "Like cancer."

Chapter 9

Cristy, Autumn, and I strolled leisurely through the neighborhood, making our way back to Autumn's house. That night, the full moon shone brightly; we hardly needed the streetlights to see our path. I was amazed at how large the moon appeared as we traveled closer to the equator. Its gentle light was always reassuring to me—it was the only type of light I truly enjoyed.

The city slowly dissolved into the suburbs, where large buildings and businesses became family bungalows nestled in amongst the shrubbery and semi-tropical greenery of southern Florida. The place was utterly silent during this time of night, free from the obsessive lawn care and rowdy children that plagued it like locus in the daylight. I had always been under the assumption that Florida was full of old people, but that hardly seemed to be the case. I saw young people with their families or tourists coming from all over the country to soak up the sun, or in many cases, immigrants from neighboring Cuba looking to make a life in this supposed great country. The entire town was a confused mess, struggling for its identity.

As the night wore on, Autumn became less withdrawn with her cousin and more vocal, smiling and giggling at our jokes in that still somewhat meek manner that made her so damn cute. The laughing abruptly stopped as Cristy began to squint in pain. She put her fingers to her temples and grimaced.

"What's wrong?" Autumn worried.

"I… don't know," Cristy said. She quickly searched the surroundings.

"Are you okay?" I asked.

"Yeah...I think so," she said.

A smile returned to her face like nothing had happened, "So, whose kick-ass car is that in Autumn's driveway?"

I peered ahead and saw none other than my mother's sleek black beast in the Alexander's driveway. The lights on the back lit up as it backed out and tore down the street with a thunderous roar.

"It's... my mom's," I said.

"Really? Sweet!" Cristy said.

"What the hell was she doing here?" I asked. I knew the answer to that question, but I was reasonably confident Cristy and Autumn didn't.

As we walked up to her house, Autumn yawned, "Man, I'm beat."

Cristy stretched, "Me too. Autumn, you look like you've had one hell of a day; why don't you head up to bed? I'll make sure Carrie gets home. These back streets can be confusing if you haven't lived here a while."

"Are you sure?" Autumn said.

"Yeah, I want to get to know Carrie a bit better anyway. Get upstairs and get your beauty sleep." Cristy laughed and jokingly punched Autumn in the shoulder. "Not that you need it."

"Okay...I guess. Good night, guys," Autumn turned and went up the stairs.

I couldn't help but stare at her as she walked into the house.

"She has a gorgeous ass, doesn't she?" Cristy turned to look at me after Autumn closed the door behind her.

"Ah... yeah. Caught me, huh?" I said, blushing. I had never blushed as much as I did that day.

"Yeah, but I didn't need to. Carrie, you are the first person outside of my Uncle William and Aunt Cassandra I'm going to be straight with," Cristy peered around to see if anyone else was around.

"What do you mean?" I cocked my head.

Once Cristy confirmed we were alone, "Let's put it this way: it wasn't a coincidence my sister started barking like a dog today."

"I had a feeling, so I take it you're far from normal," I said as we turned toward my home.

"Yeah, and I know Autumn's secret. And I knew who you were before I even met you today."

70

"Wait... okay... I can get that you know Autumn's secret. I bet your whole family knows, and she doesn't. But how the hell did you know about me before we met?"

"Well, I'll start at the beginning," Cristy expelled. "You see, as you can probably guess, I can read minds and manipulate them. Thus, my sister bark like a dog."

"Does she know you're the one who did that?" I asked.

"Nope, only Aunt Cassandra and Uncle William know that secret. Oh, and Autumn's Aunt Mina too. The rest of this damn family can't be trusted with that information. The last thing I'd need is my dad dragging me to Vegas to help him win card games."

"I get that," I nodded. "That still doesn't explain how you knew about me before I even showed up at your school."

"That has to do with Autumn. We were all stuck in Aunt Cassandra and Uncle William's basement a couple of years ago, weathering out a hurricane. After everyone fell asleep, Autumn sat up in her sleeping bag and blankly stared at me. It was the strangest fucking thing I'd ever seen. Her eyes were glowing in the dark, I shit you not. She then asked, "Where's Carrie?""

"What!?" I exclaimed.

"I asked her who Carrie was, and she replied, "My Tala'har." And you can imagine I asked her what the fuck was a Tala'har, and she explained that you were some type of magic bodyguard. That is all accurate, right?"

"Yeah, to the letter," I said, mouth wide open.

"It gets worse, though. She then said she was scared. When I asked her of what, she said 'The man in black.' I said who the hell was the man in black, and she didn't know anything about him, that his 'identity is hidden by Oblivion herself,' whatever the fuck that means."

"You mean she knows who I am!? That doesn't make any goddamn sense."

"No, I don't think so. The next morning, I asked her if she remembered talking to me in the middle of the night, and she said she didn't. So, I'm assuming this has something to do with her soul because her mind was entirely blank as

71

she talked to me. That isn't even possible. If you talk about something, your mind is thinking about it, regardless. I would know."

"Wow... that is just strange," I said. "I'll have to ask my mom about it." I took a moment to absorb it all. "Back to you. You know what Autumn is because you can read minds?"

"Yeah," she said.

"Does your sister know?" I asked.

"Unfortunately, yes," Cristy said. "She accidentally overheard our parents talking to Autumn's about it shortly after they moved here to Miami. All she understands is that Autumn is 'special,' and she isn't. She also doesn't like that Autumn is prettier and taller than her. My sister's desire in life is to be a model. Models are, of course, tall, and Autumn has her beat by a good seven inches. Autumn is also both muscular and curvy at the same time, which makes my sister unbelievably jealous. At first, it was bad enough for her to know Autumn was special. But when Autumn started to 'fill out,' she got really terrible and started spreading rumors. Not your normal, tit-for-tat shit either. She started telling people that Autumn has all sorts of diseases and is a complete whore, right down to soliciting tourists. Does everyone believe this shit? No. You have no idea how many guys in that school have a crush on Autumn. They are all afraid to ask her out because of Sophia."

"I figured as much. So... you know about... my attraction to Autumn?"

"I don't need to be a mind reader, honey," Cristy said. "Plus, if she and I weren't blood-related, I'd want to do her."

"I see," I couldn't muster more of an answer than that. The things Cristy knew were just a little hard to swallow.

"And to be honest, you can't protect her alone. I don't know the specifics about my cousin's destiny, but I know it will be rough. You and I need to build her up and get her ready for it—something I should have been doing for years. You made me realize that. In a way, I owe you a lot."

"I didn't do anything but my job," I replied.

"Bullshit, you did more than that. You're the first real friend she's had in I don't know how long. I let my hang-ups get in the way of that. She's family, amongst other things. I should have had her back from day one."

"You shouldn't beat yourself up too much about it. You're here for her now; that's what's important," I replied.

"Now, the ten million dollar question: what will we do about my sister? I can only make her bark like a dog so many times before she starts to suspect something."

As we left the vicinity of Autumn's house and away from her influence, I could see Cristy's aura even more clearly than I could at school. It was now a blazing pink, hinting at her extraordinary telepathic powers. I had a feeling with an aura that bright, and she had yet even to come close to reaching her full potential.

As we walked, I heard a twig break from a nearby bush. I dropped my bags, pulled out my small dagger, and crept toward it. Cristy had had the same idea and procured a far larger dagger. Where she retrieved it from, I wasn't sure.

Before we could react, a black blur, barely lit by the streetlights, dashed from the bush to another set and then out of sight. We stayed on our guard for a moment. Once it was apparent it was gone, we relaxed.

"You know that headache that I had earlier?" Cristy reminded.

"Yeah."

"Who or whatever the fuck that was caused it. I've been getting them all day whenever I'm around you and Autumn. It's whenever my mind instinctively searches for other minds around me. It's like static from a television, and it's fucking loud."

"So, we're being shadowed," I said. "I guess I shouldn't be surprised. The question is, why was it following us?"

"Autumn's too well protected right now. Whoever it is, they know better than to test my uncle and aunt. They were probably trying to eliminate us, so we can't be there to have Autumn's back."

"And we caught on before they were ready," I said.

"Sounds like it," Cristy said.

"What worries me isn't what we saw… but what I couldn't see…"

"It's aura?" Cristy said.

"You know about that too, huh?"

"Only because I could feel you examining me in a different way than a normal person, and I got curious. Sorry."

"It's cool. This is bad if I can't see an aura coming off this thing."

"Let's get you back to your house; it's unsafe for us to split up. I can call my dad and have him give me a lift home. I'll feed him some bullshit; he believes anything I say."

"Your dad doesn't seem like the brightest crayon in the box, no disrespect," I said.

"No, he's not," Cristy smiled. "But that makes him easy to manipulate when I need something."

"I suppose that's a plus," I laughed.

Chapter 10

My room was chaotic, with half-unpacked boxes scattered everywhere. The furniture included a bed, a dresser, and a desk with a matching chair. The new items I had picked up that evening were still strewn across the floor. The walls were painted a hideous light blue, which made me feel nauseous. If I were to stay here for any length of time, I would definitely repaint it. The only question was when I would find the time to do so, between protecting Autumn and keeping up with my schoolwork.

My mind felt like a merry-go-round, endlessly spinning all of Cristy's words as I lay in bed, awaiting sleep. My mind kept leaping back to 'the man in black' that she said Autumn mentioned in her trance. I was fairly certain that was who was following us.

"So, it seems you had a busy day," my mother's words exploded into the night air. She stood in my doorway with her arms crossed.

I nearly jumped out of my skin when her voice bombarded my ears, "Mom, don't scare me like that."

"Sorry, you're not usually that jumpy, and I can't normally sneak up on you like that. Is something on your mind?"

"Uh, duh. I arrive at a new school, find my charge, and, to add insult to injury, Cristy and I caught something following us on the way back to the house tonight."

"Cristy? I believe Cassandra mentioned that was the name of one of her nieces."

"That's the one. What worries me the most about this thing? I couldn't see an aura. It was like the thing wasn't there at all."

"That is worrisome. You'll handle it, though; I trust in your skill."

"I wish I did…" I sighed and then continued. What's strange is Cristy said Autumn entered a trance once. She seemed to know about me and what I am, a Tala'har, and something about a man in black who's out to get her. I think that might have been what was following us."

"You never know what her kind knows, dear. The Kar'kel are no different. They would occasionally pop out a piece of prophecy and not even remember they did it."

"Did Dad ever do that?" I asked. I wasn't expecting an answer.

Mom seated herself at the edge of my bed. I was waiting for her to find a way to avoid the question.

"Yes, he did. He predicted his own death. I never told him."

It took me a moment to swallow the statement. Mom never talked about Dad. She always avoided the questions. This time, it was straight to the chase, with no games.

"It should have been me..." Tears cascaded down my mother's face, caught only by the moonlight that peeked in through my window. I had never seen my mother cry, ever.

"Mom..."

"I'm the Tala'har, I'm the protector. He was Kar'kel. I should have been the one protecting the three of you, and he should be the one here."

"There was nothing you could have done. I remember that day more vividly than anything else..."

"It is a Tala'har's honor to die for their charge... I didn't get that honor. He died for me..." She turned red, "It's not supposed to go that way!"

I sat up on my knees in the bed, crawled over to my mother, and wrapped my arms around her, "Dad didn't die to defend his Tala'har. Dad died to defend his wife and daughters. Any good father would have done the same."

Mom cleared the tears from her eyes, "He was a good father, wasn't he?"

"The best," I said as I held her tighter.

When I awoke the following day, Mom was missing from my bed, where she had spent the night before. My cellphone's alarm was blaring the morning news because it wouldn't wake me up if it wasn't annoying. I slapped myself on the forehead, realizing that if I didn't hurry, Autumn might walk to school by herself and die.

76

I could smell breakfast, probably fresh from the local Dunkin' Donuts that wasn't too far off. Although, for some reason, it smelled far better than usual. Mom rarely cooked. She was far better with a sword than a kitchen knife. The poor woman could slice a man in two but couldn't roast a turkey if her life depended on it.

My mind was buzzing with thoughts of the previous day. So much had happened; I didn't know how to digest it all. As I showered, I daydreamed about wrapping my arms around Autumn and gently kissing her neck. I snapped myself out of the fantasy and tried to focus on getting ready. The longer I took to get ready, the longer Autumn was left without her Tala'har. With this thing that was following us, I wasn't sure if I wanted to let her out of my sight any more than I had to...

I completed my morning ritual by sliding my knife into my boot. It was the latest trend off the black market. It was completely undetectable by metal detectors and sharp as a razor. I was surprised that Cristy also had a knife on her, but it was some odd ornate dagger that was far more ancient than my modern marvel. I made a mental note to ask her about it and how she kept it hidden from the detectors at school, but that would come in time. I didn't want to alarm Autumn of the danger, at least not yet. She, after all, had no clue what she was and would start asking questions I didn't want to answer if she knew someone was following us around.

I rushed downstairs, careful not to trip on my long black pants. I wanted to get to Autumn's house before she could walk to school by herself. The stairs wound around the center of the house and led down between the kitchen and the living room. I took a left into the kitchen and was surprised to find Autumn seated at the table with my mother, eating what looked like a piece of homemade toast.

"Hi, Carrie," Autumn said in a chipper tone that almost reminded me of her mother.

"Hi..." I said, letting my lack of words be rather apparent. The fact that Autumn was sitting in my kitchen was surprising enough; what she was wearing was shocking. She was seated at the table with her legs crossed, wearing a lavender spaghetti strap shirt, a violet skirt that went down to the knees, and a pair of knee-high, black leather boots. If I were male, my eyes would have popped out of my head. They weren't far from doing that anyway.

"Oh, the clothes. Mom insisted I dress like a girl today. I had a sweater to go with it, but Mom refused to let me take it, saying it was far too hot for that. I've been fighting her on wearing this outfit for months, so I guess she won today," Autumn said meekly.

"I arranged with Autumn's parents that we would be the ones to bring her to school," Mom cut in. "There has been talk of people sneaking around at night, and her parents didn't want to take any chances, so I volunteered."

"How did you meet them, Mom? We saw you pull out of the driveway last night," I said, curious about the story my mother would tell.

"Judy called me about the prowlers sneaking around and hooked me up with Autumn's parents. Since you two seem to get along so well, you wouldn't mind if I took Autumn to school."

"That's fine," I said as I sat at the table beside Autumn, trying not to stare. I was failing miserably, but she didn't seem to notice.

"Mrs. Alexander sent some lovely baked goods and some homemade. She's so thoughtful, I've already explained that I'm a dreadful cook," Mom explained.

"I would try to disagree with her, but that's the truth. Starving Ethiopians would turn down her food," I laughed.

I took a slice of bread from the handwoven basket and spread it on what appeared to be homemade blackberry preserve. I took one bite and realized it must have been the most delicious piece of bread I had ever eaten. It was just bread. I could imagine what this woman could do with an actual meal. With food like this, I was shocked Autumn didn't look like Chubby Bitch from school. I once again mentally reprimanded myself for making fun of a girl's weight, even though it was just in my head. That was not the person I was anymore.

"I'll be right back; I have to go upstairs and get my keys," Mom said as I munched on my bread and jam.

"Carrie?" Autumn said.

"What's up?" I said, realizing my mouth was full.

"I don't look like... a slut, do I?" she said, eyes adverted to the table.

"No, I'm not even sure that's possible," I comforted.

"Well, this is just way more skin than I'm used to showing and..." she trailed off.

I put my arm around her shoulder. The touch of her bare skin was near electrifying, but I tried to play it off, "Autumn, beauty is something the Creator, whoever he or she may be, gave us women because men usually get more of the physical advantages. And just because you happen to have those advantages too doesn't mean you shouldn't show off what the God or Goddess gave you."

"Yeah...I understand that, but I don't want to confirm..." Autumn said as I put one finger of my free hand over her lip, interrupting her.

"Remember what I said about your cousin? Don't worry about her; she's of no consequence anymore."

I made the mistake of looking Autumn directly in the eyes while saying that. Her beautiful crystalline blue eyes were almost hypnotic, nearly overriding every bit of reason I had within me. I caught myself right before I did anything stupid and removed my arm from around her.

"Are you two ready to go?" Mom said as she came down the stairs. I was too busy staring at Autumn earlier to notice that my mom actually matched today. She was wearing a simple red dress and red heels. She looked a little dressed up to take me to school, but I suppose they were the only items she owned that weren't fluorescent and matched.

"Yeah, sure," I said. I spread another piece of toast and took it to the car. Autumn quietly followed along. I hoped she didn't notice what I desperately wanted to do when I had my arm around her shoulder.

I turned to her as I opened the door and sat in the seat behind the driver, "What's wrong?"

"Nothing, I was just thinking about what you said. I just feel nervous. I get enough grief already. The last thing I need is more."

"Go ahead and get shotgun; you're the guest here," I said, somewhat ignoring her comment.

Autumn shook her head and sat in the front passenger seat of the car. As my mother pranced out of the house and opened the car door, someone was running down the sidewalk.

Autumn turned and looked out the passenger window, "Is that Cristy?"

Sure enough, Cristy took the most significant strides her short legs would allow. It was almost strange seeing her run. She seemed like the type of girl who wouldn't run if her life depended on it, but there she was, dashing down the street.

"Hey, wait up!" she yelled.

"Is that your cousin, Autumn?" my mom asked.

"Yeah, that's her. What she is doing is beyond me," Autumn said.

Cristy finally arrived at the car and hunched over, "Hey, would it be possible to get a lift with you guys to school?" She turned to my mom and said, "Hi, Mrs. Abbey, I'm Cristy."

"I've heard wonderful things about you, dear. Go ahead and get in the back with Carrie," Mom said. "And please, call me Karen."

Autumn opened the car door and stepped out.

"Oh wow, who are you and what did you do with my cousin?" Cristy gasped as she scanned Autumn's clothing.

Autumn smiled gently and returned the seat, "We're going to be late if you keep gawking."

Cristy took the hint, ducked, and stepped into the back of the car. Even though Cristy was tiny, it was still a bit of a squeeze. The car was never really meant to seat four people.

Autumn nestled herself back in the car and closed the door. Mom ignited the engine, causing the Lamborghini to come to life. It stretched its massive paws, ready to stalk its prey.

Autumn turned back to Cristy and me and said, "I thought you had a car, Cristy. What's up?"

"Oh, nothing," she said. "Didn't feel like driving alone. I'm not fond of driving to begin with."

"I see," Autumn said. "That made you dash all the way here? It would have been faster to go straight to school."

"Well, I went to your house first, but your mom said you were here, so I came here," Cristy said.

"We're glad to have you," my mother interjected.

Chapter 11

The rest of the car ride was relatively quiet. I couldn't take my eyes off Autumn. It was hard not to stare at her. Since she was facing the other direction, she never seemed to notice. As we got closer to the school, her gaze shifted more and more to the floor. Out of the corner of my eye, I spotted Cristy with a wide grin on her face. Even though I had known Cristy for less than twenty-four hours, I recognized that smirk all too well.

We pulled up to the school, and it looked no different than it had been the day before.

"You girls have a good day at school; don't get into too much trouble," Mom said.

"We won't," I said.

"My ass we won't," Cristy giggled.

Autumn stood up and got out of the car, pulling the passenger seat forward to let Cristy and me out.

"Bye," my mother said in that exaggerated, chipper tone she was known for.

I took a step, glanced at Autumn, and noticed her feet were cemented to the sidewalk.

"Come on, no one is going to bite you. Cristy and I have your back today. I just want to see someone try to fuck with you," I said.

"That's right," Cristy agreed.

Autumn finally started to move toward the door, eyes still adverted to the ground.

Just as we arrived at the top of the steps, the sound of brakes squealing, followed by a light thud and a familiar voice yelling, emanated from behind.

The three of us turned to see Joseph's white car slam to a stop, inches from the bumper of another car dropping off students. The car's abrupt stop left black skid marks. Sophia kicked the passenger door open.

82

"Goodbye, Father!" Sophia squawked as she stood up from the seatless passenger side. She turned to the school, and it was apparent she had spotted us watching her.

She stomped as angrily as her high heels would allow her as she raged her way up to the school.

"What, the fuck is wrong with our father?" she yelled as she stomped up to us. "And why are you hanging out with these losers?" she hissed as she tried to straighten her disheveled hair. She unconsciously rubbed the red mark that was on her forehead as well.

"Not that it's any of your business, sister, but I didn't feel like driving, so I decided to get a ride with them," Cristy said with a near-sinister grin.

"You know what? I am so fucking pissed right now that I'm going to pretend I didn't see you here. What is wrong with our fucking father?" Sophia growled.

"I don't know. What did he do now?" Cristy asked.

"I caught him flattening my tires with his sword," she said. "By the time I snapped him out of it, he didn't even remember doing it. And because someone didn't leave her spare keys in the kitchen like we always do, I had to get a ride with that lunatic. And for some fucking reason, he took out the passenger and back seats out of the car, so I had to ride on the floor!"

"Sucks to be you," Cristy laughed.

"I swear, little sister, one of these days," Sophia stomped off ahead of us.

"Uh, Sophia," Cristy said.

"What!" Sophia turned with a snarl.

"Your skirt, in the back," she said.

Sure enough, a massive tear was going up the center of Sophia's mini skirt. Her ass was almost exposed.

"Oh, my God!" Sophia yelled. That's it; I'm going home!" Without another word, she stomped off in the direction she had come.

As soon as she was out of earshot, the three of us broke into laughter.

"I've heard of Uncle Joe doing some strange things, but slashing Sophia's tires? That is odd even for him," Autumn said.

"I don't know what's been getting into Dad lately," Cristy said with a smile. "He's been doing all sorts of weird stuff. Lately, he's been taking the car to drag races and taking out the seats to lighten it."

"I suppose he did that last night; that's why the car had no seats," I said.

"Yeah, he was off being a dick and getting chased by the cops. They never catch him, though, thanks to some of the features of that car. He never did properly thank you for it," Cristy said as she looked at Autumn.

"Thank you?" I said to Autumn.

"Yes, I put the car together," she said.

"Why? And you can do that kind of stuff?" I said.

"I've spent much time tinkering with mechanical stuff, including cars, when I'm not busy working to hone my sword skills. Speaking of which, I'm going to my great grandfather's dojo when Dad gets home. If either of you would like to join me, that would be great."

"Sure, I'll go," I said.

"Sorry, I'll pass," Cristy said. Krojo gives me the creeps. Maybe it's that whole 'we're not blood-related, and he's a complete perv' thing. I don't have any room to talk, but he's a thousands of years old, pervy ninja. A girl has to draw the line somewhere."

"Is your Dad the only man in your family who isn't a deviant, Autumn?" I said.

"My brother isn't," she took a deep breath. "I really miss him."

"We better get to class, or Mrs. Jenkins will have a fit," I said.

"Let the old bitty scream all she wants," Cristy snickered.

We walked toward our classroom, and I could see nearly every eye staring at Autumn, especially the boys. I could see the jealous looks on the girls' faces as we passed as well. Off to the side, I saw Susie talking to her loser lackeys, and the blood rushing to her face as we passed. I smiled and waved at the bitch as we continued. I could see it in her eyes that she wanted to lunge at
84

me, but she let us through unhindered. This made me smile; she obviously took Judy's threat seriously, plus seeing me, Autumn, and Cristy together probably made her think twice.

I didn't like being spiritually blind around this many people in an enclosed space. People's auras can hint at their intentions, and spotting threats is difficult without that ability. I took a deep breath and kept searching for a threat, but I was pretty confident no one here posed a physical danger to Autumn, especially with myself and Cristy by her side.

When we arrived at the classroom, I examined the people present. I immediately noticed the boy sitting in Autumn's seat yesterday. Autumn said nothing and sat down next to him, which was fine because plenty of seats were available in the front. I sat beside Autumn, and Cristy took her usual spot in the back.

"It's nice to see you on time today, Miss Abbey," Mrs. Jenkins said from behind her desk. "Miss Cristy is also on time; maybe you're rubbing off on her."

Cristy stuck her tongue out at the old woman. Mrs. Jenkins ignored the gesture.

"I'd like to think so," I said with a grin. I guess if I took anything from what Cristy said last night, I was.

The class eventually filled to near its total capacity. I wasn't sure if the kid sitting in Autumn's seat was new or someone absent yesterday, but I would find out soon enough.

"Good morning, class," Mrs. Jenkins squawked after the bell rang. We have yet another new student," she said as she gestured her hand to the boy sitting in Autumn's seat. This is Jacob Lewis. Some of you may know his sister, Lisa. As I said yesterday regarding Miss. Abbey, please treat him with the same respect you'd like to be treated with."

I took another glance at the new kid. He was cute in that quiet, reserved way. He was wearing a shirt from an anime I wasn't familiar with, and I had no idea what its name was because it was in Japanese. He also wore a pair of slightly tattered blue jeans. By the look of him, he may have been Autumn's type, if she had one at all. The thought of her dating anyone immediately made me feel the pains of jealousy. Yet, I knew that this wasn't about my happiness; it was about hers. If she liked this guy, we could rope him into our little circle before Sophia's nasty mouth got to him.

The class continued usually, with the new kid only speaking when spoken to. After class, I could see him staring at his schedule. Before I could say anything to him, he departed the classroom.

"Hey guys, I need to use the restroom; I'll meet you at our next class, Carrie," Autumn said.

I wouldn't say I liked the idea of Autumn going anywhere alone, but I had some questions for Cristy that Autumn couldn't hear.

"Okay, see you there," I said.

She half-dashed down the hall. I could see her trying to avoid eye contact with people, which immediately angered me, but it would have to be a concern for another time.

"So, you manipulated your father into slashing Sophia's tires, ingenious," I said to Cristy quietly as we started walking down the hall.

"Thank you," she smiled while mockingly bowing. "Why do the dirty work when you can manipulate your asshole father to do it for you?"

"How about the seats being missing? Was that a coincidence or something you set up?" I said.

"I just gave him the idea to go racing last night; no mental manipulation is needed," she giggled.

"That was so fucking great," I said. "What do you think of the new kid?"

"He's cute," she said. "I'd say I could show him a thing or two, but I have a feeling there is more there than meets the eye…"

"I mean for Autumn?" I said.

"I could see that," Cristy said. I doubt he would have the guts to ask her out. He probably thinks she's out of his league. I did catch him looking at her here and there."

"I think we should befriend him and try to hook them up. No mental manipulation, though," I said.

86

"Of course not! I would never use my abilities like that!" she said with mock disdain.

"I know; I just thought I would throw that out there," I replied.

"I'm surprised you're even suggesting this. I figured you'd be a bit jealous if she got a boyfriend."

"Yes, but that's something I must get over. This is about Autumn, not me. Right now, she needs a pleasant distraction."

"A boy would be good for her," Cristy said. "We just have to get to him before Sophia's lies do."

"I'll invite him to sit with us today at lunch. I doubt he'll have anyone to sit with."

"Wow, won't he be shocked when he gets invited to sit with three hot chicks?"

"Yeah, I could imagine," I said as we approached Cristy's classroom.

"Well, this is my stop," Cristy said.

"I'll see you later," I said to Cristy as she meandered off to her seat in the class.

At lunch, Cristy was waiting for us at the table we had used the day before. She crossed her legs, kicking her foot up and down as she popped gum.

Autumn and I sat down with our lunches, but I wasn't paying attention to the conversation she was having with Cristy. Instead, I was busy scanning the cafeteria for the new kid. When I spotted him leaving the lunch line and looking for an empty table, I waved him over. He approached us.

"What's up," he asked.

"Why don't you come over and sit with us?" I said.

"I don't think I should..." he said.

"Why, we don't bite," Cristy said with a wide grin. "Okay, I know Autumn doesn't bite, and I don't know about Carrie."

"I think you know the answer to that question, Cristy," I smiled, showing teeth.

"I don't think I should," he retracted.

"Why not?" I asked.

"Because you are..." he gulped air; "...three really pretty girls, I'm sure you guys could find better guys to sit with you."

"Two really pretty girls," Autumn mumbled.

"Hush you," I turned and said to Autumn. I returned my gaze to Jacob, "We wouldn't be asking if we didn't want you to sit with us. You are just fine; park it."

"Okay," he resigned. He sat in the empty seat between Cristy and Autumn. "I'm new here, so I don't have any friends yet. Thanks for letting me sit here."

"No problem. I'm new here, too. I only have a day for you," I said. "These two are all I got and all I need."

"Carrie, how rude of you," Cristy mocked. "You didn't introduce yourself or us."

"Ah, sorry," I said with a wide smile. "I'm Carrie, the vertically challenged one here..." Cristy giggled a 'Hey' over my introduction; "...is Cristy and Miss Legs over there is her cousin, Autumn."

"Hi," Autumn said.

"He...ll..o, I'm...Jacob, yeah, that's it," he stumbled.

"It's nice to meet you, Jacob," Cristy smiled.

I looked at Autumn and could see her blushing. I was starting to wish I could read minds; I was inquisitive to know what she was thinking.

"Why don't you tell us about yourself, sweetheart," Cristy said.

"Well, I just moved here, so as I said before. I'm not sure what else to say."

"What do you do for fun?" I said.

"Since I don't know anyone yet, I've done nothing but play video games since I've got here."

"What do you play?" Autumn said, her eyes finally meeting the boys.

"Ah, nothing you probably know. A lot of fighting games, RPGs, usual nerd stuff."

"Final Fantasy?" she said. Her interest seemed to be offsetting her natural shyness.

"Of course, I love all of them, played everyone," he said.

"You too? I have only been able to play the hand-me-downs from my brother," she said. "Which is your favorite?"

"Seven," he said. "The story was just incredible."

"Me too!" Autumn exclaimed.

Cristy nudged my shoulder, "It is nerd love already."

"Cristy!" I whispered.

"What kind of music do you listen to, Jacob?" Cristy asked.

"Oh, mostly the classics, none of the mainstream crap. You know, Hendrix, Guns 'n Roses, Metallica, all that good stuff."

"Tell me about it, you too!" Autumn said. "I can't stand most new music. It's not all garbage, but good stuff can be hard to find."

Autumn and Jacob continued to talk throughout the lunch period. It was amazing how much they had in common. I was unaware Autumn was that much of a geek, but hey, she was my geek. The more I learned about her, the more she intrigued me. As physically active as she was, I didn't even fathom she was such a gamer. Not that it's a bad thing; I love them myself. I just didn't see it in her. With all the things she was invested in, I was surprised she had the time for it.

The bell rang, and we cleared the garbage from our table and headed to class. Jacob left ahead to get to his class on the other side of the building. Autumn, Cristy and I headed toward ours.

"So, what do you think? Nice guy, huh?" I said.

"Yeah," she said in a breathy tone I recognized all too well. Someone had a crush.

"I've never talked to a boy that long. I've always been shy. I hope I didn't make a fool of myself."

"No, you were just fine. So, you hope he asks you out?" I said.

"Carrie! I couldn't possibly hope that. It would just be stupid," she said, eyes to the floor.

"Autumn, did you see the way he looked at you? I've seen some boys fascinated by a girl, but he was downright in awe of you, especially when you finally opened your mouth."

Cristy playfully slapped Autumn on the back. "He literally couldn't help but sneak glances at you, especially those legs. And a few other parts…"

"Cristy!" Autumn exclaimed. She then sighed, "You're just saying that."

"No, no, we're not. Remember, I don't just 'say things', I mean them," I reminded.

"You really think he likes me?" she said. Her beautiful eyes sparkled with a glimmer of hope.

"Does a duck swim?" Cristy chuckled.

Autumn stopped and turned to us, "I'm not getting my hopes up, am I? I know I just met him, but I like him. I've never really thought about boys. Now here I am, hoping one asks me out."

I put my hand on her shoulder. "Autumn, I'm sure you're not being silly. Just have some patience. Or you could always ask him out yourself. It is the twenty-first century, you know."

"I'm too old-fashioned for that."

"Have it your way," I said.

"I'm sure we haven't seen the last of him," Cristy giggled.

Later that day, I reported to Judy's office for detention. When I entered the room, she read a magazine at her desk. She put it down and turned her attention to me.

"Sorry, I'm a little late," I said as I sat before her. I instinctively started fiddling with my ring.

"It's fine, dear. How have your first two days of school been?" Judy said.

"It's been interesting, to say the least," I laughed.

"How interesting?" Judy inquired.

"I've found myself starting my duty already. I've found something has been following Autumn and me and probably wants to kill both of us."

"Dear God! I knew someone was stalking about, but to hear you've confirmed it is another matter! Where is she now?" Judy said.

"How did you know about that…"

"Instinct, dear. You don't get as old as I do without a proper feel for the environment around you."

"Why do I feel like you're dodging the question."

"Because I am," she said with a stern tone. "Moving on…"

I let out an exaggerated sigh. This was typical of Judy. She always knows more than she's telling but was blunt about the fact she wasn't saying shit else. I took a deep breath and said, "Fortunately, her mom came to pick her up. I have a feeling her parents know she's being shadowed too."

"Yes, your mother was worried about such a thing, so I introduced her to the Alexanders. I wasn't expecting a confirmation of our suspicions so quickly."

"Thanks for introducing them. This is a big job when Autumn has no idea what's going on," I said. "I don't even like her going to the bathroom in the school without me there, but I suppose that's a bit paranoid."

"Maybe a bit," Judy said. "Have you worried about yourself for a second since you met Autumn?"

"Not really," I said. "Tala'hars do not worry about themselves, ever. Plus, someone is already trying to kill her; how can I be worried about me?"

"The real question is, why now? Especially since you are now in the picture. You must consider that."

"You mean, I might be part of why they are after her?" I replied. "I couldn't possibly fathom why that would be. What importance am I to whoever is watching her?"

"Dear, I cannot answer that question. You'll have to figure it out on your own," Judy said. "Now, let's not worry about this business. I'm sure you have homework, and you should spend your time here doing it so you have more available to protect your charge."

After a grueling but necessary homework session with Judy, I was finally free. As I approached the front of the school, a familiar voice entered my head.

"Carrie, it's Cristy," the voice said. "I'm out in front of the school. It looks like there is more to this person watching Autumn. Come out here with me, and don't say a word."

"Okay..." I tried to reply.

"Yeah, I can hear your thoughts, so you can talk to me like this if you know I'm listening," she said.

I arrived at the front of the school and saw Cristy sitting on the railing, smacking bubble gum.

"Good, you're here," she told me in my head. "Apparently, there is more than one of those guys watching us. I could feel the 'interference' following Cassandra's car when they left. There is another one of these interferences up in the trees ahead. I can't see them, but I know they are there. They must be using some optical camouflage."

"It's more than optical if I can't see their auras and you can't read their minds."

I took a brief peek at the trees and saw absolutely nothing with both my physical and spiritual eyes. The wind blew gently through the leaves, not giving away the spy amongst them. Whatever type of camouflage they used was better than the military quality I had read about. Even if the current technology I had heard about was real, it could never replicate leaves like that, especially ones that move. And that isn't even to mention blocking out my spiritual sight or Cristy's telepathic abilities.

"Okay," I said mentally. "So, it seems we are of importance to them as well, at least one of us."

"Seems so."

"I'm glad you're with me on this. I wouldn't have seen these guys at all without you."

"No problem, I owe Autumn big time, and you guys are more fun than my moron sister any day," she mentally giggled.

"I'm going to Autumn's now so we can go to that dojo she was talking about."

"Are you going to be okay by yourself?" she said.

"Yeah, if whoever this is starts crap, I'll be perfectly willing to finish it," I replied.

Before I could step off the school's stoop, my mother's black Lamborghini slid to a halt in front of us. She pushed the passenger door open.

"Get in," she growled.

"Okay, Mommy," I barbed. I slid into the car and shut the door behind me, tossing my book bag in the back. "You wanna come?" I said to Cristy verbally.

"Nah, I'm good. Dad will be here soon," she said. I shut the door as I sat down in the front seat. "See ya later!"

After I waved to Cristy, I turned to my mother, "So, is there a reason you think I'm incapable of walking to Autumn's by myself?"

"This isn't about you. This is about Autumn. If something happens to you while you are alone, that leaves her to fend for herself, and we can't have that. Remember, we don't know if these people are after Autumn at all. For all we know, it could be you they are targeting. Autumn's parents hadn't noticed a thing until we showed up."

"And what could they possibly want with me? I'm a freakin' glorified bodyguard, there isn't anything special about me. Autumn has godlike powers, or at least the potential to have them. It would be a safe bet to think they are after her. For all we know, we might have led them to her."

"That is also a possibility. Still, we mustn't take unnecessary chances. I don't impose too many rules, but I will insist you follow this one. You are not to walk anywhere alone, ever. Driving places is fine, but not walking. You are too vulnerable out in the open, unarmed."

Chapter 12

We arrived at Autumn's house in minutes. I knocked on the door and was greeted by Autumn's mother. "Come in," she said as she gestured to me. I saw her peek out of the door, and she shut it behind me.

"Autumn is upstairs, changing," she said.

"You know about them too, huh?" I whispered.

"Yes, I'm afraid so," she whispered back. "It seems your mother knew they were there; she wouldn't say exactly how. I've yet to see anything myself."

"So, what did my mom tell you?" I asked.

"She told us about you and your duty and where you are from," she said. "I'm glad Autumn has someone like you to look out for her. William and I cannot be everywhere."

"So, when are you going to tell her?" I said.

Cassandra's eyes widened, "I don't know if she's ready, dear. We would have told her years ago, but she deals with enough already."

"I know that, but her not knowing is endangering her. It's hard for me to protect her from secret."

"I understand that, but if she finds out we've been keeping this from her, she may isolate herself, and that will make matters dramatically harder," she said.

"I've thought about that myself. I won't claim to know your daughter better than you do, but at this point, we can't afford her to run off and get picked off by these guys while we can't get to her," I said.

Light footsteps could be heard coming down the stairs. Autumn appeared a moment later, dressed in her usual garb, with a duffel bag over her shoulder.

"Hey, Carrie," she looked with a slightly tilted head. "Where are your gym clothes?"

"Oh crap," I said. I was so bent on getting to Autumn's that I forgot to stop at home.

"It's no big deal; we can stop at your place on the way to the dojo. I never thought to ask before, but do you have a sword? Dad and I practice with live steel. If you're uncomfortable with that, we can use bamboo ones."

"Yeah, I've got a blade. Haven't used her in a while. It will be nice to break her out for a little practice. I hope I'm not too rusty."

The sound of a car pulling into the driveway could be heard from outside. "Thanks!" a male voice said as the car drove off.

"Oh, good. Dad's home. I hope he's in the mood to get to practice right away. I'm itching to pull out my blades," Autumn said with a massive grin.

"'...blades?" I gawked at her, puzzled. "You dual wield?"

"Yeah, Dad's puzzled by it, too. I've always preferred using two blades. I'm okay with one sword, but I'm really comfortable with two."

The back door could be heard opening and shutting. William strolled into the living room. It again took me by surprise how handsome he was.

"Hello, dear," Cassandra said as she kissed him on the cheek. He returned her peck, wrapped his arm around her waist, and faced us.

"Hi, Dad. Carrie is going to come with us to practice," Autumn said.

"That's good; I'm quite interested in seeing what she can do," he smiled gently. "Just allow me to change, and we will be on our way. Cassandra, love, can you call and let my grandfather know we are coming? I'm sure he has forgotten. He always does."

"Sure," she nodded.

William left the room and returned moments later wearing sweatpants. We made a brief stop at my house, where I hurried to my room and opened my massive chest. I only kept one item inside, of course. Within the chest was an engraved case from my homeland. Although the case was nearly ancient, the blade inside was only as old as I was. The case featured intricate engravings of Tala'hars battling the forces of evil to protect their Kar'kel. I would often stare at the casing, trying to piece together the stories told by those images. Then, the gravity of the situation hit me. Nothing the ancient Tala'hars did, nor anyone

96

they protected, was as important as my current responsibility. I began to question my worthiness to stand by her side. While I lacked experience, it was important to remember that all Tala'hars started without it. That was simply the way of things. However, the fate of all existence usually did not rest on the shoulders of the charge. But if the fate of everything was on Autumn's shoulders, then, by extension, it was on mine as well.

I took a deep breath and opened the case. The sight of her always made me smile. Karithian, known as the Queen of Darkness in an ancient, likely forgotten language, lay before me. Its sister blade, Korithian, or the Queen of Light, was in my sister's possession. One of the few stories my mother told me about our homeland was that a master swordsmith forged these two blades along with a third blade, Kardathian, the King of Balance, before taking his own life.

According to the tale, the ruthless King of Morander wanted him to create weapons of this caliber for his army, but the smith refused. Knowing he would be tortured to death, he entrusted the sister blades to my parents and the brother blade to the parents of the Tala'har who would one day wield it, before ending his own life.

My mother believed that Karithian was the last blade he ever created. I found it funny that the 'Queen of Darkness' chose me for her wielder, not my older sister. I suppose it made sense. It was the youngest of the three blades, so it would probably choose the youngest sister. Or maybe it was because I was just infinitely more pissed off (and thus darker) than my big sister.

I picked up the Karithian and ran my hands over her black hilt. In terms of weapons of this world, Tala'har blades looked almost like a katana, except the vanguard of the blade was a very different shape. Instead of the traditional circular hand guard, our blades had a small, straight, flat guard that jutted out to each side and then veered off at angles back toward the blade. This design made the blade less defensive but had some other advantages for use with our unique abilities.

I stuffed some gym clothes into a duffle bag and tucked the 'Queen' under my arm. I would have rather put her in a bag of her own, but I didn't want to leave Autumn and her father waiting longer than I had to. The only time I did not worry about Autumn was when she was around her father and mother.

"Sorry it took so long," I said as I stepped into the back seat of William Alexander's sedan.

"It's fine," William said. "According to Cassandra, Krojo has 'company,' and the longer we take to get there, the more time he'll have to be 'finished' with them."

"He didn't just say what I think he said, did he?" I looked at Autumn.

"Yes, he did. My grandfather is a notorious lecher," she sighed.

"Yes, I'm assuming this 'company' is female," I said.

"And most likely of the young, less than virtuous type," William said.

We pulled up to the dojo and parked on the street. A simple sign stated "Krojo's Dojo" above the door. Other than that, there were no other signs that it was a place of business. The place had almost no windows and a sign on the door that said 'Closed.' If Krojo really taught martial arts here, I had a sneaking suspicion he didn't do it very often.

As we approached the door, a twenty-something woman pushed the door open and yelled back into it, "I'm not that kind of girl! That's disgusting!" She stomped away down the sidewalk.

A man who didn't look a day over twenty-five followed her out the door, "Come on, baby! If you are going to advertise it, you have to sell it!"

Considering the way the woman was dressed and from my less-than-conservative angle, she was barely wearing anything; he had a point. I had two thoughts on the matter. First, I felt a woman should dress how she chooses, and it shouldn't infer that she's a slut or not. Yet, another other part of me thought if you were going to be a whore, be a whore. Don't walk around barely wearing anything and expect people not to think you're easy. I want to believe the world should be like my first point, but I knew reality was the second.

"Oh, it's you guys. Sorry about that," the man said. He looked at me, "Well, hello there, young lady."

"Hii-ojiisan, I swear..." Autumn let out in a low growl.

My eyes exploded open like a deer in headlights. Apparently, the kitty did have claws, so to speak. I was shocked to see her take that tone with one of her elders, yet I felt I knew why. She was defending me. That was not her job, but this girl could use any backbone she could get. I glanced at her father to see his reaction; apparently, this wasn't new.

"Oh, sorry, Autumn. Force of habit," he said. He walked away but hunched and made smaller footsteps instead of the lively pace he displayed just moments ago. It almost looked like he should have had a cane and a massive beard.

"Welcome to Krojo's Dojo," he said in an authentic, almost elderly-sounding Japanese accent, far from the young, American-accented voice he had used just a moment ago. As you have probably guessed, I am the proprietor of the dojo, Krojo."

And he was a poet and probably knew it.

"Nice to meet you," I said with a false smile.

"Grandfather, I hope we didn't interrupt anything," William said.

"Nope, she was just leaving," Krojo said. "Feel free to use any of the equipment. I will lie down; I've had enough excitement for one day."

Autumn audibly sighed, "Sorry about my great grandfather. Like I said before, he is a bit of a pervert. If Dad had said something, he wouldn't have taken it seriously. For some reason, I get the idea that Grandpa is afraid of me; I can't understand why."

That was most likely because the old lecher was smart enough to recognize a force of nature when he saw one.

"Autumn and Krojo have a special relationship," William chuckled. "You ladies should go get changed."

Autumn sighed again, "I have forgotten my gym clothes in the car. I'll be right back."

Before I could say anything, Autumn dashed to the car, leaving me alone with her godlike father. As I watched her run off, William turned to me.

"She'll be fine for a few moments, Carrie; you can't be everywhere," William said.

"I know," I replied. "That doesn't mean I don't want to be."

"I've spent the duration of Autumn's life trying to prepare her for whatever the future brings. Throughout this time, I've worried my daughter would meet these challenges alone. I'm not sure by whose grace you have been brought to us; your mother was rather vague, but I am now at ease that you are here to lend your blade to Autumn's cause, whatever that may be."

I now saw the leader Autumn spoke of. He wasn't talking to me like he would to his daughter's friend; he was talking to me like a great general speaking to a soldier before an important battle.

"Sorry about that!" Autumn yelled as she ran up to us. "Come on, Carrie, let's change while my grandfather isn't around."

Chapter 13

I followed Autumn into the women's changing room, and my worst fear came true; it had a locker room-style setup. As Autumn began to take off her T-shirt, I quickly looked down at my sneakers, trying not to be too obvious about it. If I was going to see her topless, I wanted it to be under different circumstances. It wouldn't have been fair to her, and it felt no different than if I were a boy in a locker room. By the time I slowly untied my sneakers, Autumn had already changed into her sweats. It felt like the slowest minute of my life. She sat on the bench and started putting her shoes back on.

I took my shirt off and glanced up at Autumn. Part of me was hoping she was watching, but she was neatly tying her shoes. If Autumn returned my feelings, it would make so many things so much easier. That was wishful thinking, of course.

I reached back to take my own bra off and couldn't quite get it unhooked. I had never had a problem taking off another girl's bra, but when it came to my own, I looked like a total idiot trying to do it.

"Here, let me help you with that," Autumn chuckled. She walked behind me and began to unfasten the hooks. It was good that she was behind me because my face was an embarrassed shade of crimson.

"I hate these things," I sighed.

"Yeah, me too. I normally wear sports bras, but occasionally, Mom gets me into a normal one. You should have seen me today. I was jumping around my room, trying to unlatch it for nearly half an hour. Mom finally came up and helped me."

I would have liked to have seen that. As I blushed again, I realized I needed to keep my mind clear of the gutter. It was finding itself clogged there quite often.

After the latches came loose, Autumn said, "I'm going to start warming up with Dad. You take your time. You don't have to change as fast as I did. When you are a warrior's daughter, you learn battle doesn't wait for you to unsnap your bra." She laughed as she turned and walked out.

After the embarrassment washed away from my face, an exclamation mark might as well have appeared over my head. I had never seen Autumn this comfortable in any environment. Of course, only knowing her for a few days limited the number of environments I saw her in, but there was something very different about her here. She was laughing and joking at my expense, which I found funny in retrospect. She even threatened her grandfather. This was a taste of the true Autumn Alexander. She was a strong, happy girl who could kick a little ass when necessary. I almost felt stupid for feeling so worried about it.

I changed as fast as I could and rushed back to the main dojo floor. For a martial arts dojo, there were a massive number of weapons of all types on the walls. Dojos generally do not contain live weapons, but not this place. Everything from katanas to broadswords, from flails to maces, it was all here. This place didn't look like a dojo; it looked like an ancient armory.

Although the dojo was loaded with authentic weapons, it still had all the necessary facets of a standard dojo. The walls were padded, and mats covered much of the hardwood floor. A few wooden practice dummies were scattered about the room, a climbing rope hung from the ceiling, and a circular bin held numerous bamboo training swords.

I turned to Autumn and her father. Autumn readied her dual blades in a dual-wielding stance, with one blade out in front of her and the other held slightly above her head pointed forward. She swung the blades a few times with a few light swings, her footwork dancing around in a small circle. The blades seemed to dance in her hands until she brought them both in for a single, powerful, perpendicular offensive swing. She followed through and let the momentum of the swing take her around, bringing one blade up in a defensive position and the other forward in an uppercut motion. She brought the blades together in front of her as she went into two cartwheel kicks. As she came down from the last kick, she went back into a reverse cartwheel and back forward with a dual blade, jumping uppercut-type swing. My mouth hung open.

"Sorry, Dad warned me about showing off," she blushed.

"It's okay..." I muttered. I had seen grand masters who don't handle one blade that well, let alone two. I almost felt like a complete 'noob' in her presence. She would probably never need my assistance if she could handle herself half that well in battle. I then realized that was fool's talk. No matter how powerful the charge may be, a Tala'har should never assume they won't require assistance.

102

"Carrie, shouldn't you warm up before we start practicing?" William asked.

"Oh, yeah, sure," I said. I put my arms out and moved them in circles. I always felt stupid doing these things. I touched each toe with the opposite hand. After doing that a few times, I stretched backward and stood up to full height, bringing each foot, one at a time, to the small of my back to stretch my calf muscles. Once my warm-up was complete, I stepped over to where I left Karithian and took her out of her sheath.

"That is an absolutely beautiful sword!" Autumn exclaimed. "May I see?"

"Oh, sure," I handed her the blade without thinking twice. She held the weapon and inspected it like an expert, checking it for straightness by peering down it from the hilt end and then holding the hilt in the palm of her hand to check the balance.

"I've never seen anything on this level of craftsmanship short of Dad's blade," she commented. She studied the weapon's blade closely for a few more moments. And I don't recognize the metal it's made of... that's... odd."

I froze. I should have known that she would notice the blade wasn't made of any material you could find on Earth. I had just broken one of the biggest rules of being a Tala'har: Never underestimate your charge. Another one of those rules was never telling your charge 'no' unless it's for their own protection. I was between a rock and a hard place. I knew she was waiting for an answer; that's when William opened his mouth.

"May I?" he asked me.

His request shocked me out of my mental lockdown, "Sure, go ahead."

He took the same expert's eye to the blade, testing its balance and checking its straightness, just like Autumn had. "I've seen such a blade only once before. I, unfortunately, fail to remember what alloy it was made of or what master craftsman forged it. Such a blade should have its creator credited in the mind of the warrior that wields it."

"Yeah, I asked Mom about it once before; she doesn't even remember where she bought it," I said. I didn't know how, but I would have to pay Autumn's dad back for that cover story. I doubt he had really seen a blade like mine before. For a man who seemed to be the living embodiment of trust and honor, he was a damn good liar.

"Oh, okay!" Autumn nodded.

William handed the sword back to me, and I continued warming up with the blade. Once I was finished, I turned to Autumn's father and asked, "What's next?"

"I would like to see you ladies sparring if you don't mind," he said. "I understand if you're uncomfortable with live steel sparring, so we may use a few of the dojo's bamboo practice swords if you prefer."

"No thanks. Mom and I use real blades whenever we practice. If you're careful, it's not a problem," I said. I may have looked cool on the outside, but I was nervous as hell on the inside. Usually, I would have been worried about hurting Autumn accidentally, but seeing her skill level made me concerned about not making a fool out of myself.

I turned and faced Autumn. In the tradition of Asian martial arts, she bowed to me. I returned her bow and readied my sword. Gazing into her eyes, I was shocked by what I saw.

The timid, repressed young woman I had known over the past two days vanished. The eyes of a hardened warrior replaced them. If that gaze were supposed to fool her opponent into thinking that she had killed a man, no one would be the wiser. For all I knew, she had. Either way, the person holding those swords was a different being altogether. For the first time in my life, I was afraid for my well-being.

I just seemed to blink, and she already was off to my right, bringing the blade she held over her head down at me. I held up my blade, but at that moment, I realized that the first attack was a ruse. The weapon soared in at an angle, never intending to hit its target. I immediately parried low as I spun away from her. Our blades connected, and I saw that a slight smile escaped her lips. I steadied my footing and went on the offensive. I decided to try a trick of my own. I dashed toward her, bringing my blade around my back, spinning while lowering myself to my knees and spinning around for a knee-high slash. She stepped back, parried my low attack, and brought her other blade down to strike. I rolled on my back out of the way of the incoming blade and took to my feet.

We continued playing this cat and mouse sparring for another few minutes as William's well-trained eyes observed us. I could feel him examining my every move, probably judging my ability to watch his daughter's back. It was unnerving, but any pointers he could give me would be well received.

"That's enough, ladies," he said. "I'm quite surprised you can hold your own against Autumn, Carrie. It is a testament to your mother's teaching ability and your skill."

"Oh, it's nothing," I panted, my chest heaving. "My mom and I had little to do in the past, so we did this a lot."

"I see," he said. He turned to Autumn, "You should try to predict your opponent more efficiently. A few of your parries came almost too late."

"When did that happen?" I thought to myself. She seemed to read me almost too well. Something didn't make sense.

"Yes, father," she said. "I'll try to do better."

"Autumn," he reprimanded. "We've talked about that word before. 'Try' should only be used for 'trying' something new. There is only 'doing' and 'not doing'."

"Sorry, Dad," she apologized. "I'll do better next time."

"That's better," he said with a slight smile. "Why don't you get us some cold water from the kitchen?"

"Sure," she said. She put her blades on the padded floor and trotted to the kitchen.

"To be honest, Carrie, it was your parries that were a bit on the slow side, not Autumn's," William whispered. "I'd prefer not to correct you in front of her because I want her to have the utmost confidence that you can protect her if the need arises. I don't want my teaching to instill doubt in her mind. As for telling her that her parries are too slow, I only did that because I couldn't find a flaw in her technique. It's hard to teach someone whose skills may already surpass your own."

"I was wondering why you said that," I whispered back.

"The last thing I need is for her to be overconfident. So, I struggle to find flaws in her skills to give her something to work on and improve. I've never seen a more graceful, powerful fighter than my daughter."

"You're telling me," I said. "I struggled just to keep up with her."

"I'd like to spend a bit less time here from now on. She doesn't need me anymore, at least when it comes to teaching her swordplay. There is far more that she can learn from her mother."

"I see, but as you can see, I need some help," I said, finally catching my breath. "I don't believe I'll ever be 'good enough.' There is no such thing in my eyes."

"That is a good attitude to have. Remember, there is a thin line between believing you can always improve and doubting your abilities. Doubt can lead to death."

I cocked my head, "Why does it feel like you were reading my mind?"

"Cristy isn't the only one in the family," he slyly grinned.

Autumn appeared out of a door on the far side of the dojo with a tray of three glasses and a pitcher of ice water. It took me a moment to realize what Autumn's father told me. If he could also read minds, he might know more than I wanted him to know about my feelings for his daughter.

"You okay, Carrie?" Autumn worried.

"Oh, yeah. I'm fine; I just zoned out again," I said, trying not to show that this new information concerned me.

"Autumn and I can take the next match," William said. "Since you use a single sword, Carrie, you should watch my movements and see if there is something you can pick up. I know a talented fighter like yourself can learn new things much easier this way rather than me teaching you. After all, I'm not sure what you know and what you do not."

The evening went on, and we took turns going against Autumn. She was constantly in combat yet didn't show any signs of fatigue. Autumn probably just took the constant exercise as a nonverbal signal that she needed to improve.

If I learned anything that evening, I needed to talk to the Alexanders alone, without Autumn around.

106

Chapter 14

William and Autumn dropped me off at my house. As I waved goodbye, an idea struck me: I could talk to Autumn's parents without her finding out. I went inside and found my mom passed out on the couch. I gently draped the neon pink blanket hanging over the back of the sofa over her and quietly grabbed the cell phone beside her. I saved Cassandra Alexander's number in my phone before heading upstairs to take a shower.

I spent yet another shower trying not to think of Autumn, especially the incident in the locker room. It was inescapable, and I found myself blushing in the shower. I felt like a giddy little schoolgirl. Well, I was, sans the giddy part.

A few hours later, when I knew Autumn would be asleep, I called Cassandra's phone.

"Hello?" she answered.

"Hi, Mrs. Alexander, it's Carrie. Look, I know it's late, but I can't really talk to you and your husband with Autumn around. There are some things I need to know. Can you meet me somewhere?"

"I know you must have many questions, and you can't continue to do your job until you get the answers. William and I will pick you up if it's okay with your mother."

"I think she'll be fine with it," I said. "She's out cold. I wouldn't worry about it; I don't have a curfew."

"I see; we'll be there as soon as we can," she said as she hung up the phone.

The Alexanders' sedan pulled up to the front of my house fifteen minutes later. They drove an older car whose brand had been retired by its owner. It was as white as one of Cassandra's dresses and well-maintained, probably by Autumn. I entered the back seat and shut the door behind me.

"Hello, dear," Cassandra greeted me from the front passenger seat. "It's good to see you again. And before you ask, Autumn isn't at home alone. My sister-in-law, Mina, is there. She's good protection."

"I see," I felt stupid. I never thought about Autumn being by herself.

"I'll drive to a secluded spot I know of," William said. "Until then, you can think of the questions you want to ask us."

"Okay," I said.

The ride seemed to last forever, stretching out into what felt like the longest ten minutes of my life. I had so many questions for the Alexanders, and I tried my best to organize my thoughts. Eventually, the car slowed and came to a stop in the parking lot of a small park on the outskirts of town.

"We're here," William said as he disengaged the engine, and the automatic windows rolled down simultaneously. "Ask away, Carrie."

"Alright, I guess I'll start with the obvious. Don't take this as me calling your parenting into question, but why haven't you told her? It makes my job much harder with her not knowing what she is."

"There is a good explanation for that," Cassandra explained. "We planned on telling Autumn when she was thirteen. The night we planned on telling her we set up a nice dinner. I made a meal of all her favorite foods. She was strangely quiet that day. Before we knew it, she was face first in her food, and we were rushing her to the hospital."

"What happened?" I said. My heart was genuinely racing.

"She attempted to commit suicide," William said. "We're unsure where she found the pills to do it, but she had to have her stomach pumped. We checked her into a psychiatric clinic the next day. It turns out she suffers from severe depression. Before then, she never let on that life was so difficult at school. I do my best not to wander into my daughter's mind, to give her privacy. Reading her thoughts without permission wouldn't be right."

I was in absolute shock. I struggled to find words.

"Judy told me about the girl she sent to the hospital," I said. "Was this incident before she tried to kill herself?"

"Yes," Cassandra said. "That was the only trouble we had heard of at the time. We were clueless of how harsh school was for her."

"This is why we haven't told her," William said. "Her mental state is still fragile; I can sense that much without reading her mind."

108

I still couldn't believe what I was hearing, but it all made sense. The weight of existence resting on your shoulders would shake anyone. For someone who had already attempted suicide, it might be enough to push them over the edge.

"Child, you have no idea how much of a difference you have made," William continued. "I've never seen her quite this happy."

"I'm glad to hear that," I said. "And since you can read minds, I take that you know about my...feelings."

"Sweetheart," Cassandra turned back to me. "It did not take a mind reader to see that. It is obvious that you adore her."

"Wow, I didn't realize I was that obvious," my mouth dropped. "I know Cristy knew, but I have spent a good amount of time with her."

"You were wise not to let Autumn know you feel this way. She is rather naive in the ways of the world, and it could scare her," William warned.

"How... do you guys feel about it?" I said. My heart was still pounding, feeling it might burst out of my chest.

"We aren't going to tell you how to feel," Cassandra said. "As for how it relates to Autumn, if she returns your feelings, that's wonderful. We won't allow society to tell our daughter how to live and especially who to love."

"We still think it's best you let Autumn figure this out on her own," William added.

"Yeah, I agree with you there. I'll try to hide it better," I said. "So, how can you read minds? Cristy can; I know that much. I would say it's a family trait, but you guys aren't blood-related."

"Cristy and I have two very different gifts. Hers originates from the Telosian blood that she gets from her mother. Mine is a side effect of my immortality. I can only read minds; she can manipulate them, as I'm sure you know."

"I've seen her use it before," I giggled. "What is a Telosian?"

"Telosians are an ancient race of people, mostly women, who were born with magic back in the days of ancient Greece," Cassandra said. "Our little family is the last of what remains of the Telosians since Zeus destroyed most of them."

"Why are they mostly women? I asked.

"We aren't sure, but males born from Telosian females are scarce. Autumn's brother is a rarity," William answered.

"And thus, this is why most of the family is female," I said. "What about the blonde hair, fair skin, and blue eyes? That's not typical of Greeks."

"That is another Telosian trait," Cassandra said. "Those are the norm, except for the males, who tend to be the tall, dark, and handsome type. Jason looks like that."

"So, what type of magic do you have?" I looked at Cassandra.

"Mostly healing, light-based magic, and other assorted types," she said. "I think it's time Autumn learned more about her Telosian heritage. I can start teaching her spells from an ancient spell book that was said to belong to the original Cassandra."

"You mean Cassandra of Troy?" I said.

"Yes, she was a Telosian, and thus, that is where she inherited her gift of prophecy, not from an Olympian god curse. She wasn't originally from Troy. She was a Telosian who was hiding in Troy during the war. I believe that Zeus allowed the war to go on because he wanted Cassandra brought back to Greece, where she could live out her grim destiny."

"Wow, that's cruel," I said. "I guess the Olympian Gods are jerks. Sort of chilling to know they are real. Speaking of jerks, what is the deal with Autumn's Uncle Joe? Why does he hate her so much?"

"I have yet to figure that out," William said. "He didn't act this way when Jason was born. I assume it has something to do with Autumn being a Balanced One. He has been known to be very jealous. He probably felt he was the 'special' one in the family due to his history and magic sword. At least in his eyes, Autumn seems to have inherited that position."

"How did he ever find out what she was?" I questioned.

"He and Megara were present when she was born. Not long after Autumn was born, a pair of... how should I explain this... angelic beings

110

showed up and explained to us what she was," Cassandra explained. "They told us that normally, a person finds out on their own that they are a Balanced One, but they said Autumn must be prepared to save all that exists. She would have a weight on her unlike any that came before. Of course, I saw Joseph's face during the encounter, and he looked furious. I never understood why. He has always dodged the question."

"I wish I would have confronted Joseph right then and there," William lamented. "Maybe then he might have been willing to explain why he hates her. If I had been more diplomatic about this, maybe Autumn's life wouldn't have been as laborious as it is now."

"You can't blame yourself for the past," I said. "And even so, Sophia would have still found out, eventually."

"True," William said. "She might have a more difficult time doing what she does to my daughter if her father was keeping her in check like he should."

"Parents can't control what their kids do at school," I said.

"Good point," William said. "I keep attempting to blame myself for Autumn's predicament when, in reality, it cannot be helped. My brother-in-law and my niece will do what they do, and there is little I can do about it sans killing them both. I would never do such a thing. I feel rather guilty about the numerous beatings I've given Joseph over this matter..."

"We need to worry about the present here, though; the past can't be helped," I said.

"You are wise beyond your years," Williams said.

"What are we going to do about these guys following Autumn?" I said. "I can't even keep track of them. The only ones who can are Cristy and, I'm assuming, you, Mr. Alexander."

"Yes, I get the same 'white noise' Cristy gets when she notices one of them," William confirmed. "I'm not sure who they are, but we can be sure they mean to harm both of you."

"All we can do for now is to make sure Autumn is never alone and wait for them to make their move," Cassandra said.

"I suppose that's what must be done," I sighed.

"Which is another reason why we brought you here," William said.

"William and I must leave town this weekend to go to the house in Pennsylvania. I left the spell book there for safekeeping. I wouldn't have dared to bring the book to Miami. The power it emits is immense and would likely attract the attention of the wrong people. It is too late for that, so it is essential for Autumn to learn from it."

"I see," I said.

"We need you to stay with Autumn at our home. You won't be alone; Mina will be there, but I don't want her to be left defending Autumn by herself for that period of time," Cassandra explained.

"Why not just bring her to my house?" I asked. "The only thing better than one Tala'har is two."

"That was my first thought, but your home lacks the protective barriers that our home has," Cassandra said.

"I never noticed anything like that," I said.

"That is the point," Cassandra said. "I ensured the protections were nearly invisible to even a trained eye. Remember, there are more than just beings from the physical realm that could be out to harm our daughter. Spiritual attacks can happen, especially while she sleeps, and although they probably can't hurt Autumn, they could prematurely awaken her."

"Awaken?"

"As in awakening her spiritual senses and thus possibly scaring her. The last thing the poor thing needs is to wake up one day and start seeing things from the spiritual plane and not understand what she's seeing," Cassandra explained.

"I can get that. It took me a while to get used to my spiritual sight, although Mom said I have a very 'bare bones' version of the ability and can only see the spiritual world's outermost layer. In other words, enough to identify my charge, keep track of her, and maybe identify threats," I said.

"Do you have any other questions?" William asked.

"Yeah, Mom said Autumn is a 'Balanced One.' I know that is something important, which means she is very powerful, but what else is there to it?"

"At first, we didn't know much other than what those beings had explained, which was rather minimal. We have a friend who makes a point of studying their kind, and she explained that Autumn is an 'incarnate' of a Balanced One, a spiritual being that rarely shows up on the physical plane. These incarnates are the part of it that is born here," Cassandra said. "We were also told there are four balanced ones, two males and two females. The Balanced One that Autumn is a part of is called Alexandral."

Alexandral... I found it a hauntingly beautiful name, yet for some reason, the mention of the name brought up emotions of anger that I couldn't explain. I idled on the thought for a moment, becoming more angry as I focused on the name.

"Carrie?" Cassandra broke me out of my preoccupation with these strange feelings of rage.

"Oh, sorry, Mrs. Alexander," I said. "Please, continue."

"Autumn is amongst ten mortal incarnates that are part of a Balanced One. Each is a different shade of light or dark regarding personality and temperament. There have been balanced ones incarnated as the most holy of individuals and the most ruthless of killers. "

"Wow, that is pretty crazy," I said. "Anything else you might happen to know about them, or maybe just Alexandral?"

"We know she is considered the 'Warrior Queen,'" William said. "Any accounts of her that I've heard described her as rash, destructive, and easily angered. If what I've heard is true, she is the type of warrior that enjoys the kill as much as the battle itself."

"Oh, Carrie, there is one other fundamental rule you must know about Balanced Ones," Cassandra said, in a very 'warning' tone. "More than one can never be simultaneously in the same plane of existence. Under normal circumstances, it is said that if more than one were to show up in a single plane of existence, it would be like two magnets tearing apart a pile of metal dust.

"That sounds pretty scary," I stuttered. "I guess it makes a lot of sense. If these beings are balanced, they probably serve as the center point for each plane they inhabit. Something can't have two centers."

"While that is true, it's a bit worse than that," she continued. "If you see more than one of them in the same place, that means special conditions in the universe have been met and thus... how to put this in a way that won't scare you..."

"The end is near?" I guessed. "Some final battle is on the horizon where more than one of their power is necessary?"

"Exactly," she said as she took a deep breath. "Although, with the way the "angels" were talking, it would not surprise me if these conditions had already been met." She took another deep breath and exhaled. "Anything else? Hopefully, nothing that involves the end of all there is."

"I think that covers most of the essential things," I said. "Oh, what about that 'history' you mentioned, the stuff relating to Joseph? I heard something about his sword before, but what exactly is that guy about?"

"My brother-in-law was once a servant of the Olympian gods," William said. "He helped defeat the Titans when they attempted to overthrow the Olympians. Because of this, he was granted immortality and his magic sword. Eventually, he grew tired of living under the Gods' beck and call, so he changed his name from Brathamas to Joseph, a Christian name, to anger them and began ignoring their calls. They occasionally send servants to destroy him. Partially thanks to my blade, he still lives. I continue to help him because he and I have a long-standing friendship, and he is married to Cassandra's sister."

"Pretty shitty friend, if you don't mind me saying. The guy is a complete dick," I said.

"Yes, that's always been part of his personality, but he has always been someone I could count on, believe it or not. I wish he would let this dislike of Autumn go. I'd like to have my old friend back and one less tormentor for my daughter."

"I think it would be easier to kill him," I said.

"Trust me, as I've also mentioned, it's been tempting," William said. "No matter what I do, he continues his abuse of Autumn and encourages his daughter's. I'm thankful Cristy seems to have more sense than her father and sister."

"I'm not sure what I would do without Cristy," I admitted. "Without Autumn knowing, this becomes a more-than-one-person job. School is the biggest challenge, and it is where Cristy can help me the most. Oh, and speaking of school, I know I shouldn't talk to you about your daughter's personal life, but I think Autumn might have a male admirer."

"So, that's why she came home beaming today," Cassandra said. "I figured she would have been a bit grumpy from me making her wear that outfit."

It looks like she caught the attention of a guy who's new to the school," I said. He is a bit geeky, but that seems to be her type."

"How does this make you feel?" William said.

I swallowed hard. For some reason, I didn't even foresee this being brought up.

"Uh...that's ill-relevant. What is important is Autumn's happiness, not my feelings. She needs a distraction, and I think a boyfriend would be a good one. Let her worry about something other than Sophia slandering her daily."

"I agree," said Cassandra. "Now, I know this is going to sound like the protective mother we all know is in me, but this boy can be trusted, right?"

"I had Cristy with me when they met, so I'm assuming so. She would have kicked his ass right then and there if he couldn't be trusted."

"Good," Cassandra exhaled.

"Cristy and I are going to try to get him to ask her out," I said. "Don't be surprised if he shows up at your front door."

"Thanks for the heads-up," William said. I think that's enough for tonight. We should get you home and in bed so you can get some rest before school tomorrow."

Chapter 15

The next day began like any other. Just this morning, I knew Autumn would probably be waiting for me downstairs, likely making idle chit-chat with my mother. I hoped Cristy would join us for the ride to school again today. I enjoyed her company, and knowing she was physically intact would be reassuring. I wouldn't say I liked the idea of her walking home from school alone any more than I was fond of Autumn doing it.

After getting out of the shower and dressing, I found Autumn and Cristy waiting for me at the kitchen table. Seeing Cristy brought a sigh of relief.

"You okay, Carrie?" Cristy said.

"Yeah, was just glad to see you two," I said.

Once again, Autumn's mother packed us an excellent breakfast. Autumn dressed normally, wearing her huge, faded shirt and beaten-up baggy jeans. I hoped she would dress up again—not really because I liked seeing her in that kind of clothing, but so she could keep her new admirer's attention.

I had a feeling she dressed this way because of him. She likely wanted to see if he really liked her because if he were going to be around her, he would see her dressed like a boy in rags, more or less.

The ride to school went without incident, but I knew it wouldn't last. Sophia would be there when we arrived and would probably open her mouth about Cristy hanging out with us.

I wasn't sure what Cristy planned on saying to her, but I was sure it would be enjoyable.

When we pulled up, I saw Sophia loitering with her crowd in front of the school. She likely picked the spot so she could confront her sister.

Sophia strutted up to us after my mom drove away.

"Cristy, I could have sworn I told you I didn't want to see you with those losers," she hissed.

"Yeah, that's why I stopped hanging out with you and those dickheads," her sister said. "I prefer my current company. You know, the kind with a brain."

116

"Look, child..." Sophia said.

"You were born ten minutes before I was!" Cristy snarled.

"I wasn't talking about how I was born before you; I meant how you look like a child, shorty," Sophia said.

Cristy opened her mouth but didn't get a chance to say a word. Autumn stepped up to Sophia and glared down at her. Sophia's eyes opened wide as she gawked up at her cousin, who towered over her by more than half a foot.

"Sophia, I don't give a shit what you say about me, but when you start spitting trash about my friends, and yes, your sister is one of my friends, that's where I draw the line," she growled. "So, if I were you, I would shut your mouth if you know what's good for you."

"I'm... just going to... go over here," Sophia said. She returned to her group of friends almost as fast as her heeled shoes would carry her.

"Holy shit," Cristy expressed. "Why the hell don't you do that when she starts with you?"

"Because I'm not worth protecting," Autumn said. She turned and walked into the school without saying another word.

I was dumbfounded, although it made sense why she would do such a thing and reply to Cristy the way she did.

Cristy was about to run after her, but I put my arm across her chest.

"Let her go," I advised.

"But she can't go on thinking she's worth nothing!" Cristy exhaled.

"I know, but it's not easy to convince someone who has looked down on herself for that long with just a few words. I'm not sure how to handle this," I said.

I leaned closer to Cristy and asked, "Have you ever actually read Autumn's mind, you know, rooted around in there, about her past?"

"No, that would be an invasion of privacy; why?" Cristy said.

"Apparently, not long after she moved here, she tried to kill herself," I said.

"Fuck..." Cristy said. "That would explain why she was gone for those few weeks in eighth grade. I knew what Sophia did had bothered her, but I had no idea it was that bad. Anyone else would probably do the same thing."

"I'm starting to think that she lets people like Susie hit her because she feels she isn't worth anything," I guessed.

"How are we going to help her?" Cristy said.

"I have some ideas," I said. "Part of them has to do with her getting a boyfriend."

"Okay, well, we should get to class," Cristy said. "Yeah, I know; you probably never thought you'd hear that out of my mouth, but you need to get your seat close to Autumn."

We entered the classroom and noticed Autumn with her head down on her desk. The new kid sat in the seat he had chosen yesterday, his eyes focused on her. Since Autumn didn't seem to notice him, he stood up and walked over to Cristy and me.

"Is something wrong with Autumn?" he said. "I tried saying something to her, but she didn't notice. Either that, or she's ignoring me."

"Not a possibility, I promise," Cristy comforted. "She's just had a tough morning."

"Oh, okay. I'm worried about her. She's been like that since I got here and hasn't moved."

"I'll make sure she's okay," I said. "Can I ask you something?"

"Yeah, sure," he replied.

"Look, she needs something to pep her up, and I was going to try to be a bit slyer about this, but oh, well. You like her, right?" I said.

"Well...I....yeah, I do," he stuttered.

"Good," I affirmed.

"Yeah, but I don't think I'm really in her league," he said. "There is no way a girl like her would ever go out with me. The girls only liked me in my old school because I was an oddity. Hell, I'm an otaku, but the novelty of my race was too interesting to them."

118

"I don't think you get it," Cristy said. "She really, really likes you."

"You guys are just messing with me," he dismissed.

"No, we're not," I said. "She likes you. It would make her day if you would ask her out."

"I don't know," he hesitated.

"I promise you, she will say yes," I said.

"Yeah, she will," Cristy added.

"Okay, I'll try. I don't know why she would want to go out on a date with someone like me."

"Trust us, Jake," Cristy said. "You're just her type."

Jacob went back to his seat, and the bell rang. I sat next to Autumn, and Cristy went to the back of the classroom. Mrs. Jenkins took attendance, but Autumn only raised her head when she was called on. The rest of the class went on as usual, but Autumn didn't raise her hand to answer a single question and only spoke when she was spoken to.

The bell rang its harsh tone, signaling the end of the period. Autumn stood up to leave her seat. I waited to see what Jacob would do. I had to give the guy credit; he had more guts than I thought he would. He approached Autumn before she left the classroom and tapped her shoulder. The other students walked by Autumn, giving her the usual dirty looks on the way out.

"Ah, Autumn," he said quietly.

"Oh, hi Jacob, I didn't even notice you there. You didn't try to speak to me, did you?" she said.

"Yeah, I did," he said. "I was a bit worried about you."

"Sorry, I didn't mean to be rude; I've just had an upsetting morning," she said.

"Your cousin and Carrie said something like that. Look, Autumn, I hope I don't come off as too forward, but I don't think I can wait much longer. Would you like to go out and do something sometime?" he said.

Autumn's eyes widened, and she blushed, "You mean, go out on a date?"

"Yes, I guess that's what I'm asking," he said.

"Well, I don't know," she said. Her face continued to become even redder. She looked back to me, and I gave her a slight nod and smile, which I hoped would reassure her. After a pause that had to feel like an eternity to Jake, she said, "Yeah, sure, we can."

"Great, when would you like to go?" he said. "I'm free any time after school today. I have practice tomorrow, but I'm free afterward."

"Today would be okay, I guess," she said.

"Great, how does seven sound?" he said.

"Wonderful," she grinned.

"I'll be at your house at that time. I'd offer to pick you up, but I don't have a car," he said.

"That's fine; I don't have one either," she said.

"Where do you live?" he said.

"I live at 625 Raccoon; do you know where that is?" she said.

"I think so. I'll see you at lunch; I have to get going to class," he said before he dashed out the door.

Cristy and I finally stood up from our seats and headed toward Autumn.

"What did you guys have to do with this?" she said.

"Nothing, really," I said. "We just suggested it to him, that's all. Not like we held him at knife-point to do it. He does like you."

"Autumn, you can believe me when I say it. I know when a boy likes a girl, and he's really into you," Cristy confirmed.

"If you guys say so," she sighed. "What am I going to wear?"

"I haven't known you that long, but I'm betting this is the first time you've worried about that," I laughed. "Don't worry, me and Cristy will help you out. I'll buy you something if I have to. I still owe you that outfit, remember."

"Yeah, I know," she sighed again. "I think Mom has more clothes she wants to get me into. Maybe she has something. I wish she would take them back."

"Well, I'm off to class," Cristy said. "I'll see you two at lunch."

Autumn and I walked to our next class together. I glanced at her and, for the first time at school, noticed that she was walking with her eyes facing forward and a slight smile on her face. I usually disliked expressions like this, but seeing her like that warmed my heart. I found myself wishing that I was the one who had made her smile that way.

The rest of the morning went as normally as possible, except for Autumn's cheerful mood. She brushed off the dirty looks people gave her as she walked by. Susie stepped in front of her as they were about to pass, snarling, "What the fuck are you smiling about, Alexander?"

Autumn ignored her and continued to grin. She moved around the little bully and continued down the hall. I could hear the little fuck having a conniption as we breezed by. Yet, Autumn disregarded it all. I turned around and briefly stuck my tongue out at her, and that made her face grow even more red with anger. I let out a hearty chuckle.

We left our last morning class and went to lunch. Cristy and Jacob were waiting for us, exchanging conversation at the table.

After retrieving my lunch and her milk, we sat down at the table. Autumn smiled slightly at Jacob as she seated herself. I sat on the other side of the table, crossed my legs, folded my hands, and put them under my chin.

"So, I hear someone has a date tonight," Cristy giggled.

"It's not a big deal," Jacob said.

"Sure, it is; it's my cousin's first date," Cristy said. "Oops, did I just say that out loud?"

Jacob turned to Autumn, "Is this really your first date?"

"Afraid so," she replied, cheeks crimson with embarrassment.

"Wow, I just can't believe a girl like you has never been out on a date before," he said.

"What do you mean, a girl like me?" Autumn asked.

I smiled a big grin because I knew exactly what he would say.

"You know, a girl as pretty and smart as you are," Jacob said, his cheeks looking a bit red, too, as he attempted not to make eye contact with Autumn.

"You're just saying that," Autumn replied, looking more abashed than ever.

"No, really," Jacob said. "I just can't believe other guys aren't interested in you. I mean, look at you. You're... beautiful."

Autumn's face was more ruby than a box of Lucky Charms.

"Well, they have," Cristy cut in. "Plenty of guys have been interested in her, I would know. Of course, they fear my sister too much to talk to her. Not everyone believes my sister's crap, but they know she's not a bitch to trifle with. Unless you enjoy getting your ass kicked by the football team, that is."

"Nice going, Cristy," I said to myself, in my mind, with the off chance that Cristy was listening.

"Don't worry, that won't scare him away," Cristy replied mentally. "Let's just say I've broken my rule and rooted around in his head while you guys were getting here. Had to, for Autumn's sake. He has nothing to worry about at all. Sophie's cronies, on the other hand…"

"Eh, I'm not too worried about your sister, Cristy. I don't care what she does," Jacob leaned back, putting his hands around his head. "I've dealt with that sort of stuff at my old school; it has always been part of my life."

"I don't think you have much to worry about myself," Cristy smiled.

122

Chapter 16

The rest of the day went on without incident. School let out, and Autumn briskly maneuvered her way through the hallways with Cristy and me in tow. Her smile had yet to fade despite the sneers and glares pointed her way at every turn.

Susan saw us and began to move to cut us off. Cristy bared her teeth at her, and Susan stopped dead in her tracks. We continued out the doors of the school and into the surrounding streets.

The streets looked no different than on other days, with the spring sun hanging high in the sky. The streets were quiet, and less obsessive grooming of lawns occurred than I felt was usual for the area. The occasional car passed, but other than that, the quiet was almost eerie.

"Carrie?" Cristy said to me in my mind.

"Yeah," I replied.

"They are following us. We really can't get a break, can we? I only notice them when I'm around Autumn or you, so they are probably just interested in the two of you."

"Is it just me, or does it feel like we're being followed," Autumn whispered.

"Yeah, I've been feeling that way," Cristy said. "Not sure by who or what."

"It gives me the creeps… and pisses me off," I added.

Autumn turned around and yelled, "Whoever you are, we're not afraid of you. I know you've been following us for the last few days. Come out now, coward!"

Silence filled the suburban street.

"Oh well, I guess they are just cowards, too afraid to face three unarmed girls," Autumn said, with her hand on her chin and her other one on the small of her back, under her long shirt. In one quick, deft motion, she pulled a dagger that was tucked away in the back of her pants and hurled it up into a nearby tree. The dagger hit what appeared to be thin air. The air flickered, revealing what appeared to be a person in black for a short moment. It faded back into the air after only a fraction of a second.

We all stood in defensive stances: Cristy with her relatively large ornamental dagger, Autumn weaponless, and me with my small dagger.

Silence again filled the streets.

"They're gone," Autumn relaxed. She walked over, picked up her fallen weapon, and tucked it back into her jeans.

"How did you know they were there?" Cristy said.

"Instinct, I guess," Autumn said. "I first noticed them when Carrie and I walked home that first day."

That was long before I knew they were there. There was nothing like your charge having the heads-up on you to make you feel like an inadequate piece of shit.

"Wow, Autumn, those are some finely tuned senses," I marveled.

"Thanks. I figured that since the first day I saw them was when I was with you, they are probably after you," Autumn said. "They did follow me home yesterday when I was with my parents, so I don't know what to think."

"These guys don't worry you?" I said.

"Nah, I've been through stuff like this before. You tend to watch your back when you have an uncle on the Olympians' hit list. Hit men come after us all the time," Autumn dismissed.

"Tell me fucking about it. You know how many of those psychos have tried to kidnap me and Sophia?" Cristy said. "When we were kids, they got my mom once."

"We're Alexanders; we're used to danger, Carrie," Autumn said with a gentle smile. "I just want you to know if these guys are after you, I'll make them wish they were never born if they lay a hand on you."

I internally sighed and thought, "Great, she thinks she's my protector. I suppose it's better than trying to hide that these guys are after us." I figured she could think what she liked for the time being. Then again, I suppose I had no proof they weren't after me.

124

"Thanks, Autumn," I said.

Then she stepped up, wrapped her arms around me, and gave me a tight hug. I wanted to melt as I returned her embrace.

"Ah! Group hug!" Cristy cheered as she tried to wrap her short arms around me and Autumn. Autumn and I let her into our little huddle. It was a moment that felt like it came right out of a sitcom, but I couldn't have been happier. It was the first time in my life that I was content, and I knew where I belonged. If Autumn and Cristy were close, I wouldn't care what the world threw at me.

We left our little hug and smiled at each other.

"Hey, Autumn, we should stop by my house, and I'll pick up my makeup case. I have some awesome stuff you must try on," Cristy suggested.

"I don't know, Cristy, I'm not sure how much I'd like wearing makeup," Autumn said.

"Oh, come on," Cristy prodded. "I just want to add some color, that's all, none of that concealer crap or anything overly flashy. You've got great skin and features, so there is no need to hide it under a bunch of muck. I want to add a few highlights to bring out those beautiful eyes of yours."

"I'll think about it," Autumn conceded.

"If you don't like it, you can wash it off, you know," Cristy poked.

"Yeah, it's not like it's permanent," I added.

"I swear, you two are dying to play Barbie with me," Autumn grinned.

"She caught us, Cristy," I said.

"Caught red-handed," Cristy replied.

"To be fair, she sort of looks like a Barbie, doesn't she?" I laughed.

"That's not funny; she was modeled after a sex doll!" Autumn mockingly exclaimed.

Cristy blew up her cheeks and smirked, ready to say something.

"Hush you!" Autumn chuckled.

After a brief stop at Cristy's house, where Autumn and I waited outside, we headed for Autumn's. Cristy looked like she could barely carry that massive makeup case of hers.

"Geez, Cristy, what do you keep in there, a dead body?" I said as we entered Autumn's home.

"A girl can never have too much makeup," she said.

"But you don't seem to wear a lot," Autumn said.

"I said you can never have too much makeup; you can definitely wear way too much," she giggled.

"Oh, hello, ladies," Cassandra greeted as she lounged on the couch, sipping tea from a neat little cup and saucer.

"Hi, Mrs. Alexander," I said.

"Hi, Aunt Cassy," Cristy said.

"Mom, I have great news," Autumn beamed. "We don't have any plans tonight, do we?"

"No, dear, why? What is going on?" Cassandra said.

"Good, because I was asked out on a date tonight!" Autumn said.

Cassandra nearly dropped the cup and saucer but was able to recover it. She put her tea on the coffee table before her and stepped up to Autumn.

"Oh, sweetheart, that's wonderful!" she rejoiced as she wrapped her arms around her daughter. "I hope we get to meet this young man."

"You should; he's going to stop by to get me at seven," Autumn said.

"That's good. I'm interested in meeting him," Cassandra said, returning to her couch and tea.

"Mom, do you know where some of those clothes you bought that I wouldn't wear are?" Autumn asked.

"Yes, dear, in the hall closet. I knew you would want them someday," Cassandra smiled.

Autumn sighed in reply, led us upstairs to the closet, and opened the door. Inside was a box marked 'Autumn' amongst the bed, bath towels, and other linens. Cassandra was obviously a fan of bleach because all her whites were nearly blinding. The sight of the whites reminded me of my mother's first attempt at using bleach when we first came to this world. We threw away a lot of clothes that day. None of the linens in our home were white simply because of my mother's sheer hatred of bleach.

Autumn retrieved the box and went to her room. I realized I had never been in Autumn's room before, and I had no idea why the thought of going there gave me goosebumps.

She opened the door to her room, and I was assaulted with posters that plastered the wall. They were posters for what I assume were old games to legendary rock stars, such as Ozzie Osbourne, Metallica, Elvis, the Beatles, Jimi Hendrix, and many others. Most of the posters were in terrible shape, and some looked like they had been old advertisements from stores, signaling that she had not bought them but fished them out of the garbage.

In open spaces on the walls hung swords that appeared to be Autumn's previous training weapons. None of them were ornamental, and most were in extreme disrepair. In other spots in the room were boxes of parts for everything from computers to automobiles. A computer with an old CRT monitor was on her desk, which was expectantly neat. It was the only piece of technology I had seen in the house.

"It's sad," Cristy lamented. "I've known you my entire life, and I don't think I've ever been in your room." An immediate look of shame followed. "I'm sorry."

"You already apologized," Autumn comforted. "It's over and done with. The important thing is you are here now."

"Yeah, I guess so," Cristy said as she plopped on the bed. "So, let's get to work enhancing those natural good looks of yours."

"Now you are just trying to make me blush," Autumn replied.

"Am not! Tell her, Carrie!" Cristy said.

"The woman speaks the truth," I proclaimed.

"I should probably take a shower first," Autumn said. "I'd like to smell nice for him, at the very least."

"Why don't you try on some of that perfume your mom wears," Cristy said. "She has great taste!"

"We'll see," Autumn said. She opened her closet, and it was just as tidy as I figured it would be. She selected a robe that hung on the back of the door. "You two behave while I'm gone," she giggled; "Me Casa, su casa." She closed the door behind her.

"This place depresses me," Cristy sighed after knowing Autumn was out of earshot.

"Why?" I asked.

"Because it's obvious how old everything in here is," Cristy sighed. "Example: the mattress I'm sitting on has to be at least twenty years old. I would bet good money that it belonged to Jason. And that computer over there might be even older, or at least the monitor is. I knew Uncle William and Aunt Cassandra had it tough, but I didn't know it was like this. Autumn must really not let them spend a penny on her."

"You've seen her clothes, right?" I said. "Most of them are faded to an insane degree. She said she gets most of her clothes from a thrift store, and being rather tall, I'm sure most of her stuff is men's."

"Nothing wrong with wearing men's clothes," Cristy glanced down at her leather jacket. "Yet, I get the idea she doesn't do it exactly because she enjoys it. So, how are you feeling about this?"

"What do you mean?" I replied.

"You know, the whole 'Autumn going out on a date' thing. I know how you feel about her. And I know a simple crush when I see it, and that's not what I see out of you."

"How I feel doesn't matter. The only important thing here is how she feels," I said.

Cristy sighed and slapped her forehead, "I swear, you are as bad as Autumn. Of course, how you feel is important. Do you think you will really be able to protect her if you're depressed all of the time?"

"Tala'har are trained to work through such feelings," I explained. "Our charge is the number one priority. Everything else is secondary."

"So, will you hide this from her forever?" Cristy said as she stood up off the bed and put her hands on her hips.

"If I must," I replied. I sat on the bed, and Cristy sat beside me. I closed my eyes and let a tear escape from my left eye.

Cristy put her arm around me, "I'm not sure what to say to you. So, when all else fails, I hug." She put her other arm around me.

Cassandra slipped into the room quietly and shut the door softly, "I'm not interrupting anything, am I?"

"No, Mrs. Alexander. Everything is fine. What's up?" I said as Cristy removed one of her arms but held the other over my shoulder.

"We have a change of plans, ladies," she explained. "William and I cannot wait until the weekend to get the book; we must leave as soon as possible."

"Book?" Cristy said. "Oh, that book! So, you are finally going to start teaching Autumn?"

"That's the plan, but I'm a bit worried," Cassandra sighed. "One of the proximity alarm spells that guarded the house has been tripped. As far as I can tell, the book is still there, but I won't feel better about it until we have it in our hands."

"Are you sure you and William should go alone?" I said.

"I'm afraid we are the only ones available. Autumn's Uncle Daniel is nowhere to be seen, and I need his wife, Mina, here to keep guard. As for Krojo, asking him to do anything is to encounter a barrage of excuses. Joseph might draw more attention to us, so he isn't an option either."

"I can stay the night with Autumn," I volunteered.

"I was counting on that," Cassandra said. "Mina won't be here until late."

"I see," I said. "I plan on shadowing Autumn tonight during her date. If these guys are going to try something, it will probably be while you and Mr. Alexander are out of town. If they do, I'll be there to ensure nothing happens."

"I'm coming too," said Cristy. "Been itching for a reason to get out the new rifle I got for Christmas. You might need some cover fire since there is more than one of them."

"Rifle?" I raised an eyebrow.

"Oh yes, she's a beaut!" Cristy grinned. "Not that I need a scope to hit my mark, hehe."

"I just hope her new friend doesn't get caught in the crossfire," Cassandra said.

That was something I hadn't considered. I was so focused on making Autumn's life bearable that I didn't think about what might happen to Jacob if those jerks attacked when he was with her.

"It's not like we can close her up and protect her from getting close to anyone outside of us," Cristy said. "Anyone she's near is in danger; it can't be helped. If she knew these guys were after her, she wouldn't be willing to have a social life. She'd probably close herself up in the house, which isn't good for her."

"I suppose you're right," Cassandra lamented.

"Right now, she thinks these guys are after me," I said. "I suppose it is better that way. You can be assured that we won't let anything happen to her."

"Thank you," Cassandra said. "Both of you are a dream come true. I better get going; Autumn takes notoriously short showers." She turned to leave the room but then spun back to both of us. "Oh, and if you have time, please get her to play something on the guitar. We tell her she's wonderful at it, but she doesn't believe us because we're her parents." She left the room.

I looked at Cristy, "She plays the guitar?"

"I'm just as surprised as you are," Cristy laughed. "Is there anything she doesn't do?"

130

"Do what?" Autumn questioned as she came into the room. She was dressed in her robe, and her hair was still wrapped in a towel. My eyes were immediately drawn to her.

"We're talking about you playing the guitar." Cristy grinned mischievously.

"Oh, Mom told you, right?" she rolled her eyes.

"Yep," I said as I tried to avert my eyes.

"I'm not any good," she said.

"Your mom says otherwise," I said. Why don't you get it out and play something?" Not staring but trying not to look away noticeably was becoming more challenging by the moment.

"Do we have time for that?" Autumn begged.

"He's not going to be here for another few hours," Cristy reminded. "I think we're good."

"If you insist," Autumn admitted defeat. She turned to the closet from which the robe was removed and procured a guitar case. She seated herself on a chair, pulled from the side of the room, and gently placed the guitar case on her lap. She opened the case and revealed the most beautiful guitar I had ever seen. It was a sleek electric guitar with a shiny black finish.

"My brother bought this for me for my thirteenth birthday," Autumn said as she leaned over and plugged the guitar into a cord that was neatly wrapped up by her desk, which I assumed was plugged into a hidden amp. "I thought it was too expensive, but he thinks I'm good and deserve a good guitar. Girls, meet Meimegami, the Dark Goddess..." She let out a mischievous grin. "...of Rock."

"So, what are you going to play for us?" I said.

"I can play 'Paint it Black' by the Rolling Stones. I guess I consider it the guitar's theme song since she's black, and well... you get the gist. Sorry about my terrible singing; I have a hard time playing without doing it," she said. She took a breath and started to play the song. I expected Autumn to be good, but I was literally bewildered by her skill with the strings as she played through the song's introduction. She then opened her mouth to sing, and I was just as impressed.

She had an excellent voice. There was no reason Autumn couldn't be in a band as both the lead singer and lead guitarist.

I was expecting her to play something more cheerful, but then again, Autumn had spent her teenage years gripped by depression. I have always liked this song, and it sounded just as good coming from Autumn as it did Mick Jagger. Autumn's voice added an element of beauty even the most confident diva would be jealous of.

Autumn concluded the song, and we both clapped enthusiastically.

"That was awesome," Cristy cheered.

"Yeah, I agree," I added.

"You guys are just saying that," Autumn dismissed.

I sighed and shook my head. "How many times do I have to tell you, girl? I don't just say anything. We should start getting you ready for your date."

"It's just weird hearing that, you know, me going out on a date," she unplugged Meimegami and placed her back in the case. She stored the guitar back in the closet.

"Get used to it," Cristy laughed. "When we are through with you, you are going to have guys pounding down your door, to pound you, actually."

"Cristy!" Autumn exclaimed.

"Oh, come on, Autumn. Why stay a virgin for longer than you have to?" Cristy poked.

"You're an immortal, too, and you know exactly how I get away with having so much sex. We don't get pregnant unless we want to. So, why wait till marriage when you can have fun now?" I added.

"I never said I was going to wait. I just want to find the right guy, that's all," Autumn said with her cheeks beat red.

"We can hope the 'right guy' is the one you're going to go out with tonight," I said. "So, what do you want to wear this evening?"

"I don't know," Autumn said with a look of relief washing over her face. She opened the box that she had left on the bed, revealing a large number of clothing articles.

132

Autumn gently removed each piece from the box, spreading them across the bed. I had to give Cassandra credit. She had taste. Nothing looked like something a mother would buy her daughter to wear, but things the girl would choose for herself. Once the clothes were neatly displayed on the bed, Autumn turned to us.

"So, what should I wear?" she said.

"What about this black one-piece?" Cristy said.

"That's a... little revealing," Autumn stuttered.

"Yeah, we should probably go a little more conservative for the first date. She can save that number for later," I said. I looked down at the bed and spotted the perfect piece. It was a light purple dress with spaghetti straps.

"How about this?" I said as I lifted it by the straps.

"That isn't much different than the black one, except it has straps," Autumn said.

"That's why we add this," I said, picking up a dark purple lace shirt. The shirt was designed to go over a dress as it was somewhat see-through. "This, plus this purple skirt and those boots you wore to school yesterday. What do you think?"

"I like it," Cristy said. "A little on the modest side for my taste, but hey, it looks good."

"I think this will work. Purple and black are my favorite colors," Autumn said.

"Black?" I said. "I figured you would like some lighter colors."

"No, not really," she said. "I'm going to take these and get dressed, be right back."

Autumn went to her drawers, pulled out what appeared to be a lavender bra and panty combo, and left the room.

"You should get an Oscar for this," Cristy said. "I don't need to be a mind reader to tell you are screaming inside."

"What can I do?" I said.

"Tell her how you feel," Cristy said.

"Yeah and take the chance of her distancing herself from me because the whole idea of being with another girl makes her uncomfortable," I said. "You saw her face when you brought up sex. I'm sure the idea of a lesbian relationship will cause a similar, yet worse reaction."

"You're probably right," Cristy sighed.

"Her parents said it would be best if I kept my feelings to myself," I said. "Not because they had a problem with them, but because they might make her feel uncomfortable around me, and that's something I can't afford."

"I guess you holding things back is the right thing to do; I just hate to see you in pain. And don't fucking lie to me, I know you are," Cristy said.

"My mother always told me, 'Pain is the life of a Tala'har.' You don't want to know what I've been trained to endure," I said.

"I refuse to dig that deep. You can keep that stuff to yourself if you want. If you want to talk about it, I'm always here," Cristy said.

"Thanks, Cristy," I said. "I'm not sure if I could do this without you."

"No problem," Cristy replied. "Protecting Autumn is a family affair, and I've been absent too long."

Chapter 17

The next few moments were filled with silence as we waited for Autumn. I really did want to scream. I had only known her a few days, but every fiber of my being wanted to wrap my arms around her and ask her not to go. To kiss her, to hold her, to tell her that I would make sure nothing bad would ever happen to her. The feeling of jealousy wasn't something I was accustomed to. I had never been jealous of anything or anyone before, not even my big sister. I had never cared enough about love to be jealous, and I now longed for someone I couldn't have. The more I learned about Autumn, the harder it was to stop loving her.

"So, how do I look?" Autumn asked, snapping me out of the internal dialog. She was already dressed in her black knee-high boots, purple dress, and lace over-shirt. I attempted to not stare; she looked stunning, and I was at a loss for words.

"You look awesome, cous'," Cristy said.

"Yeah..." I expelled.

"Okay, I'll take you guys' word for it," she said. "I guess you are going to insist on putting makeup on me, aren't you, Cristy?"

"Only a little, with a complexion like that, you really don't need a lot. I've always found it funny that none of us had ever developed acne. I wonder if it's a genetic thing."

"Don't know," Autumn said as she seated herself at the dresser with a mirror attached to it. "You okay, Carrie?"

"Yeah... I'm fine," I said. "I think this heat is getting me. I'm glad it's nice and cool in here."

"I've caught Mom keeping the air conditioning off while Dad and I are gone. She says she's fine without it and always tells me growing up in the Mediterranean makes Miami look like the Arctic."

Cristy opened her makeup box, dug through its contents, and pulled out a palette of mascara and eyeliner pencils. She sat on the bed, close enough to Autumn to apply the makeup.

"I think I'm going to get something to drink," I said.

"Just ask my mom; she can help you out," Autumn said, attempting not to fidget.

"Sure," I said. I left the room, paused a bit down the hall, and leaned against it. I peered up to the ceiling with my head resting against the wall.

"Is she okay?" I heard Autumn say.

"I think so," Cristy said. "This place is new to her, and it will probably take some adjusting. She always puts up a tough face, but she's human, just like you and me. Hell, maybe she's a little lonely and could use a date nearly as bad as you do."

"I just don't like seeing her like that," Autumn said. "She's always thinking of me, and I feel I should do something to say I'm grateful."

"Eh, I don't think you need to do anything special. Just enjoy yourself tonight and try to have fun for once," Cristy said.

I stopped eavesdropping and went downstairs as quietly as I could. I wandered to the kitchen and found Cassandra playing solitaire at the table. Without a word, she stood up and put her arms around me.

"I know this is hard on you," she whispered. "All I can say is William and I are eternally grateful for everything you have done. You have no idea how long it's been since I've seen my daughter truly smile. I want you to know that I am here for you. If you need a shoulder to cry on or need someone to talk to, I'm here. Our home is your home. We would be honored if you would consider yourself part of our family."

I said nothing and only hugged her back.

Cassandra pulled back, "Now, is there something you need?"

"Yeah, a glass of water, if that's okay," I said.

"Certainly," she said. She turned to the refrigerator and took out a clear glass pitcher of water. With her free hand, she grabbed a cup from one of the cupboards next to the fridge and poured me a glass. After handing it to me, I sat down at the table.

"This is becoming more difficult than I expected," I expelled. I immediately felt guilty about the comment. I was doing something a Tala'har should never do: let her feelings get the better of her. "Mrs. Alexander, I'm feeling jealous. I've never been jealous, ever. There is just something about her... I know you should probably be the last person I talk to this about, but I don't know who else to turn to. I wish I could dismiss my feelings as a simple crush, but it's more than that; I know it. Your daughter is... incredible."

"I wish I could say something to make this easier," Cassandra said. "The only thing I can say is this, and I probably shouldn't. Autumn will love you... someday."

"Wha..?" my mouth slacked open but a full word couldn't escape.

"Every so often, she will wake up in the middle of the night, eyes glowing, asking about you and telling us how much she misses you... and how much she loves you," Cassandra said. "She never has any recollection of these incidents."

"I knew about the waking up in the middle of the night thing; Cristy told me about that. But how much she loves me?" I said with my mouth still agape.

"Yes, and this was long before she met you," Cassandra explained. She shifted her weight in her seat and continued, "I'm not sure what you can do with this information; I can't even guarantee she'll ever express these feelings to you, but I am fairly certain that someday they will be there. I can't tell you when."

"I'm not sure if that will make this easier or harder," I said.

"I understand," Cassandra said.

I could hear a door open and shut upstairs, signifying that Cristy had completed Autumn's makeup. I stood up and walked into the living room, followed by Cassandra. After a few moments of moving around upstairs, Cristy appeared and came down the stairs.

"Ladies and... well... ladies," Cristy announced from the bottom of the stairs. "I present to you the lady, no, let's be straight about this, 'babe' of the evening, Miss Autumn Alexander."

I heard a soft sigh from upstairs as Autumn slowly came into view, gracefully stepping down the stairs with one hand on the banister. She looked simply stunning. The outfit we had chosen for her looked even better against the subtle hints of color that Cristy had applied to her face. The makeup was almost imperceptible, which is the mark of skillful application. There was just enough color around her eyes and lips to make her eyes stand out while perfectly complementing her outfit. Cristy must have also convinced her to style her hair because she had a butterfly pin securing a flawless butterfly knot at the back of her head. The rest of her hair fell neatly to the small of her back. She was blushing deeply as everyone admired her.

"Well, how does she look?" Cristy said.

"Wonderful, you look absolutely wonderful," Cassandra joyfully expressed.

"Agreed," I added.

"Sorry, I didn't ask about borrowing the hairpin," Autumn said. "I didn't think you would mind."

"Oh, sweetheart, you don't need to ask to borrow anything of mine. What is mine is yours," Cassandra said. "I think your outfit needs one more thing, though." Cassandra dashed up the stairs, which looked slightly unbefitting for a woman of such feminine grace. A silent moment passed, and she hopped down the steps holding a small velvet box. She held the box out to Autumn.

"Here, this is for you. I was going to save it for your wedding day, but since it would look so lovely on you right now, I cannot resist giving it to you," Cassandra said, tears coming down from her eyes.

Autumn took the box and opened it gently. She lifted from it a silver bracelet with light purple gems woven into it. The bracelet was entirely woven silver, with the gems seated at intervals. At first glance, I thought they might have been amethyst, but I wasn't so sure after getting a better look at it. The bracelet matched her clothing perfectly.

"Oh, Mom, it's beautiful. Are you sure?" Autumn said.

"I'm positive," Cassandra said. "It was handed down to me by your grandmother and has been handed down to each woman in our family throughout the ages. That bracelet is likely over two thousand years old."

Our three sets of eyes widened. She shouldn't be wearing it; it should be in a museum.

"Unfortunately, it and the matching earrings and necklace are probably the last surviving Telosian artifacts. My sister has the other pieces. This bracelet is our family's heritage, and it warms my heart to hand it down to you," Cassandra said. She turned to Cristy, "Sorry to ruin the surprise. You now know something about your inheritance."

"I wouldn't worry too much about it, Aunt Cassy," Cristy said with a grin.

"Mom, something about this... feels kind of strange," Autumn said as she slid her fingers over the bracelet's surface.

"Yes, I know. It was made by an enchanter, like all Telosian jewelry and weapons. They do have some strange powers, although I can't really be certain what power that bracelet holds. You are a young lady now and have earned the responsibility of such power and beauty."

"Thank you, Mother. I'll treasure it always," Autumn said. Glancing at the bracelet with a broad smile, she wrapped it around her right wrist and hooked the clasp.

"It is instinct to want to tell your child to take care of a handed-down heirloom," Cassandra mused. "I am unsure that applies here. There is a belief that these jewelry pieces are virtually indestructible. I would be honored if you would wear it daily if you like."

"Why didn't you?" Autumn said.

"I don't know. I guess I never bonded with it, but I have a feeling you will," Cassandra smiled.

"Oh, I'm sorry, Carrie, you probably have no idea what a Telosian is, do you?"

"I gave her mother a bit of a rundown on it," Cassandra said. "She told you about it, I hope?"

"Yeah, she mentioned a few things," I said, fiddling with my ring. "I can hear about the specifics later."

"We still have some time until Jacob comes to pick you up, Autumn, so what we gonna do in the meantime?" Cristy said.

"We could play cards," Autumn suggested.

"Sounds good to me," Cristy said. "Carrie, you okay with that?"

"Sure," I said, "as long as Mrs. Alexander plays with us."

"I'd love to if you girls will have me," she said.

Chapter 18

We were seated around the kitchen table, playing the game Cristy suggested: poker. Autumn reclined in her chair with a calm face, laughing and joking with the rest of us. She was clearly focusing on the game instead of the approaching date. I couldn't stop looking at her. She was stunning. There was just something about her that made my insides squirm.

The kitchen was much like the rest of the house. It was in a pristine order that most homemakers would envy. There were no stray crumbs or dirt on the kitchen's white linoleum floor, which shined, showing signs of recent waxing. The walls were done in white wallpaper, with spaced-out light blue pinstripes. The countertops were made of a simple oak and shined, with a complete lack of scratches and dents that most well-used kitchens exhibited. The cabinets were wooden painted cream with no indications of wear. The ceiling was done in stucco that was a brilliant shade of white, with no dust to be seen.

The table looked handmade and created from the same oak as the countertops. The refrigerator was a gleaming white but looked to be extremely old. I had difficulty gauging how old it was because this was the first time I had seen one like it, which meant it was far older than the length of time I had lived in this world. As for the stove and oven combo, it also looked ancient and looked to be gas on closer inspection. It had removable coils that one would need to take off and clean underneath. Even though it appeared very old, like the rest of the place, it was immaculate.

Considering Cristy was on a losing streak, she was not cheating with her abilities. She had more willpower than I would if I had such powers. Cassandra looked like a pro handling the cards, even though she had won only a few hands. Autumn was the big winner so far.

"I swear, girl, you have no tells," Cristy gasped. "Most of the time, you are an open book; what gives?"

"Oh, it's just something you learn when you train for battle as much as I do. It comes in handy in many situations," Autumn said as she examined her recently dealt hand.

"Where did you learn to play poker, anyway," I asked.

"Mom taught me, isn't that right?" Autumn said as she threw in her bet for the current hand.

"That's right, I taught her most of what she knows about the game, although I can't take credit for her poker face. That's all, William," Cassandra said as she sat down her bet.

"Where did you learn, Mrs. Alexander?" I asked.

"Oh my, that was a long time ago," she reminisced with her head tilted back. "During World War II, I went to New Orleans to find a job while William was off fighting the war. A good friend of mine there taught me."

"Wow, New Orleans during World War II," I mused. "That seems like so long ago. I guess since we're all so young, the idea of immortality hasn't even sunk in yet. You must have learned to do a lot of things during your life, Mrs. Alexander."

"That is a lesson you all need to learn," Cassandra said. "I don't mean cards, though. We must not be specialists; we are immortal women. We must learn to do as many things as possible because the world always changes, even though we change very little. As a young girl, I was a baker with my father. The war broke out in my homeland, and I became a medic. After I married Autumn's father, we traveled to America. I did a myriad of jobs to help us get by, anything from being a seamstress to again a baker in the colonial and Revolutionary War days when I wasn't tending to those on the battlefield to a bookkeeper at a bank during the Civil War to being a barmaid in the days of the Old West, to working in weapons factories during both World Wars. Most of this was while William was away, fighting in the wars. The fact is, we must always be self-sufficient. The world is cruel, and there may be a day we will be on our own and must fend for ourselves."

"Seems like Mr. Alexander fought in many wars," I stated.

"Yes, he couldn't stay away from combat. We helped found this country and thus felt responsible for its well-being. It's our home, you see. Whenever the country was truly in danger, William volunteered for combat," Cassandra said. "The last war he fought in was the Vietnam Conflict. After that, he never felt the same about fighting for our country. It just didn't feel to him that he was protecting our homeland anymore."

142

"I see," I said. "How did you feel about Autumn's brother joining the army?"

"Proud. We would never look down on those who are willing to die for the place they were born and raised. I know Jason would never do anything immoral like they tried to force William to do during Vietnam," Cassandra explained.

"Yeah, I heard about stuff like that," Cristy said. "What did Uncle William do?"

"He refused. Being he was a decorated soldier during the Korean conflict, he had some sway and was able to stop himself and others who had refused from being court marshaled. Instead, he and the others were given an honorable discharge."

The sound of William's car pulling into the drive could be heard.

"Sounds like Dad's home!" Autumn exclaimed. "You think he'll like how I look?"

"I'm sure he'll think you look lovely," Cassandra assured.

"I've never really talked to Dad about boys," Autumn said. "I don't know how he will react to this."

"Hello," William came in the back door. "How are my four favorite ladies?"

"Hi, love." Cassandra bounced up, kissed William on the cheek, and wrapped her arms around his neck as he put his around her waist.

Autumn stood up to greet her father. She looked nervous but smiled warmly anyway.

Cassandra turned and put one arm behind his back while he kept one arm around her waist, side by side.

"And there is my lovely daughter looking more lovely than usual. What is the occasion?" William said.

"Ah, I'm going out on a date tonight...if that's okay with you," Autumn said, letting her nervousness slip out.

"So, some young man finally found the courage to ask you out?" William chuckled. "I do get to meet this boy, don't I?"

"Yes, sir," she said.

"Autumn," he said, with a slightly stern tone.

"Yes, father?" she cocked her head.

"I thought we talked about calling me 'sir'," he said. "This isn't the army. I'm your father, not your boss or superior. I've always thought the practice was too rigid for family life."

"I understand. Sorry, Dad," she said. "Is my outfit...okay...I mean, if you want, I'll go upstairs and change into something that shows less skin if you like."

"Autumn," he sighed.

"Yes?"

"Calm down, you look lovely, and you are dressed quite appropriately," he replied. "You are not a little girl anymore. I have no right to tell you what to wear. You could walk out of this house half naked if you chose, and I would say nothing."

"I would never do that, Dad," she laughed.

"That's not the point," he laughed. "You are old enough to make your own decisions. I refuse to lord over you like an overbearing dictator. I trust my daughter and her decision-making ability."

"Thanks, Dad," she said. She stepped toward him and hugged him.

The doorbell rang.

"That's him!" Autumn exclaimed.

"I'll get the door," Cassandra almost giggled.

"I can get it," Autumn said.

"No, Autumn," Cristy said. "Don't you know anything about boys? You make them wait. You and I are going to go upstairs and 'get ready.' Carrie, why don't you stay here and keep the guy calm? Sorry, Uncle William, but the sheer sight of you can be pretty intimidating to a teenage boy."

144

"I understand," William said with a laugh.

"Okay," I agreed. I followed Cassandra to the living room as Cristy grabbed Autumn by the wrist and dragged her upstairs.

"Coming," Cassandra rang.

"This is starting to feel like an old sitcom," I laughed as I positioned myself on the couch and crossed my legs. She opened the door, and Jacob stood with a bouquet in hand.

"Hello, Miss," he said. "Is your sister home?"

"Oh, dear," Cassandra chuckled. "I'm not Autumn's sister; I'm her mother, Cassandra."

"Oh, I'm sorry, ma'am," he stumbled. "I'm Jacob. You look so young, I didn't think you could be..."

"It's alright," she said. "I will take it as a compliment. Most people confuse us for sisters. She's upstairs, finishing getting ready. Come in, please."

Jacob meekly stepped in the door past Cassandra and surveyed the home.

"Oh, hi, Carrie. I wasn't expecting to see you here," he said.

"Are you kidding," I said. "I wouldn't miss this for the world."

Of course, that was a blatant lie. I would prefer not to be here for this. I would also choose not to trail him and Autumn for the evening, but I knew it would be too dangerous to leave them on their own, unarmed.

"Hello, son," William walked into the room.

"Uh, hello, sir," Jacob looked up at William.

"I'm William, Autumn's father," he said, handing Jacob his hand. Jacob paused momentarily, then took William's hand and shook it. "You do not need to be nervous. I don't plan on giving you the third degree or anything of the sort. Sit down, please."

"Sure," he said. He sat down next to me on the couch. I looked over at him. He wore a colorful, anime-inspired button-down shirt with some sword-wielding, character-design, and khakis. He was adorable but not the type of guy I

145

was into. I had always been into the bad boy when it came to men. Usually, that's how it was with the girls, too, but there was something different about Autumn. Something about her drove me wild.

"So, Jacob," William said. "How long have you lived in the Miami area?"

"Not very long, sir," he said. "I just moved here. My father and sister have been here for years, though."

"Moving is always difficult," Cassandra said. "William and I have done quite a bit of it ourselves."

"I hope you can make this place your home," I said.

"Where did you live before you came here?" William asked.

"Japan, sir," he said.

"Really?" William said. "I'm from there myself."

"Oh?" Jacob said. "What part?"

"A small town located at the southern end of the country. I doubt you've heard of it," William said.

It was unlikely that the town still existed.

"What brought you to America?" Cassandra asked.

"My mother died; I lived with her," Jacob said.

"Oh, I'm sorry to bring it up," Cassandra said.

"My condolences," William said.

"It's alright," he said. "She was rather ill for years. I'm just happy she's at peace now and not having to worry about me."

There was something about the reference to his mother being ill that almost brought up a memory of something else, but I couldn't put my finger on it. It felt like I should have remembered something, but I couldn't. It was like looking for something in the dark. The object would be there, but it was unseen by the naked eye. It felt very wrong, but I mentally shrugged it off and kept my mind on the conversation.

146

"Got into a lot of fights?" William said.

"Uh...yes, sir. How did you know that?" Jacob said.

"Because people of partial Japanese descent are generally looked down upon," William said. "I've been in my share of those fights, too; I'm half British."

"I never let it get me down," Jacob said.

"Son, I can look in your eyes and tell the kind of man you are," William said. "Just do me a favor and try not to get into too many fights on my daughter's behalf."

"I'll do whatever it takes," Jacob said. He began to sit up straighter. "I've heard a bit of what these people at our school say about her from my sister. I won't tolerate it, regardless of the kind of relationship she and I have. At the very least, she's a friend, and I don't let people talk about my friends like that."

This guy was starting to sound a lot like me. I wasn't sure how to feel. Autumn did deserve a man to fight for her honor, yet I couldn't help but feel like he was stepping on my toes.

William smiled, "I had a feeling you would say something like that."

A few silent moments passed, and then Autumn hurried down the steps slowly, followed by Cristy. She looked no different, but she still took my breath away. I could see she did the same to Jacob. She came down the steps smiling, her cheeks slightly red. Either she was not used to being looked at like this, or she had heard what Jacob said.

"Hi," Autumn exhaled. It didn't seem like she could say much else.

"Hi, you look...wonderful," he said. "Oh...here." He handed her the bouquet. Her eyes widened at the gift. They were a collection of light purple flowers, but I didn't know what they were. I never did learn much about flowers. I know what roses are. Roses aren't a first date thing, and I was betting Jacob knew that.

"Thank you so much. Purple is one of my favorite colors; how did you know?"

"Lucky guess," he said. He glanced over at Cristy. That girl was always up to something.

"Mom, can you put these in some water?" she looked over to her mother.

"Yes, dear," Cassandra took the flowers from Autumn.

"Excuse me," Jacob took a flower. "May I?" he said to Autumn. She smiled and nodded her head in agreement. He broke off part of the stem and placed the flower in Autumn's hair. This guy was good. He was either smooth or the last real gentleman left on the planet. I looked over at Cassandra and saw her wipe a tear from her eye. Cristy was smiling and rolling her eyes all at once.

"Well, I think the two love birds should get going before it gets too late," Cristy said.

Autumn turned to her parents, "What time do you guys want me home?"

"Anytime, dear, feel free to stay out for as long as you like," Cassandra said. "We trust you and your new friend."

"Yes, whenever you want. It's so rare you get out, so you should try to make the most of it," William agreed.

"I hope you don't mind, but we have to take the bus," Jacob said. "I haven't had a chance to get an American license yet, and I still need a car."

"It's fine, I like the bus. You get to see so many interesting people," Autumn said.

"Cristy is probably right," Jacob said as he pulled out his smartphone and observed the time. "The bus will be here soon; we should be getting going."

"Have fun," Cassandra said.

"Yes, please do. It was nice meeting you, Jacob," William said as he put his hand out again to him. Jacob shook it more firmly this time.

"You too, sir," he said.

"We're going to follow you two out," Cristy said.

I followed Cristy, Autumn, and Jacob out of the door. After I shut the door, Autumn turned to Cristy and me and said, "So what are you two going to do tonight?"

148

"Hang out," Cristy replied. "Carrie and I have some havoc to cause somewhere."

"What sort of trouble do you plan on dragging me into?" I said.

"Nothing you and I can't handle," Cristy said.

"Good, that's my favorite kind," I said.

"It's good to see you two again," Jacob said.

"Don't do anything I wouldn't do...and that isn't much," Cristy warned with a grin.

Autumn rolled her eyes.

"See you guys later," Autumn said. Jacob raised his arm, and Autumn gawked at him momentarily. Then she realized what she was supposed to do and wrapped her arm around his. They began to walk toward the bus stop.

Once they were out of earshot, Cristy turned to me.

"Man, he is good," Cristy said. "I had a feeling he'd be smooth when he got up the nerve, but that was just damn impressive."

"Is the whole 'gentleman' thing genuine?" I said.

"As genuine as the leather this jacket is made of. And if you're wondering, yeah, this is real leather," Cristy laughed as she put her grabbed onto her jacket. "I don't like sifting through people's minds, but I checked this guy out. Trust me, he's the real deal. And he is absolutely crazy for her."

"That makes two of us," I sighed. "How the hell do you manage to wear that jacket in this heat? Are you one of those people who are always cold?"

"Yeah, and it looks boss," Cristy said. "Plus, even though my sister has more than a few inches on me, people would still mix us up unless I wore the jacket. That's what started me wearing it all the time."

"It's really nice," I said. "Where did you get it?"

Cristy took a deep breath, "I don't really like talking about it, but you and I are tight. You asked a question, and damn it, you're going to get an answer to it."

"You don't have to tell me if you don't want to," I said.

"No, I do," she said. "Just give me a bit."

"Okay," I said.

"I don't think it's a good idea we tail them unarmed, or we won't be much use. I will try to catch up with them while you go back to your house and get your blade. The bus stop they are on their way to is on the way to my house, so I will stop by and get my car and my rifle. I'll call you and get you when they are in a public place. I don't think these guys will mess with them with a bunch of people around," Cristy said.

"Good idea," I said as I turned toward my house.

Chapter 19

I started running as fast as I could. It was times like these that I regretted loving the color black so much, as the sun was turning my shirt and pants into a cloth oven. I knew every moment Cristy was tailing them unarmed was a chance for something to happen. I hoped Cristy could get to her house and get me in time.

A red light appeared in the corner of my eye, and before I could react, it nailed me on the foot. It knocked me off my feet, but I recovered my footing and spun around a tree. I examined the foot that was hit. The buckle on my boot was singed with a blast that had to be from some beam of light. The weapon couldn't have been powerful because a belt buckle shouldn't have stopped it. I couldn't believe my luck. Either whoever was shooting at me had terrible aim or was purposely trying to disable me.

I peeked around the tree and saw nothing with both sets of vision. I loathed not knowing where these guys were. I peered behind me and saw my house only yards away. I took a step to make a run for it, and a blast came from up in the trees across the street, once again aimed at my legs or feet. The blast narrowly missed that time. I was sure of it. They wanted to take me alive.

I searched the street and found no one, even though I was in the middle of a normally busy suburb.

As I scanned for places to move to, the familiar noise of a chain rubbing against metal filled the still air. I turned just in time to see a figure in the street holding what appeared to be spear, pointed downwards with a chain attached to the other end. The chain was hurling toward a tree on the other side of the street. On the end of the chain, a scythe blade was attached. This was a weapon I knew very well. It was the Dharg'syth, my mother's Tala'har weapon, the Raven of Death. The weapon's blade sliced through a large tree branch, causing it to crash to the ground and knock down part of a fence. A thunderous crash reverberated through the empty yards and street.

"Go, now!" my mother yelled.

I sprinted into the house, and she followed. I shoved through the partially open door, and she shut it behind us. I peered out of the window around the neon pink curtains. The area was still. The owner of the tree and fence my mother had just damaged must have been away.

151

I bent over to catch my breath chest heaving. I looked at my mother and saw her signature scythe that hung on her back. For a woman with such tacky taste in clothing and general household design, she had one bitchin' weapon.

"Are you hurt?" she said finally.

"No, they hit my boot buckle," I said. "I swear my luck has never been that good before. How did you know where they were?"

"A little trick I picked up from Cassandra," she said. "I was talking to her on the phone before you went over there. She mentioned she could radiate energy waves to find them, like radar. I figured we could use a similar technique, but of course, through our weapons. If they bounce back to us and something isn't there visually to match it, we know someone is there. I was using the scythe to test this technique, and it worked. Just in time."

"This is all well and good, but how can I use this to protect Autumn when I can't carry my sword around in public?" I said.

"Your ring," she said.

"Oh," I said, gazing down to the gryphon-shaped Tala'har signet ring that always occupied the ring finger on my right hand. "That's right! My ring is made of the same metal as my sword. It's going to be hard to radiate those kinds of waves out of something so small."

"That's why you'll want to practice with your sword first, then the ring," she replied. "So, since you are here, I take Autumn is at home with her parents?"

"No," I said. "She's actually out on a date."

"Really?" my mother replied. "That means she's unprotected right now?"

"Not exactly," I said. "Cristy is tailing them. She will pick me up in her car when she gets a chance. I better get upstairs, get 'the Queen,' and be ready for her to pick me up. The less time Autumn is by herself, the better."

"And do you not remember the talk we had yesterday? About you walking around alone? It could have got you killed."

"About that. It's obvious they wanted to take me alive. It didn't seem they would chance hitting me high; they kept aiming for the feet."

152

Mom rolled her eyes, "Well, I suppose that is useful information. Just don't do it again."

My phone began to ring in my pocket. I pulled it out, flipped it open, and answered it.

"What's up," I answered.

"We have a problem," Cristy replied.

"What now?" I said.

"Thomas," Cristy stated simply.

"Who?" I questioned.

"I'll explain when I get there. Be ready."

Cristy pulled up to my house within minutes, and I jogged out of the house with my sword in a duffel bag. Cristy drove a cherry-red Ford Mustang, last year's model, which was a pretty sweet ride overall.

I opened her passenger door, pulled the seat forward, and tossed my duffle bag in the back.

"So, who the hell is Thomas, and why am I going to have to kick his ass?" I said as I pulled the seat back to its original position, sat down, and closed the door.

Cristy sighed loudly as she put the car in gear and started driving, "Thomas is a dickwad that's been haunting our family for longer than I even know. When I say 'haunting,' I mean it. He's basically the living dead, in a way. He's a walking, slowly rotting corpse that has the idea that if he drinks an immortal's blood dry, he will gain that immortality as well as a normal body. I don't know if it's true, but he sure as hell thinks it is."

"So, he's after Autumn to drink her blood?" I asked.

"Yep, but to be more accurate, any of us," she answered. "I'm sure he picked Autumn as a target because she's with someone who isn't a part of the family, and she's mostly unarmed. I think Autumn is his favorite target. His major beef is with her father, and since Uncle Will kicks his ass constantly, he wants to get back at him by killing his daughter."

"It would have been nice if someone would have mentioned this guy earlier!" I exclaimed.

"Sorry about that," Cristy apologized. "I guess no one brought him up because dealing with him is normal in our lives. Even while she is unarmed, he's not much of a threat to Autumn. It's her reaction to an attack tonight that has me worried."

"What do you mean?"

"If he attacks Autumn while she's with Jacob, Autumn won't go out with Jacob, or anyone else, ever again. She probably hasn't even considered the possibility of Thomas coming after her while she's out with Jacob, and it should stay that way."

"Oh shit," I said. Then, a wave of relief washed over my face uncontrollably. I immediately shook the thought of Autumn being permanently single out of my head.

"I wouldn't feel bad about it; it's totally human to feel that way," Cristy said.

"Yeah, but I shouldn't," I said. "I'm her Tala'har, her protector, and her friend. I shouldn't wish something bad on her for selfish reasons."

"But you are also human," Cristy replied. "You can't punish yourself for feelings. You can't act on those feelings; that's the important part."

"I know," I sighed. "So, how do we deal with this Thomas guy?"

"I have an idea," Cristy said. "Autumn and Jacob are going to eat downtown. Once they go into the restaurant, we'll make our move. Thomas will likely wait outside the place for them. We'll have a little surprise waiting for him. The question is, can you drive stick?"

Chapter 20

We entered the downtown scene just as it was beginning to wake up. Usually, Miami was my kind of town, especially at night. It attracted people from all over the country who came to party. I loved how the urban landscape was intertwined with tropical scenery. The large, modern buildings blended seamlessly with the palm trees scattered throughout the area.

As I observed the crowds on the sidewalk, I noticed a diverse mix of people from various creeds, races, and nationalities, most of whom were there for one thing: to party. I couldn't help but gawk at the many attractive individuals around me. The girls were dressed in barely-there outfits—bikinis, short skirts, halter tops, and other skimpy clothing. Many of them had perfect bodies, and I suspected that most of it wasn't entirely real.

The guys were either very well-dressed or hardly dressed at all, proudly displaying their six-packs and muscles. The crowd was filled with an abundance of superficial flair. While I found it entertaining, I also had my reservations. These people could be fun to engage with, but they weren't exactly enjoyable to be around for long.

Wherever I looked in the downtown area, clubs thrived. Neon lights lit up the skyline like the Aurora Borealis. I could think of a plethora of things to do here if I had the free time. This was my kind of town, and, at the same time, I dreaded the place. With so many people in one area, a threat could appear from anywhere, and I may not recognize it in time.

Autumn and her family felt out of place in this wasteland of superficiality. For all their strange history, they were comparatively ordinary, honest people. Nothing was shallow about them, like the crowds that thrived in these clubs. I would expect them to live somewhere quieter. As for Cristy and her family, I could see why they wanted to stay here. I wondered if Autumn, deep down, resented her parents for bringing her here. Her life turned to hell overnight, by how it seemed to me.

"There they are," Cristy said, snapping me out of observing the surroundings. Jacob was taking her into a quiet little restaurant that looked somewhat fancy. After they entered the restaurant, my eyes scanned the sidewalk to find this 'Thomas' guy. Finding him wasn't as hard as I thought it was going to be. A man wearing a brown trench coat and a derby hat was off by himself, smoking a thick cigar. If he was trying to look inconspicuous, he was failing at it miserably. His aura was even worse. It was like mud blended with blood in color. It would be called 'Swampy Gore' if it was a crayon.

"I assume that's him," I said.

"Yep. Let me warn you about three things. First, he is nothing but rotting flesh and bone. My family believes the magic that keeps him alive propels his bones. The more his flesh falls off, the faster he can move."

"Ugh," I expelled.

"Second, he carries a cutlass and a handheld shotgun, most times," she said.

"Got it."

"Last and most importantly, he smells horrible!"

"I probably should breathe out of my mouth when confronting him," I nodded.

"The reason this is most important is he almost killed my father once because the idiot took too good of a whiff of him and vomited. Fortunately, my father's sword moved his arm up to block the incoming swing."

"This is going to be fun," I sighed. Cristy moved the car into a side alleyway. I exited the vehicle as she slid into the passenger seat. I took my spot in the driver's seat and prepared for what was to come.

Cristy leaned into the back seat and removed her sniper rifle from a guitar case. If you wanted to carry a rifle without being suspected of having one, that would be the way to do it, even though it was a bit cliché. She opened her moon roof and climbed up out of it. She brought the rifle up out of the roof. We were far enough into the alley that only Thomas could see us once we gained his attention. Cristy paused for a moment before she let off the shot. I barely heard it and wouldn't have noticed it if it wasn't for the kick jarring Cristy's body back. I glanced through the rearview and saw the shot hit Thomas in the shoulder. He sneered at his shoulder, then at us, and began his pursuit.

"I think you pissed him off," I called back.

156

"Good," she said. She let another shot off as he entered the alley. That was the cue for me to ram the accelerator. With as fast as this car was, I couldn't understand why Cristy wanted me to drive through a narrow alley at full speed. It did not take me long to figure out why. Thomas was amazingly quick. He kept up with us far better than I expected, and her shots weren't slowing him down much. I saw him reach into his coat. Cristy lowered herself immediately down into the car and slid into the passenger seat as the blast of his hand-held shotgun was heard. I felt some of the blast nail the back of the vehicle. A second shot rang out, hitting the back windshield. The blast did nothing to the windshield. It must have been bulletproofed.

"That cocksucker!" Cristy spat.

I weaved through the alley as fast as possible, letting Cristy keep track of Thomas. As Cristy promised, we came to the back end of a construction site. As we approached, I hit the gas to get a bigger lead on Thomas. As we reached the gate, I slammed on the brakes.

"Run!" Cristy said as she flipped a few switches I just noticed on the dash. There were quite a few strange switches on the dash that I knew weren't factory.

As we dove out of the car, we could see Thomas advancing toward us. We climbed over the fence and landed on the other side just as Thomas reached it. Cristy kept running, and I retreated a few paces. Thomas leaped over the fence in a single bound.

"I don't know what you girls think you are up to, but you are going to pay for that," he said in a raspy voice tinted with a British accent. He sniffed the air, "Well, well. Lookie what I have here. Two little immortal bitches, one of them is Joseph's little cunt. Hey, little, short bitch, I'm not here for you today. I'm not familiar with you, Miss Spooky, but that doesn't matter; you'll be coming with me!"

"Like I'd go anywhere with you," I snarled, "Not with a stench like yours!!"

"Have it your way, love" Thomas growled, pulling his blade from his jacket. It was just as Cristy mentioned before. He used a medium-length cutlass, just small enough to hide in his coat.

I drew my blade and dropped the sheath to the ground. Just as the sheath hit the ground, the bastard was already on top of me with an arcing downward slash. I spun out of the way, retreating further back. He continued his attack, slashing in quick, quick bursts. My larger blade made retaliating almost impossible, but that was fine. I had never planned on being offensive at that point.

As I withdrew, I began to prepare Karithian for use with my abilities. She never wanted to accept my power, and today was no different. Most Tala'har my age would already be well-synced with their weapons. Yet even though the Karithian chose me as her wielder, she never wanted to cooperate without a fight. She was a cantankerous little bitch.

Thomas's shoulder jolted back. That must have meant Cristy was in position. He glared up into the partially constructed building and growled. He resumed his attack, trying his best to ignore the hail of bullets raining down upon him, each finding their mark. One even landed directly in his crotch. Knowing Cristy, that was no accident. I kept moving back as he swung furiously. He was no longer paying attention to where we were going or would have noticed what was coming. We continued up a ramp as he hacked and slashed. Soon, I found myself turning around an L-shaped curve on the scaffolding and with my back to a wall. More bullets came down keeping Thomas at bay.

"Looks like ye have nowhere to run, bitch," Thomas howled as he was being pumped full of lead.

"Oh, I'm not trying to run anymore," I said as Karithian finally allowed my magic to flow through her. I came at him with a horizontal slash, releasing fire energy into it in a way only a Tala'har could do with their special blades. As the blade chopped into his trench coat, he caught fire. He screamed out into the night. I was astonished he could still feel pain. As he flailed around on fire, Cristy hit him with a few more bullets, causing him to stumble back a few steps. I dashed toward the bastard and jump-kicked him in the chest, sending him plummeting off the scaffolding directly into a portable trash compactor. I jumped down from the scaffolding and engaged the machine.

"I'm gonna to git you, you fucking lil' cunts!" he screamed as the machine chewed him apart as he burned. Hopefully, no one could hear him.

While I watched our handy work with a grin of satisfaction, Cristy made her way down from the building and stepped up next to me.

158

"Now, I know how it feels to be an Alexander. You know, kicking the enemy's butt and protecting others while doing so."

"Yeah," I expelled. "I now really know how it feels to be a Tala'har." Thomas's screaming was gurgled; his vocal cords were being crushed. "He's going to come back from this, isn't he?"

"He always does. Oh, by the way, nice touch lighting him on fire. I was wondering if Tala'har have any special abilities."

"Yep, we can release magic through our weapons," I said. "To protect a wizard, you must have the magic to keep up. At least that's what my mom says."

"Very cool. Did I hear right? Did he say he was here for you?"

"Yeah… so does that mean he was just tailing Autumn to draw me out?"

"I'd like to sit here and hope he screams some more and figure this all out, but the smell is really getting to me. Burning rotting flesh sucks," Cristy said as she started to cough.

"We shouldn't be here when the police arrive either."

Chapter 21

As we drove out of the alley, I took this time to catch my breath. I couldn't hear Thomas' muffled screams anymore. The world around us seemed unaware of what was happening only a few hundred meters away. The car pulled out of the alley and back into the main street.

"Hey, Cristy. What were those switches you hit before you jumped out of the car?" I asked.

"Oh, one covered my license plate," she said as she flipped that switch again.

"And the other engaged an electronic jamming device to get rid of any security cameras the construction site might have." She flipped the other switch off as well.

"I assume your Dad had this stuff built into the car?"

"Yep, along with some other tricks. Thomas is always a problem, amongst other things. The Olympian gods send assassins after my father from time to time. He wants us to be protected if they decide to target us."

"I see he's not a complete moron," I said.

"No, don't get me wrong, he's a good dad. He's a horrible uncle and probably a pretty bad person in general, but he's a great dad. He always makes sure Sophia, Mom, and I are protected, like any good father would."

"Yeah, well, everyone needs redeeming qualities," I said.

"Hey, we should probably take this chance to get something to eat. I don't know about you, but I haven't had jack but those chips since lunch," Cristy said.

"Good idea," I said. "I doubt Autumn is in any real danger at the restaurant. It seems like these guys try to be pretty stealthy about everything."

We drove through a little mom-and-pop fast food stand and picked up some sodas, a cheeseburger for each of us, and a large fry to split. Cristy drove the car back to the restaurant, parking in the side parking lot, where Autumn and Jacob would unlikely see us.

"Are they still here?" I asked.

"Yeah, they are. This is a pretty nice place; Jacob's got style. I'm sure Autumn tried to talk him into something cheaper, though," Cristy said.

"Autumn is rather thrifty," I said. "Growing up with money always being an issue can do that to you." I put my head to the back of the seat and took a long drink of my soda. "Any idea what that Thomas guy wanted with me? You are the mind reader, after all."

"No clue, really. That would have had to take some digging into his head, and I had to focus on shooting him. His mind is a mess, anyway. I've tried controlling him, and it tends to throw him into a rage. I didn't want that today. I can only tell that he kept telling himself not to kill you."

"Great... so someone IS after me. Think it has anything to do with the guy in black?"

"You got me. It wouldn't surprise me."

"But that means he really is after me, not Autumn," I sighed as I bit into my burger. After a few moments of chewing, I turned to Cristy, "So, when are you going to tell me where you got that jacket?"

"Oh yeah, that," Cristy sighed. "Well, I figure I owe it to you. Only my sister knows where I got it. I plan on telling Autumn, too. This jacket is my most prized possession. It can never be replaced."

"If you don't feel up to telling me, I'll understand. Some things are hard to talk about."

"Yeah, but you've done all this sharing with me, and I haven't told you a damn thing about myself. There really isn't a lot to know, I suppose," Cristy said.

"Are you trying to say you are shallow?" I said. "Cause trust me, that's not the case."

"I was shallow, and I did it on purpose. I ran around with my sister, played her sidekick, and hung out with her friends; I gave up any friends of my own. Did all the stupid shit on social media. My selfies are seriously legendary, though."

We both laughed. Cristy took a deep breath and shifted her weight to face me in her seat.

"It was easier that way. In reality, I have no interest in popularity and things like that. I've always just wanted a few close friends that had my back. I guess I was just afraid to have feelings, any type of feelings, for anyone again. I even pushed away the one friend I did have."

"I'm not sure what you are getting at," I said right before I took a bite of my cheeseburger.

"It has to do with this jacket...and my abilities...and someone else," Cristy struggled.

"A guy?" I asked.

"Not just any guy, the guy," Cristy said. "Back when I was thirteen, I met this guy from another school. It was all innocent shit at first, emails and text messages back and forth, and then we went out on our first date, just like Autumn is doing tonight. It was incredible. You see, Carrie, I know you love Autumn because that's how he felt about me. He was completely in awe of me; I know I'm a mind reader. It only took one date for me to realize this was the guy I was going to spend forever with. That was when I decided I wanted to make him my first. I didn't want to be a whore, but I knew how he felt about me, and I knew how I felt about him, so I didn't see a reason to beat around the bush about it. So, we made love that night while his parents weren't home. For the first and only time that night, I tried something I call 'mind-melding. ' "

"What's that?" I asked.

"It is when you literally join your mind with someone else, and thoughts, feelings, and emotions flow freely between the two of you."

"Sounds incredible," I said. I wondered what it would be like to mind-meld with Autumn. "Did you share your immortality with him?"

"Oh, no. I wanted to give him a chance to back out if he wanted to. Was going to save that for marriage. It was really tough trying to keep spending forever with him out of my mind while that was happening. And, as you can probably imagine, he saw everything. He understood who I was and understood my feelings for him. We agreed that we would spend forever together afterward. He walked me home that night, and it started raining. He put this very jacket around my shoulders, and we ran to my house. We shared one more kiss before we parted. He insisted I hold on to the jacket."

162

"Wow. That is all just so romantic. What happened next?" I said. It just didn't seem to me that Cristy was interested in that type of relationship, but I knew the person who was the aftermath of what she told me about, not the love-struck thirteen-year-old.

"Well, things were good for the next couple of months. Then..." Cristy trailed off.

"What?" I said. Tears streamed down Cristy's eyes. '

"He cheated on me," Cristy said.

"Oh, I'm so sorry," I said.

"No, that's not the bad part," she continued. "His brother carted him to this party while I was sick. He apparently got drunk and had sex with some chick. He came to me the next day and broke down in front of me. He wouldn't tell me who the girl was, and I respected him too much to find out for myself. I knew he was telling the truth about it being an accident, and to be honest, I didn't care. I loved him and was almost glad he got a taste of someone else. I know being with someone for an eternity can be pretty boring."

"So, what happened?" I said.

"Well...I hadn't heard from him from the time he confessed. So, after he wouldn't answer my calls or text messages for a few days, I went to his house to see him. I walked up to the house and saw smoke coming out of the garage. I ran into his house and went in through the garage door. I found him in his parent's car, with the engine on, holding a suicide note."

"Oh...I'm so sorry," I gasped. The tears that were trickling down her face began to flow faster.

"I pulled him out of the car, and the last thing he said to me was, 'I'm sorry,'" she said.

"The suicide note said that he couldn't live with himself after what he did to me."

Cristy obviously couldn't hold it together much longer and just began to bawl. I wrapped my arms around her the best I could from the car's passenger seat.

"So..." she continued, sniffling. "That is why I am the way I am. I absorbed myself in my sister's phony world to escape reality, pushing away anyone who had meant anything to me. This way, I didn't have to think, only to go along with her and her loser friends. I sleep with anyone that will sleep with me because I'm bored. Sex with other people never means anything. It's a hell of a lot of fun, but it isn't very meaningful. I'll never love someone else. He was it, my soul mate. The one person in this world I opened my soul to, and he responded back."

I said nothing but continued to hold her.

"Now, I have you and Autumn. I think that's all I need," she said. She gazed deeply into my eyes and kissed me. Before I could even contemplate what to do, my world went blank. No other thoughts were in my mind; it was just me, Cristy, and this kiss. She pulled back after an undetermined amount of time, still looking me in the eyes.

"Remember that's there for you if you ever need it," she said as she placed her index finger upon my lips. I could hardly move. I was still stunned by the ordeal. I eventually withdrew back to my seat.

"That's the first time in a long time that a kiss actually meant something to me," she said. "It's a token of my affection toward you. You and Autumn are all I need. I think it would be fun to share my body with you. It would be fun and meaningful."

"Thanks," I said. I could hardly muster a word beyond that.

"I know how lonely you are," she said as she stared out toward the restaurant. "It's difficult not being able to be with the person you love. And when you love someone like the two of us do, it's impossible to love anyone else."

"Yeah," I said. "Cristy?"

"What's up," she said, wiping the tears off her face.

"Thanks for everything."

164

Chapter 22

Soon afterward, Cristy turned the key of the Mustang without muttering a syllable, and the car roared to life. I knew this must have meant Autumn and Jacob were done with their meal and on to their next destination, wherever that might be.

"They are going to the theater down on Oak," Cristy said. I was feeling increasingly certain that this job would be impossible without her.

"Hey Cristy, my mom showed me a way to find those people who have been following us, but I haven't been able to sense them since they attacked me on my way home."

"They attacked you?!" she exclaimed.

"Oh yeah, I forgot to mention that, didn't I?" I said. "My mom scared them off. She taught me a method I can use with either my sword or my ring to see if I can find them. I've been trying to use the ring since I can't openly hold my sword in the car. So far, I'm not getting anything."

"They haven't been around," Cristy said. "Everything is pretty clear."

"Now it just feels like we are snooping in on Autumn's date," I said. "You know, with no bad guys around."

"Feels?" Cristy laughed. "Hell, I've been listening in. Things are going well. I'd let you listen in too, but it might make you sick... and extremely jealous."

"So, they are getting along?" I said. "Yeah, like I thought they wouldn't."

"It's going to be more sitting around, but I don't mind," Cristy stated.

"Same here, and I'd go in to see a movie too, but I have too much on my mind right now even to pay attention," I said.

Cristy directed the car out into traffic and kept enough distance from Autumn and Jacob. The movie theater was within walking distance, so it wasn't likely they were going to get on a bus. They passed a few clubs as they exchanged conversation. I wondered what they were saying, but Cristy was right; I didn't want to know.

My phone started to ring.

"Hello," I said.

"Hi, Carrie," Cassandra said from the other end of the phone.

"Hi, Mrs. Alexander, what's up?"

"William and I are on our way out of town as we speak," she said.

"Okay, thanks for the heads-up," I said.

"You mentioned you would stay the night with Autumn, and you're with Cristy, right?" she said.

"Yeah, she's here," I said.

"Good, she has a key to our house," Cassandra said. "Feel free to make yourself at home once Autumn is on her way back from her date. I didn't tell her we were going out of town; I didn't want to distract her."

"I'll make sure to relay a message. What should I tell her for?" I said.

"You can go ahead and tell her I'm going back for the spell book; just make sure to leave out the part about the spell sensor being triggered. I wouldn't want her to worry."

"Sure, I won't say a word," I said.

"Okay, Mina will be over later tonight, so you don't have to sleep with one eye open. Feel free to stay the whole weekend if you like; she won't mind."

"Will do."

"Please be wary. Your mother told me about what happened out in front of your house. I'm worried about everyone at this point."

"That wasn't much compared to our run-in with that Thomas guy."

"Thomas? Oh, no, not now. What happened?"

"We caught him following Autumn," I said. "We put an end to it before she noticed, I think."

"Good, she deserves to have one somewhat normal night. Are both of you unharmed?"

"Yeah, we're fine. I'm a little concerned, however. He wasn't after Autumn; he was attempting to capture me."

"That's strange… I can't imagine why, but I doubt it's for anything good. And it's even more worrisome that he knew you would be tailing Autumn. Just keep an eye out for him; he can be persistent. I must be going now; I, too, must keep an eye out for potential threats…"

"Thread carefully, Cassandra. Bye," I said.

"Goodbye," she said as she hung up.

"You have the key to their house, right?" I said to Cristy.

"Yep, don't leave home without it. They never gave Sophia one. I don't think either of them trusts her. The fact is no one should."

As I turned my interest back to Autumn and Jacob, they arrived at the theater, and we pulled into an out-of-the-way portion of the parking lot. I laid my head back on my seat. It was going to be a long night.

"So, what now?" Cristy said.

"I'm not sure. I suppose we don't need just to sit here," I said.

"There is this seventeen and under club right across the street here. We can go check out some boys …or girls," Cristy giggled.

"Sounds like fun," I said. "Not dressed how I'd normally look to go into a club, but hell, who gives a fuck?"

Cristy and I exited the car. She opened the back seat and removed the black jacket, allowing her black halter top and black leather skirt to be more noticeable. As we walked to the club, I could see her turning heads as we passed people on the sidewalk. As we entered, it was plain to see teens dancing in every spare inch of the club. We weaved around the dancers to the bar and found a pair of seats.

"A Coke for me, please," I said to the bartender.

"Give me anything with a ton of caffeine," Cristy said. She turned to me, "See anything you like?"

I surveyed the club and saw many good-looking people, but my mind kept drifting to Autumn. We quietly hung out at the bar, people-watching. My mind kept attempting to return to her, no matter how incredible the crowd looked. The club was simple in design. It was a rectangular room with a bar on the left and a DJ table in the back near the restrooms. The roof was covered with mirrors so the crowd could look up at themselves, and I was assuming so that guys could look down girls' shirts. They played standard club fare, mostly bass-heavy electronic dance music or dance remixes of popular Top 40 songs, in other words, dreadful music. The establishment was like every other dance club I had seen in this world. It was dark and featured strobing colorful lights exploding everywhere around the room. I enjoyed these clubs because of the opportunity to play with the people they attracted, not the places themselves. I was more into a bar that played hard rock, preferably live if possible. The ones I wasn't old enough to get into.

Movement near the door caught my eye. A tall, dark-haired guy dressed in a black dress shirt and khaki pants entered the scene. An equally good-looking girl tailed him. She had to be wearing the skimpiest clothing out of all the girls in attendance. She was clad in a black skirt that hardly covered her ass and a gold top that slung over her shoulders, barely covering her breasts, made of a net material covered in sequins.

"Holy shit, did you see those two?" I said.

"Yeah, they are both pretty fine," she said. "By the looks of it, they aren't dating. You should go say hello to one of them."

"Nah," I said. "I'm in more of a 'look, but not touch...or talk' mood."

"If anyone comes up, let me handle them. I'm in the mood to be a bitch," Cristy grinned.

It didn't seem like I was going to get my wish. The guy was heading straight over to Cristy and me.

"Hello, ladies," he said as his partner passed by.

"Hi," I said.

"Maybe you should go away," Cristy said.

"What? I just wanted to talk," he said.

"Well, we aren't feeling chatty," Cristy said. "Now, scram."

"Fine, if either of you change your mind, I'll be hanging out with my sister over there," he pointed to the other side of the room. The scantily clad chick who had arrived with him was standing right next to Sophia herself. He walked away.

"Want to go outside for a minute?" I said after I finished my drink.

"Yeah, sure," Cristy said. We headed for the door and went around the corner, where a deserted alleyway was beside the club.

"Did you know she was here?" I said.

"No," Cristy said. "It's not like I scanned the whole place, but I usually notice someone I know so well when I enter any place. Although, this wouldn't be the first time she's passed under my radar. I'm not sure how she does it. Maybe it's part of her Telosian gift."

"What is her gift?" I said.

"The full extent of it isn't known, but she sees things."

"What kind of things?" I asked.

"You name it. Dead people, auras, all sorts of stuff. As far as our parents know, her gift hasn't shown its face yet, but I know better."

"How long has she been able to see this stuff?" I asked.

"Since we were kids," Cristy said.

"Wow, I guess that would fuck up anyone," I said.

"I wonder if that has something to do with why she's such a colossal bitch," Cristy said. "I mean, it goes beyond torturing Autumn, shit I don't even feel like telling you about. When they say she runs that school, she does. She probably has more control than Judy, in reality."

"I didn't think it was that bad," I said. "I thought it was the whole 'no one wants to cross the most popular chick in school' type of thing."

"It's that and more," Cristy said. "She's president of the Student Council, my dad is the biggest contributor to the athletics program, and she even goes as far to fix the games in our team's favor."

"How the hell does she do that?" I said.

"Different ways, depending on the situation. Everything from sleeping with coaches to blackmailing star athletes. It's really sick," Cristy said. "She tried to rope me into that crap, and I told her to go fuck herself."

"Damn," I said. "It seems like keeping up this little charade about Autumn being a dirty slut is child's play compared to the other shit she's doing."

"It started with that," Cristy said. "Then slowly became much worse."

"Fuck… It's more than Autumn suffering here," Carry gasped.

"Yeah… like my new friend, Liz," Cristy said. "Liz's brother and sisters are prominent athletes. She's trans, but still in the closet."

"Sophia could use that as a hook into her siblings, right?"

"Yeah… my sister is such a hypocritical bitch. She's bi, it's pretty clear. She has had sex with a lot of girls… and used it as blackmail… Liz isn't even the only trans person that is in danger of being outed by her. I can't even hang out with Liz; she needs a friend. Especially with her other problem, she's got another soul attached to hers that's slowly taking over."

"I think I saw her my first day… until Autumn's energy overtook hers."

"We have to do something about Sophia… she's wrecking so many lives," Cristy said. "I don't know what yet."

A frustrated silence materialized between us. Neither of us knew what to say or do.

"So, do we want to go back in there," I broke the silence.

"Yeah, I'm sure the bitch knows we are here now, and I don't want it to look like I'm leaving just because of her."

"Good point," I agreed.

We returned to the club and danced by ourselves for a while. I would occasionally look over my shoulder, and there was Barbie-cunt, who was giving me nasty looks from across the dance floor. I was almost ecstatic that my very presence was pissing her off.

Cristy tapped me on the shoulder and leaned close to my ear, "We better move it; Autumn's movie is ending."

"I was getting bored anyway. Pissing off Sophia loses its novelty after a while," I said.

"I learned that at a young age," Cristy giggled.

Chapter 23

We strutted out of the club and back into Cristy's car. From across the street, I spied Jacob and Autumn strolling toward the bus stop. I glanced down the street and spotted the bus heading toward the stop.

"We can probably just get going; I'd like to get to Autumn's house before she does," I said.

As neither of us sensed any disturbance, we departed from them and headed back to Autumn's house. We pulled into the driveway, and Cristy turned off the car.

We stepped out of the car and walked to the house's door. Cristy opened the door with a key attached to the ring that held her car keys, and we entered. Not seeing Cassandra on the couch was strange, as she always seemed to be waiting for someone to come through the door.

"Want to see something cool?" Cristy said.

"Sure," I said.

Cristy walked over to what looked like a handmade cabinet and opened it. She picked up a remote inside. She pressed a button on the remote, and the top of the curio slid open. A small flat-screen television rose from within the curio.

"I was wondering if they had a TV," I said.

"William and Autumn made this thing," she said. "I used to sit here and lift it up and down while my parents visited. Autumn usually stayed up in her room," Cristy said.

Cristy turned on the television with the same remote. After flipping through a few channels, she sighed.

"Now I remember why I never watch television over here," she said. "They don't have cable, and it's not a smart TV." She turned toward the door. "Looks like our love birds are almost here. Let's go watch."

We peeked out the window and saw Autumn and Jacob, arm in arm, strolling down the sidewalk. I saw the wide-eyed look on Autumn's face when she saw Cristy's car. She noticed the extensive body damage Thomas's shotgun had inflicted on the vehicle. She turned back to Jacob and smiled. After exchanging a few words, Autumn started to turn toward her house, then spun around, pulled Jacob close, and kissed him. He returned her kiss as they placed their arms around each other. I would have been envious if it wasn't so adorable. This was perhaps Autumn's first kiss. I was astonished that she initiated it. After a few moments, they left the kiss and hugged. She left him a peck on the cheek and glided toward the door.

Cristy and I bounced away from the window and onto the couch. Cristy began to flip channels as Autumn slowly entered the door, cheeks still red.

"Hi guys," she greeted. "Are my parents here? I didn't see their car out in the driveway."

"Nope," Cristy said. "They didn't want to disturb you on your date, but they made a last-minute call to get 'the book' back at your place in Pennsylvania."

"Really?" Autumn said in a quiet tone. "It's strange of them to do something so impulsive."

"Your mom called me to let us know," I said. "She also said your Aunt Mina will be coming by later."

"Oh, okay," Autumn said. "So, did you guys enjoy the show?"

It took me a minute to figure out what she meant. She beamed and blushed profoundly.

"You knew we were watching?" Cristy said.

"I'm pretty good at that. I'm surprised I did it myself. I don't know what came over me," Autumn said. "Speaking of strange things, what the hell happened to your car?"

"Oh, that," Cristy replied. "Thomas."

"You have got to be kidding me," Autumn said. "I hope you made him pay for that."

"Yeah," I smiled. "We did."

"I pumped him full of lead, Carrie lit him on fire and kicked him into a garbage compactor."

Autumn laughed, "That's awesome. So, when can I start work on it?"

"You?" Cristy said. "Nah, don't worry about it. Dad can spend his money and get his guy to fix it. You have better things to do than fix my car."

"You mean that guy that's not as good as me?" Autumn said.

"That would be the one. It's not like I need a performance enhancement; I'm sure he can handle some bodywork. Like I said, you have better things to do."

"If you insist. I shouldn't be so cocky, Louie does good work," Autumn said. "Poor thing, I know she's a Ford, but she deserves better than what happened to her."

"Hey, what can you do?" Cristy said.

I turned my attention to the television and saw a news report featuring the construction site where Cristy and I battled Thomas.

"Hey, Cristy, turn it up," I said.

"Around eight-thirty p.m., police responded to a call about blood found on the inside of a trash compactor at this downtown construction site. Police responded to the call, and the two officers were brutally murdered by a man who appeared to have crawled out of the trash compactor. The suspect seemed to be wearing a costume to make it appear as if he was decaying like a corpse. He was also wearing a long overcoat that was torn to shreds. Channel Eight News has acquired a tape of the brutal killing, but due to its graphic nature, we will not be showing it on air."

"Fuck," I said.

"Crap," Cristy said.

"Guys, you can't blame yourselves for this," Autumn said. She seated herself on the couch between us. "Thomas is a monster; it's not your fault he killed people that were in his way."

"I know that," I said. "I still can't help but feel responsible."

"If we wouldn't have fought him there, those officers wouldn't be dead," Cristy sighed. "So, in a way, I guess it's our fault."

"Yeah, and it's my fault that your sister makes my life hell," Autumn said as she put an arm around us. "Look, you guys did what you could. There was nothing you could do, and regardless of how you dealt with him, there was always a chance something like this could happen. At least now, the police will be looking for him. Hopefully, they catch him, and he gets used as a lab rat."

"I suppose you're right," Cristy sighed. "Still sucks. I should get going. After seeing that on the news, I'm sure my mom and dad are worried. Plus, I must break the news about what happened to the car, and I'd prefer to do that in person."

"Hey, Autumn, mind if I stay over?" I said. "I will have to tell my mother about the whole Thomas thing, and if I could put it off for a night, I'd prefer it."

"Sure, like I said, me casa su casa," Autumn replied.

"I had fun tonight, Cristy," I said. "Even with that crap with Thomas. That was a blast, except for what happened after we left."

Cristy stood up from the couch, "Yeah, it was fun. Now, you two behave."

Autumn grinned and rolled her eyes, "I don't think we will be getting into any mischief tonight. It sounds like Carrie has had quite a night already."

"Just a warning, Autumn, boys are addictive," Cristy said as she skipped toward the door. "They are like potato chips."

"I'm happy with just one, thank you very much," Autumn said as she tailed her.

"I guess I can't do much more damage around this popsicle stand; I'm outta here," Cristy blew a kiss into the air said as she left. Autumn waved and shut the door behind her.

Chapter 24

Autumn drew and expelled a deep breath before slowly returning to her spot on the couch. It just occurred to me that I was alone with Autumn. A strange tension seemed to engulf her. The whole thing gave me goosebumps.

"Carrie, can I talk to you about something?" Autumn exploded into the night air, shattering the silence.

"Yeah, sure, what's up?" I said. I couldn't imagine what she was about to say. I started to fidget with my ring once again.

"Well, it's about tonight. I didn't want to say anything about it while Cristy was here because she's so gung-ho about sex," she began.

"Not that I'm not," I said.

"You're not quite so, how should I say, vocal about it," she said. "While I was out with Jacob, we had dinner. He took me to this nice little place downtown. He didn't have to, but he insisted. Then we went to a movie. It was great; the special effects were awesome. I haven't been to the movies in so long..."

"Autumn," I cut her off.

"Yeah..."

"I think you're avoiding the subject."

"You're right. Sorry," she said. "I don't know how to say this..."

"Take your time; we've got all night," I said.

"...let's just say I had urges to do more than kiss him... especially in the movie. I barely held myself back," she said, now turning ruby red.

That was the last thing I was expecting her to say. I knew this had something to do with sex, but I didn't think it would be anything like this.

"That's natural; I'm sure you were just excited to be out on your first date," I said. I had no idea what to say to her.

"Can I be honest with you?" she said.

176

"Of course," I said.

"It's on my mind...a lot. A lot more than I think is natural," she said. "It actually...scares me."

"Autumn, you are sixteen years old. It's natural to think about sex. We all do," I said.

"No, I don't think you understand. I do... way more than I should," she said. As the conversation continued, I noticed she slowly retracted to the other side of the couch.

This was confusing. She said right in front of Cristy that she didn't think about boys and was most likely telling the truth. Cristy was a human lie detector and didn't mention anything about her lying about that. Then again, Cristy does her best to stay out of the minds of her friends. It also could mean Autumn didn't mean thinking about sex with boys...

"I don't think it's anything to worry about," I said. "So, when you said you don't think about boys, was that a lie?"

Autumn's eyes diverted to the ground, "Yes, I'm sorry.... you're not mad at me... are you?"

I laughed, "I'm not going to get mad at you for something so trivial. That's your business."

"Okay... I don't think the urges I had tonight were... normal," she said. "I just hope I can keep my hands to myself until I'm ready." She took a deep breath. "Can you promise me something?"

"Sure, you name it," I replied.

"If I start acting like... a total slut... you'll stop me, right?" she said, her eyes remaining anchored downward.

"My definition of a 'total slut' and yours may be two different things," I said.

"Okay, perhaps I should be clearer. I'm not asking you to stop me from having sex. I'm asking you to stop me from doing things like, I don't know, cheating on my boyfriend, stuff like that."

"So, you and Jacob are official?" I said.

"No... no... I'm getting ahead of myself. That's just an example. Please, promise me you'll stop me if I go too wild."

"I will, I promise," I said. "So, otherwise, I want details. What happened?"

"Okay, okay," Autumn said, her body loosening, and her back finally met the couch cushion. "On the way, we talked a lot. We have so much in common, more than I thought. Did you know he used to live in Japan? He's fluent in Japanese. We spoke in it half the night."

"He mentioned something about that to your dad," I said.

"He wasn't too hard on him, was he?" she asked.

"No, he was cool," I said. "He warned him about not getting into too many fights on your behalf."

"I suppose that's my dad," she said.

"What else happened?" I said.

"Not much. We talked about a lot of geeky stuff you're probably not into. I had a good time," she said. "He put his arm around me during the movie. I really liked that. I'm just glad I was able to control myself."

"You need to stop thinking about it," I said. "You just have to come to terms with your hormones, and you'll be fine."

"I don't know, Carrie... the feelings can get seriously intense. The last thing I want to do is prove Sophia right."

I had a feeling that was what this was actually about.

"Autumn, to prove her right, you'd have to go sleep with a bunch of disease-ridden guys. Even if you did do more than you did tonight, that would be a far cry from what she says you are."

"Yeah, I know. I didn't think about her tonight... until we left the theater," she said.

"Why?" I said. I pretty much knew the answer to this.

"I saw her standing outside that club across the street from the theater while we waited for the bus. What's worse is I know she saw us. I can't wait to hear what she makes up tomorrow," Autumn rolled her eyes.

"I wouldn't worry about it too much. Jacob knew he would get on her bad side if he went out with you. I'm sure he's prepared for whatever she throws at him."

"I'm not so worried about him. I'm worried about what I'll have to do to her if she opens her mouth about him. I won't tolerate her talking about him like that. Or you or Cristy, for that matter."

"Why don't you stick up for yourself?" I said.

"I'm just not worth it; let's leave it at that," she said as a tear fell from her left eye.

"Okay, I'm sorry. I didn't mean to upset you," I said.

"It's okay. Sorry to get emotional," she said, wiping the tear off her face.

"Anyway, did you bring something to sleep in? The only thing I see here is your sword... and... why is that even here in the first place...."

"Just in case Thomas showed up again," I laughed nervously. "And as for clothes, I guess it slipped my mind."

"I might have some old stuff that might fit you. There was a time when I was your height."

She stood up, and I followed her to her room, first retrieving my sword propped up near the door. The whole thing felt surreal. It was me and her alone. I was hoping I could keep my hands to myself.

Before we went to her room, she paused at the linen closet and retrieved a blanket and pillow. We entered her room, and she went to her closet. She lifted a box from the top shelf and sat it on the bed. She yanked out some pajama bottoms and an oversized, plain-colored shirt. They were lilac, not something I would typically wear, but they were just pajamas.

"Thanks," I said. "These should work fine. I'll be right back."

I was about to leave the room, and I turned to hear my name.

"Uh, I need some help with this bra. I'm all thumbs when it comes to these things," she said.

I giggled and pranced over to her. She turned away, took the over-shirt and the top she was wearing off, and set them on the bed. I tried not to pay attention to her mostly naked body. I was sure her face was red with abashment. I unfastened the bra for her and left the room.

A few minutes later, I returned to her room dressed in the pajamas she loaned me. They were still pretty big on me, but they worked well enough. I had my clothes folded, tucked under one arm, and boots in another. I entered her room and found her dressed in her pajamas, sitting on the bed, legs crossed. She wore a long white shirt with a design on the front, but it was so old I couldn't tell what it was; it had long since been worn off. The bottoms were a dark purple flannel pattern. It was a bit ridiculous that she still had the makeup on from this evening. Even like this, she was stunningly gorgeous.

"I hope you don't mind going to bed right now," she said. "I've just had an eventful day. Plus, if I stay up any longer, I'll start to worry about my parents. It is strange for them to just up and leave so suddenly."

I seated myself on the bed beside her and put my things on the floor.

"I'm sure they will be fine," I said. "Yeah, I'm beat myself. Oh, Autumn?"

"Yeah?"

"Your face…"

"Oh, I should go wash this off!" she exclaimed.

"Bingo. I slip on washing off on my lipstick, but my poor lips must be used to it."

She quickly left for the bathroom, and I took a deep breath. My heart pounded as I sat on the bed, trying not to let my mind wander. It only took a moment before she appeared back in the doorway. I noticed how her pajamas hung off her curves, which was incredibly alluring. I noticed the difference between her wearing a bra and not was pretty minimal, which was astounding considering her rather large endowments. She had the proportions of a comic book heroine, and I was utterly in awe of her.

180

"You okay?" she said with head cocked.

"Yeah, I'm cool," I shook my head as I searched my mind for something to divert the subject. "Oh, something I didn't get to tell you about." I lifted my boot from the floor and showed her the burned buckle. "Our invisible 'friends' tried to take me captive today, or at least I think that is what they were trying."

"What happened?" she exclaimed as she examined the boot.

"They had me pinned down behind a tree before my mom came out of the house and attacked."

"What type of weapon did they use to do this?" she asked.

"Looked like some light beam. I guess you could call it a 'laser,'" I struggled. "This just gets stranger and stranger."

"Maybe you really shouldn't be left alone," she said. "I don't know what I'd do if something happened to you."

"I'll be fine," I sighed. "You don't need to be worrying yourself about me. We better get to sleep. I get a bit cranky if I don't get enough sleep. Speaking of which, where should I sleep?"

"You can sleep up here with me," she said.

"I don't know..." I said.

"Oh, come on, I don't bite. I'm not Cristy," she laughed as she scooted under her blanket and pulled it over to her side of the bed.

It wasn't her I was worried about biting.

"Okay, if you insist," I said. I stretched out on the bed and put the pillow under my head. I covered myself with the blanket she picked up from the hall closet. Autumn approached the nightstand behind the bed and turned off the light.

"Oh, Carrie, I might want to warn you about something. I can be a bit of a cuddle bug. I tend to do it in my sleep, so I hope it doesn't bother you."

I almost laughed that she used the term 'cuddle-bug.'

"That's fine," I said. "I can probably use a good cuddle."

"Oyasuminasai, Carrie-chan," Autumn said.

"Goodnight, Autumn," I said. "That was goodnight, right?"

"Yep."

Chapter 25

As exhausted as I was, I couldn't sleep. I lay next to Autumn, trying to be as motionless as possible. I couldn't be sure how much time had passed; Autumn's head was blocking her alarm clock, and I didn't want to move and disturb her. After an undetermined amount of time, Autumn sat up, back straight, eyes facing forward.

"What's up?" I said to her.

She said nothing.

"Autumn? Are you okay?"

She said nothing. She turned to me. Her eyes illuminated a bright blue. I sat up and put my hands on her shoulders.

"Autumn, are you okay?" I exclaimed as I shook her slightly.

"Carrie?" she said, in a light, dulcet tone.

"I'm here," I said.

"Where have you been?" she said.

"I've been right here," I replied.

"I missed you," she said. She wrapped her arms around me and kissed me. I was stunned for a moment. I was in ecstasy. It was the single greatest moment in my life. This was what every part of my being wanted. I could have kissed her forever, but I realized it was wrong. She was never going to remember this. This wasn't the Autumn I knew; this was the Autumn from another time, one who loved me. This Autumn, as far as I knew, didn't. And this Autumn was using my Autumn's body to kiss me. Either way, it just wasn't right. Yet... I had a more difficult time than I should have to resist her. Guilt flooded my mind like a dam had ruptured. My conscience and hormones were having one hell of a tug-of-war. My body didn't want to listen to anything but my urges. It took every bit of fortitude, but I pushed back the need to ravage her.

I finally gathered enough resolve to push her away. It took my all to nudge her gently, "No, you won't remember this, sweetheart. It's just not fair... to you."

"You don't love me?"

A wave of crushing, alien sadness floated into me alongside the obvious guilt. I struggled for words.

"Autumn... I... what about Jacob..."

"Jacob...he's..." she said as a tear fell.

"He's what?" I said.

Autumn did not reply. She laid back down, and her eyes returned to their standard shade of blue. I also rested my back against the bed, trying to wade through my emotions. As soon as her eyes stopped glowing, I felt the sadness vanish like it was never there. I didn't understand it at all. I was hoping that things would start to make sense over time. For every answer I received about Autumn, a million questions replaced it. I didn't know what to think anymore.

I fruitlessly attempted to sleep for some time, yet again, I couldn't distinguish. A noise from downstairs jarred me out of my reflection.

"Autumn," I whispered as I nudged her. She continued to sleep, motionless and breathing very deeply.

I stood up and retrieved my sword from against the wall. I crept out of the room, opening the door as gradually as possible. I drew my sword as I gently stepped down the staircase. I heard another noise, this one coming from the kitchen. The house was pitch black, and my spiritual sight was of no good being this close to Autumn, so I hoped the intruder had just as difficult of a time seeing as I did. I found my way to the kitchen and saw a figure moving toward me. I saw a bit of sudden movement and swung my blade. My blade met another as the lights came on, nearly blinding me.

"You must be Carrie," the short woman said. She was the one on the other side of the kunai blocking my blade.

"Oh, you must be Autumn's Aunt Mina," I said as I retracted my blade and put her back in her sheath. "Sorry, I've had an interesting night. I forgot you were coming over."

"Eh, better safe than sorry," she said as she tucked the blade into her boot. I just realized I was holding a sword to a woman wearing a 1950s-style pink poodle skirt with a button-up pink blouse to accompany it.

184

"Ugh," she said. "Yeah, I guess you are gawking at my uniform. I work at that cheesy vintage diner downtown. I hate this thing."

"Sorry…hey, you do what you gotta do. Although I would probably rather starve than wear that getup," I laughed. I noticed she had no hint of a Japanese accent, which was interesting, coming from a woman who was so clearly Japanese.

"Here, kiddo," she said, "sit down, and I'll make you some coco."

"That would be great," I said.

"I'm just surprised Autumn wasn't down here with you; she usually wakes up if someone drops a pin in the house unless... Hey, she didn't have one of those trances again, did she?"

"Yeah, she did," I said. I realized too late that I was blushing.

"Is there a reason you're blushing?" Mina said as she opened the cupboard and removed the cocoa mix.

"Wow, you don't miss anything, do you?" I said. "Yeah... because... Autumn...kissed me while in that trance."

"Not surprising," Mina said. "She's been talking about you for years in those trances.

"How did you know she had a trance?"

"Because it's the only time she sleeps deeply. Any other time she sleeps like any kunoichi sleeps: lightly."

"I take by the fact that you have a kunai in your boot. Does that mean you are a shinobi?" I said.

"Got that right," she said as she placed the two cups of cocoa in the microwave. "William and my husband, Daniel, were also trained as shinobi."

"Autumn said something about that."

"Dan wishes he was as good as I am," she said. "As for William, the guy is too big to be a shinobi. Otherwise, I couldn't hold a candle to the man."

The microwave beeped, and Mina removed the cocoa and handed me a cup. She sat across the table from me and began sipping at her drink. She

185

removed the hair clip from the back of her head, letting raven hair cascade down her back. Her green eyes seemed to peer right through me, which was unnerving.

"So, when will I get to meet your husband?" I asked.

"Your guess is as good as mine," she said. "Bastard is off somewhere, fucking some big-titted whore."

"He cheats?" I said.

"Never caught him," she sighed as she played with her hair. "He disappears every so often, sometimes for months at a time. He's always been like this. He can't stay still."

"I hope that isn't the case. I'm not sure what's worse, a guy who cheats or a guy who is never there. Is he really a husband if he's never around?" I said.

"Honey, I ask myself that every day," she said. "I don't want to keep you up all night with my problems; you've got enough of your own. Protecting Autumn is not going to be easy."

"Tell me about it, especially when she doesn't know what she is."

"If everything I hear about you is true, you can do it," she said. "I hear you are pretty handy with that sword."

"I suppose," I said.

"Fortunately, Cassandra picked a good weekend to do this; I'm off until Monday. You can go home and sleep in your bed tomorrow."

"...not that staying here is a bad thing. I like to be as close as possible to her... for obvious reasons."

"Beyond protecting her," Mina said.

"Why do all of you women in this family read me like a book?"

"It probably has something to do with being around for a few centuries," she said.

I said nothing else as if finished drinking my coco with a real live, hundreds-of-years-old ninja dressed in a poodle skirt. I wasn't sure my life could get any stranger. I did my best to avoid eye contact and avoid giving away some other secret I didn't want to be verbalized.

Once I had finished my drink, I looked up at Mina and said, "I probably should get to bed. Whether or not I'm up to it, I'm going to school. Being close to her is my top priority."

"Good luck," Mina said. "At least relax tonight. I'll be awake until you guys leave to keep watch. I'm so wired after work that I usually can't sleep anyway."

"Thanks," I said as I stood up from the table. "It was great meeting you."

"You too. I'm glad my niece has someone so vigilant to watch her back. Spirits know she'll need it."

I went back upstairs and laid down in Autumn's bed. Autumn's breathing had become lighter since the last time I had been there. A few minutes after settling into bed, she rolled over and curled up next to me, resting her arm over my stomach. I wrapped my arm around her and silently began to sob.

The following day, I awoke to Autumn's alarm blaring, and she was nowhere to be seen. I popped out of bed and fumbled with the clock to stop the racket.

"Where could she be?" I said to myself as I fumbled with the device to shut it off.

I left the room and went downstairs. Autumn was seated at the kitchen table, fully dressed and eating toast, with Mina and my mother chatting.

"Hi, sweetheart," Mom said. "I brought some clothes and things you need to get ready. I left them in the living room for you."

"Thanks, Mom," I replied.

"Did you sleep well?" Autumn asked.

"Yeah, I was fine," I said. "Gotta hurry, don't want to make us late." I turned to the living room and picked up my clothes and bath supplies.

After my shower, I dressed, put on the lipstick my mother included in the package, dried my hair with a blow dryer laid out for me, and rushed down the stairs.

When I arrived, I found Cristy seated amongst the ladies at the kitchen table.

"Let's roll," I said as I headed to the door.

Chapter 26

When we arrived at school that day, I could see from the car that Jacob was waiting for Autumn on the school steps. We strolled up the steps, and he stood up.

"Hi, ladies," he said.

"So, what's up, Romeo," Cristy said.

"Hi," Autumn glimmered.

"What's up?" I said.

"How are you all this morning?" he asked.

"Not as good as Autumn," Cristy said. "She looks like she's going to float off the ground any second."

"Cristy!" Autumn falsely scolded. "It's nice to see you, Jacob. I had fun last night."

"I did, too," he said. "Can I carry your backpack to class?"

"Oh, you don't have to do that," Autumn blushed. "I can carry it myself."

"What you can do is let the guy be a gentleman," I added.

"Okay," Autumn sighed. She removed her book bag and handed it to Jacob. We strolled into the school, and I observed the glares of the people around us. I could see the bitches around us talking in hushed tones and the guys looking jealous but attempting to hide it.

The vicious cunt in me was hoping Sophia was in the hall so that we could rub Autumn's new boy in her face, but I was glad she wasn't. Autumn was in a perfect mood, and I didn't want her to spoil it.

We entered our homeroom and found our usual spots. Everything went normal throughout the day, except Autumn and Jacob made googly eyes at each other whenever they could. I knew the calm wouldn't last for long. Sophia would eventually open her mouth, and either Autumn was going to put her in her place, or I was.

We grouped up after classes ended for the day and began to leave the school. There, standing with her clique, was the bitch herself. This time, more guys with letter jackets seemed to be standing around her than usual.

"So, what do we have here?" Sophia hissed as she sauntered over to us. "Look, new kid, I don't know how much you know about my cousin..."

"Why don't you go fuck yourself, okay?" Jacob said. "I don't care what you have to say."

Sophia sighed, "I didn't want to have to do this." She turned to walk away, "Guys, teach the new kid how things are done around here."

Four jocks stepped toward Jacob. Autumn attempted to step forward, but Cristy put her arm in her path.

"He'll be fine," Cristy whispered.

One of the jocks took a swing at Jacob, and he delivered a swift, short kick to the stomach. The other three rushed him, and he punched one in the face, delivered another kick to the stomach to a second, and then caught the punch of the third and slammed him into a locker.

"Oh, Sophia," he said as Sophia turned back to see what had transpired. "Next time you open your mouth about my lady, I might break my cardinal rule about hitting girls." He turned to Autumn, "You are my lady, right?"

She just smiled and nodded.

"I hope it doesn't come to him attacking my sister," Cristy said telepathically.

"I didn't think you'd give a damn," I replied.

"No, it's not that. She's out of practice, but she's nothing to sneeze at regarding physical force. I doubt any of the three of us would have a difficult time with her, but Jake or any of these jocks would get smashed."

"Thanks for the heads-up. I'll try to stop him if he attempts it. Also, I probably shouldn't take her lightly myself."

Heels could be heard pounding their way down the hall.

"All five of you, in my office," Judy growled from behind us. Sophia began to walk away.

190

"And Sophia, I'm not stupid. I know you instigated this. Next time, I'll ensure it's not just the people fighting who get punished."

Sophia didn't acknowledge the principal as she sauntered off.

"Look, Principal Angler, this is my fault," Autumn said.

"No, it isn't," she said. "We'll talk later."

"I'll be waiting for you outside her office; I'm so sorry," Autumn told Jacob.

"You have nothing to be sorry for," he said with a grin.

It was all so sweet it almost made me sick.

We waited for Jacob outside of Judy's office.

"That was pretty cool, Autumn," Cristy said. "I mean, I had a feeling he could defend himself, but he's a certified badass."

"He would have to be," Autumn said. "He's half Japanese, and he went to a Japanese school. Japanese are not kind to people who are konketsuji, which is someone of two different bloods. It's seen as chic in media and maybe a fascination of teen girls, but that's not the case in society, especially with some male youth. It's probably because the whole idea is popular with girls."

"Your dad was talking about that," I said.

The four jocks exited the office, and each gave us their version of a nasty look while they instinctively rubbed sore areas of their bodies. They stomped off together, bitching about the papers they held, which I assumed were suspensions or detentions.

Jacob exited the office, holding a similar document.

"So, how did it go?" Autumn asked.

"No big deal, detention. I've got a lot of these at my old school. Don't worry about it. I had to let it be known I don't take crap eventually. Better to do it for your honor," he said.

"Looks like you've got a knight in shining armor, Autumn," Cristy giggled.

191

"And her knight in shining armor better try to avoid these fights from here on out," Judy said as she seemed to materialize in the doorway.

"I told you, Principal Angler, I can't promise anything," Jacob said.

"Yes, I know. That is the second time I've heard that this week. It would be best if you kids got going. I wouldn't want your parents to get worried about you."

Autumn was silent but did smile. The rose color on her cheeks spoke for her. I thought that the more people to help me watch Autumn's back, the better, but I was sure he didn't know what he was getting into.

As we strolled down the hall, I realized I might be getting my jealousy under control. Maybe it was just that Autumn was beaming even more than she was last night after her first kiss. I was happy she had a hero other than her father. Just because she was a powerful woman didn't mean having a man stick up for her didn't feel good. I understood how she felt, but I couldn't pick out why. I knew I had a man stand up for me that wasn't my father, but my memory of who came up empty.

I glanced over to Autumn and Jacob and saw them holding hands.

"I need to get home; Dad is taking me to karate practice," Jacob said. "I'll wait until afterward to tell him about the detentions."

"I'd like to see where you live," Autumn said.

"Me too. Can I come?" Cristy said.

"Sure, ladies, you're all welcome; I'm sure my dad would like to meet you all," Jacob said.

We walked over to Jacob's house, just a short distance from the school. It was a house similar to any other in the neighborhood. It was decorated with a white paint job and blue shutters on the windows. A man stood out in the driveway, working on what looked to be a classic, dark blue 1960s-era Corvette.

As we approached, the man stood up. He was a tall, slim man in dirty overalls. He turned to greet us while brushing his hanging brown hair from his brown eyes, which were reminiscent of Jacob's.

"Hi, Jacob. I see you've got friends with you," he said.

"Dad, this is Autumn, my girlfriend," Jacob said. "And this is Cristy and Carrie."

"Well, it's nice to meet you all," he said. "I'd shake your hands, but mine are dirty." He showed us his oily hands.

"Hi," I said.

"What's up, Mr. L," Cristy said.

"Mr. L?" I said. "What are you, the Fonz?"

"Yep," she said, raising the collar of her leather jacket. She pointed her index fingers and said, "Hey."

"You're a little young for that reference," Mr. Lewis said.

"Please excuse my insane friends. It's great to meet you, Mr. Lewis. So, what do you have there, a '67?" Autumn said.

"Yeah, good eye," he said. "I'm just having a hard time getting it to start."

"May I take a look?" Autumn said.

"Sure, why not," Mr. Lewis replied.

"It looks to me that this engine wasn't taken care of; it's a shame," Autumn said. "How much mileage does she have on her?"

"Two hundred thousand miles," he said. "I just bought it for a good price. I knew about the neglect of the engine. You don't find a car like this every day, though."

"It looks like, at least at a glance, that you need a new distributor cap, possibly a new transmission, and probably a few other things," Autumn said as she peeked at the partially disassembled engine.

"Wow, I wasn't expecting you to be so knowledgeable on cars... and tall," Mr. Lewis laughed.

"Autumn is a real Renaissance woman," Jacob smiled.

"Yeah, she built my father's custom sports car," Cristy said.

"Wow, seriously?" Mr. Lewis gasped. "You must know a lot, definitely more than me."

"You didn't mention that," Jacob raised his eyebrow.

Autumn sighed, "That car isn't something I like to think about. But this one, on the other hand, has me interested. If you need help, I'm not doing anything tomorrow," Autumn said.

"That would be great, but I don't think I can do this myself. I tried to hire a mechanic, but they all wanted too much to work on a car like this," Mr. Lewis said.

"I'll do it for free, sir, if you can trust me at work," Autumn said.

"Yeah, sure. If you can build a car, you can work on this one. Better than trying to do it on my own like I have been for the last week," Mr. Lewis said. He turned to his son. "See her son, you have found the perfect woman. She likes cars and looks like she just walked off a runway..."

Autumn appeared to be struggling for words.

"...and can kick a lot of ass," Cristy said.

"As I was saying, son," Mr. Lewis said as he laughed. "Don't ever let her go."

"Don't plan on it, Dad. I hate to cut this short, but I need to get to karate practice," Jacob said. "Sensei hates it when we're late."

"Let me go wash my hands, and we'll go. It was nice meeting you ladies."

"You too, sir," Autumn said. "Ja-ne, Jacob-kun"

"Ja-ne, Autumn-chan," Jacob returned.

"See you later, Jacob, Mr. L!" Cristy waved with a goofy amount of excitement.

"Bye, guys," I said.

Jacob followed his father into the house, and we headed down the street toward our homes.

"So, what now?" Cristy said.

"I think I'm going to go home and nap," Autumn said. "I've been rather worn out today; I don't know why."

"Then it's just you and me, chick," Cristy said, slapping me on the back.

"Sounds fun; what should we do?" I said.

"Find some guys? And none of them being a walking corpse named Thomas," Cristy said with a laugh.

"I'd like to avoid that tonight," I laughed.

We dropped Autumn off at her house and set off on our own.

Chapter 27

The area around us was the same as it usually was: lawnmowers mowing, stupid children playing, and the occasional high school student driving by blaring terrible music. I closed my eyes and focused through the ring, hoping to use the technique my mother mentioned, even though I still lacked the practice I needed with the Karithian to make it work properly. I felt nothing, and I was sure Cristy would have said something if they were around.

"So, what happened after I left last night?" Cristy looked at me as we slowly walked down the street.

"Well, let's put it this way," I started. "You weren't the only Alexander I kissed last night."

"You kissed her?" Cristy said. "Oh, she was in a trance, wasn't she?"

"Bingo," I said. "It killed me, but I had to push her away. It just wasn't right. Otherwise, it was the best kiss... ever."

"There is nothing like kissing someone you truly love," Cristy said as she stretched.

"When I pushed her away, she asked, "Don't you love me?" I said.

"Ouch," Cristy said.

"The strangest thing happened at that point. A potent, foreign feeling of sadness just overtook me. It wasn't my sadness. Mom said that with the 'Tala'har link,' you can feel the emotions of your charge, but only slightly. This was all-consuming, so I don't know what it was."

"'Tala'har link? What's that?" Cristy asked.

"It's a link Tala'har eventually gains with their charge. I haven't known Autumn long enough to develop the link. It lets us know where they are and what they feel to a small extent. Nothing like what I felt last night."

"Who knows if that's how it works when protecting a Balanced One. The rules might be entirely different. Tala'har protect wizards, right? I doubt any Tala'har has ever protected someone as powerful as Autumn. Your link might have developed early and could be more powerful than a normal Tala'har link."

196

"You could be right," I said. "I hope not." I took a deep breath, "So, what now?"

"We go get my car and head out for a night on the town," Cristy said. "It looks like you have the evening off, so you should take advantage of it."

"Tala'har never get off days," I furrowed my brow.

"Right now, Autumn is being watched over by one of the most powerful ninjas...ever. Her Aunt Mina is a badass. She was babysitting Sophia and me once, and Sophia wanted to put her hand in water while she passed out cold on the couch. As she was pouring the water into the bowl in the bathroom, we heard from downstairs in the living room, 'Don't even think about it.' A mouse could sneeze in that house while she's asleep, and she'd hear it."

"I figured as such." I signed. "I still feel guilty shirking off my duties."

"It's not shirking off if you aren't needed. I'll grab some clothes when we stop to get my car, and we'll go over to your house and get all sexy for tonight. It will be fun, better than last night. My bitch of a sister is off at some stupid jock's birthday party tonight, so we'll have the town to ourselves."

I stretched my arms upwards, "Let's just hope we don't have any other uninvited guests. Does your family have any other enemies that might be popping up that I should know about?"

"Unless the Olympians try to take another shot at my dad or me, no."

"I guess being the daughter of a notorious dick has its consequences."

"You're telling me. What I don't get is why they never go after my sister," Cristy rolled her eyes. "If they target anyone in my family that isn't my dad, it's me or Mom. I've had a few close calls."

"I'm not sure how you put it up with it all," I said as I put my around her.

"Sometimes, I'm not sure how I deal with it either," Cristy sighed. "When I was growing up, I was kidnapped a lot. Half the time, it was Uncle William who saved me. My dad is useless without his sword and even with it sometimes."

Two cars were parked in the driveway when we arrived at Cristy's house. One was Cristy's Mustang, and the other was the one I saw in front of Autumn's house the first day I met her. It was incredibly sleek and compact, only having room for a single passenger. It was still missing the passenger seat, as it had been when Joseph had dropped off Sophia at school.

"No wonder Autumn doesn't like thinking about this car. It's beautiful sans the fact that it's white," I said.

"White is just the default color. It can change color on command. White is the default because Autumn called it 'Angel,' I think it references a video game or something. He doesn't deserve this car. She should be driving it."

"Nothing we can do about that," I sighed.

"My sister isn't here right now, so you won't have to worry about dealing with her. My father is always here but in the basement, probably playing cards with Uncle Kartarus."

Uncle Kartarus? Who's that? Another relative I haven't met?"

"Pretty much, but to be exact, he's my father's sword. Poor guy was his best friend long ago, but my Dad was a dumbass and got him ended up sucked into a magic sword right after it was forged."

"The more I hear about your dad, the more of an idiot he appears to be. Oh, and how the hell do you play cards with a sword?"

"He floats and can levitate small objects. He doesn't seem to mind being a sword... except when he mentions that he hasn't been laid in a couple thousand years."

"Yeah, that would suck," I agreed.

"He bitches out Dad when he and my mom start getting it on in front of him. There is nothing like waking up as a kid at three in the morning and hearing your father arguing with a sword because he can't keep his dick in his pants around him."

"I pity you."

"Yep, growing up as my father's daughter was strange. My mom is the most normal one in the house, and she's a Telosian."

As we walked in the door, Megara was sitting on the couch, legs crossed, watching the massive television that blocked out the windows in the front of the house. It had to be the most massive television I had ever seen in a home. It was too large to hang on a wall and had to sit on the floor. The house was just the opposite of Autumn's house. Around the big television was a vast entertainment center littered with electronics, from video games to what looked to be a ridiculously expensive surround sound system. The house was dust-covered, a testament to the inhabitants' disdain for cleaning. The furniture was black leather and probably very expensive.

Megara wore a black, strapless dress. Black high heels completed the outfit, one of which she bounced around on her toes, exposing her heel. She looked as if she was dressed up to go out, but I figured she always dressed like this. She was adorned with a different collection of gaudy jewelry than what she was the last time I saw her. Before, I was close to Autumn, so I could not see her aura. Today, I found that her aura was almost as bright as Cristy's but was golden. There was hidden power inside her. Her eyes grew wide when we entered the home.

"Hi, Cristy. I was expecting you to be spending the day with Autumn. It's nice to see you again, Carrie."

"Hi, Mom," Cristy said. "Autumn was feeling tired, so she's at home with Mina. We're just stopping by so I can grab some clothes and the car."

"It's nice to see you too, Mrs. Alexander," I said.

"Oh, please," Megara said. "Just call me Megara. Mrs. Alexander makes me sound so old."

"Mom," Cristy said. "You're a couple hundred years old. I think that classifies as 'old.'"

"But I don't look it," Megara grinned.

"We're just going to be up in my room," Cristy said.

"If you could give me a moment with Carrie, I'd appreciate it," Megara said.

"Sure, Mom," Cristy said. She pranced up the stairs that led out into the living room.

"You needed to speak to me, Megara?" I asked.

"Yes. First, I would like to thank you for being there for Cristy," she let out a compact grin. "I'm just glad she has someone other than Sophia to hang around with."

"No problem," I said. "I'm not sure how I would get by without her sometimes. Is there something wrong with her being around Sophia?"

"I hate saying this, but yes," Megara let out a drawn-out sigh. "Sophia is a... how should I put it... a bit too much like her father for her own good. I swear, she's lost all concept of what is important in life. With the way Cristy has been following her around for the last few years, I was afraid that Cristy would lose what makes her 'Cristy.'"

"You mean a heart and general concern for the wellbeing of others?" I said with raised brows.

"Exactly. I really shouldn't talk about my own flesh and blood like this. Yet, I'm not blind. I know what goes on at that school, and it disgusts me. It's hard to punish Sophia for hearsay, and it doesn't help that her father encourages her behavior."

"I can see how that might be difficult," I replied.

"I just can't help but feel..." she stuttered. She hung her head down a bit. "I just can't help but feel that what my niece goes through is my fault. I should be a stronger woman and a better mother, like my sister. I should have put a stop to all of this when it started."

"I wouldn't blame yourself too much," I comforted. "It's hard to control someone whose very nature is to control everything around her. I'm wondering if it's the fact that she can't control Autumn is why she attacks her like that."

"Maybe, although I know she feels inferior to her," Megara sighed. "When the girls were little, we frequently visited Cassandra, William, and Autumn in Pennsylvania. On our way home, Sophia would ask me if she was prettier than Autumn during the whole return trip. I didn't want her getting a big head, and I would tell her she was just as pretty as Autumn, and of course, my idiot of a husband would tell her that she was leaps and bounds prettier than that 'psychopathic little brat.' I'm unsure where he got the idea that she's a psychopath, but he's always called her that, even as a small babe. I don't understand it all. Sophia was never this way with Cristy. Usually, little girls are competitive with their sisters, not their cousins."

200

"Everyone is different," I said. "You can't expect anyone to adhere to certain normalities that humans usually follow."

"I've asked to talk to you for a reason," she continued. "I want you to do whatever it takes to protect my niece from my daughter and husband. Anything short of killing them. My niece is important and has a difficult life ahead of her. She doesn't deserve this. I'm asking you to have the strength I never did. I understand this may require you to make Sophia miserable, but so be it. Something must be done, and you are the only one in the position to make a difference. I won't hold anything against you and will do what I can to help you."

"Thank you, Megara. Hearing that from you at least makes me feel better. I know I will end up making myself an enemy of Sophia and your husband; I'm just glad I won't be getting on your bad side."

Cristy skipped downstairs with a bag of folded clothes and her colossal makeup case.

"Gee, Mom, what are you doing, giving her the family history?" Cristy said.

"No, just getting to know your friend," Megara said. "You two should get going. Have a lot of fun tonight!"

Chapter 28

Within minutes, we were in my driveway. On the way in, I noticed my mother's car was absent. I assumed she had headed out early for the evening.

I opened the door with my keys and let Cristy in. The house was in its usual half-unpacked disarray—a disheveled mess but still moving closer to livable. A few lamps were unpacked and ready to be used. I noticed a few pieces of Mom's art, pictures of sunshine, rainbows, and unicorns, were freshly placed on the walls. My eyes rolled nearly to the back of my head as I passed them. Cristy glanced up and smiled at the one with the unicorn. We headed up to my room, where fewer sparkles would be found.

"Welcome to my room," I said as I opened the door.

Cristy jumped on the bed and held her head up with her hand.

"Haphazard decorations? Check. Everything here is black? Check. So, this is your room." She turned to me. "You've got me in your lair now, Carrie," she said with an over-the-top, seductive voice. "Take me!"

"Don't tempt me," I said as I shut the door.

"Why not? Not like we have to go out."

I was curious to know if she was kidding or being serious.

"Maybe later," I smiled.

"Yeah, we should tease some boys tonight," she said. "Well... maybe more than tease."

"You are insatiable," I said.

"And you're starved," she replied.

"How do you know that?" I laughed. It didn't take long to realize that was a dumb question.

"I don't need to be a mind reader to know that. On top of that, you've been teased by Autumn enough lately. Not that it's her fault."

"And you," I said.

"Okay, I'm guilty of it too. I can't help that I'm sooooo fine."

"Help me pick out something to wear," I said.

"Ooooh, yay!" Cristy hopped off the bed. "I love looking through goth girls' drawers. Both kind, actually."

I rolled my eyes and smiled. Now I was feeling like Autumn.

"I would wear some of the stuff you wear, but to look right, I'd have to dye my hair, and I just can't do it to these beautiful locks," she said as she ran her fingers through her luxurious hair.

"Fortunately, I don't have to dye my hair; it's naturally this black," I said as I opened my top drawer and sifted through my folded shirts. Cristy opened the drawer next to it.

"I don't think I need help picking out my underwear," I said.

"I'm just curious," Cristy grinned. "I knew it!" She pulled out a black thong. "I figured I'd find one of these in here and knew it would be black."

"If you haven't noticed, nearly everything in there is black."

"Yeah, l soooo knew you had one!"

"Can we get back to the task at hand?"

"Sorry, underwear causes me to have a case of temporary ADHD."

"You are strange."

"Yeah, but I'm hot."

"What does that have to do with you being strange?"

"Nothing; I just thought I would throw that out there." She lifted a black corset from the drawer I was looking through. "You should wear this. I would love to be able to pull that off."

"Not a bad idea. The skirt I bought when I went out with Autumn would work well with it. You should have seen what I did to her in the mall. I got her to try on this dress at that gothic apparel store. She was not happy."

"But I bet you were. How did she look?"

"Awesome, it just wasn't really 'her,' if you know what I mean.

"So, where do you want to go tonight?"

"Not sure, I'm new here, remember. I don't know the town."

"I'm sure we can come up with something to do."

"I'll be back, so feel free to get dressed here while I'm gone."

"You could get dressed in here."

"Are you always this horny?"

"Yes, you should have learned that about me by now."

I pulled out a pair of lace, see-through arm covers from another drawer and left for the bathroom with the corset, skirt, and thong Cristy picked out. After I dressed, I returned to my room to find Cristy had also changed. Now, she was wearing one of the skimpiest halter tops I had ever seen and probably the shortest skirt legally allowable.

"Not leaving much for the imagination?" I laughed.

"I'm not the creative type," she replied.

"That barely makes sense."

She shrugged, sat on the bed, and tied her tennis shoes. I noticed that she always wore sneakers regardless of what outfit she wore.

"I'm surprised you don't have heels to go with that," I said.

"I hate heels. I prefer to be comfortable. Plus, when you are as short as I am, I consider it a form of false advertising."

Chapter 29

We cruised downtown, searching for something to do in Cristy's beastly hotrod. The hum of its engine almost drowned out the organized chaos of the metropolis. The city was already alive with its neon lights and loud music. Part of me wanted to sneak into one of these clubs, get some dope to buy me drinks, and wash away all my feelings. I knew that path wasn't a wise one. The last thing Autumn needed was a drunk bodyguard.

Cristy hit the touch screen on the car's dash and put on some hard rock. I put my head back and soaked in the music. The song that came on was about dragging yourself out of the gutter and turning your life around. It was a great tune, and I felt nostalgic listening to it, although I couldn't pick out why and who it reminded me of.

"Thanks for this; I doubt it's your kind of music," I said with my eyes closed.

"You'd be surprised what I listen to," Cristy giggled. Autumn and Jason weren't the only ones bitten by the rock bug in the family. My tastes in music are as diverse as my tastes in people."

"How do you like 'em?" I asked.

"I don't know, sexy…" Cristy shrugged. "And sexy can mean anything I feel like it is at the time. For example, there was this dude who was totally passionate about mecha anime and I found that hot."

"Mecha anime?" I raised my eyebrow.

"Hey, passion is sexy. If you don't get passionate about something, you'd be boring. His sister was passionate about it, too," she winked at me.

"You did not…"

"Oh, I did…Don't worry, she was his step-sister, and I think they were just looking for an excuse to get down, and I helped give them that, so I figured it mission accomplished," she shrugged with a devilish smile.

"I bet you have a lot of stories like that…" I sent Cristy a sly eye.

"Ohhhh, I do, but I'll keep you guessing," she giggled. "So, how do you like your people? Other than, you know, the tall, voluptuous force of nature-types."

"I…." I found myself at a loss for words. In my mind, I kept looking for traces of someone I was really into other than Autumn and had to dig back a few years. "I guess… alt.. like myself. Not the depressive, sad types, though. I had a girlfriend once… she was a bit more on the emo side, though. So, no more of that. Then, again, at the time, so was I."

"We all have our phases. Speaking of which, hey, want to go skating?" Cristy said as we hit a stop light.

"You sort of said it yourself. Maybe when I was thirteen."

"No, really, this place is great. Imagine a kicking club with a roller rink in the center. It's awesome, I promise you."

"You're the expert. Let's get some chow first. I'm about as hungry as a feral dragon."

"'Feral' dragon?" Cristy glanced at me, puzzled. "I didn't think there was any other kind."

"There are back where I came from. There are ferals that roam the wilds, and there are dragons that co-exist with humans."

"Cool, I'd like to meet one someday. Ask the ladies if the boys are ribbed for their pleasure."

"You're too much," I giggled.

We pulled into a restaurant that was a hot spot for partygoers. It was a twenty-four-hour chain that caters to people our age and college kids. The outside of the atypical exterior was entire groups of young adults loitering about. The place was made of white brick, and the large windows showed it was nearly packed with diners. There were no notable auras in the restaurant, only the dull colors of typical humans.

"Oh look, the vultures have already sniffed us out," I said as I noticed the guys around the restaurant immediately turn their collective attention to us.

"Oh, come on, you love the attention, or you wouldn't dress like that," Cristy said.

206

"I want to attract guys, just not all of them," I said.

"You have the gift, just like me," Cristy laughed.

"Sometimes I feel it's more like a curse..."

We exited Cristy's car and started strutting into the restaurant. Cristy swung her hips, almost reminding me of her sister. I preferred that the guys pay attention to her and ignore me. Her tactic seemed to work, as most male eyes we passed followed her swaying behind.

I had a feeling that the type of people I liked to cohort with didn't hang around a city like Miami. I was well aware that the way I dressed and acted was a fetish for some sleazy guys. Yet, that would not stop me from looking how I wanted.

We entered the little diner and waited for a server to lead us to our seats. A cute brunette girl with hazel eyes, dressed in the place's drab dark green uniform, stepped before us.

"Welcome, two, right?" she said.

"You betcha, cutie," Cristy flirted.

"I'm Aileen, not 'cutie,'" she sighed. "Do you always have to flirt with me when you come here, Cristy?"

"I wouldn't be me if I didn't, girl. Plus, I wouldn't say it if it wasn't true," Cristy said. "My usual table available?"

Aileen rolled her eyes, "Sure, this way."

We trailed Aileen to the table. Cristy was leaning to her left, making a huge show out of staring at Aileen's ass. Aileen saw a few people staring at her, turned her head, and rolled her eyes again. She led us to a corner booth away from the main dining area.

"So, what can I get you guys to drink?" Aileen said. "We're short on waitresses tonight, so I'll take care of you myself."

"Oooh! My favorite hostess is my waitress! I smell a big tip for her... and maybe some digits if she plays her cards right," Cristy grinned.

"Cristy, I've had your phone number for nearly as long as you've had a cellphone," Aileen pulled out her cell phone and revealed her contact list with Cristy Alexander near the top of the list.

"Oh crap, now what am I going to leave other than money? Money is so impersonal," Cristy grinned. "I'm not attached to the underwear I'm wearing right now..."

"I'll have a cola," I said before Cristy wore down Aileen's last nerve.

"I was waiting for you to say something. What is your name, sister? I'll give props to anyone who can hang out with this pest."

"I'm Carrie. It's nice to meet you, Aileen," I said.

"Nice to meet you, too. Does she flirt with you like this, too?" Aileen asked.

"Afraid so, I somewhat like it, but don't tell her that," I said.

"I'm right here," Cristy chimed in.

"You're all right, Carrie. Most goths that come in here seem to like to make a giant show of being 'so miserable.' Glad to see not everyone that wears black like that isn't a complete bitch," Aileen said.

"Yeah, I do my best. I think those 'goths' you're referring to are posers. Sounds more like bloody emos to me," I laughed.

"Yeah, you're probably right. Everyone in this city likes to pretend to be something they aren't. Now that you are done making an ass of yourself, Cristy, what would you like to drink?"

"Cola," she smiled. She leaned closer to Aileen and loudly whispered, "Just go ahead and write that love note you promised me on the napkin. Don't worry, I won't tell your dad."

Aileen again found the near top of her head. She laughed and walked away.

"Damn, I hate to see that girl go, but I love to watch her leave," Cristy said as she intently gawked at Aileen. "I love fucking with her. Or fucking her. I'd like that too."

"So, does she have any idea that your flirting is serious?" I said.

"I'm sure she does. She has a boyfriend, sadly. I've tried to talk her into a threesome, but I think she's the jealous type."

"You are too much," I laughed as I picked up my menu.

"This wouldn't happen to be that friend you say you distanced yourself from?"

"Bingo," Cristy said. "Hanging around with Sophia prevented me from being around her, which was by design. She doesn't need to deal with my shit... well, the old me's shit. I like coming here, though, because it's the one place my sister won't show her face in this city."

"Why?" I said, face hidden behind my menu.

"Because Aileen's dad owns the place, and she hates Sophia's guts. She and Sophia had it out in here one day, and her dad threw Sophia and her whole gang out. For the most part, she can't do jack to Aileen because she goes to a Catholic school across town, so all of Sophia's little tactics to get even don't work there. What's even funnier is Aileen is my next-door neighbor. They sneer at each other at least once or twice a week. It's great."

"Aileen seems cool. We should invite her to hang out sometime," I said.

"I'm away from Sophia now, and Aileen deserves an explanation as to why I was such a cunt."

"I'm sure she'll understand."

Cristy said nothing but smiled and stared into thin space.

"Cristy?"

"Oh, sorry. Was just imagining Aileen in her school uniform. That girl can rock a plaid skirt better than almost anyone. I have been late to school several times because I would sit on the porch and wait for her to leave for school. Damn, she looks good. Second nicest ass on a girl I know."

"Who is the first?" I asked, almost not wanting to know.

"I almost feel ashamed for looking. You should know who I'm talking about. You spend enough time staring at her yourself. I'd probably be all over her if the girl weren't a blood-related cousin. Autumn has a fantastic ass."

"With all the working out she does, it's unsurprising," I said. "I hope she's okay. I bet she was tired because of her trance last night."

The memory of the kiss Autumn and I shared popped into my head. I tried desperately to replace it with another memory but failed miserably.

"She should be fine. The time I saw one of those trances, it was the same way the next day. She lasted until about mid-afternoon and then went to bed. She'll wake up refreshed tomorrow from all the extra sleep."

Aileen appeared with our drinks. She placed two napkins from her apron on her waist before us. Cristy's had "Go Away" followed by a big smiley next to it written on it with red lipstick. Aileen clearly knew how to play the game.

"I love you, Aileen," Cristy said.

"Right back at you, pain in my ass," Aileen smirked.

"Get it right, I'm a pain in your sweet, sweet ass," Cristy grinned.

"On to subjects that don't include my ass, what would you ladies like to eat tonight?" Aileen said.

"I'll have my usual," Cristy said. "I'd ask for your phone number, but I already have that."

"And for you?" Aileen looked at me.

"I guess I'll have a chicken salad bread bowl with ranch dressing."

"I'll get that right in for you guys," Aileen said as she scooped up our menus.

"Hey, I was wondering," I said as soon as Aileen was out of earshot. "Have you felt the presence of those guys that were following us lately?"

"Nope," Cristy said. "They just...disappeared. I hope that doesn't mean they followed Aunt Cassy and Uncle Will. Not that they can't protect themselves. I suppose it gives us a break, though."

"Yeah, but if they did follow them, they aren't only interested in me. I'm not sure if that is a relief or more worrisome."

"Who knows? Right now, enjoy your day off. Who knows when you are going to get another one."

210

While we waited for our food, Cristy pulled out her cell phone and started playing a game. I observed the restaurant and saw nothing out of the ordinary. The entire situation was causing me to feel uneasy. Did these people stop following us, or did they find a way to hide their presence? I hoped they weren't watching Autumn, although I was confident in Mina's ability to defend Autumn if she had to.

Aileen eventually appeared with a large tray of food. On the tray was my bread bowl chicken salad, what looked like a barbecue burger, which was loaded with the aforementioned sauce, onion rings, lettuce, tomato, and, for some ungodly reason, more onions. It was placed next to a large portion of fries covered in cheese and bacon. A bowl of macaroni and cheese was also on the tray, with more bacon strewn throughout it. A few large hot dogs had their own plate and their own portion of onion rings. Along with all of this was a giant chocolate milkshake.

"Carrie, you had the Chicken Salad Bread Bowl," Aileen said as she put my food in front of me. "And Cristy... you had your usual." She placed the numerous plates of food in front of Cristy and, finally, the milkshake. "Enjoy," she said as she walked away.

"What the hell is all that?" I exclaimed.

"My dinner?" she said. "What do you think it is?"

"Enough food to feed a small army," I said. "You must have the metabolism of a hummingbird."

"That's what my mom always tells me. If I were a normal human, I'd probably have to worry about it slowing down, but since my body isn't likely to change much... ever, I'm pretty sure I can eat like this for the rest of my life."

"Must be nice. The rest of us girls need to watch our figures," I said.

I thought Cristy would take a long time to finish her meal, but I was wrong.

She was done before I was. Where she had the room for it all was beyond me.

"So, skating next?" I said.

"Yeah, as soon as Aileen gets her cute ass back here with our bill," Cristy said.

Almost as if she were summoned, Aileen approached with the black cushioned folder that held our bill.

"I can take care of this whenever you guys are ready," Aileen said. As I opened the small purse I kept with me whenever I wore an outfit like this, Cristy yanked out a credit card, placed it in the folder, and returned it to Aileen.

"Don't worry about it; I'm a rich bitch, remember. Save your cash," she said.

"I've learned not to argue with you," I said as I put my wallet back in my purse.

"I'll be right back," Aileen said. Cristy again watched her stroll away.

"I'm starting to wonder if there is more than a physical attraction to her," I said.

Cristy just shrugged her shoulders and sat back in her seat.

A moment later, Aileen returned to the table with the receipt on a small tray with a few mints. Cristy took the receipt, scribbled her name and the amounts, and returned it to Aileen. Aileen began to walk away and stopped dead in her tracks as she looked at the receipt. She turned around and came back.

"You left me a two-hundred-dollar tip. I'd say you made a mistake, but the total is right," she said.

"Yeah, that's for being so fine and a good waitress," Cristy grinned.

"Let me guess. There is no way I can talk you out of this, right?" she said.

"Nope, unless you have some process of getting your fine butt in a doggie bag, no," Cristy laughed.

Aileen turned her eyes upwards one more time, "Thanks. Have a good night, guys."

212

Chapter 30

We left our seats and started working our way out of the restaurant. The guys inside also seemed to study our every move as we went. I caught one particular guy starting and shot him a glare, just for the hell of it. Once in the car, Cristy turned the key and then made herself comfortable with the seatbelt. The Mustang started its massive engine, and we immediately pulled out of the parking lot. She drove the vehicle south, delving deeper into the city. It was only a short time until we pulled into the parking lot of the club-skate rink combo. I wasn't thrilled about the idea of skating, but I decided to try it before I knocked it.

We parked, and I saw many people our age around the place. It was amazing how many of these people were downright hot. Fantastic-looking teens surrounded the place, not an unkempt one in sight. No wonder Cristy enjoyed it here.

"I'm surprised you don't like sneaking into actual clubs," I said.

"Nah, pretending I'm older than I am is my sister's deal, not mine. I like partners my age anyway because someday, I won't be able to find any."

"Let's see what fun we can have in this place. I don't know how into skating I am. Plus, rented skates smell."

"Who the hell says we're renting skates? This place has a badass skate shop. Last time I was here, there was a pair of knee-high skates that would look awesome with what you are wearing."

"I have a feeling you just want to see me on skates," I said.

"You can read me like a book, Carrie. Oh, and I'm buying your skates. No arguments," she grinned.

"Are you ever going to let me pay for anything while I'm out with you?" I said.

"Highly unlikely. You'd be surprised how much money I have. It's no fun having lots of money if you can't blow it on real friends."

"Fine, just keep buying me stuff. I'll pay you back with some massive birthday present. Remember, I have money to blow, too."

"Make sure it's something sexy, and you've got a deal," Cristy laughed.

We stepped out of the car and immediately drew attention. I ignored it while Cristy waved to all the boys and girls. Before the actual skating rink entrance, there was a thin hall with a ticket booth. Cristy paid our way in, as I figured she would insist, and continued inside.

We entered the skate club to find it darker than any other skate rink I had been to. The music was thumping with a club mix of a popular pop song. Teens danced on the rink itself and on a good-sized dance floor. The place was stuffed to the brim with people our age dressed to impress someone. As for the spiritual end of things, it wasn't very interesting. All this superficial flash meant little on the other side. It was undoubtedly a fun-looking place, but if Cristy hadn't accompanied me, I would have found all of it completely bland. I found myself quickly losing interest in even the most exciting places. My mind kept trying to drag me back to the Alexander residence.

Cristy yanked me by the wrist, snapping me out of my musings to the skate shop, a small enclave off the dance floor's left. It was a room that consisted of pairs of skates all over the walls, a small counter that held the register, and a clerk behind it. I immediately saw the skates Cristy spoke of. They were rollerblades, black, and knee-high, the kind that roller derby players wore. They were very similar to the boots I was wearing now, which was why Cristy thought they would look great with what I was wearing. She was absolutely correct.

Cristy snagged a simple pair of black leather standard skates. She paid for both sets of skates, and we headed out to find a place to sit. After lacing up our new skates and tucking our shoes in a locker, we surveyed the club.

"Let's go do a few laps around the rink. Maybe we'll catch someone's attention," Cristy chuckled.

"Sure, why not," I replied.

We skated over to the rink. It had been years since I had worn skates, but it took me little time to get accustomed to them again. We glided along, side by side, around the rink, observing the eye candy among us.

"I think I'm going to check out what is going on in the rest of the place," I said loudly, trying to talk over the music.

"Cool, I'm going to skate a bit more. My ass needs the exercise," Cristy replied.

214

"I don't know, looks pretty good to me," I flirted. Just for the hell of it, I playfully slapped her on the butt and darted off. I loved giving that girl a taste of her own medicine.

I found the 'bar' on the other side of the dance floor. It had a glossy oak finish and a chrome bar surrounding it. In front of it, bar stools were bolted to the floor. Black pleather covered the seats.

"Quick, bartender, give me a soda before my friend shows up and insists on paying for it," I said as I sat on a bar stool and slapped a pair of dollar bills down. The bartender was a girl probably about my age. Like most female bartenders, she was extremely attractive and showed a healthy amount of cleavage through a black V-neck shirt. They always received the best tips for apparent reasons.

"Coming right up," the bartender said with a grin. "Usually, most girls don't want to pay for their own drink."

"My friend has too much money to blow, and I can't get a dollar in edgewise with her around."

"At least you don't have guys hounding to buy you drinks here. I don't see that too often in this place. Guys tend to keep their money to themselves if they don't have the prospect of getting a chick toasted enough to sleep with them."

"Most guys are pigs. Except..." I trailed off. I felt like there was a name that I would normally say at the end of that sentence. Yet, at the time, I could not come up with it. It was maddening.

"You okay?" the bartender said.

"I'm fine. I'm new to the area, and I think it's just the heat frying my brain," I said, taking a hard draw of my drink and nearly draining the cup.

"You'll get used to it. We all do; my family is from Alaska."

"Holy shit," I chuckled. "Makes Seattle seem like it's just across town."

"Is that girl drunk or high?" the bartender made an offhanded comment as her eyes followed Cristy with one leg almost straight in the air, showing the world her panties while rolling backward.

"Nope, just high on life," I laughed. "That's that friend I was talking about."

"Oh, sorry," the bartender said. "I didn't mean to insult your friend."

"It's no big deal. She doesn't take things too seriously, and you didn't mean anything by it. If I didn't know her, I'd think the same thing." I drew a final drink from the straw, "It was great talking; gotta jet before my mental midget comes looking for me."

"Have fun!" the bartender smiled.

I slid back to the rink and went around a few laps. Cristy found a few people to skate-dance with, and she appeared like she couldn't be happier.

As I moved around the rink one last time, I felt an excruciating wave of emotions crash into me. It was absolute terror, with hints of ecstasy and bloodlust all in one. It was so powerful it sent me crashing to the floor, face first.

I remember little of what happened over the next few moments. I remember Cristy skating quickly toward me and random people hovering over me. I heard Cristy's phone ringing, and she deftly answered it, spoke on it quickly, and hung it up.

"Carrie, we gotta go. Something is wrong with Autumn," I heard her say.

"Oh shit," I mumbled as my world spun.

Cristy and some guy helped me off the floor and to the lockers.

"I'm sorry, Cristy, it was fun while it lasted," I muttered, still in a daze.

Cristy snatched our shoes and my wrist and led me out the door.

My head was circling, and I felt like I was in one of those g-force test units that the space program used. I could hardly stand, and my skates weren't aiding the situation. I must have blacked out on my feet because, by the time I came to, I found myself in the car, skates still on, and Cristy driving barefoot.

"What happened?" I asked.

"To you or Autumn?" she replied.

I turned to her with furrowed eyebrows and a grimace.

216

"Mina says she's having some sort of panic attack. She told me it used to happen a lot when she was younger, and Cassandra is usually the only one who can calm her down."

"Cassandra isn't here," I said while attempting to focus on a single point.

"That's exactly why she called us. I don't know what we can do, but we're the only ones she could call. Are you okay?"

"I have no fucking clue. I felt a wave of emotions flood my head. It was so powerful it knocked me on my ass."

"Shit," Cristy said. "I think that link of yours is going into overdrive."

"I had a feeling this wasn't a coincidence. I told you Tala'har don't get days off."

Chapter 31

I hoped I would recover as we drove to Autumn's house, but I was wrong. The waves of emotions continued unabated. I had to keep reminding myself that these emotions weren't mine, and I needed to keep my head intact. The strangest aspect of the feelings was that arousal was mixed in with them. I could feel my temperature elevating. I wasn't sure what I wanted to do. I either wanted to cry, scream in terror, slit someone's throat, or force Cristy to pull over so I could rape her. I don't think me raping Cristy was even possible. You can't rape the willing.

We pulled into the drive, and I forcefully lifted my legs and dropped them out of the car. I did my best to unlace the skates in my current condition, but Cristy had to assist me. My breathing was labored, and my movement was far from graceful as I slid my boots on. I stood up to get out of the car and nearly fell over, but I was able to catch myself on the vehicle. I took a deep breath and attempted to focus as I carefully wobbled toward the door. I then lost my footing and slammed into it, cheek first.

"Are you okay?" Cristy asked.

"Ask me later," I murmured. Cristy helped me up on my feet.

Cristy opened the door with her key. Mina was rushing down the stairs as we entered. I nearly lost my footing again but steadied myself on the couch.

"Carrie, are you alright?" Mina said.

I took a breath, "I'm fine. Where is she?"

"On the floor in her room. We better get up there; she was asking for sleeping pills, at least from what I could understand of it."

Cristy aided me up the stairs slowly. I could hear Autumn sobbing from the stairs, and it broke my heart. As we approached the room, I could see Autumn wearing a white nightgown on the floor, her face soaked with tears. She was beside the bed, her back up against the wall, her knees against her chest. In her hands was a bottle of nighttime acetaminophen she was struggling to open.

"Stay here, Cristy," I said. "With her state of mind, she may associate you with your sister, and I don't want her to do anything rash. I am not sure if I can stop her."

"Yeah, maybe that's a good idea," Cristy said.

I stepped into the room and felt the foreign feelings melt away. Autumn was so intent on trying to open the acetaminophen that she didn't notice my approach.

"Honey, give me the pills," I said.

Her eyes slowly drifted upwards and grew as I approached.

"Carrie?" she gasped. The bottle slipped from her hands and fell onto the floor. She pushed herself off the wall to stand up. She wrapped her arms around my neck, and we both tipped backward. Then, I fell on top of her. She clung to my neck for dear life as I was stuck on top of her. I couldn't help but enjoy her holding me like this, although it was pretty painful.

"Autumn, let go.... you're squeezing me too hard," I finally gasped.

"Oh," she released her hold. "I'm sorry."

I rocked back and sat on my butt. I took a deep breath.

"Are you okay?" I asked. It felt stupid to say, but I had nothing else.

"Yeah, I think so now."

I waved Cristy over. She sat down on the bed.

"What happened, Autumn?" Cristy asked.

"I had a dream... I guess it was more than a dream...." she said.

"Do you want to talk about it?" I asked.

"Yes, I suppose. I was... killing people..."

"Killing people? You mean you were in battle?" I asked.

"I guess you could say that. To me, it was just killing people. They were fighting back if you could call it that. They didn't stand a chance."

"Autumn, just because you are stronger than another warrior doesn't make it murder," I said.

"No, that's not what made it murder," she said. "I mean, I was enjoying it. It was... bliss.... and... this isn't easy to say... sexually arousing. I loved it. I didn't want it to stop. I just tore through their flesh with my blade; I could feel the bones cracking as I slashed... I nearly......while it was going on. I loved every bloody, gruesome second... and it terrified me. I'm a bad person... a monster..."

"It was a dream, Autumn; you're not a monster or a bad person," Cristy said. "No one died."

"That's not the point!" she raised her voice. She paused for a moment. Her eyes sunk to the floor. "I'm sorry, I had no right to yell at you."

"It's okay," Cristy comforted.

Autumn looked at me inquisitively, "Carrie, are you okay? Your elbows are bruised."

"Oh, I fell while skating. It's no big deal; we're here to worry about you."

"I'm sorry for interrupting your evening," Autumn said. "I know I'm a burden to everyone."

"Don't talk like that," Mina reprimanded from the doorway. "You are not a burden to anyone, Autumn Elizabeth Alexander, and if I hear you say that again, I'm going to kick your ass. You may have a foot and a half on me, but I've got a ton of years on you. Understand?"

Elizabeth. What an elegant middle name. That was the first time I had heard her middle name.

"Yes, Aunt Mina," she said, eyes returned to the floor. She looked up once again, "May I talk to Carrie alone, please?"

"Oh, sure," Cristy said. "Just holler when you need me; I'll be on the couch."

"Give us a yell if you need us," Mina said as Cristy followed her.

I was almost sweating bullets. What could she want to talk to me about alone?

Autumn steadily pulled herself onto the bed and crawled onto it. I, too, grabbed the bed and lifted myself on it.

"If you don't want to tell me what happened to you, that's okay. I mean, you fell on top of me; something more must be wrong."

220

"Okay, you got me. I haven't been feeling well tonight. I got a bit lightheaded right before Mina called us. I fell at the skating rink," I said while saying a silent prayer that she bought that story, although it wasn't entirely a lie.

"Are you okay? I have been worried the heat of this place would get to you. Is that it?" Autumn's eyes grew wide.

"I think so. Maybe I haven't been getting enough sleep. It's been an exciting week, I guess."

"You worry about me too much. You should have gone straight to a hospital, not here."

"I'm fine now, so don't worry about it," I said.

A light knock on the door was heard.

"Can I come in?" Cristy said meekly. "I know I said I would wait downstairs, but I need to talk to you, Autumn."

"It's okay, you can come in," Autumn said.

Cristy entered the room timidly. I had only known her for a few days, but I didn't think this woman could look that meek. I couldn't help but wonder why.

"So, what's up, Cristy?" Autumn glanced upward.

"I just think it's time I told you a little secret of mine. Right now, very few know, and I feel you should be one of them."

"Okay, go on," Autumn nodded. "You know I won't tell anyone."

"I wanted to tell you about my Telosian ability," Cristy said slowly. "It's something I have kept from everyone for the most part, especially my father and my sister. See, I'm one of those Telosians that can read minds... and stuff like that."

Autumn's eyes grew wide, "You can read minds? Well, I suppose that makes sense. I take it's more than just reading minds; you can manipulate them too, right?"

"Yeah, how did you know?" Cristy tilted her head.

"A couple of reasons. First, your sister doesn't normally bark like a dog. Also, your dad slashing her tires isn't like him."

"Yeah, you caught me," Cristy laughed. "Don't worry, I try not to read my friends' minds; it's an invasion of privacy. Although I did take a peek at your boy toys, and let me tell you, he is the genuine article. A real gentleman, probably one of the last."

"I suppose you wouldn't have let me date him if he hadn't been," Autumn said.

"Are you kidding? Me and Carrie would have kicked the shit out of him."

"I feel honored that you are willing to share your secret with me. I assume Carrie already knew?" Autumn said.

"She told me that night she made the bitch bark. I think she knows I'm a human lie detector," I grinned.

"Although, now it makes me worry even more about you," Autumn added.

"Why do you say that?" Cristy shot up an eyebrow.

"I have a theory that the Olympians didn't destroy the Telosians because of their destructive abilities. I think they destroyed them because of the ones with your ability type. It's a stretch, but it could be possible for you to control a god."

"Knowing how paranoid I hear Zeus is, I wouldn't put it past him," Cristy said. "You really shouldn't spend your time worrying about me; I'll be fine."

"Until they find out what you can do," Autumn said. "Really, Cristy, be careful. Cause I swear, if that blowhard of a wannabe god tries anything, I'll make him wish he hadn't."

Autumn exuded an extraordinary amount of confidence. After all, we were talking about a god, and she was threatening him. The vibe I was getting from her told me that she wasn't just kidding around. Autumn never seemed like the type for false hubris.

222

"There is something else I wanted to talk to you guys about, specifically Cristy. Carrie and I already discussed this last night... sort of. I think I've been thinking about..."

"What?" Cristy said after an awkward moment passed.

"I've been thinking about sex way more than natural. It's starting to worry me."

"I can see why you didn't talk to me about this before. How exactly is this a problem?"

"It is because I have urges that are nearly overpowering. It scares me. And with that dream I had, it terrifies me more now. I'm afraid I might..."

"Take your time," I added after silence filled the air for more than a few moments.

"I'm afraid I might... take advantage of Jacob," she finally spat out.

"Autumn, honey, you have a lot to learn about guys. It's not very easy for girls to take advantage of them. That's not the way it works," I said.

"That's not exactly what I mean."

"You mean..." Cristy said.

"I'm afraid I might force myself on him," Autumn said.

"Okay... I'm not sure that would work..." Cristy said.

"Yeah, Autumn, it's difficult for a woman to force herself on a guy. It requires him to be aroused, which usually means he's willing. I'm not saying it doesn't happen, but Jake does care about you," I said.

"It all still concerns me. These... dreams... They are so violent, and I revel in it... at the time. I fear that violence will manifest itself in... other ways. And as for the arousal part...I'm afraid I might instinctively use some Telosian magic... I've done it before; I'm just afraid I'll do it again."

"Whoa," I cut in. "You've used your Telosian abilities before?"

"Yeah, I was alone, and Thomas managed to get me into a compromising position. I thought I was done for... and somehow, I struck him with lightning."

"When was this...and what does that exactly have to do with sex?" Cristy said.

"When I was... thirteen," Autumn said. "It wasn't too long before I tried to kill myself."

That wasn't something I was expecting. Cristy and I shared the same shocked expression, but not for the reason Autumn probably thought.

"It's part of the reason I tried to kill myself. My hormones... haven't stopped since. I don't know why. Sex is constantly on my mind, and it doesn't feel natural. That's why I need your help. Jacob called me earlier and said his dad got called out on business for the weekend, so we can't work on the car. So, he asked if I could come over anyway. He said I was welcome to bring you guys if I wanted. I need you two there. I can't trust myself. I barely held it together in public, and this will be in private. He said there is a possibility his sister might be there, but she might not be."

"Okay, I don't know about Carrie, but I'll come," Cristy said.

"You can count on me," I said. "And you never really answered the question. What exactly does your Telosian magic have to do with sex, other than it seems to incite your hormones."

"Telosian magic... has a... sexual school. And from my understanding, regardless of ability type, any female Telosian can use it."

"Holy shit," Cristy said. "You're fucking serious, aren't you?"

"Wow, you learn something new every day," I said.

"Part of Telosian magic is used during the Festival of Womanhood."

"How come I have never heard about this shit? So, what is this festival all about?" Cristy said.

"As for why you don't know much about this stuff, I don't know. As for the festival, you see, I don't know how much you know about my bloodline, Carrie, but males are rare. Because of this, for the race to procreate and... enjoy themselves, they must have the Festival of Womanhood, where every woman of childbearing age has sex with the few non-related males amongst them...and each other. So, before you say it, Cristy, yes, it's a big orgy."

Cristy opened her mouth wide, and I placed my hand over her mouth.

224

"So, what does that have to do with the magic?" I said.

"Since there are only a few males and many females, Telosians had to use sexual magic to keep the men... going."

"Oh," I said. "Now that makes sense."

"You are afraid you might... accidentally use some of that magic on Jacob... and force yourself on him?" Cristy said.

"Yes..." Autumn said. "I know this may sound stupid, but I know I'm capable of some violent things, and I don't want to hurt him... or anyone else for that matter."

Cristy gazed up at the ceiling, "That festival sounds awesome. It would suck the rest of the time. I mean, with so few guys, what do you do with yourself?"

"Well... I guess that's why most Telosians are bisexual," Autumn said. "They are usually married to another woman while a lucky few get to marry the few males... if they survived the festival."

"You really do learn something new about yourself daily," Cristy said. "That might be why I dig chicks. That's kind of cool. The question is, Autumn, do you like girls?"

Autumn's face immediately flashed a deep crimson. Silence flooded the room.

"Autumn, you don't have to answer that question." I turned to Cristy. "Just because she's from a bloodline that is usually bisexual doesn't mean she is," I said and then turned back to Autumn. "I know these things are hard for you to talk about, and I'm honored that you are comfortable enough with me to talk about them."

"Now let's get back to this whole 'you trying to kill yourself' thing. What the fuck, girl?" Cristy said.

"I just... couldn't take it. On top of my hormones, I had a lot of...internal...problems I was dealing with."

"I take your parents think it's because of what you go through at school?" I said.

"Yes, for the most part. I haven't told them about any of this stuff. I don't know how to, so it's easier for them to think it's all because of school. I will admit, it is a little of it, but not as much as they probably think."

"You haven't tried again, have you?" I asked.

"No, I've concluded that fate won't allow me to die. I just wanted to be released from all of this," she said as tears started to flow. "Why me? Why can't I just be normal? I'd give up everything to live the life of a normal girl. I could live the rest of eternity alone if I could escape all this..."

She began to sob so heavily that I wasn't sure if she was saying words anymore or just crying.

Cristy scooched closer to Autumn and wrapped her arms around her, "I know you've gone through a lot of shit, and I can't promise that it will be over any time soon. What I can promise is that I will be here for you, and I'm sure Carrie feels the same. Never feel like a burden, you hear me. We're here for you just like you're here for us. You have a shoulder or four to cry on if needed."

I said nothing and put my hand on Autumn's shoulder. I shut my eyes and could feel her sorrow closing in on me. I turned away so Autumn couldn't see my tears. It wasn't just her sorrow that caused these tears.

"So, you'll both come?" she said once she stopped crying enough to speak.

"Sure," Cristy said.

"Yeah, I'll be there. Just give me a call," I said, attempting not to sound like I've been crying.

"Is something wrong, Carrie," Autumn's voice picked up.

"It's hard to see you in so much pain," I said. That wasn't the reason I was crying, but it was true, nonetheless.

"I'm used to it; you shouldn't worry about it. I'm talking silly, to be honest. 'Normal' is impossible for someone like me," Autumn said.

"I think 'happy' is more important," Cristy said. "And who wants to be normal? Normal sucks. I've been hanging around my sister my whole life, who tries to be normal but seeing spirits and other assorted shit isn't really in the realm of normal."

"That's her Telosian gift?" Autumn asked.

"Yeah, I think. It's tough to say what it truly is. She only told me she would see ghosts when we were kids. I knew she wasn't just imagining it, not because I could read her mind, which is extremely difficult to do, but because I could read the thoughts of the ghosts she saw. That never scared me. What is freaky is when you're used to being able to tell where everyone is around you by the presence of their mind and soul, and she pops out of nowhere. Most of the time, I can't tell she's there. Now that's scary."

"That sounds terrible being able to see the dead," Autumn said. "It might have been what warped her so much."

"I know she's been able to see them most of her life, even before I could read minds. She would show up in my bedroom late at night and ask if she could sleep with me. She made me swear I wouldn't tell our parents. I don't know what bullshit she's fed, Mom. I'm sure she is convinced neither of her children has gifts because I know if I tell her about mine, Dad will find out. She has a notoriously big mouth."

"Hey, Cristy. Something I've been wondering about," I said. "You've said Sophia wants to be a model. Don't models usually start modeling in their early teens? Unless she does model, and I don't know about it."

"No, she doesn't. I don't get it either. She has talked about being a model her entire life and still does. Mom and Dad got her gigs when she was young; everyone said it looked promising. Yet, when she should have started, probably when she was thirteen, she seemed to opt into wanting to be the queen bitch of the school instead. She spends all her time doing that. Even the party she's at right now is her being there to control the situation. I know she doesn't have fun. Hell, she doesn't even really drink; I've seen her pour her drink into plants or whatever she can find to get rid of it so her buddies don't know. It's all about image with that girl."

"I know what happened," Autumn hung her head low. "I know why she stopped modeling."

"Why?" Cristy said.

"I showed up here when we were thirteen. As far as I know, most of her behavior started when I moved to Miami. So, I guess it is my fault."

Cristy's eyes grew wide, her brows furrowed as she clenched her teeth, "Don't you ever blame yourself for what that bitch does!" Her fists were wrung tight as she shook.

Autumn inched away, her eyes fully open and her mouth ajar. It was amazing that Cristy could intimidate her.

"Hey, chick, calm down," I said.

Cristy took a deep breath, "Sorry... I don't know what came over me. Please forgive me, Autumn. It's just..."

"It's okay," Autumn said after waiting for Cristy to finish her sentence, but it never came. "So, what is it?"

"It's just... she does blame you. I know I probably shouldn't tell you that. She thinks... fuck, I don't even know what she thinks. Her train of thought doesn't make sense. I asked her why she wasn't modeling, and she handed me some half-assed excuse about you. I didn't understand it, so I don't even bother to remember exactly what she said."

Autumn hung her head with a sigh and said, "You know, I remember when we were kids, and your parents would bring you guys up to see us. Sophia would do nothing but talk about how she was going to be this famous model, and I could never be one because I was ugly. I kept telling her I didn't want to be a model, and she didn't care. She always seemed like she thought I wanted to compete with her, and I didn't and never have. I would be happy to be like my mother, a good mom. I don't want to be famous."

My heart sank when I heard that she wanted to be a mother. I could never give her a child. It wouldn't be fair to her, even if she loved me. I realized my silence was the best gift I could give her. Jacob could give her a child. She'd get her wish to be a mother and have a bit of normalcy in her life.

"Sure, but being famous would be a lot of fun," Cristy said. "I mean, not like my sister wants to be. She wants to get by on looks alone. If you were famous, you'd be famous for your guitar or something like that."

"I don't know. I don't think I'm good enough for anything like that. I've always just played the guitar as a hobby."

"That's always how it starts," I added. "Most of the greats never aimed to be famous. That's something a poser does and never accomplishes that goal. You play the guitar because you love it, not because of what it can get you."

"That's true," Cristy said.

"We could start our own band. You know, not to get famous or anything like that, but for kicks," I said. "I can play a little bass; Cristy, can you play any instruments?"

"Not yet. Give me a few weeks," she smiled. I just have to find a good drummer."

"Someone to teach you?" Autumn said.

"....eh, something like that. You don't worry your pretty little head about it," Cristy's grin grew wider.

Autumn finally smiled and rolled her eyes, "I suppose I don't want to know, do I?"

"I'll tell you when it's all said and done," Cristy said.

"Oh!" Autumn perked up. "Jacob can play the keyboard. His mom always made him practice the piano because she thought he would be some prodigy. He always liked the keyboard better, though."

"I was hoping it would be us three girls, but a keyboardist would be cool. Got to have some eye candy for the girls, if you know what I mean," I said.

Autumn gave me a stern look.

"Autumn Alexander, is that a bit of jealousy I'm detecting?" Cristy said.

"He is her boyfriend," I said.

"I guess so," Autumn said. "It's just weird saying it. I have a boyfriend. And yes, that was jealousy. I haven't felt that before... it's so... weird."

I knew exactly how she felt.

"Wouldn't worry about it; it's natural to feel jealous. He's a great catch," Cristy said.

"I just feel I should be better than that, that's all," Autumn said. "I suppose it's my insecurity talking."

"Trust me, honey," I said. "You have nothing to be insecure about."

"I'm worried," Autumn said. "...about Sophia. If she can't bully someone, the next step is usually seduction; if they are a guy, that is. And if they are in the closet, probably girls too... I overheard that she slept with another school's quarterback and then blackmailed him. If he didn't throw the game, she'd tell his fiancé."

"Here we are talking about my bitch of a sister again," Cristy said. "Forget the bitch, Autumn."

"If she even flashes her eyelashes at your man, I'll bash that pretty little face of hers into an unrecognizable mess," I said.

"I should be the one hurting her, Carrie, not you. I can't let her push me around anymore. Now that Jacob and you are in my life, more than I will suffer. I can't let myself be the school punching bag because you all will be in the same boat by association. I know you don't care, but I do. It's not even just us. Everyone, even the slightest bit different, with any secret to hide, is at risk. Like your friend Liz, Cristy."

"How did you know about Liz?" Cristy shot an eyebrow up.

"I.... thought I saw you two hanging out..." Autumn stuttered.

"We've only hung out at once... it was a football game," Cristy said.

"Oh... well I couldn't have been there... I'm not sure how I knew that..." Autumn said.

"I'm sure it's just those finely tuned instincts of yours," Carrie added.

"Don't sweat it, cus, maybe I mentioned her and don't remember," Cristy patted Autumn on the back.

"Point being, too many suffer because of her. She has to be stopped," Autumn growled.

"So, what exactly are you going to do?" Cristy said.

"I'm not sure yet, but this has to end," Autumn sighed. She took a deep breath. "Okay, I'm a big girl. I'm fine now. You two should head home."

230

"We can stay," Cristy said.

"For sure," I added.

"No, I insist. I'll be fine, I promise. No more attempting to take medicine, which I probably shouldn't. It never has predictable results, anyway."

"She'll be fine," Mina peeked in the door. "Now, shoo. "

"Okay," I said. "But if you are having problems again, you ring the fuck out of us."

"Will do, I promise," Autumn nodded.

Chapter 32

As Cristy drove the car to my house, I could tell Autumn was sleeping soundly. Before, it was just raw emotion I could feel through the link, but the more time I spent with her, the sharper the information through the link became. I turned my attention to the environment around me. Using the method my mother had taught me, I tried to sense the world around me and found nothing out of the ordinary. I knew I would have to ask Cristy if they were around before the end of the ride, which made me feel completely useless.

"You okay?" Cristy said, breaking me out of my reflection.

"Yeah, I guess," I said. "Any of our 'friends' hiding in the area?"

"Nope, not that I can tell," she stopped momentarily. "I know some of the things Autumn said tonight weren't easy to hear."

"Tell me about it."

"Like that, she wants to be a mother."

Cristy always had this way of hitting the nail on the head. I had been trying to avoid thinking about that part of the conversation.

"You got it... I hope she gets her wish, though."

"If her life can ever be calm enough to raise a kid. Let's face it: she's got hell to go through before she can live in peace. Shit, she may never get that kind of quiet in her life."

"I wish I could do something for her. You know, before she has to face her destiny. She deserves some joy before everything goes to hell."

"Maybe starting that band would be a good idea. Give us all something else to think about," Cristy said.

"Sounds fun," I said.

"I still have no idea how she would have known about Liz. I mentioned her to Aunt Cassy, but Cassy would have never mentioned her to Autumn because that might have led to the team of mercenaries that tried to kill us... well her...kidnap me...and if you haven't noticed, Autumn is a bit protective..."

"What the fuck?" Carrie muttered.

"Zeus sent them. It wasn't a huge deal," Cristy shrugged. "Also... how the hell did she know Liz's chosen name... I'm really going to have to ask Aunt Cassy."

Before we knew it, we were in my driveway. I noticed my mother's car was absent. "Well, it looks like Mom is out again tonight. Do you want to stay the night?"

"Planned on it," she smiled.

"How did I know you would say that?" I replied.

We exited the car, and I opened the door and let Cristy in first. The house was dark, so I flipped the light switch by the door, illuminating the living room. My mother must have returned home while I was gone. I was amazed she had managed to unpack as much as she did in such a short period. The place was starting to look livable.

I took a deep breath and closed my eyes. I could feel Autumn's consciousness. She seemed to be still asleep but dreaming about something. I could feel feelings of euphoria that were obviously hers. I felt she was dreaming of Jacob, but I couldn't be sure. Then, the sense of arousal I should have seen coming showed up.

"You okay?" Cristy asked.

"Yeah, I think Autumn is having a good dream," I said. "Wish I knew what it was about."

"That's...odd," Cristy said. "I don't detect any mental activity coming from her. It seems like she's in a dreamless sleep to me. That's fucking weird. You sure?"

"Yeah, I'm pretty sure," I said.

Cristy shrugged, "Oh well, not going to strain my brain on it. I'm going to go use your bathroom, okay?"

"Sure, I'll be in my room," I said.

I trotted upstairs and entered my room. I glanced about my barren walls and found a distaste for it. I had been so busy that I hadn't had time to set the place up. I knew I would eventually have time because I wasn't moving anytime soon.

Before I could even take a boot off, Cristy appeared in the doorway of my room. She was no longer in the clothes she wore for the evening but a silk, red, strapped nightie that barely covered her crotch. She was wearing nothing else.

"So, I hope you weren't expecting to get any sleep during this 'sleep-over,'" she said as she sauntered toward me. "Cause I knew I was going home with someone this evening," she pressed against me and slowly wrapped her arms around my neck. "I'm glad it was you."

Before I could say anything, her lips locked with mine, and my mind again went blank. Even the link was gone. The only emotions I could feel were my own, and at that point, Cristy was driving me crazy.

"Are you going to allow me to take off my boots?" I said once my lips were free.

"Leave them on," she said in a breathy tone.

Before I knew it, she was kissing my neck as her hands deftly undid the strings on my corset. I slid my hands down her toned body until I reached her ass and gave it a squeeze. It felt the way I expected, nice and toned with just enough squish, like the rest of her.

My corset fell to the floor, and Cristy playfully pushed me onto my bed. I was amazed that someone so small had the strength to do this. When she pounced on me, I realized that I was wearing nothing but my boots. When she managed to get my skirt off, I wasn't sure. I also noticed I was being somewhat submissive. I was typically dominant in situations such as this, but something about Cristy disarmed me. It felt wonderful to surrender control for once.

She landed on me and kissed me again. Our hands seemed to both go for the other's breasts at the same time. Her breasts were substantial but plush, and their general feel did nothing but turn me on more. The way she touched mine was terrific. She knew exactly what I liked. It was never uncomfortable, and she used just the perfect amount of pressure. Her right hand slowly made its way south, as I was still bloody fascinated with the girl's breasts. I felt her index and middle penetrate me, and a moan escaped from my mouth. It had felt like it had been years since anyone had touched me.

234

After a moment, I felt like returning the favor, and one of my hands worked its way down to her crotch. What I found left me shocked. I had never known it was possible to be this smooth in that area. I found it a strange thing to think about in the throes of passion, maybe because of how much of a turn-on it was. My mouth moved to the nape of her neck. She gasped in ecstasy as I kissed her neck softly, and my fingers entered her. Only after a few seconds did her insides contract, and she moaned loudly as one of her hands found its way to my shoulder and lightly dug her nails in.

She gazed at me intensely, "Why, you naughty girl! I wanted to make you come first. It looks like I'm just going to have to punish you..."

She stood up and grabbed my still-booted legs, slid them long ways on the bed, and crawled between my legs up to my mouth. She forcefully kissed me while groping my breasts. She began to kiss her way down my body lightly...

After the most physically exhausting sexual experience of my life, I sat up next to Cristy, my boots still on, and she was completely naked. My heart pounded from the exertion, and my head spun. I lost count of how many orgasms we both had, but it felt like Cristy was having them every minute or two. I had never seen someone so sensitive. It was then that her apparent addiction to sex started to make sense. The more she had them, the more she drove me to my own. It was incredible. The sex had never been this good since the last time I was with...

"Lucas..." I gasped.

"Who's that?" Cristy said, groggily.

"My boyfriend... in Seattle," I said. "He was the love of my life. What the fuck?"

Cristy scooted herself up higher on the bed and wrapped her legs and arms around me from behind.

"What's wrong?" she said, putting her head on my shoulder.

"I haven't thought of him... at all... since I got here," I gasped.

"You've been busy; I wouldn't worry about it," Cristy said.

"I don't think you understand, Cristy," I said. "He literally hasn't crossed my mind. I even told Autumn that I didn't leave anyone in Seattle. I was heartbroken when we had to part. I feel like I'm losing my mind. It's like I forget he even existed."

I couldn't help it; I started to cry. After a few moments, I realized these feelings were mine and mine alone. I couldn't feel Autumn's presence at all. I went from heartbroken to terrified in an instant.

"Cristy, the link... it's gone!"

"Oh, I know," Cristy said. "Ever since we started 'having fun,' I've been blocking it. I should have said something. I didn't mean to freak you out. Plus, I know you said that it's a one-way thing, but let's face it, it isn't exactly acting like a normal Tala'har link, so who knows if Autumn can feel what you are feeling? I don't think either of us wanted to explain to Autumn why we were having sex. She might not get it."

"I don't even want to think about that conversation. I feel bad. I lied to her when I didn't have to. I want to share as much as I can with her. I already feel so far away from her because of all the lies I must tell her."

"Tell her about him tomorrow; I'm sure she'll be all happy that you are sharing with her. That type of thing seems to make her day."

"Speaking of which, I should probably call him tomorrow. Lucas will want to know about her. He knows all about what I am and who I'm here to protect." I turned my face to Cristy. "Can I take my boots off now?"

Chapter 33

After a stop at Cristy's house for her to shower and change, we met up with Autumn at her home for the walk over to Jacob's. I started wondering if the heat was affecting me, so that day, I carried a black umbrella to keep the sun from directly beating down on me. As we strolled down the street, Cristy and Autumn were busy conversing, and I thought back to when I awoke that morning. Cristy was tucked under my arm with her arm around me. My first waking thought was about Lucas. I sighed heavily and closed my eyes as a few tears escaped. Being without him was almost crushing, which was strange because I hadn't thought of him for nearly an entire week before.

At that point, I was still unable to feel my Tala'har link. The link kicked back on when I crept out of bed and lost physical contact with Cristy. I wasn't sure if it was the fact I had gone a while without it, but it seemed to come back stronger than it had been before it went away. If I concentrated hard enough, I could tell what Autumn was doing.

I glanced over to Autumn into those amazing eyes. What about her made me forget everything else in my life? It felt as if my life before Autumn was just a dream. I barely remembered anything that had happened before. All of this didn't sit well with me. I felt as though I was starting to lose my mind.

"Hey, Autumn," I broke into the conversation. I was so deep in thought beforehand that I wasn't sure if I had cut one of them off. "Remember when I said I never had a steady boyfriend and didn't leave one in Seattle?"

"Yeah, why?"

"That wasn't entirely accurate. I'm sorry. I'm not sure why I said that exactly. There was someone very important to me I had to leave in Seattle."

"Why are you apologizing? It's not that big of a deal. You've had a rough week. I know when I first moved here, I was a mess. I actually woke up one morning and asked my mother when Jason was coming home from school. He had been in the military for months by that point." Autumn stopped and turned to me. "So, what is this boy's name? Is he cute? Oh, that's a stupid question; a girl like you could land any guy she wants... oh lord, am I sounding like one of those stupid gossip girls Sophia hangs around?"

I laughed, and Cristy giggled.

"I don't think that's possible," Cristy said as we started to walk again.

"Well, to answer your questions, he's good-looking. His name is Lucas. To put it simply, he is a reformed bad boy. He spent a lot of time in the juvenie. He and I met at this party the summer I moved to his neighborhood. He was... great. I miss him a lot," I said.

"It's not fair you had to let him go," Autumn said.

"His mom wanted him to come with us, but he wouldn't. His mom is dying from cancer, and he is the only one around to take care of her. He spends most of his time looking after her, to the point where he barely passes classes at school. To say she wanted him to come with us is a large understatement. She begged him; she didn't want him to see her die. Of course, Lucas being Lucas, he wouldn't go. He loves her too much."

"I think any good son would do the same," Autumn said. "He sounds like a great guy. I want to meet him someday."

"If he shows up here, it only means one thing: she's dead," I sighed. I didn't want to even think about that. As much as I loved Lucas, I didn't want him here. He would be in a lot of danger, and it would make things... complicated... to say the least. "Lucas has no living relatives he knows of, so we're about all he has beyond his mom."

"I see," Autumn said. "I just don't like that you have chosen to be my friend, which means you'll be lonely here. I doubt any of the guys at school will want anything to do with you because of me."

"I think it's for the best," I said. "I don't know if I could love another guy beyond Lucas. I still love him, and that isn't going to change." The question was, could I choose him over Autumn? I didn't even want to contemplate that choice.

I was a bit impressed that Autumn was dressed in feminine clothing today since she didn't have her mother or us to badger her. She was wearing a tight red top with a v-shaped collar that showed just a tiny amount of her stomach. She wore tight, straight-leg blue jeans and her usual sneakers. She wanted to impress Jacob, which was a good thing.

The bracelet her mother had given her was on Autumn's right wrist. It didn't match the ensemble, but Autumn clearly didn't care.

When we arrived at Jacob's house, Autumn stepped up to the door and knocked. After a few moments, a brunette girl of medium height answered. She appeared to be our age and was pretty cute.

When she saw us, she smiled gently. "Hi, I'm Lisa, Jacob's sister."

Interestingly, even though Jacob had spent most of his life in Japan, she looked more Japanese than he did, other than her very brown hair.

"Hi, I'm Autumn, and this is..."

"Carrie and Cristy, yep, I know who you guys are. It's good to see you could make it. Jacob is upstairs. Please, come in, and I'll go get him."

We entered the house and saw a relatively neat and modern home. The living room's centerpiece was a large flat-screen television that hung on the wall. Below was an entertainment center filled with movie players, game consoles, and other equipment. The place was ordinary for the most part; little stood out, maybe, except the massive amount of electronics in the living room. The fact that they were lying about, out in the open, lent itself to the idea that this was a male-dominated household. It is not that women don't like their toys too; they keep them excellent and hidden away, like Autumn's family's television. I've noticed men like their electronics out in the open to show off to everyone. The elegance of a home usually doesn't enter their mind, but I didn't know as much about men as I pretended to, being my father died when I was young... My train of thought was interrupted. My head began to spin, and the world faded out...

I was whisked back, against my will, to that day. My mother, sister, and father ran through dense woodland as fast as our legs would take us. I kept glancing back for our pursuers but could never see anything. I looked up to my mother, calm and collected as usual. She seemed to be concentrating on something else, not the world around us. Her slick, black leather-like body suit covered her neck to toe, signifying her duty as a Tala'har. Her long boots and gloves had metal guards to block incoming attacks and were her only real armor. Her scythe bounced around noisily on her back, with a black leather strap that held it there.

My sister was just like Mom: cool, collected, and calm. She also scanned the environment, looking for who was pursuing us. Like Mom, she wore similar leather body armor, but hers was a shade of gray, signifying that she retained some innocence and was still a Tala'har in training.

Beams of light flashed from behind and singed the trees around. My dad would occasionally turn and counterattack with a quick fireball. He appeared even more frantic than usual, which told me this was bad.

My little legs barely stepped over the large roots that protruded from the woodland floor. I kept getting whacked in the face by low branches, even with my sister's best attempt to keep them out of my face. She held my hand tight, and I could feel her tremble slightly, her body giving away how frightened she was. I glanced up, and she smiled instinctively, her hazel eyes gleaming. She was always so strong, even when things became terrible. I always wanted to be like her and grow up as the Tala'har that I knew she would be soon enough.

My gaze returned to my father. His old, ragged robes gave him a shoddy appearance, but to the trained eye, they were a mark of his high rank as a wizard. Truly great wizards, like my father, did not require fancy robes. They wore humble garments to signify their understanding of the world and their place in it. I had never seen my father look so panicked. He was usually jumpy, but this was different. Typically, my mother would be speaking soothing words to him to keep him calm, but not a word escaped her lips this time.

I felt blazing heat pass us as my mother pushed Gwen out of the way, allowing the blast to hit the scythe's handle on her back without looking back. I nearly fell from her nudge but regained my footing and kept running.

I peered back and saw something black working its way through the wood, gaining on us rapidly. I yelled to my mother and father, but it seemed like it took an eternity for the words to escape my mouth. My mother turned to meet the aggressor, pulling the scythe from her back and swinging its blade into the locked and ready position. A clash of blades was heard as the attacker rushed her. The force knocked her back; she tumbled backward and landed on her feet, still sliding back a few inches. I finally received my first good look at our pursuer. He stood up to full height, revealing that he was amazingly tall and dressed in jagged black body armor from head to toe. His headpiece was the most frightening thing of all. It was made of two metal plates that joined at the center of his face. On each side was a slit for eye holes. No other holes were on the mask. This same pattern of near-flat metal plates was on his boots and gloves. The rest of his black suit was covered with metal plates to protect his body. I immediately remembered hearing my mother's scythe clash with steel, but I saw no sword on the man.

"Karan, go," my father said as my mother slid to a halt.

"But, I can't..." she replied. "I'm your Tala'har."

"Go! The future and destiny of our children are far more important than my life. And only you can teach them what they need to know to meet their destiny. I love you all, don't forget that."

My father's hand grasped toward us, shielding Gwen and me from more oncoming blasts.

A tear escaped from my mother's eye as she nodded in agreement and turned to run. She latched onto my sister's arm and yanked her along, with her and I watching Father. Light beams continued to rain down on us as we ran.

"It's my turn to protect you," he said as Mom yanked us into a dark cave I had not noticed before. My father rushed the attacker, flinging fast-casting spells at him but missing the man as he sped around him at speeds I didn't think were possible. The last image I saw was the stranger sticking his knee into my father's stomach. A long blade protruded from my father's back as all faded to black.

"Carrie?" Autumn's voice rang as reality rushed back into view.

"Wha?" I said. I came to with Jacob, Cristy, and Autumn, all standing around me with concern painted on their faces.

"Are you okay?" Autumn said. "We've been trying to talk to you for the last five minutes."

"Yeah, I think I might just need some water," I said. "Can I sit down?"

"Sure, make yourself at home," Jacob said. He turned and left for the kitchen.

I sat down on the couch in front of the television. Cristy sat next to me, and Autumn next to her.

"Carrie, is the heat bothering you?" Autumn said.

"I am so sorry," Cristy whispered, eyes holding back her own tears.

"How much did you see?" I whispered back.

"Enough," Cristy said.

"What?" Autumn said.

"We'll talk about it later," I said. "I'm fine for now."

Jacob quickly walked back into the room and handed me a glass of water.

"Thanks, I'm fine now," I said before taking a sip.

An awkward moment of silence filled the air. I glanced at Cristy, hoping she would get the signal to say something.

"Autumn, I've yet to see you even give your man a hug," Cristy teased.

"Oh, sorry," she stood up and wrapped her arms around Jacob. "Just Carrie scared the living hell out of me."

"I think she scared us all," Jacob said.

"Is she okay?" Lisa said as she came down the stairs, cell phone in hand.

"Yeah, she's okay," Jacob replied.

"Times like this make me wish we had a home telephone line. Two cell phones were in the house, and it took me that long to find one of them," Lisa remarked.

"You won't need it, I assure you," I said.

"Okay, if you say so," she said. She turned to Jacob and Autumn, who were still in a loose embrace. "You two do look cute together."

"Thanks," Autumn laughed lightly. "I'm surprised you aren't horrified I'm dating your brother."

"Please," she waved her hand. "Like I believe anything that whore has to say. No offense Cristy, but your sister is a whore."

"None taken, just glad there are people that agree with me," Cristy replied.

"And if you two want to get all lovey-dovey, go for it; I don't care," Lisa said. "I hope to talk to you about something if you don't mind."

"I knew she was up to something..." Jacob rolled his eyes.

"Aren't you forgetting something?" Cristy entered my mind.

"Um... no," I replied to Cristy.

She took her hand, lightly touched mine, and said in my head, "Think about it harder."

I immediately noticed the link was missing. I concentrated on what Cristy was talking about. I looked about the room, and my eyes caught Jacob and Autumn together on the small couch.

"Fuck! I forgot about Lucas...again. I was supposed to call him, wasn't I?" I said back to Cristy.

"I think that link is fucking with your mind, girl," she said to me.

"I'll be right back; I need to make a phone call before I forget again," I said aloud..

"Are you sure, Carrie?" Autumn said. "I'm worried about the heat…"

"I'll be fine, I promise," I said.

"I think Carrie should hear what I have to say, too, so I'll wait," Lisa said. "Take your time."

"But not too long!" Autumn beaconed. "You have to watch the heat!"

"I'll be fine, trust me, okay mom?" I smarted as I opened the door.

I stepped outside back into the smothering sun. I opened my umbrella and received some shielding from it. For the first time since the first day I met Autumn, I thought about hating the sun. I started to hope what Cristy said wasn't true, that I was just being absent-minded, but the proof was piling up that being forgetful in a usual way wasn't the case.

Chapter 34

I pulled out my smartphone and unlocked it. A picture of Lucas holding me from behind was on the phone's wallpaper background. If I didn't feel like I was losing my mind before, that was the piece de la resistance. I found his number in my favorites and dialed it. The phone began to ring as I placed it against my ear.

"Carrie?" his familiar, comforting voice rang.

"Hi, Lucas. I'm sorry I've been out of contact. A lot has been going on."

"I didn't bother texting; I knew you'd be busy. I understand, what's up? How is the new place and the new school?"

I wanted to say everything was great... but it wasn't.

"Things... are interesting, to say the least."

"Interesting good or interesting bad?"

"A bit of both?"

"Care to explain? I know your mom does that vague shit, and you know it won't fly with me."

"Yeah, I know. I found my charge."

"That's awesome!"

"It's not as simple as that. She doesn't know what she is, as far as I know. So, I must protect her without her knowing I'm doing it."

"That doesn't sound easy."

"It's not. I'm just glad I have her cousin Cristy to help me out. She's great, you'd like her."

"So, what is this charge of yours like? What is her name? How old is she? What does she look like? I suppose I've heard you talk so much about wanting to meet this person. Now I want to, as well."

"Well... she's... beautiful." I stopped short. My mind drew a blank. It was all I could really say at the moment.

"Carrie... do you like this girl?"

"Yeah... I guess... I think... I don't know anymore. Actually, I don't know much right now. Lucas, I have to come clean. I haven't thought about you at all for the last week or so. I don't know why..."

"Carrie, love. It's okay. You've had an exciting week..."

"No, it's not just that. I think it's the 'link'."

"What link? Oh, that link. Shit. What do you mean?"

"My link with her has developed rather rapidly. It's doing a lot more than it is supposed to. I can actually feel her emotions. And when it's not active, I return to normal. The first time it wasn't there, I finally thought of you. Whenever it's active, it seems like she is all I can think about. I'm so fucking confused right now. I'm not sure how I feel about anything. I love you so much and think I might love her too. I know that's not right, and I don't even know if it's real now; I just..."

"Carrie..." he interrupted me. "It's okay. If you have feelings for her, so be it. I mean, look at your mom. Her charge was your father, right? So, maybe this is meant to be."

"Well... it's more complicated than that. She doesn't seem to return my feelings. I doubt she's even aware of them, but everyone else seems to be. She is a bit naive, at least regarding 'love' and stuff like that. So... I set her up with a guy..."

"You did what? Why would you set up someone you have feelings for with someone else?"

"I'm not sure. At the time, I felt that if I told her how it might scare her away, and that's the last thing I need. Her life is complete hell, and I felt she needed a pleasant distraction. Now, I must watch her with this guy, and it's tearing me apart. And then there is you; I love you so..."

"Carrie. We had this talk before you left. Don't worry about me."

"I know, but..."

"But nothing. Continue, please. What is so bad about her life?"

"It's Cristy's sister, Autumn's other cousin, Sophia. To make an extremely long and complex story short, she has basically turned the entire school against her. It seems like most people believe this poor, virgin girl is a disease-ridden whore."

"That's horrible. How could anyone do that to family?"

"I don't know, but that isn't all of it. Someone is watching us. I don't know who, and I don't know what they are after. I assumed they were after Autumn, but their only aggressive movement was at me when I was alone."

"You didn't get hurt, did you?"

"No, just damaged an awesome pair of boots, no big deal. Fortunately, Mom was there to bail me out. I don't know what to do. I'm just... so confused. And the heat is killing me. That link seems to have me so focused on Autumn that I don't even notice the sun making me sick. I just seem to ignore it. I'm just... so stressed... I guess. I didn't notice until now. Maybe that's what Cristy meant when she said I needed it."

"Needed what?"

"Oh," I laughed for what felt like the first time in a century. "Cristy and I had some... fun last night. You know, just for fun, I guess. No romance or anything like that."

"I'll try to keep myself from thinking about that too much, or I might have to walk there. Since I am male, I must ask if she is hot."

"Extremely. Not normally the kind of chick I'm attracted to. Short, blonde, but has curves in the right places. Her and Autumn's mothers are twins, so they look much alike. Except Autumn is... how should I put it... a lot taller and... oh man, this is going to sound so cheesy, but more like a goddess... oh fuck I'm doing it again. I'm just..."

"In awe of her?" he completed my sentence.

I let out a sigh, "Yeah..."

"It's the same way I feel when I see you. I understand."

"Shouldn't you be the slightest bit jealous? I know she's a chick, but I've been spilling my guts about how I might love her."

246

"Carrie... understand something. Our time on this Earth is short... okay, let me rephrase that...my time on this Earth is short. I've learned that I must enjoy the time I get with the people I care about. Any time I have with them is a gift, and that's precious. My time with you was the best in my life. If you have to move on, so be it. Just don't forget, I'll always be here for you in any capacity you need me. I won't tell you to ignore how you feel for my sake. That would be selfish. There may have been a day in my life that I would have done that, but not now and never again."

"Lucas... I don't know what to say..."

"Don't say anything. Just do what you feel is right, and don't worry about me. Just know I love you and will do what I can to help you if that's anything."

"I don't know what I did to deserve you... I must have sucked off an angel or something like that..."

"If you did, that is one lucky angel."

When I returned to the living room, I hoped no one would notice the slight smearing of my makeup from the tears that came while talking to Lucas. I had done more crying than any other time in my life... well, not any other time... but close.

I looked up and saw tears streaming from Autumn's eyes and her arms visibly shaking with Jacob holding her close. Cristy held her head down. Lisa shuffled her foot, obviously uncomfortable.

"Carrie, something happened to Aunt Cassy," Cristy said. "She's badly hurt and is in a hospital up in Youngstown. Uncle Will just called. He's already called your mom and mine. Your mom will pick us up here; we'll grab my mom and head up there now."

I was speechless. Unsure what to say, I said the only thing that came to mind.

"Where the fuck is Youngstown?"

"Northeastern Ohio," Cristy replied.

"Fuck..." I gasped.

Chapter 35

My mother pulled up to the house within minutes. She was driving the car we called 'Old Reliable,' the first car she picked up when we first came to this world. It was a maroon, older Buick LeSabre. It was almost a living room on wheels, as far as sedans go, at least. I thought my mom would never drive it again, but it was not like we all fit in the Lamborghini.

"Hey, Autumn," Lisa said as Autumn was ready to get in the back seat. "I really hope everything works out. I'm so sorry."

Autumn just nodded in understanding. Jacob walked up to her, put his arms around her neck, pulled her close, and whispered a few things I couldn't hear, but I was sure it was something to the degree of 'It will be okay' and other comforts of the sort. Autumn did nothing but nod and ducked into the back seat.

"See you later, guys," I said.

"Later," Cristy said.

"And guys," Lisa said. "Don't even worry about what I said I wanted to talk about. It's not important."

Cristy nodded, "We can get together when we get back."

We both got into the back seat. Cristy went first and sat in the middle, and I followed. My mother pulled the car into drive and drove off.

"Autumn, I already stopped at your house and grabbed a few things from Mina. She packed your blades and some clothes," my mom said.

"Why would she need blades?" I asked.

"The same reason yours and mine are also in the trunk. Cassandra and William were attacked when they arrived at the house. The place was on fire. By the way I understand it, William met the attacker head-on while Cassandra ran into the house to get the book she was after. Once she secured the book, she returned to assist her husband. The attacker knocked her down a hill with a bladed weapon. I think it was a slash to the stomach."

"Oh no," Autumn muttered. "Not that hill."

"Oh shit, if it is the hill I'm thinking of, that is one long tumble," Cristy said.

"We need to get your mom, Cristy, because Cassandra may need a blood transplant for the surgery required to remove the debris from her wounds."

"Why can't they just find another donor?" I asked.

"Apparently, Telosians like Cassandra have a special blood type, according to William. Even though she and Megara are twin sisters, her doctor is afraid they might have very different blood because of their different ability types," Mom continued. "So, Autumn might be a closer match because she and Cassandra apparently have more similar abilities. "

"Who the hell is her doctor? What would they know about Telosians?" I said.

"Theresa," Cristy said. "Theresa has been the family doctor long before we were born. She delivered me, Autumn, Sophia, and Jason, and she has cared for us all when there has been a big problem. She's an old friend of my dad's."

"She's an immortal, I take?" I said.

"Yep, slightly older than Dad, I think. She still treats him like a kid, but that could be because of his size. That's why Aunt Cassy's in Youngstown. Theresa has been working at St. Elizabeth Hospital for a long time."

"I just hope this car holds up for the trip; it is ancient," Mom said.

We then pulled up to Cristy's house. My mother beeped the horn, and Megara rushed out of the door, holding a suitcase and a duffle bag. Joseph tailed her out of the house.

"I can take you. You don't need to ride with them!" Joseph said.

"No, Joseph. I don't want you upsetting my sister. Now go back to the house before you make a scene."

"Joe, shut the fuck up and get back in here," an unseen male voice echoed from within the house.

"When have I ever given a shit about making a scene?" he replied.

I could almost see the eyes rolling from the back of my mother's head.

"He wants a scene; I'll give him one," she mumbled as she stepped out of the car.

"What is she doing?" Cristy asked.

"I don't have the foggiest," I replied.

"Uh… Joe… get back in here… now," the unseen voice warned.

My mother stomped up to Joseph and socked him in the jaw, sending him tumbling to the floor. He gawked up at her, flabbergasted.

"That's for hitting on my teenage daughter!" she said. "Come on, Megara, we have to go."

"Does she do that to every older guy that hits on you?" Cristy asked.

"Nope, this would be the first. If she did, she'd be in jail... a lot."

"Goodbye, Joseph," Megara called out as she entered the car's passenger door.

Mom hopped in as well, and soon we were on our way.

"I'm sorry for him hitting on Carrie; he can be such a slimeball sometimes," Megara said.

"Oh, I didn't hit him because of that. I just felt like it, and he was getting in our way," Mom replied.

"I won't argue that he deserves it sometimes," Megara sighed. "I know we haven't been formally introduced. I'm Megara, but you can call me Meg."

"I'm Karen, and I'm sure you've met my daughter, Carrie," Mom said.

"Yes, she and I had a nice little chat when they stopped at our house yesterday," Megara said. "Autumn, how are you holding up, dear?"

Autumn simply nodded her head.

"Karen, if you wouldn't mind stopping, I can fit in the back better than Autumn. With her long, beautiful legs, she should be upfront."

"It's okay, Aunt Meg, I'm fine back here. Let's get to Mom as fast as possible," Autumn finally spoke.

250

"All right, if you insist," Megara replied.

"Get comfortable, ladies; this is going to be a twenty-hour drive," Mom said. "I just hope Cassandra can last that long without a transplant. We really should be flying in, but it would be tough getting our weapons by the TSA. Are they really worth risking Cassandra's life for?"

"She'll be fine for the moment," Megara said. "Theresa has some healing abilities to keep my sister stable while we make it there."

"Just let me know when you need me to take over," I said.

"Not necessary," Mom said, in that 'Tala'har business' tone I remember her using with Dad occasionally. "I've made longer drives than this, you know that."

"Since you have at least two other people with licenses in this car, there is no real need for you to drive the entire length," I argued.

"Karen, maybe you should listen to her," Megara said. "I know I'm a guest here and appreciate what you are doing for us, but I think you should take turns driving with Cristy and Carrie. We'll have a better time if each driver gets some rest."

"Mom, it's touching you want to take care of everyone like you used to take care of me, Dad, and Gwen, but please, share some of the burdens," I said.

"Fine, I guess you are right," she sighed. "Megara, you want a turn?"

Cristy immediately laughed.

"No, sorry, I can't help. As you can guess by my daughter's laughter, I'm an atrocious driver," Megara sighed. "I've failed the driver's exam more times than I can count."

"Are you ready, mom?" Cristy said before whistling a nautical tune.

"Don't you start, young lady!" Megara mockingly scolded.

Cristy burst into laughter, interrupting her tune.

"I don't get it," Mom said blankly.

"You don't want to know," I chuckled.

"I'm assuming it's kind of mean," Mom laughed.

"It's okay," Megara said. "I've been trying to drive ever since they came out with the automatic transmission. So, I'm pretty much a failure when it comes to that."

After that, things went quiet. I glanced at Autumn and didn't need the link to know how she felt. A constant state of worry hung over her mind, completely evident on her face. Cristy eventually took Autumn's hand and clasped it in her own. I would occasionally peek up into the front seat and examine my mother. I could see her eyes scanning the traffic around us. I wondered what she was thinking, but I was fairly certain Dad was on her mind. I know she didn't want Autumn to lose one of her parents. She didn't want her to feel what Gwen and I felt.

I spent most of the initial ride in an uneasy sleep. While I was asleep, I found myself nearly overwhelmed by Autumn's roller coaster of emotions. She continued to slide from constant worry to rage.

I eventually fell victim to sleep as well and woke about ten hours into our drive when I felt the car stop. I found Cristy with her legs on me and her head on Autumn's lap. Autumn's head hung low, and her hair fell before her eyes, so she looked asleep. My link told me better. I could feel her mind racing. What about what, I wasn't entirely sure. I was certain some of those thoughts involved tearing apart whoever hurt her mother.

"Okay, ladies, if you need to use the restroom or grab a snack, now is the time," Mom said from the driver's seat.

"Mom, I'm driving next, okay?" I said.

"If you insist, kiddo," she said.

"I'll get in the back then," Megara said. "I'm not much use up here in front; I'm not a very good navigator."

"Hey, shorty, wake up," I shook Cristy.

"But Mommy, I don't want to go to school... I wanna stay and snuggle with Aileen," Cristy said with her eyes shut. '

I shook her a bit harder, just to be playful.

"Wha?" she awoke with a snap.

"You weren't awake?" I said.

"No, why?" Cristy said.

"Cause you said you didn't want to go to school and you would rather stay home with Aileen."

"Well... I would... so sue me," she laughed.

"I swear, girl," Megara said. "I've been saying for years that your fascination with that girl's behind is more than just a fascination with her behind."

"Is not!" Cristy stuck her tongue out at her mother.

"You just keep telling yourself that, dear," Megara said. She turned to the back seat. "Autumn, honey, are you awake?"

"Yes," Autumn replied simply.

Everyone left the car, and we found ourselves at a truck stop as the sun began to set. Attached to the gas station was a McDonald's. Mom grabbed the nozzle from the pump beside the car and refilled the tank. The rest of us found our way into the gas station portion of the facility.

"I don't know about you," Cristy turned to me, "but I'm in the mood for some chicken nuggets."

"So 'some' means something like fifty, right?" I said.

"Oh, you know me too well," she giggled.

"No more than thirty, missy," Megara chimed in. "I don't know where you keep it all, but the last thing you need is for your metabolism to slow down before you stop aging."

"But... but... Momma... I'm a growing girl!" she whined.

Megara couldn't hold a straight face, and neither could I. We both burst into laughter. I wasn't sure, but even Autumn might have cracked a smile.

"What? I am too growing!" she almost sounded genuinely wounded.

"Maybe in increments only Smurfs can measure!" Megara laughed even harder.

"That's not funny, Mommy!" Cristy mocked. "I'm not going on no more trips with you, ever! Daddy doesn't make fun of my height!"

"Daddy," I said. "Doesn't have room to talk."

"Yeah, at least I'm small and cute.... he's small and something, I'm just not sure what," Cristy remarked.

"I could probably come up with at least fifty 'somethings,' but I'll keep my mouth shut," Autumn grumbled.

There were those claws again.

"Autumn, you can speak your mind in front of me," Megara assured. "Anything you can say about my husband he most likely deserves, tenfold."

"I'd prefer not," Autumn replied. "The more I talk about it, the more I'll think about it, and the more likely I'd end up taking it out on Sophia since I see her daily, and I don't think anyone wants that."

"But bottling it up isn't healthy, either," Megara said.

"I'd smash his car to bits if I didn't put my heart and soul into its construction," Autumn growled.

"You didn't have to build that for him," Megara replied.

"Yeah, but we were going to lose the house if I didn't, and Dad wouldn't have taken the money from him any other way."

Megara just sighed and let the subject go. We stepped up to the counter and placed our orders. Despite her mother's protests, Cristy did order her fifty chicken nuggets, two large fries, and a large drink. Autumn left the line and found a table without ordering anything. I wasn't sure if I'd be hungry either if I were in her shoes. Mom eventually joined us in the line, and we all joined Autumn with our food.

Megara glanced over to Autumn without any food before her and sighed again.

"My mom blames herself for most of the crap Autumn goes through," Cristy spoke to me through my mind.

"I know, she told me while you were upstairs yesterday," I replied in my mind.

254

"I wish she wouldn't take all of this so hard. It's not her fault. She can't control Sophia or Dad," Cristy said.

"I told her that myself," I said back.

"It doesn't do any good. In the end, she's an Alexander, through and through. Stubborn as fuck but beautiful, so she gets away with it," Cristy's words bounced into my mind.

"Is everyone in your family this stubborn?" I asked mentally.

"Well, you've met just about everyone but Jason, Autumn's Uncle Dan, and Uncle Kart, so, yeah," Cristy said telepathically. "Dan's nearly as bad as his brother, sometimes worse when it comes to this stuff. He has always had enough money, even for being an unemployed drifter. I really do owe it to Aunt Mina to find out where the fuck he goes. She doesn't deserve this shit."

"Men, you can't live with them, and you can't kill them, either," I said.

"Who says you can't?" Cristy said.

"Good point. At least ones like Autumn's uncles, you can't," I said.

"I don't know… with my dad's shenanigans, I've fought off the urge to send him on a one-way walk off a cliff…" Cristy replied.

Chapter 36

We quietly ate our meal. I wished I could have persuaded Autumn to eat something, but I knew she wouldn't. I hoped she would eat something before she passed out.

Mom rushed into the driver's seat before I could get to it, and we left the truck stop and started our quiet drive north. As we traversed the central portion of the United States, the rolling hills became larger and larger. The scenery became less tropical and more frequently coniferous the farther we drove north.

"Okay, Mom, hand it over," I said after about twelve hours had passed on the road.

"I'm fine, Carrie," she said.

"Pull over…" I growled. "You were supposed to let me drive hours ago."

Karen rolled her eyes and brought the car to a stop on the shoulder of the road.

I jumped into the driver's seat, and Mom took the passenger's seat. Megara took my place in the back.

"The rest in the back did me good. I figure I would be okay for eight hours, at least," I said. "You okay with taking the rest of the way, short stuff?"

Cristy replied with a thumbs up as she assumed her stretched-out position over her mother and cousin's laps.

A few hours later, we found ourselves twisting and turning through the mountainous curves of West Virginia as we passed midnight and headed for the morning. I had never visited this part of the country and was in awe of the beautiful, forest-dense, hilly countryside. Majestic conifers lined the mountain slopes with oak and other types of trees spread throughout the thick forests. It was spring in this part of the country, so the deciduous trees were already awakened from their winter nap and spreading their thick green plumage. I could only see what the car's headlamps would allow, but what I saw was breathtaking. It made me reminisce about the world I came from and the world I still couldn't help but miss.

"Carrie, we're being followed," my mother snapped me out of envisaging.

I glanced at the rearview and saw a large semi-trailer truck barreling toward us.

"Who the fuck is that?" I exclaimed.

"I think it's obvious," Cristy said. "It's gotta be Thomas." Cristy then winced in pain.

"Are you okay?" Megara exclaimed when she saw Cristy's flinch. Cristy nodded in the affirmative.

An arm appeared from the driver's side of the cab, with a sawed-off, handheld shotgun, and attempted to hit our back windshield. The pellets hit, but with not enough force to even cause cracks. Megara and Cristy ducked instinctively, but Autumn remained motionless.

"Wasting ammo is almost as bad as wasting food," Cristy spat as she slid between Autumn and Megara. "Only Thomas would be dumb enough to fire one of those at that range."

"Can we get to the trunk from the backseat?" Megara asked. "Cristy might be able to take out his tires if she can get to her guns."

"He's got mental shielding now, Carrie, I can't do shit…" Cristy said to me telepathically.

"If we can't get to them, I have my Deringer. I can always try with it," Cristy said out loud.

"You're not going to need to do that, honey. I told William I would get you safely to Youngstown, and I'm a woman of my word. Let me handle this. Carrie, speed up and keep going straight," my mother said.

I did as I was told and rammed the accelerator. I was starting to outpace the giant truck. We sped past a pair of police cruisers. As the massive truck rolled by them, they tossed their lights on and took up pursuit.

"Well, that's convenient. I'm not sure what they can do about it at the moment. I'm not stopping…" I said.

As the police approached the truck, Thomas jerked it into a slide and released its trailer. The trailer tipped over, tumbled, and smashed into both tailing police cars.

"Those poor men..." Megara mumbled.

"He was planning that. You can't release a trailer like that. It takes preparation," Mom said.

"How the hell do you know that?" I said.

"I've spent some time with some rather... handsome truckers..." she replied.

"Why the fuck did I ask?" I reprimanded myself.

Without the extra weight of the trailer, Thomas's truck began to move faster, quickly closing the distance.

"We aren't going to be able to outrun him like this," Mom said. "And I don't know how long this old car can handle this stress. Carrie, get off at the next exit and use the curve to get us some space on him."

"Right," I nodded. I glanced behind me to see how close Thomas was and caught another glimpse of Autumn. She still hadn't reacted. She sat in a slouched position with her head down.

"Pull over, ladies, you can't outrun me with that piece o' rubbish," Thomas's grizzled British accent could be heard over a loudspeaker. "Gimme, Carrie, and you all can live for another day."

"Since when is he after you?" Mom exclaimed as she produced a small dagger from the glove box.

"Since the last time we saw him..." I trailed off.

"And why didn't you tell me that?!" she growled as she held the dagger tight, and it began to glow. "I swear you and I are going to have a nice long talk when all of this is done."

"Hey, a lot of shit has happened lately, gimme a break," I swore.

An exit finally appeared, and I took it. It curved around a hill, which I navigated as fast as possible without throwing us off the road. Thomas struggled to keep up, ramming into the railing but still falling behind as his rig couldn't keep up with the nimbler handling of the old luxury car.

As we sped away from Thomas, he struggled to recover speed from the exit. Mom rolled down the window and stood up out of the car. As Thomas's truck finally started to catch up, I saw the small glowing weapon speed toward the truck. It stuck into the big rig's grill. Even more light emanated from it, and it exploded, setting off a fiery reaction that turned the massive vehicle into a fireball, which tumbled from the road and down a hill. An explosion lit up the night sky after the truck rolled out of visibility. Smoke rose into the sky, clouding the clear night.

Everyone but Autumn let out a collective sigh of relief as we sped away from the disaster.

Chapter 37

Most of the rest of the trip north went by faster than I thought it should have, but I was busy navigating the vehicle. I occasionally checked for our invisible 'friends' and found nothing. I wondered if the method was working because I never had a chance to practice using my sword instead of the ring. I kept looking behind us, expecting Thomas to show up with another big truck. First-degree burns probably weren't enough to slow him down. Fortunately for us, it never happened.

After about five hours on the road since our last stop, Autumn finally fell asleep. It was probably far past when she was used to going to bed. I spent a good deal of time hoping she didn't pass out due to hunger. I didn't know if she ate that morning, but I did know she hadn't had a scrap since.

Stretched out over Megara and Autumn was Cristy, with her arms wrapped around her mother's left arm. Megara used her free hand to caress her daughter's head with a gentle smile. Megara was obviously focusing on her daughter to keep her mind off her possibly dying twin sister.

"I love you, Mommy," Cristy mumbled in her sleep.

"I love you too," she replied.

We finally crossed the Ohio border around eight a.m. on Monday. As I was reaching my endurance limit, I searched for a good place to pull over and get breakfast.

"Carrie hit the next exit. There is a wonderful little restaurant right off the highway," Megara said from the backseat.

"Sure," I said. I looked over to Mom and was surprised to see her asleep. "Wake up, people, we're stopping in a minute here."

As Megara had said, once I pulled off the freeway, we found the restaurant directly off the exit. It was a quaint-looking place, built from logs. It appeared surprisingly busy; the dirt parking lot was loaded with cars. I pulled into the small dirt lot and parked in one of the few available spaces in the back. My passengers slowly awoke as I disengaged the engine.

"Wow, that nap felt good," Cristy said as she stretched. "I forgot how comfortable you are, Mom."

"Well, I've got big enough pillows," Megara replied as she looked down at her chest.

The fact is, all the Telosians I had seen so far had rather large 'pillows.' It was funny how they all had the same breast size relative to their body size. In other words, Autumn's could be classified as weapons. Learning to fight with those monsters hanging from her chest had to be a tremendous task.

We entered the small restaurant, and a husky, elderly woman approached us.

"Five?" she said, in a slightly raspy, 'I've smoked far too much in my life' voice.

"Yes," Mom nodded.

"This way," the waitress turned and weaved through the small, crowded restaurant.

This establishment mainly attracted travelers. Everyone here looked like how we felt, tired and sick of being in the car. Beyond the travelers, mostly, older people seemed to frequent the place. I was sure Cristy and I were quite the eyesore for these people. They were likely disdained by the fact that I was a goth and Cristy was wearing barely anything under her leather jacket. The halter and skirt she wore left visible far more than it covered.

The place was simple in design; it was a large square room with tables and chairs. The walls were papered with a simple striped pattern that was rather dingy, probably signaling it was applied long before I was born. The tables and chairs all looked like they were made from the same oak, whose luster had long since been worn away but were all still structurally sound. Each table had a small lantern lit with a tiny oil-powered flame. On the far end of the room was a brick fireplace with smaller tables near it. The smell of the place reminded me of home, back when we all huddled around a fire at night while Dad told us stories that Mom constantly reminded us were nothing but hogwash. It took everything within me not to sink into an abyss of depression.

The waitress showed us to our table, and we all sat down. She handed us menus and pulled out her pen and paper tablet.

"What can I get you ladies to drink?" she asked.

"I think I'll go with some coffee; the stronger, the better," Mom said.

"Same here," Megara added.

"Orange juice, please," Cristy chirped.

"I'll go with some milk," I said.

"Just water," Autumn mumbled.

"I'll get that for you while you look over the menu," she said. She stopped dead in her tracks and turned around.

"Miss," she said, gazing directly at Megara. "Did you used to come in here with your mother, sister, and father?" she asked. "If so, you grew up to look just like your mother."

"Yep, that was me," Megara nervously laughed. And these two lovely young ladies are my cousins."

"Oh, yeah... cousin, right," Cristy said.

"It's good to see folks from all over coming back, especially when they were here as kids. Reminds us we're doing our jobs." The waitress walked away.

"I sometimes forget that I don't age," Megara whispered. "I hate making up stories like that."

Mom shrugged, "Eh, what can you do? You can't just avoid going places you used to go just because someone might notice you haven't aged."

"I guess you're right," she sighed. She looked over to Autumn, who was staring into the face of the table. "Don't expect to leave here without eating, missy. When your mother and father aren't around, you know the rules. I'm in charge, and you are eating something, do you understand?"

"Yes, ma'am," she said in a near whisper.

"Oh... my... god," Cristy said, gawking at the menu with mouth wide open and eyes nearly bulging out of her skull. "They have venison as a topping for omelets.... I think I died and went to meat heaven."

"You had the same reaction when you were a little girl... then you asked your father when you could go out and hunt a deer," Megara reminisced.

"Yeah, that idea was dropped fast when I found out that I would have to cover myself in deer piss to attract one."

"I think he just made that up, so he didn't have to get up early," Megara said.

"Crap..." Cristy sighed.

The waitress eventually returned with expectant eyes and lorded over us, "So, what can I get yins?"

"I'll have the omelet with everything on it," Cristy said. "A plate of pancakes with fruit on top, a side of home fries.... oh, and can I have some bacon and sausage, along with some French toast, too."

The waitress opened her mouth but never got out a word.

"And I also want some scrambled cheese eggs with a side of toast and some ham... yeah, don't forget the ham," Cristy rattled off.

"Honey, is this all for you?" the waitress grinned.

"Yes, ma'am," Cristy said with a massive smile.

"How does your mother afford to feed you? More importantly, where do you keep it all?" the waitress laughed.

Megara sighed.

"How about you?" the waitress looked at Autumn.

"Just some toast..." Autumn said quietly.

Megara said nothing but sent a sharp glare at Autumn.

"...and some sausage, with syrup," Autumn added on.

"Are you sure you don't want anything else, child?" the waitress questioned. "I know a tall drink of water like yourself needs more than that to eat."

"She'd like a plate of pancakes as well," Megara cut in. "You know us girls, always worried about our figures."

The waitress gargled a laugh that could rattle paint off of a car, "Oh, sweetheart, if I ever had a body like yours, I wouldn't worry too much about it. The worst thing you have to worry about is growing taller."

We left the small restaurant as soon as everyone was finished eating. Megara could force Autumn to get more food but couldn't force her to eat it. She barely ate any of the pancakes that Megara added to her order and only half of the toast and meat. As for Cristy, she once again packed all of her food away faster than anyone else. She skipped to the car like a little girl, joyous about her encounter with the salty temptress that was venison. She even picked up some venison jerky they sold at the counter and carried its plain brown paper bag like a child holding a new toy. Sometimes, it seemed as if the girl only thought of two things: sex and food. I knew it wasn't anywhere near accurate, but how things appeared was amusing.

Cristy slid into the driver's seat and adjusted it to accommodate her small stature. Mom sat in the front passenger seat again, and I was between Autumn and Megara. I took my arm and wrapped it around Autumn, pulling her closer. Autumn bent her head toward mine and started crying as Cristy turned the key.

I couldn't help but love being this close to her, even though it was the worst of occasions. I could spend the rest of my life holding her. I just hoped that one day, it would be because she wanted to be held by me, not because she was engulfed in sorrow.

I should have paid more attention to the surroundings as we traveled northward. My entire focus was on Autumn. When I finally glanced out the window, I saw that Ohio didn't look too different from other places we had traveled through. The only thing that struck me was the number of farms in this state. Even with the little bit I had been paying attention, I had spotted at least a dozen farms, and around half had corn crops.

About an hour into our Buckeye State trip, Autumn finally said, "What if she dies?"

"I'm sure that won't happen," I replied, not knowing what else to say.

"But what if, Carrie? She always tried to teach me to be prepared for anything, but I'm not prepared for this. There is still so much she hasn't taught me and so much I haven't told her. Sometimes, I wonder if she knows me at all..."

264

"I don't think any of us tell our mothers everything," I said.

"But I should have..." Autumn cried. "I'm a coward. I'm just afraid... afraid of so much."

"You're not a coward. We can't predict the future," I explained. "We just have to try to do better once we know we're wrong."

"It feels like Dad can tell the future," she said. "The day before they left, he sat me down and talked about what would occur if something happened to either of them. He said I should stay with you and your mom if anything happened to them."

"We did discuss that; I thought it was strange, too," my mother chimed in.

"I hate to say it, sweetheart, but it would be best if you did that. You know I can't give you the sort of home you deserve," Megara said, staring out the window. I didn't need to see her reflection to know tears started to stream down her face.

"What's really strange," Autumn wiped her eyes with her wrist, "is that even if something happened to only Mom, he would want me to stay with you guys."

At first, I couldn't fathom why the hell he would say that. Of course, the more I thought about it, the more it made sense. I had no idea how to convey it to Autumn without saying too much.

"I just don't understand why he wouldn't want me around..." Autumn cried.

"I don't think that is the case," my mom said.

"Then what could it be?" she said with a harsher, frustrated tone.

"Honey, how much do you know about your own abilities?" Mom asked.

"Not much, I'm afraid. Only the little bits my mother has told me about."

"You, my dear, are essentially a sorceress," Mom explained. "This gives you all sorts of wonderful abilities, some of which I'm sure you can't even fathom. But it also makes you vulnerable."

"Vulnerable to what?" Autumn asked.

"Spiritual attacks," Mom answered. "Most magic users get their power from having an open connection to the spiritual world through 'the veil' that protects most people. Because of this connection, you have your powers, but it leaves you without the veil's full protection. Without knowing how to protect yourself from such attacks, you are very vulnerable, mainly while you sleep. So, your mother placed shields around wherever you and your family dwell to protect you from outside attacks. Without her, these shields will fall."

"Why hasn't she told me about these shields?" she asked, tears still falling.

"Autumn, I have known you for only a short time, and I can tell you are very much a 'worry wart,' Mom said. "She most likely didn't want you to have to worry about things of that nature if it wasn't necessary."

I was always amazed at Mom's ability to skirt the truth without telling a single lie. This time, the item being skirted was what could happen if Autumn were attacked from the spiritual world.

"I still don't understand. Why you guys? There are no shields without Mom, so why does it matter that I'm with you and not him?"

"Honey, it's because of what I am," my mother continued. "I am what is known as a Tala'har, a protector of wizards from the world I came from. That's how I was able to send that charged knife at that truck."

"From the world you came from..." Autumn stumbled.

"Yes, as in, Carrie and I are not from this world. I hope you are not too upset about her not telling you that. It isn't something we make common knowledge."

It may not have shown, but I was sweating bullets. If Autumn eventually put two and two together about me being a Tala'har, then she might realize the reason I was there in the first place. I wasn't sure how she would react to that.

"So... you can protect me from these things?" she said.

"Better than most can, yes. My order has special measures. I have been taught that if one of our charges becomes vulnerable like you are now, I will

266

have to set up a temporary means of protecting you tonight, for most likely, we will be staying in a hotel."

I realized my mother never taught me these 'special measures.'

"I see... I don't want you to get me wrong," she wiped more tears. "I think I could enjoy living with you and Carrie... just my father was being so vague, I was afraid that he wouldn't be able to look at me if Mom was gone. I just felt like he was... rejecting me."

"I can assure you that is not the case. And I'm sure your mother will be fine as soon as we get you and your aunt to Youngstown," Mom reassured.

After that, the ride was silent. I held Autumn close, and I could feel her nervousness and the rest of her emotions seeping into my consciousness. I wondered if what my mother had said about spiritual attacks scared her, but more than likely, it was the fact that her mother could die, and her life would change forever. I couldn't help thinking how it would be to live with Autumn, but I didn't want that ever to happen. That would mean Cassandra would have to die. The last thing I would like is to see Autumn grieve her mother. I knew what it was like to lose a parent, and it was something I didn't want to ever wish on someone else, especially someone I cared for as much as her.

Chapter 38

As Cristy navigated the twists and turns of the freeway, I could tell when we had entered Youngstown before I saw the sign that welcomed us to that hole-in-the-wall city. I could see decrepit old storefronts from the highway and houses that looked like they hadn't been occupied in years, causing the whole ride to take to a new level of depression. The highway seemed to plunge directly into the city's center. An oddly well-cared-for university was in the town with a massive stadium that loomed overhead, visible for miles. The bright red letters of YSU were illuminated on a tall building, showing rather brightly even in the late morning sky.

When we exited the freeway, I wondered how long it would take to get to the hospital, but the question answered itself. A tall building with a blue cross stood vibrantly on the skyline. For a city that was so desolate, it seemed proud to advertise its hopes in the sky.

Around the hospital was what looked to be low-income housing, many of which were falling apart. I found it odd for such a facility to be in such a neighborhood, but I was sure the neighborhood grew around the hospital, not the other way around.

Cristy seemed to know exactly where she was going when she pulled us into a parking garage. The automatic gate opened, and she pulled the car through and found a parking spot.

Autumn sprung to life out of my arms and the car. Everyone else slowly stretched their legs and stepped out. Autumn was about to walk ahead but stopped and seemed to think better. We crossed the street together and entered through hospital's main entrance.

Just inside the main entrance was a counter with a few secretaries to answer people's questions. Just before we could approach them, William appeared from our left. If it was possible for the man to age, he must have deteriorated twenty years in the last few days. His hair was more disheveled than usual, and he was heavily bearded. Black circles surrounded his eyes like whirlpools.

"Dad!" Autumn cried as she lunged into his arms. He wrapped his arms around his daughter.

"How is she? Where is she?" Autumn scrambled in tears.

"She's stable, but Theresa is afraid if they don't operate soon, we could be facing major infections."

Almost on cue, a shapely, beautiful, dark-complexed brunette in a white lab coat appeared behind Autumn and William.

"Hello," she said to us. "I'm Dr. Theresa Smith, Cassandra's doctor."

There was no way this very Greek-looking beauty had the last name 'Smith,' at least natively. It was obviously an alias if it wasn't her married name. What was it with everyone associated with this family being hot as hell?

Before we could say anything, the doctor said, "There isn't much time. Autumn, Meg, I will need blood from both of you. I'll have to test for compatibility on both, and we won't have time to waste if Megara isn't compatible. There is a lot of debris that has worked its way deep into her wounds, and we must operate as soon as we can. I don't know if she's strong enough to fight an infection."

Autumn and Megara said nothing and followed Theresa. William let them go and held his hands out in front of the rest of us.

"I need to talk to all of you while they do that," he said.

Cristy stared into William's eyes, "Is this the asshole that hurt Aunt Cassy?"

"How... did you know? Where did you see this man?" William stuttered.

She stepped close to her uncle and said softly, "I pulled that image I showed you out of Carrie's mind. It's the same asshole that killed her father."

"What?" my mother and I said simultaneously.

"Let's go someplace where there are fewer prying ears. The intensive care waiting room was empty the last time I was there. Let us hope it remains that way."

William led us to an elevator. Fortunately, when we entered, no one was in it. I looked over at Mom and saw that she was utterly shocked.

"William, this man you saw... killed my husband. I've explained to you that we are from another world. Does that mean he followed us here... and we've brought him on to you and yours?" Mom muttered.

"If anything, it was your future association with us that brought him on to you," William said.

"I always assumed it was one of King Gregor's men... but I've never seen anyone who worked for him fight with such skill... and his strange armor didn't feel like it was from our world either."

"Then my presumption is probably correct," William sighed. "I'm sorry."

"You have nothing to apologize for," I said. "When we catch this dick, he'll be the one held accountable."

The elevator came to a halt, and William led us through a few turns until we found the waiting room. It was deserted just as he had said.

"It's hard to say what this man wants," William said as he sat down. "He's attacked you and us. Also, when I was battling him, he had the same sort of mental protection as those pressuring Autumn and Carrie. So, we can't be sure of his motive, but I'm sure Autumn has something to do with it."

"And Thomas has it too now," Cristy said. "I tried to control him on the highway. It hurt."

"Thomas was after you on the way here!?" William exclaimed.

"Yeah, but Mrs. A. handled him like a total badass," Cristy said.

"And he made it clear he was after my daughter," Mom glared at me.

"So that must mean he is working with the man in black armor, but what does he want? Why attack us?" William said.

"I don't care what he wants," I said. "I want him dead."

"A bullet through that fucker's brain does sound good," Cristy added.

William let out a long sigh, "I should have put an end to this when I took him on, but I'm afraid I do not have the skills to defeat him. As you know, he fights with retractable blades from the hands, knees, and even on both feet, extending from his toes. His hand-to-hand combat was unparalleled. Had that
270

been his only talent, I could have been victorious... but I'm afraid he also has magic at his disposal."

"What type of magic?" Mom asked.

"He seems to favor lightning," he replied. "He can use it for both offense and defense as well. I did score a hit on him, but some sort of lightning shield repulsed my blade. It took all my effort to keep it in my hands."

"We have our own magic to fight him with," Mom said. "I just hope I've improved enough to take him on myself. What happened next, William?"

"Cassandra came from the house, attacking him as well. If you weren't aware, she has a few offensive spells at her disposal. He was able to slash her in the stomach and send her reeling down a hill that runs alongside the property. He then retreated into the trees."

"So, he didn't take the book?" Cristy asked.

"No... he injured Cassandra and left..."

"It was to lure us here..." Mom said. "But he would have to incredible knowledge of your family for that theory to pan out.

"Why go through all that trouble when he could have just come after us in Miami while you were gone?" I said.

William sat silently for a few moments. He seemed to be contemplating something.

"He doesn't want to engage Mina or Krojo..." William finally spoke.

"Why?" I cocked my head.

"Because Mina is a powerful kunoichi with jutsu at her disposal, and Krojo is the master who taught her. I excel at the physical sides of the art of ninjutsu, but they can use the spiritual weapons that made shinobi the talk of legend. My grandfather has told me that the mental powers I received from birth interfere with my ability to my ability to use those spells. Daniel is gifted with telekinesis, and he, too, has difficulty with jutsu. Mina and Krojo have no such difficulties and could easily disable his lightning shield with counter-jutsu."

"All that work to avoid Aunt Mina and that pervy old man..." Cristy said. "She's so going to want to hear this. And we won't hear the end of it..."

"It also put us on the open road, where Thomas was given a chance to take Carrie," Mom sighed. "Could they just be after her?"

"I sure it's more complicated than that, Mom," I reassured. "I'm a glorified bodyguard. And if he was really after me, he would have ignored Dad and followed us into the cave. But he spun around Dad and...." I couldn't continue the sentence... I fought hard not to choke up.

Mom put her hand on my shoulder, "All we can say conclusively is there is much we don't know."

We sat silently in the waiting room for a moment. William hung his head low and eventually spoke up.

"I'm afraid I'm a failure as a husband... and a father..." he said quietly.

"Where do you come up with?!" Cristy exclaimed.

"I couldn't protect my wife, and I cannot protect my youngest... I could barely provide for Jason...and..."

"William," my mother said, touching his shoulder. "This world and its rules aren't made for the fair play people like us expect. I had an incredible amount of help to ensure we could survive here. And I know you are too proud to take that sort of help."

"Yes, and that is yet another one of my failings..." William trailed off for a moment. He looked at me, "Not to change the subject, but I do have some bad news that, in the end, will make your job easier in the short term. Did Autumn tell you that I asked if something were to happen to Cassandra in specific, that she would have to come to stay with you and your mother?"

"Yeah..." I said. "And we also had to dispel the idea she got in her head that if her mother died, you would want nothing to do with her."

"Oh... my," William sighed. "I must be more careful in how I speak to her. She's far more fragile than I expect sometimes. I don't need to defend myself by saying her perception is incorrect. If anything, I would want her closer. I wasn't sure how to tell her the truth without revealing more than I intended to."

"Well, you are rather fortunate that Mom is very adept at that," I replied.

"I'm not sure if that's a compliment or an insult..." Mom said. "To make a long story short, I said because she is essentially a sorceress with an open connection to the other side, she is vulnerable to spiritual attacks, mainly while she sleeps unless she is shielded."

"Which is true. I didn't think to put it that way," William sighed again. "The point being, with Cassandra being so weak, Theresa had to remove the shielding from our home. If Autumn stays there, she will be vulnerable. I will unfortunately require your talents in shielding her, Karen."

"Our home is her home, as far as I'm concerned," Mom said.

William let out another long sigh, "Here I am, unable to protect her again. I am not worthy to be her father..."

"Will you stop beating yourself up, Uncle Will," Cristy jumped in. "Let's face it, Autumn is a gentle, fragile creature at heart. You've been charged into turning a gentle creature into a warrior, and, for the most part, you've done one hell of a job. Yeah, you've fucked up here and there, but what parent doesn't? The only thing I'll fault you for is underestimating her. Cause it seems like whenever you underestimate her, you hurt her in the process."

"Are you trying to say we've sheltered her too much?" he replied.

"Fuck yes," Cristy answered. "You should have told her to beat the tar out of my sister years ago, and we might not be in the mess we're in now. Yeah, she's family... so what? Family doesn't treat family like that, and Sophia deserves anything Autumn could throw at her. In other words, you underestimated her ability to use just enough force and not too much. And look what it caused."

"You must understand our reasoning for asking her to act this way..." William started. "It was when she broke that girl's hand... when we visited the girl in the hospital... she just kept rambling about Autumn having glowing fire-red eyes."

"I've seen her eyes glow blue... but not red," I said.

"Yeah, me too," Cristy stated. "What the hell is that supposed to mean?"

"It is said that when Alexandral inhabits an incarnate, their eyes glow fire-red," William said solemnly.

"Oh shit," Cristy said.

"Oh fuck," I gasped. "Does that mean..."

"Yes, it means just what you think," William interrupted. "Alexandral took control of Autumn and broke that poor girl's hand. I know my daughter would never use such extreme force for something of that sort. Alexandral, on the other hand, most likely would. That young lady who tried to punch Autumn moved out of the area shortly after her hand was broken. I have a feeling she refused to go to school unless it was somewhere else. I saw the fear in her eyes myself."

"So that's why you've told her to handle things this way," I said. "If she uses force, you fear that Alexandral will show up and overdo it."

"Exactly. Fortunately, we've never seen it happen again," William said, "but I won't doubt it will happen again for a second. Therefore, we especially don't want her fighting Sophia."

"Because Sophia could end up dead," Mom cut in.

"That is exactly our worry. I know we've kept far too much from Autumn. I've been too protective over her; now she lives in a world of lies. It isn't fair to anyone. It is our failure as parents to understand her. Now we have difficulty saying what she can handle and cannot."

"William, no parent understands their teenager," Mom added. "I've had two myself, remember?"

"Yes, I know, but that doesn't change reality. Now, thanks to us, Autumn is blind to her very nature and lives in a hostile environment. Maybe if we had told her about Alexandral earlier... let her understand what she is, and maybe she could..."

"There are many things I would have done differently with my children if I had the chance to turn back time," Mom said. "We don't have that option. We can only learn from our mistakes and try to correct what we can."

"I fear she will hate us both by the time she learns the truth about everything," William said as he hung his head to the floor.

"Autumn, hate?" Cristy cut in. "I don't know if we are talking about the same blonde Amazon here, but the Autumn I know could never hate her parents... let alone anyone."

"We don't know that for sure..." I said. "If you think about it, she believes her problems are her fault. She has no solid, concrete reason to blame

274

anyone else. Give her a reason to hate; who knows what that will do? Sure, it doesn't appear that she can hate anyone, but in all reality, does anyone know her that well?"

"I'm afraid I know little about my daughter. She is an enigma to me. I've spent too much time training her to be a warrior; thus, I know little about the woman she has grown into."

The waiting room grew silent. No one else knew what to say. I wasn't sure how to feel. I was already weary of keeping secrets from Autumn, but it seemed like there was little else to do. Any of the secrets I held from her could be potentially dangerous. The concept's weight might crush her if she was told she's a Balanced One. If I were to let her know that I'm her Tala'har and came to this world to protect her, she could believe that is the only reason I'm her friend. If I confessed how I feel about her... well... I didn't even want to think of the consequences of that action.

Chapter 39

Autumn and Megara were eventually led into the waiting room by a nurse. Other people also entered the room, so we couldn't discuss matteres further. Part of me wanted to suggest we go elsewhere to talk, but I knew everyone was anxious to know Cassandra's condition.

After about two hours, Theresa appeared through a set of double doors, dressed in surgery scrubs. A slight smile was visible on her lips, and a bounce in her step could be seen. She approached us. Everyone stood up.

"How is she?" William spoke first.

"She'll make a full recovery, but she's weak, so I must insist she not see visitors for the rest of the evening. She probably won't awake from the sedative for quite a while. I believe we've escaped the threat of a major infection. We have her on antibiotics, just in case, but even using those concerns me. I suggest everyone go up Belmont Avenue, get a hotel, and rest until she's ready to have visitors, most likely tomorrow."

The whole group let out a collective sigh of relief.

"Thank you for your help, Theresa. My family owes you a great debt," William said.

"Family does not owe family debt," Theresa replied.

Autumn said nothing but wrapped her arms around the doctor and squeezed her tight. Theresa returned her embrace and smiled. She then gently pushed Autumn away.

"Go get some rest, and I'll see you all tomorrow," she said.

"Thank you," Autumn finally spoke.

"It was good to meet you, Doctor," Mom said.

"Yeah, it was," I added.

"It's wonderful to see my friends have such good friends. Hopefully, we can get to know each other better when matters are less urgent. If you'll excuse me, I have other patients to attend to."

Theresa vacated the room. Everyone exchanged glances.

"Cristy," Mom said. "Do you know where this 'Belmont Avenue' is?"

"Sure do, we're on it," she replied. "We just have to drive up the street to get to some hotels and a few restaurants."

"Well, that makes matters easy enough," I added.

"I think I will stay here. The least I owe her is to be at her side when she wakes," William said.

"Are you sure?" Mom said.

"Yes, and Autumn, I must talk to you before you go. I'll follow you out," he said.

"What's up, Dad?" she asked as we started to walk down the hall.

"I wanted to apologize for our last talk. I spoke to Karen and the others, and it seems some things I said were misunderstood, which is my fault. You must understand that when I said I would want you to live with Karen and Carrie, I didn't mean I wouldn't want you near. If anything, I want you as close to me as possible."

We stopped at the elevator, and Cristy hit the button with a certain amount of glee, which is usually reserved for small children.

"Autumn, I love you so very much," he continued. "I just look into your eyes and am reminded of the good times our family has had together. I could never ask you to go away without good reason."

"Oh, Daddy! I'm sorry for jumping to conclusions!" Autumn wrapped her arms around him. He returned the hug around the small of her back. The elevator doors opened, and she let go and headed into the elevator.

He continued once the elevator doors shut, and William saw we were the only ones in it.

"Autumn, do you remember what Karen told you about those shields?" he said.

"Yes... why?" she cocked her head.

"Theresa had to dispel them because your mother is too weak to support them. What I'm trying to get at is that I need you to stay with Karen and Carrie while your mother heals."

"I see. I can still come over in the daytime, right? She said I'm only really in danger when I'm asleep."

"That is true, so you can play nurse to your mother all you like in the daytime, but when it's time for bed, I need you to head to Karen's so she can protect you while you sleep."

"I understand," she said. "Is that okay with you guys?" She glanced back to me and Mom.

"Of course, dear. Our home is your home," Mom said.

"You can stay in the spare room we keep for sis," I said.

"Ahh, I was hoping to cuddle with you again," she smiled for the first time in what seemed like ages. I wasn't exactly sure how to react to that comment, so I kept my mouth shut. It was just good to see her smile.

"I wanna cuddle, too!" Cristy chimed in.

The elevator opened at that moment, and Cristy's outburst echoed into the very serious-looking lobby. Megara smiled and playfully rolled her eyes. A small giggle escaped my mouth as we stepped out.

"I'll see you all tomorrow. I want to see you all well rested," William said.

As we left the hospital, Autumn looked around and saw no one in earshot, "I'm just so relieved everything went well. Surgery is a scary thing for a Telosian."

"Well, I think it's scary for anyone," I said. "Is there something that makes it worse for you guys?"

"Yes, it's our interactions with normal medicine," Autumn nodded. "Our body chemistry is very different from that of an average human, and most medicine can have unpredictable effects, at least according to Theresa. So, she was worried about putting Mom under for the surgery. I wish it weren't that way; I'm sure some normal medicine could help us with some things...."

"And that means no painkillers for childbirth," Megara added. "I'm glad I had both of my kids at once because I will never go through that again. Karen, what was it like where you are from?"

"Oh, my husband insisted on deadening my nerves with his magic both times. I told him I'm a Tala'har and pain is our existence, and I wasn't concerned. Yet he was a wizard, which generally equates to a stubborn man with magic, so he got his way."

"Sounds like Dad…" I laughed.

"Hey, Mrs. Abbey, would you be able to drive? I want to talk to Cristy and Carrie in the back," Autumn said as we walked out to the car.

"Sure, as long as I can get instructions, I don't have the foggiest where we are," Mom replied.

"Oh, and don't call me 'Mrs. Abbey.'

Cristy, Autumn, and I entered the back seat while Mom and Megara sat in the front. Mom turned on the car and drove out of the small parking deck. Autumn seemed intent on taking the middle seat.

"Take a right out of the deck and then a left on the next street. Then, keep driving," Cristy said.

We pulled out of the deck and cruised on Belmont Avenue. The area around the hospital was a prime example of the desolation in this small city. I could see houses down side roads that looked like they would fall apart if you touched them, empty lots littered with trash, and closed businesses covered in spray paint. The whole area was utterly dismal.

"I wanted to thank you all," Autumn said, taking my right hand and Cristy's left. I'm not sure what I would do without you. So, this goes out to everyone in the car. Thank you."

"No need to thank us; it's what family and friends are for," Cristy said.

"I was somewhat of a bitch on the way here..." Autumn said.

"Nonsense, no one acts all nice and peachy when their mother could be dying!" Cristy said.

"Don't sweat it. I'm glad we could be here for you," I comforted.

"And Carrie," Autumn said. "I don't hold it against you for a moment that you didn't tell me tell me you weren't from Earth. I might not tell anyone something that wild sounding, myself. And our family is one massive wild thing."

I smiled and nodded. Autumn said nothing else and laid her head back on the seat, still clutching my hand and Cristy's. In only moments, it looked as if she had fallen asleep.

We stopped at a steakhouse right before all the hotels. I wanted to wake Autumn because I wasn't very comfortable with her sleeping in the car, but before I could rouse her, my mom silently shook her head at me. I sighed and stepped out of the vehicle.

"Mom, is it okay that she's asleep?" I whispered. "I mean, she does have those vulnerabilities."

"A short nap is not much to worry about. It takes time for her to be deep enough sleep where she could be in trouble."

I wasn't paying attention to the conversation at the table; I kept my eyes glued to the car where Autumn slumbered. She seemed to be sleeping peacefully for the first time since we left Miami. Mom was right for not waking her.

We entered the car once again, and Autumn didn't even budge. As we traveled along the street, I noticed the surroundings weren't quite as drab as we first saw in Youngstown.

I realized we weren't in Youngstown anymore but one of its suburbs. It was nowhere near as derelict, and I was thankful for that. We drove only a minute or two more until we reached a hotel on the left side of the road.

"You guys go ahead and get your stuff together; Megara and I will secure rooms for us," Mom said.

"Hey, you," I gently nudged Autumn. "We're at the hotel; it's time to get up, sleepyhead."

"Don't make me tickle you," Cristy said as she tickled Autumn's ribs.

Her eyes finally opened, and a smile came to her face, "Okay, I'm up, I'm up!"

Before Cristy or I could move, she wrapped her arms around our necks.

280

"Thank you...so much," she said. I couldn't see her face, but it sounded like she started crying.

"You already thanked us, hun; now it's time to get to our rooms. I am so cannibalizing the mini-fridge if they have one!" Cristy grinned.

"Are you ever not hungry?" I said as I left Autumn's embrace and exited the car.

"Am I ever not horny?" she grinned.

I sighed, "Ask a stupid question and get a stupid answer."

Autumn giggled from within the car. She and Cristy left the vehicle, took our family-packed bundles out of the car, and headed into the hotel. Before we could even get in the door, my mom and Megara stepped out of the hotel.

"We got two rooms to split between the five of us," Mom said. "You three girls get a triple to yourselves, and Megara and I can share a single bed."

"Don't you open your mouth, missy," Megara looked at Cristy presumptively.

"Oh, come on, Mom, I wouldn't be me if I didn't make some smart-ass comment about you guys getting it on..." she giggled.

"I can assure you, Cristy, I'm completely straight," Mom said. "Not that your mother isn't a very attractive woman, but I love men way too much."

"Love?" I quipped. "I think the word 'addicted' would be a much better descriptor."

"You be quiet too," Mom laughed.

Chapter 40

The hotel was made of brick and was one of those chains that dotted the American landscape. I glanced across the street and saw what used to be a significant business of some sort, but all that was left was the parking lot. Not far from that was a small ice cream stand covered in white siding. Back on our side of the road, further down the street, was a graveyard full of well-cared-for graves. The entire place sent very mixed messages.

We entered the hotel, and I was impressed by how well-kept it was. It actually didn't look very old at all. We headed upstairs immediately, and through a couple of twists, Mom led us to our room. After showing us the way, she handed us each a key card and Megara, and she headed off to their room, which we were told was right now down the hall in 305.

Cristy opened the door, dropped her stuff on the floor, and dove for the first bed she could make contact with. The room was clean and rather dull. It had three beds, as Mom had said, with two small nightstands complete with their own lamp between the beds, a dresser in front of the room with a fairly new television, and a cable box placed next to it. Over to the left was a door to the bathroom. Near the entrance, a small table with four chairs sat.

"Ah... there is no mini-fridge, but there is a gas station pretty much next door. We can head over there if we want to get some grub later," Cristy said.

"Oh, here," I said, lifting the bag we brought from the steakhouse and pointing it at Autumn. "You, eat. It should still be warm."

"Thanks," Autumn replied.

"I call this bed and the first shower!" Cristy hopped off the bed and dove into her belongings. She pulled out a spaghetti strap night top and some shorts. "No peeking now," she grinned. "Unless you really want to, of course!"

She bounced off to the bathroom. Autumn sat down with her meal at the table and quietly began to eat.

I sat down on the middle bed and took a deep breath. I peered over at Autumn as she ate. I could see the strain of the last day or so wearing on her face, and I was sure she would feel better once she was able to get some real sleep in a real bed.

"Carrie..." she said.

"Yeah?" I replied.

"What did you see at Jacobs? You know, when you blacked out."

"I... saw the death of my father..." I stuttered.

"I see; how did he die, if you don't mind me asking?"

"When we were escaping to this world, we were chased down on our way to the portal. My father stayed back to take the man on as we got away, sacrificing himself for us. It's something I'll never forget. It was a strange man in black armor."

I realized that I should tell her about this man attacking her mother, too. I knew her father meant to and I was tired of hiding the truth. I wasn't all that great at it like my mother was.

"And... Autumn... there is something you need to know about the man who killed my father."

"What's that?"

"He was the one that assaulted your parents and hurt your mother."

"How... do you know?" Her eyes looked as wide as saucers. Her hand, which held the fork with a bite of steak on it, shook.

"Because Cristy compared the image that she saw in my mind to what your father saw in his mind. It was the same man in the same strange black armor. I know your Dad probably meant to tell you this but never really had the opportunity. I'm sorry."

"So... he killed your father and hurt my mother..."

"Yes."

"And he was too strong for my Dad to defeat?"

"He said he used some kind of magic to protect himself. Some sort of lightning shield, on top of that, other magic attacks, I think."

"I'll show him lightning..." she growled. "Carrie... if I see this man... I'll have to kill him. Nothing will stop me from killing him."

I knew her hostility was not directed at me, but it sent a shiver down my spine. Her cold determination was downright frightening.

"Autumn... I think we should just be glad your mom is alive," I reasoned, trying not to show my own intimidation. "We'll figure out what to do about this guy later. We should rest right now."

"Carrie..." she said again.

"Yes?"

"I don't want to get snippy. I'm going to try not to. The last day has been a rollercoaster, so I apologize in advance. If I get nasty, I'm sorry."

"It's okay; I'm not made of porcelain, as much as I might look like it," I chuckled.

"Why didn't you tell me Thomas was after you."

"I just didn't want to worry you. You have enough shit to deal with."

"Yeah, but I need to keep an eye out for him, and I have a right to know. He's my family's problem, and now you're a target. You should have told me..."

"I'm...sorry, Autumn..." I replied. "I'll try not to do things like that in the future."

"I don't know what I'd do if I..." she put her eyes down to the floor. "I'm so sorry for getting angry."

"You didn't do anything to apologize for. Just forget about it. You really shouldn't worry about things like that now. Just rest."

Determination appeared on her face once again. "Oh... I'll rest... and I'll be ready," she snarled and continued to eat. She growled something in Japanese; the only words I could make out were 'nakama' and 'otsan'. I knew otsan meant father, and I had heard the word nakama before; I couldn't remember what it meant.

I took out my cellphone and opened its web browser, looking up the term nakama. One of the definitions that appeared was "A person who is considered a close friend, something akin to family." Obviously, this term was not used lightly, and I was touched by her sincerity and surprised at her anger, which seemed to be more on my behalf than on her own.

I turned my attention to the link and found that same feeling of bloodlust and arousal emanating from Autumn. I peeked over at her, and her breathing was slightly labored. I could almost smell the pheromones in the room. Then, my own fear of her was being mixed with arousal... I just wasn't sure whose arousal it was.

"Holy shit, she's pissed," Cristy echoed in my mind.

"Amongst other things..." I replied to Cristy. "Did you happen to catch what she said in Japanese?" I replied.

"Yeah, it was something like 'He will pay for killing my nakama's father. Yeah, so if you're wondering, she's more pissed off about what happened to your father than what happened to her mother. And forget about her being angry with you for not telling her about Thomas; she's probably already forgotten it. Now that she knows her mother will heal, she's ready to kill this guy for you. I know you're aware that 'nakama' isn't used lightly."

"Cristy, is it really normal for her to get this attached this quickly? I mean, you are her cousin, you're family. She's known me for less than a week."

"Think about what you've done for her already, and you have your answer. It doesn't take a genius to realize that Autumn is deeply loyal. She was born and bred to fight for others. It gives a meaning to all the hard work she's put into perfecting her sword skill."

"I can see that. That's not really her job, though."

"Yes, it is, she's your nakama, remember? That's what nakama do for each other."

"Yeah, but I'm her Tala'har, and her fighting for me puts her in danger. That's something I can't have…"

"Even if she knew you were her Tala'har, do you think that would matter? She still wouldn't rest until this guy is six feet under."

"Protecting her isn't going to be easy, is it?"

"Nope," Cristy said as her voice turned to a giggle. "Hey Carrie, I'm ready to wash my 'fun parts,' wanna come help?"

"Maybe later, when Autumn's not around," I laughed.

"Oh, come on. Maybe she'll want to watch and learn a thing or two."

Chapter 41

Cristy returned from the shower dressed in the pajamas she had taken with her. Her hair was still wet and pretty much everywhere, which seemed perfectly natural for the bouncy blonde. She again leaped onto the bed closest to the door, and the force of her landing caused drops of water from her hair to spray me in the face.

"Ah... I had no Peeping Janes... how disappointing," she giggled.

I laughed, and Autumn said nothing.

"Cous', don't concern yourself with 'him' right now. Your mom will be okay, and we're three chicks in a hotel room. Take this chance to loosen up. How often do you get to hang out in a hotel with limited parental supervision?"

"He... just needs to die. I can't kill Thomas, but I can kill him. I've never wanted to hurt someone so badly in my life."

"When has revenge helped anyone?" Cristy replied.

Autumn took a deep breath and exhaled.

"You're right... I can't bring Carrie's dad back, and I can't undo what he did to mom,"

Autumn sighed. "I'm just giving into..."

Autumn stopped mid-sentence. After a moment of awkward silence, she continued. "... blood-lust, I guess. The whole idea of ripping this guy apart, limb from limb... turned me on. It's scaring me."

Cristy reached for her jacket and pulled out her mobile phone. She tossed the phone to Autumn.

"Why don't you do something with that 'lust' and call your man? He's worried sick. Maybe you can talk dirty to him while you're at it. Give him something to look forward to."

"I don't know if I should now..." she blankly stared at the phone.

"She's right," I said. "About the calling him part, not the talking dirty part. He's probably really concerned. He should at least know that your mom is okay."

"Yeah, I guess you are right," she conceded. She unlocked the touchscreen phone and stopped dead.

"I can't remember his number..." she mumbled. "I'm not sure where my phone is…"

"It's in my phone book, don't worry about it," Cristy said. "Thought it might come in handy. He doesn't know I have it, of course."

Autumn looked like she was going to say something but appeared to change her mind. After touching the phone screen, she put the phone up to her ear.

"Hi, Jacob?" Autumn said. "It's Autumn, I'm calling from Cristy's phone. She's going to be fine; I'm so relieved. I... don't want to come off too forward... but I miss you. I'm just... a bit messed up right now."

"Let's give her some privacy," I whispered to Cristy. Cristy nodded, put on her jacket, grabbed her shoes, and prepared to leave the room.

"Hold on a second, Jake," Autumn put the phone in front of her and pushed what I assumed was the mute button. "If you are leaving the building, don't go unarmed. I'm worried his hurting Mom might have been a ploy to get us away from Aunt Mina and possibly Krojo. As you mentioned, a lightning shield wouldn't hinder a shinobi capable of using jutsu."

"Good point," I said. "I picked up the separate smaller tote that included Karithian.

Cristy picked up a small pink book bag with a pink pony on it and slung it over her shoulder.

"What?" she responded to my smirk; "I'm a pegasister," she said with a straight face.

"You surprise me more and more every day…" I said. "Has the irony set in that there are guns in that bag?"

"Fully. Now, let's get out of Autumn's hair so she can talk dirty to her man."

288

Autumn stuck her tongue out at Cristy and then unmuted the phone, "I'm back; sorry about that."

After I shut the door behind Cristy, she grinned at me.

"Hey, how about we go down to this park that's less than five minutes away?" she said.

"I don't know," I replied. "I don't like leaving her alone like that."

"Oh, come on, your mom is right down the hall, and if we aren't out here waiting on her to get off the phone, she'll be more likely to stay on and maybe get her mind off this guy."

"You are right, as usual," I sighed. "Let me at least tell her we're going."

I poked my head in the door and saw Autumn still on the phone.

"We're going down to the park; we'll be back in a bit," I said. Autumn shook her head in understanding, and I shut the door.

We walked down the hall and found our mothers' room, number 305. I knocked on the door, and my mom opened it and smiled.

"What's up," she said.

"Cristy and I will give Autumn time to talk to her boyfriend. She has Cristy's phone, but I still have mine. We're heading down to the close park," I said.

"I'm surprised you are willing to leave Autumn alone," she laughed. "It's not exactly hard to keep track of her. The girl is nearly impossible to miss in a spiritual sense. Just look for the dead area. I can track her movements around town if I want to. You don't need to worry about her; I'll keep an eye out. Yet, I'm more worried about you, but I see you're armed, so I won't treat you like a child."

"Thanks, Mom," I said. Mom closed the door, and we headed down to the hotel's ground floor and out the door.

We stepped out of the hotel, and Cristy gave me a raised eyebrow.

"We're being watched, you know that, right?" she said mentally.

I put my other hand on my ring and attempted to emit the waves as I had before. This time, I felt something.

"Holy shit, it worked!" I exclaimed mentally. "Is it them?"

"No, I don't think so. I'm not getting that static, so they don't have mental shielding. I don't think they are human, though. I'm having difficulty reading them, but I can tell they don't mean us any harm."

"Okay, let's keep walking then," I said mentally again. "Maybe we'll catch a glimpse of our shy friend on our walk."

The sun began to set as we strolled down Belmont Avenue. In only a minute or two, Cristy pointed out a drive leading into the park with the wooden sign 'Churchill Park' sitting next to it. It felt slightly off that a public park would be this close to a business district and a significant highway pit stop. We walked down the drive far longer than the walk to the park. Once we started traversing the park's drive, I realized that the park was just a massive clearing in a decent-sized expanse of woodland. As we moved along the slightly curved road, we saw a baseball field to our right and a small creek in front of us, with a wooden bridge for pedestrian crossing leading to the park's central area. We crossed the small bridge, and I saw the playground equipment. The trees shaded the entire park, so even though it was dusk, I could never imagine it being incredibly bright, even in the middle of the day.

We didn't see anything of our tail, but the feeling of being watched persisted, and I could undoubtedly tell with my ring that an unseen entity was near us. Cristy made a beeline for the swing set. It was one of those swings with a bendable rubber seat supported by chains. She nearly leaped onto a swing and began to push off as fast as her short legs would allow. I sat on the swing next to her and took in the sights. Before us stood a large stone pavilion where locals held birthday parties and other events. Around the area, other pavilions were scattered, but they weren't all as well-built and permanent as the stone one. The park itself was empty, not a soul in sight. I was happy to know we could talk without being overheard here.

"I love this place," Cristy said as she stopped her swing. "No one is ever here for some reason except for special events. We used to come to Youngstown to visit Theresa and Arthur all the time. We would come and have picnics at the park, too. It was great, especially when my dad stayed home with my sister because she had the flu."

"So, as for kids, it was just you and Autumn?" I said.

"Yep, well, and Jason, too, if you want to count him. It was so much fun. Autumn probably doesn't even remember it. I love my father and sister, but they can ruin things."

"How old were you guys?"

"About seven or so, something like that. That trip sticks out in my memory for a few reasons. It was the first time we took a plane up here instead of Dad driving us. That was fun; I kept yelling, "We're all going to die!" and people would give me and Mom dirty looks. It stands out because, before that day, I was conscious of my height. Even as a seven-year-old, I was tiny."

"You? Are you conscious about anything? I didn't think that was even possible," I said.

"Yeah, I was. My sister would always make fun of me; sometimes, I let her get to me. We were at this park, celebrating Aunt Cassy's birthday. Jason was helping Uncle Will at the grill, Mom and Aunt Cassy were getting everything else ready, and Autumn and I were playing in that sandbox. She was rather quiet like she had always been, as she built her little sand sculpture. I kept trying to build this huge tower out of sand. I was getting frustrated because it would always crumble once I built the tower so high. I eventually blurted out, 'I don't want it to be short like me!'. And I swear, Carrie, this moment will always stick in my memory. She stared at me with her head cocked and said, 'Why? What's wrong with being short? You're perfect the way you are.' "

"Wow," I said.

"That remained with me from there on out. She was right. I was perfect, but not in that 'I'm better than everyone else' perfect or the 'There is nothing wrong with me' perfect, but the 'I'm just right' kind. You know, the kind of perfect in Goldilocks and the Three Bears. I'm just right for who I am, and I don't have to live up to anyone's standards, including my sister's."

"I didn't know Autumn had that kind of a profound effect on you."

"Well... it was a memory I had been avoiding lately because I was ashamed of how I stood back and let Sophia walk all over her."

"We all make mistakes."

"Yeah, but most people's mistakes don't ruin others' lives."

"Her life isn't ruined; it's just not in the best state. We can help her fix that."

"If we live..." she said, this time in my head. "They're here."

Chapter 42

I took a deep breath and attempted to still my mind, to no avail. Rage crept into my thoughts. I wanted to unleash a primal scream. My hands trembled, but I squeezed my eyes shut momentarily and attempted to focus.

"Shit..." I said. "We must find cover. How many of them are there?" I said mentally to Cristy.

"I think just two at the moment, so we might be able to take them. Might be more, but they don't look like they are going to engage. Although if that armored guy is amongst them like I think he is, we're pretty fucked," she replied back to me.

I soon realized that I was most likely going to confront my father's killer in the next few moments.

"On the count of three, we run for the pavilion and get some cover," Cristy told me mentally.

"All right."

"One... two... three!"

We dashed over to the pavilion. Cristy was far faster than I thought she would be with those short legs. Laser fire rained from above, almost on cue, barely missing us both. We turned the corner and hid behind it, facing the small bridge, for it was two walls intersecting, not a column. I removed Karithian from the duffle bag and peeked around the corner, seeing something I had only seen in my dreams for years.

The man in black armor strolled across the wooden bridge. His armor was precisely as I remembered it from all those years ago. The sight of him enraged me. Karithian was ready for battle faster than I had ever seen. It would only matter of getting close enough.

"It's him," I snarled as Cristy pulled her pair of nine-millimeter handguns from her pony bag.

Before the man could reach us, the roar of an engine could be heard tearing down the street to the park. The tree coverage blocked my view of the road, so I couldn't see what was making the noise. The masked man turned to meet the newcomer. It only took a moment to see the blade of my mother's scythe flying toward the armored man. The retractable claws I remembered so well shot out of his gloves, and he blocked the weapon with ease, and it recoiled back to her in an arc. She ran under the blade as it returned, charging with the spear-end of the scythe pointed forward. The man blocked her attack with both hand claws. After the block, she brought herself into a slide, swinging the now returned blade at her opponent. The man leaped over her and avoided the attack. They both readied themselves for the next blow; my mother was back up and turning around, with the man already ready to face her. There was a pause in the fight. They stared each other down for a moment. Before she could move, he sent out a bolt of lightning from his right arm. Mom threw up the scythe just in time, but the blast knocked her onto her back. I noticed a brown glow to the weapon, meaning she charged earth magic into it just in time.

I attempted to step forward to help her but nearly received a laser blast from somewhere in the trees. There was nothing I could do as he approached her. He lifted his arm to deliver the final blow when, somewhere from above, a katana was tossed into the ground between them. My mother quickly rolled backward over her head as the stranger leaped in retreat. The area surrounding the katana exploded with a mass of electricity, whiting out my view. When the smoke cleared, a familiar tall figure was attacking the man in black with frightening speed.

My worst fear was realized as I watched Autumn swinging her remaining katana at the man in black. Every inch of me wanted to bolt out there to assist her, but I would most likely be dead by the time I reached her with the sniper in the trees.

Autumn swung her katana at the armored man, and he lifted his bladed hands just in time to block. She slid to his right side and pressed the attack with quick swings at her opponent, each barely blocked or dodged. He backflipped away from Autumn, and she cartwheeled back, recovering her scorched katana from the ground. She spun the blade around and put it into the defensive forward position, held vertically to her opponent, while the other blade was held high, ready to strike.

I wanted to scream because I knew what would happen next. He did what I expected and lifted his hand to shoot lightning again. The shot came out but missed completely. Autumn rolled under the blast and back into his face, but instead of a blade attack, she tucked her right blade under her arm and delivered

294

her own blast of lightning at close range. The attack hit home, and the man was knocked back onto the ground. Autumn leaped at him with both blades in the air. The man still managed to lift his bladed hands to block the attack, but the force shattered his claws.

The laser fire stopped for a split second, and another shot was fired, this time at Autumn's back. She gracefully rolled out of the way, and the shot found home in the dirt beside the armored man.

"Now!" I screamed in my head, hoping Cristy was paying attention.

Cristy removed herself from the cover and fired a pair of shots into the trees. The sound of metal on metal was heard as a rifle fell from the trees. I took a step out from cover and swung my sword, letting out a blast of air up towards the tops of the trees. I shortly heard a thud with dust popping up from the ground. The sounds of a scurried roll and footsteps away followed.

Another engine, bigger and much louder, was heard from the road into the park. The squeal of breaks echoed outside the trees as a gigantic figure leaped over the creek between Autumn and her opponent. A tremendous thud radiated through the air as he landed. He squared up with the man in the dark armor.

This was the largest man I had ever seen by a long shot. He had to be somewhere near eight feet tall. He wasn't just tall; he was broad as well. Muscle definition covered his body; not an inch of fat was noticeable. His skin was semi-dark, reminding me of Theresa. His hair was short and dark brown, only partially combed back, with the rest flopping out all over. He was clean-shaven and had dark features. He wore dirty overalls and a T-shirt. He was so large that even from this distance, I could see the grim look on his face.

"Little girl, you're too young to have blood on your hands," he said, glancing back at Autumn. He turned quickly and dashed at the dark man. The man in black armor lifted his knees, revealing the blades and kneeing them into the big man. The giant didn't even seem phased as he snatched the man's armored neck and lifted him into the air. Once in the air, I saw the claws on his knees bent nearly in two.

"You're gonna have to do better than that," the big man roared.

The armored man put both hands around the massive arm holding him up. Electricity visibly flowed through the colossal man, and he let out a gigantic, gut-busting laugh.

"You have got to be kidding me!" he heartily chuckled. His hair stood on end, but he didn't appear harmed otherwise. He pitched his arm back as the man in armor's body dangled in the air like a rag doll and tossed him with crushing force into a large oak. The man crashed against the tree, the force of the crash creating a massive crack. From above, what appeared to be a dark blue-skinned female in a black, skin-tight suit that covered her from neck to toe dropped down, quickly lifted the armored man onto her back, and amazingly leaped away.

"Uncle Arthur!" Cristy exclaimed as she dashed toward the big man.

"Hey, kiddo!" the big man grinned as he turned to the seemingly miniature Cristy as she jumped up and wrapped her arms around his neck.

"Are you all right, Autumn?" he said as he looked over at her. He lifted his arm around Cristy's legs, and she sat on his shoulder like a parrot. Autumn's eyes were adrift to the ground, and I could see her digging her nails into her palms.

"I was fine. I could have finished him," she said in a low voice.

"That's the point, young one. You're too young to take a life. Does whacked out things to your mind, believe me, I know."

"Oh, crap, I didn't introduce you guys," Cristy said from atop the giant's shoulder. "This is the Invincible Uncle Arthur. He's not really our uncle, but he's Theresa's husband. Arthur, this is Carrie and her mom, Karen."

"I'm invulnerable, not invincible," Arthur said. He turned to my mom, "Oh, sorry, ma'am, I didn't even notice you there. When kids are in trouble, I get a little single-minded. You'll have to excuse me. Karen, is it? Are you hurt? You look a little... well electrified, if I do say so myself."

"It's all right, I'm fine. Nothing that a shower won't fix. It takes more than a little lightning to kill me," Mom said.

I could feel the hostility slip away from Autumn as she approached the big man and wrapped her arms around his massive torso.

"Sorry about the disrespect," Autumn said as she put her head on his chest. "I just haven't been in my right mind lately. It's good to see you, Uncle Arthur."

"Nonetheless, thank you for coming to my rescue, Autumn. Sometimes, even Tala'har allow our emotions to get to us. I was in over my head yet again."

"I can't blame you," Cristy said. "He did kill your husband, after all."

Arthur let out a low growl, "Damn. Maybe I should have let Autumn finish him. Was that the fellow that hurt Cassy as well?"

"Yeah," Autumn sighed.

"Looked pretty skilled to me; he probably would have torn me apart if I was a normal guy. Anyway, Will sent me for you. Cassy's awake and wants to see everyone as soon as possible. Doesn't seem to be too intent on listening to the doctor's orders."

"One sec," Cristy said. She ran over to where the rifle dropped and picked it up. She examined it closely.

"I don't think human hands made this," she said.

Mom moved over to where Autumn and the man fought, knelt, and found one of the larger fragments of his hand blades. She picked up the primarily triangular fragment with two fingers and peered at it.

"And I don't recognize the metal this is made of. They aren't from around here, that's for sure. And I'm pretty sure they aren't where we're from, either."

"Karen, why don't you take your car back to the hotel, and I'll drive everyone to the hospital. The van is big enough. Save your gas for the trip home, Arthur said."

"Sure, I'll get Meg while we're there," Mom replied.

"Hey, Uncle Arthur," Cristy said. "How did you know we were at the park?"

"I called your mom right before I got here; she told me what was happening."

"Oh... Mrs. Abbey, sorry about nearly electrocuting you. I was working on 'auto-pilot,' so to speak, so I really don't remember much before I threw the sword," Autumn said quietly.

"It's fine, dear; I'm alive because of you," Mom said.

I examined Autumn more closely to see if she had been hurt and noticed a few fragments of the man's claws sticking out of her arm. Blood oozed from the wounds, but she didn't seem even to notice. Since her shirt was red, it was helping to camouflage her wounds to everyone else. I looked down at her swords and noticed the one she had thrown into the ground was still intact but wholly melted. Had Mom been hit by the blast that had emanated from the weapon, she wouldn't have lived to tell the tale.

"How did you get down here so fast, Autumn?" I asked.

"Like I said, I don't remember much before throwing the sword. I know I was in the hotel room, and I hung up with Jacob, and I don't remember why I came down to the park or how I got here so fast. I'm... a bit confused," Autumn said. After a moment, she reached into her pants pocket and pulled out Cristy's cell phone. "Thanks for letting me use it; I hope it still works."

"Who cares if it doesn't," Cristy laughed as she returned holding the alien-looking rifle. She took the phone, awoke it, and laughed, "Damn, still works. I won't be able to bug Dad for another one." After a moment, a thought seemed to hit Cristy, "Oh, did anyone else see that chick that drug that guy off? She totally wasn't human. Hot as hell, but not human."

"This is getting stranger and stranger," I said as I climbed into the van.

Chapter 43

We left the park inside the massive dark blue van the big man drove. It didn't look like any make or model I had ever seen, so it was probably a custom job. The front end was big enough to have a semi-engine in it. Mom and Megara joined us, and we left for the hospital.

We arrived at the hospital. The van was comfortable enough, with its plush seats, soft fabric-coated interior walls, and ample legroom. Meg sat in the front alongside Arthur and his massive captain's chair. Behind the front seats, there were two rows of seats. Autumn, Cristy, and I were seated in the middle row, and my mom sat in the back. He pulled up to the front of the hospital.

"You ladies, go ahead and get out; I have to park this beast elsewhere. It won't fit in the deck."

We exited the van and headed for the same hospital lobby we had entered earlier. William awaited us in the lobby and smiled when we came into view. Once we came closer, a look of concern washed over his face.

"Karen....are you alright?" he said, finally noticing my mother's frizzed hair.

"Yeah... we had an encounter with him... I wouldn't be standing here right now if it wasn't for your daughter and Arthur."

"Autumn...you fought him?"

"Yes, father."

"You're wounded!" he said, noticing the dried blood.

"Oh... that I am. It's no big deal. It doesn't really hurt; I didn't even notice. More importantly, where is Mom? I want to see her."

"You never think of yourself, child. She's in the recovery unit, but she's stable and awake. She wants to see everyone, against Theresa's orders, of course."

William led us to the appropriate elevator, which we took. The ride was quiet. I could help but glance at Autumn and her wounds. Hopefully, Theresa would take care of those for her. The last thing she needed was an infection.

The elevator opened, and William led us down a long hall with patient rooms. He eventually turned right into one of the rooms, and there in the singular bed was Cassandra, looking amazingly well for nearly dying. Her skin had its usual lively tone, and she looked reasonably healthy besides her disheveled hair. She was reading a magazine and instantly put it down as she saw us approach. She let out her usual casual smile.

"Mom!" Autumn exclaimed. She was about to hug her but then thought better of it.

"Hi, sweetheart... what happened to you!" Cassandra exclaimed.

"It's nothing, Mom. Are you in pain? How are you feeling? Can you..."

"Autumn," she said sternly. "You didn't answer my question. What happened?"

"I fought the guy who hurt you... I shattered his blades, and I got some of the shrapnel in my arm, that's all."

"You fought him... why? You didn't go looking for him, did you?"

"No, he attacked Carrie and Cristy," Mom cut in. "I came to their aid, but I was outmatched. I wouldn't be standing here if Autumn hadn't shown up when she did."

"Autumn... be honest with me... did you use magic to fight him?" Cassandra said.

"How... did you know?" Autumn stuttered.

"Call it a mother's intuition," Cassandra said. "William dear, will you get it out of the car, love? It's time."

"Are you sure?" he said.

"Yes, I'm sure," Cassandra said. "She already started using her abilities without it, so I don't see the harm in her having it now."

"That is true. I will be right back," he said. William left the room.

"Aunt Cassy, you should have seen it; Autumn kicked his ass!" Cristy exclaimed.

"You would have been proud of her, Cassandra," Mom added.

"And I want to thank you, Karen. Thank you for bringing my family to me. That alone saved my life."

"No need to thank me. I am happy to help."

I realized that Megara had not moved from the doorway. Her eyes were drawn to the floor, and tears flowed from them. She finally inched toward the bed. Once she reached Cassandra, she fell to her knees.

"Don't you ever do that to me again!" she cried. "Without you... I don't know what I'd do..."

"I'm sorry, Megara..." Cassandra apologized.

" 'I'm sorry' isn't good enough! You almost left me! I'm a complete failure; I don't know what to do..."

"I don't want to hear you talk like that!" Cassandra raised her voice slightly. "You are not a failure. I'm looking at one of your successes right now." Cassandra glanced over to Cristy.

"But..."

"But nothing. You would do fine without me; don't tell yourself otherwise."

"I'm not strong enough... I have no control over my husband or my other daughter. And Autumn's been the one to pay for it."

"No one expects you to have control over this, sister," Cassandra said quietly. Megara remained on her knees, wrapped her arms around her sister's hospital-tagged arm, and sobbed.

The room was silent until William returned with an ancient tome under his arm. He was followed by the massive Arthur, who had to duck under the doorway to get into the room. Megara finally stood and stepped away from the edge of the bed, drying the tears from her eyes. William approached the bed and then handed the book to Cassandra.

"Autumn, come here, please," Cassandra said softly.

Autumn stepped toward the bed, "Yeah, Mom?"

"I've waited a long time to give this to you... It's probably too long. I feel you are old enough now to hold this kind of responsibility. My grandmother gave this to me the day after your father and I married. Now, times have changed, and you are now older than I was when I married. I wanted to save it for then, but that would be foolish, especially now that you need it. You don't need to worry about translating it; the book will appear to you in a language you understand. But first, you must answer a question for me."

"What's that?"

"Autumn, since you started using your magic, however long it's been, have there been any side effects to its use? It is imperative I know about it if there has been."

"No, Mom. There hasn't been anything like that."

"Oh shit..." Cristy said to me mentally.

Without another word, she handed the tome to Autumn.

"Thank you, Mom, you won't regret this," Autumn said with a smile.

Before anything else was said, Theresa joined us in the crowded room.

"It's good to see you all again," she said as she entered.

Arthur turned to his wife, "It's always wonderful to see you, my dear."

She lifted herself on her toes and kissed Arthur on the cheek. She then turned and closed the door behind her. The room immediately felt more stuffed.

"I'm glad you are all together because I have an announcement. Arthur and I have contemplated this decision for a long time, and the events of the last few days have solidified it in our minds. I just put my resignation into the hospital. As far as they are concerned, my mother in Florida is dying from a form of terminal cancer, and I must attend to her in her final days. In reality, I am moving to Miami to start a practice there and do what I should have done over the last four years: provide the kind of care only I can provide to my family. In other words, all of you."

"Are you sure?" William asked.

"Hell, Will, what do we have here?" Arthur said. "You guys are our family. What reason is there for us to stay?"

"And plenty of doctors in this area can treat my patients. This family has needs only I have the understanding to handle. In other words, to stay here

302

would be selfish. It is a doctor's duty to go where she is needed, and now that everyone is gathered in Miami, it wouldn't be wise to stay here any longer," Theresa explained.

"So, when are you guys moving?" Cristy asked.

"If William and Cassandra don't mind me coming along as soon as I release Cassandra, which will be tomorrow morning, judging by her current condition. Arthur will stay here and make arrangements for the actual move."

"Of course, you can come with us," William said. "You are also welcome to stay with us at our home until you get settled."

"Theresa, if you don't mind me asking," Mom said. "But how is she in such good condition? Earlier today, we were told she was close to death."

"Well... I suppose it has some to do with my healing magic and the Telosian's natural healing capabilities. I suspect she should be up and walking around within a week, but I don't think she should replace the shields she protects Autumn with until she fully recovers."

"Hopefully, I can learn to protect myself, so she doesn't have to," Autumn added.

"Autumn Alexander! How can you walk around with wounds like that? Come with me, and we'll get you cleaned up," Theresa said. She snatched at Autumn's arm to better look at her wounds. "Oh dear, it could hurt getting these out. What are they, anyway?"

"They are the remnants of the claws used to attack Mom," Autumn said.

"I don't think this metal is from Earth, Theresa, so I wouldn't leave any pieces about. People will start to ask questions if they examine it closely enough," Mom added.

"Yes, that would be wise. Come on, you and I are going to one of the examination rooms. We should be able to do this in privacy there."

Autumn and Theresa left the room.

"So, what exactly happened this evening?" William asked.

"I guess I should explain this," I started. "Cristy and I decided we would give Autumn some privacy while she talked to Jacob, so we went down to

Churchill Park. While there, that guy in the black armor attacked us along with a sniper. While the sniper kept me and Cristy pinned down, Mom showed up and took on the guy."

"Yes, I'm afraid he's too much for me. It's difficult to admit that I probably won't be able to avenge my husband myself, but it is a true testament to Autumn's skills. She did something that usually only full-blown wizards can do, at least on this scale, called 'spell attachment,'" Mom added.

"Spell attachment?" William said. "I'm not familiar with that term."

"It's just like it sounds," I explained. "It's the attaching of a spell to an object. In this case, Autumn attached some powerful lightning spell to her katana. She threw the katana between Mom and the asshole, and it created a massive explosion of electricity. It effectively ruined one of her swords, though."

"It's similar to how I apply shields to our home. How would she even know how to do something like that?" Cassandra gasped.

"Your guess is as good as mine," Cristy shrugged. "She said that she didn't remember much between when she hung up with Jacob and when she threw the sword. So, most likely, she doesn't know how she did it, either."

"How she covered the distance in such a short time is the real mystery," Mom said. "When I left the hotel, I'm certain she was still in her room. And I drove to the park. Yet, Autumn appeared no less than a few minutes after I did with no vehicle."

"Then she's using some sort of magic that we're unfamiliar with," Cassandra concluded.

"And one that even she doesn't remember," I added.

"Yeah, but back to the story," Arthur said. "When I showed up, she gave that guy the what-for, and I got between them. Someone that young shouldn't have blood on her hands, and I told her so. Of course, as you know, his little lightning tricks don't work on me, and his blades might be made of some fancy metal, but they still weren't sharp enough to cut me. I haven't found anything sharp enough to do that. I threw the bastard into a tree, and his little lady sniper friend scooped him up and ran off."

"And about that chick," Cristy said. "She had this weird skin color. It was like a dark blue."

304

"And her strength was greater than any human," I said. "She put the guy on her shoulder and leaped straight into the air. She must have jumped into the trees. That was one hell of a leap."

"So, is it safe to assume neither of them is human?" Cassandra said.

"No, I think the guy in the armor is human," Arthur said. "I had the guy with his arms around my wrists, and he was strong but not anything beyond what a human could be."

"My question is, why does he hide everything? Few wear armor that covers every inch of skin without having something to hide. Masks like his obscure vision and thus are more of a liability than an asset in battle," Mom commented. "

"The sniper wasn't wearing anything over her face," I added.

"Don't forget their mental protection," Cristy said.

"Yes, this indicates that they knew about our abilities beforehand," William commented. "The disturbances these devices create tend to give away their positions. If they knew that this would happen and still used them, this also means that they have much to hide."

"We do have some clues," Cristy said. "But I'm not sure how much the chick's rifle and some parts of the claw will tell us."

"Otherwise, I think we can sum all of this up to the idea that even though we've encountered the enemy and have some more clues, the fact remains that we still don't know shit," I said.

Cassandra sighed, "And my daughter is still a mystery to me."

Epilogue

A large red fox peered from the bushes along the park's edge. It watched the man in black armor approach Cristy and Carrie. It spied the beams nearly strike them as they took cover. The fur on the back of its neck stood up. It spun around as it saw a gout of flame come at him. A golden shield appeared as it snuffed out the flame. It dashed off into the thicker brush.

A woman in a dark red coat, wearing a large black hat with a thick veil over her face, stood in the clearing behind the bush with her gloved hand extended. She took a step forward but quickly realized the fox was long gone.

She spun to see a man in a long, dark, hooded robe with an outstretched hand covered with dark blue skin emitting a golden glow.

"I cannot allow you cause a fuss that would interrupt what is transpiring, child of Kain," the man stated quietly.

"You disrupted my hunt!" she snarled from behind the veil. She lifted her red-painted clawed hand out toward the hooded man. Fire began to emanate from her fingertips.

"Your pursuit of a simple fae does not trump our mission. We were sent here by a partner of your very master," the man said.

"You speak of the prince, wizard?" she hissed. More flames began to rage from her outstretched hand.

"That is correct, and I suppose by this world's standards, I am a wizard."

"If he is an ally of my master, he should not be working with you. Lilith and my master have very different aims," she said as she pulled her hand into a fist, flame now engulfing half her arm. The flames left her clothing unsinged.

"I believe our missions are not incompatible. We can work together. Our briefing included information regarding this very fae. He means to contact the Balanced One as per instructions of his queen."

"Should this be allowed?" she said as she extinguished the flame from her hand and crossed her arms.

"It would be advantageous for both of our masters if this contact is permitted," he replied. "Yet, it likely requires the fae to meet them in Miami. You must tread lightly in Miami, even more than we do."

"Why so? All I gaze upon turns to ash unless I have meddling wizards getting in my way. I fear nothing."

"Even the famed vampire hunter, Mina Kurotsuchi?"

The woman hissed, "Mina…"

"She's not the only shinobi in Miami. Her master resides there as well. It is well known what a formidable force he is."

"Which is why I needed to catch the fae now!" she let out a loud hiss, throwing her head forward and arms back, her hands briefly catching fire.

"I could not allow you to interrupt the Dartraxian's attempt at capturing the Tala'har. Unfortunately, he is unlikely to succeed. I sense the elder Tala'har on the move and another party on their way. To complicate matters, the Balanced One has likely sensed the battle by now. The Dartraxian believes he can best her, but I have my doubts. Alexandral's incarnates tend to have an innate control over time, fire, and lightning. This one's Telosian blood and combat training makes her even more formidable. If she were as easily defeated as my comrade believes, we would not have need for her."

"So, what do you propose?" the woman rolled her eyes and put her hands on her hips.

"We can cover you while you attempt to capture the fae. We'll draw out the shinobis and keep them occupied. I propose that while our targets are together, we should support each other's missions."

The woman let out a loud sigh. She was silent for a few moments. She began to gag and held her nose.

Another man stepped into the clearing from behind the wizard. His tattered trench coat stuck to branches that he effortlessly ripped the coat from and moved into the clearing alongside the wizard. He spat out a cigar butt and snuffed it with his foot.

The woman let out another hiss, "I thought I smelt your filth here, ghoul."

"Ain't no ghoul, darlin'," Thomas spat. "Just suffering from a bit of ye ole curse. Best listen to magic-hands here. Bloody Alexanders and their kin are challenging to deal with. Been doin' it for centuries now. With 'em Tala'har, tis even worse. Left me all knackered up twice in the last week. Best calm them fangs and hear the lad out."

A loud explosion echoed from within the park. The woman's hair stood on end. She turned and gazed through the bush that the fox was peering through. She viewed a ruined, smoking katana stabbed into the ground between the Dartraxian and a tall blonde girl with long hair. A woman with a giant scythe lay on the ground, attempting to recover. She turned back to face the hooded man.

"This looks like more trouble than even I can handle," she snarled. "You're on, wizard. I will assist you with your mission if you assist me with mine. Just keep me downwind of that heap of rotting flesh."

www.ingramcontent.com/pod-product-compliance
Lightning Source LLC
Chambersburg PA
CBHW070807180626
46818CB00001B/147